He s ... ped
forwar ... he
said. "Olivia, I love you. I've never felt this way before
about anyone. If I were to leave without seeing you,
without letting you know how I feel about you . . ."

Before either of them could think more about the
matter, he took her in his arms and kissed her, his lips
hot on hers, his hands—strong young hands, gentle and
insistent at the same time—running up and down her
back and sending delighted chills through her . . .

THE RIVER QUEEN

MELANIE DANIELS

CHARTER/DIAMOND BOOKS, NEW YORK

THE RIVER QUEEN

A Charter/Diamond Book / published by arrangement with
the author

PRINTING HISTORY
Charter/Diamond edition / November 1990

ISBN: 1-55773-413-5

Charter/Diamond Books are published by The Berkley Publishing
Group, 200 Madison Avenue, New York, New York 10016.
The name ''CHARTER/DIAMOND'' and its logo are trademarks
belonging to Charter Communications, Inc.

PRINTED IN THE UNITED STATES OF AMERICA

10 9 8 7 6 5 4 3 2 1

Book One

Chapter 1

Olivia Soames woke at the first bell, blinking and rubbing her eyes, then sitting bolt upright while the echo of the sonorous clang hung still in the chill night air. Almost immediately the pounding of the engines, deep in the bowels of the big side-wheeler, came to an abrupt halt, and the great steamship settled into an almost silent glide.

Olivia reached for her robe and, pushing one bare arm into a heavy sleeve, slipped down to the floor, feeling the sudden shock of the deck's chill on her bare feet. Struggling into the robe, she ignored the cold and padded over to the shuttered window and opened it slightly at one corner, just as the engines started again and the great wheels reversed themselves, backing water powerfully.

What she looked out upon, however, was not the colorful scene of bustling dockside life she might have seen at a landfall some twelve hours earlier or later. The landing ahead was shrouded in thick fog, and only dim lights ahead in the darkness marked the shore. Beyond these she could see nothing, nothing at all.

She bit her lip, hesitating for a moment; then the impulse came upon her, irresistibly strong, and as her heart beat a little faster at the thought she gave way to it. Casting off her robe, Olivia reached instead for her heavy topcoat draped over a chair beside her bed. With this formidable garment buttoned and buckled around her, she abandoned all thought of other clothing, leaving her long white drawers and petticoats hanging in downright indecent disarray by her bedside.

3

She slipped her chilled feet into warm slippers before stepping out silently through the cabin door to the boiler deck.

With the door open, the chill hit her immediately; she shivered, holding the high collar of the coat up around her neck to shield her face from the freezing fog. But bravely she forced herself to the starboard rail to peer out into the icy gloom.

Up ahead there—"up for'ard," as the men on the boat said—lanterns waved, and dim figures became visible. The big steamboat, still backing water, approached the dock, slowing visibly. Olivia marveled once again at the pilot's skill as he steered the ungainly vessel to dock, coming to a stop just before the dock disappeared below her boiler-deck field of vision. She leaned forward, her eyes eagerly searching the darkness.

Yes: Cairo. This must be Cairo, Illinois, where the two great rivers met, where the last leg of her epic journey would begin as the boat finally went out on Mississippi waters . . . yes, yes! And that would be the point, the place where the Ohio joined the great river. The Mississippi! The Mississippi at last!

Despite herself, Olivia grinned happily, a child's unguarded grin that hid nothing, held back nothing. It had been *so* long. She hadn't seen her father since her mother's death six years ago, when he'd shipped her back East to stay with her aunt and go to a girls' school in Baltimore. And how she'd changed in that time . . . why, her father likely would have changed as well. Would she recognize him at first sight? she wondered, not for the first time. Would she know Wyvern Plantation anymore? Would she recognize Uncle Driscoll?

Olivia's attention was caught by the activity on the dock. By the light of the lantern that hung from a pole at the point where the dock touched land, she could see a pair of richly appointed carriages pulling up: a tall rockaway and a black landau with a cover-up. Servants jumped down from the high seats, one to open the side doors, one to begin wrestling with luggage stored to the rear of the passenger compartment. And now the passengers themselves began to emerge.

There were several men, all of them expensively dressed. Even the livery of the black servants was costly and of a stylish cut, and the clothing of the men of quality was breathtakingly styled after the latest French fashion. The man nearest Olivia, standing tall and thin and straight as a ruler, wore a raglan coat of stone-gray cloth, open to show its lining of a gray-check pattern. Under his coat he wore a brown cutaway with a white waistcoat and pale gray trousers. His cravat was of spotted green; black shoes and a black silk hat, the latter worn at a severely conservative angle, completed his stunning turnout. As he turned his face to look up at the vessel standing before him, Olivia could see the strong character of his sharp features between prominent black sideburns.

Now he turned and began to hand a woman down from the coach; she was dressed all in black, even to the glove that took his hand, even to the shapely soft slipper that was the only other part of her that could be seen. But it was a stylish black as far removed from mourning as anything Olivia could have imagined. She was hooded; the heavy coat she wore veiled nearly any impression one might have drawn of her except what was dictated by her proud, dignified, even regal bearing. As she stepped gracefully now from dock to plank and paused for a moment to speak softly to someone on board, someone Olivia could not see, a portion of her face could be seen: a firmly rounded chin and a mouth made only more bewitchingly lovely by its generous width and red lips—and, for no more than the blink of an eye, a single tress of startlingly, flamingly red hair could be seen as well.

Then, to Olivia's surprise and shock, the lovely face turned up, up—and for a moment a pair of eyes as green and as bright as emeralds looked sharply upward from beneath angled brows at *her*—Olivia! Their eyes met; a faintly mocking, completely understanding smile flashed suddenly across the wide and beautiful mouth, and the smile made much of wide cheekbones and a noble, even haughty nose. Olivia gasped, her hand to her throat, and started to shrink back. But the woman turned away, a twinkle still in that jewellike eye, and swept aboard the vessel, followed by the man in gray.

Olivia shivered inside her thick coat, as much from the excitement as from the chilly air. Who *was* the beautiful red-haired woman who had just boarded, attended by handsome and aristocratic-looking retainers? Who was she that the mighty side-wheeler *City of Newport* would make a midnight stop for her alone? And what business could she have that would bring her out at this time of night, when steamers plied the Two Rivers at virtually all hours of the day?

Now, however, the powerful engines, silent these ten minutes or so while the red-haired woman had boarded with her companions, began to pound once more to life. And the night chill hit Olivia again, shocking her back to reality. Why, look at her! A decent, well-brought-up young woman of twenty-one, about to be presented to Delta society for the first time, and here she was, out on the boiler deck of a river steamer at midnight, unchaperoned, no more than half dressed. She shivered again and, giving the receding sight of the Cairo docks a last quick glance, hurried back to her little stateroom.

But after she had once again undressed and slipped between the chilly sheets, the heavy blankets now pulled up tight under her chin, the thought that haunted her all the way to sleep was of the mysterious red-haired woman she'd seen, with her queenly grace and bearing, with her haunting, mocking smile, and with those deep, intelligent eyes that had looked so boldly into Olivia's soul—and seen . . . seen what? She didn't know. But the spirit behind those emerald eyes had been one that understood her, knew her.

And when Olivia finally slipped off to sleep, it was to dream of romance, adventure, midnight trysts and intrigues, of the dark mysteries and exotic things that had already begun, little by little, to add a strange and bafflingly attractive spice to her great journey back to the lands of her birth.

Breakfast was Olivia's worst meal aboard the *Newport*. Something about the forced camaraderie of the morning meal invited in her elders a familiarity that unsettled her, unused as she was to the ways of the grown-up world after years at school. Olivia would gladly have skipped the first meal altogether if she had not learned by now that the action would provoke others to come after her, inquiring as to her health. So, stoically, she sat through the hateful meal, pecking daintily away at food she neither wanted nor enjoyed, keeping to herself as much as she could.

It was no use. The older people at the table had a way of bringing her into the conversation. Now the terrible Mrs. Bertrand, who claimed to have known Olivia's mother some years before, was introducing her to the new man at the table, a retired steamship pilot named Henry Flythe. And Olivia fidgeted under his fatherly gaze and heard him say, "Soames? Well, pardon me, ma'am, but you wouldn't be related in some way to Driscoll Soames?"

Olivia, uncomfortable as the center of attention, found herself blushing, to her surprise and embarrassment. "Why, yes . . . he's my uncle." She forced herself to look him in the eye, ignoring the others' stares. "I've been off in school in the East."

"Here," Mr. Flythe said, "I didn't mean to disconcert you, miss. It's just that . . . well, it's a small enough world, and it'll get smaller as you go farther downriver. Particularly if you're the daughter of . . . let's see, it'd be Dwight Soames, wouldn't it? Why, yes, I've done business with him once or twice, in Nyorlins. And your uncle and I have played piquet together. You see, folks of some quality tend to know one another—"

Mrs. Bertrand broke in, her rasping baritone voice full of amusement. "If you don't mind me changing the subject . . . you won't guess who came aboard last night in the dark of night." She looked around, amused, as if counting the raised eyebrows. "Mrs. Clifton, dear, could I trouble you for the peach preserves? Why, thank you." She looked down at the jam she was spreading onto her biscuit; then, almost ingenuously, she looked back up and around again. "Why, Aurora Brand, that's who! I had a peep out of the window, no more . . . but under the lights on the Cairo docks I couldn't fail to recognize that hair. At midnight! And trailing an entourage as long as your arm: servants, riverfront bullyboys—and that handsome young Jew lawyer of hers. What's his name, now?"

"Hmm . . . that'd be Ben Samuels," Captain Frye said from farther down the table. "My word. I wonder what in tarnation she's up to, boarding the *Newport*? A ship of another line? Why, there're two steamers of the Brand line due

through Cairo before noon. Why couldn't she wait for one of
those? Passage for that large a party would cost her a pretty
penny, I'd say.'' He raised a graying brow. ''Hmm. Fireworks
ahead if she finds out some of Rathbone's party are aboard.
Oil and water. But why?'' He was talking to himself now.
He patted his mouth with his napkin and shoved back from
the table. ''I wonder . . . shoal water downstream? Snags?
But how would she know ahead of time? Well, if she did, the
pilothouse might know. Mr. Flythe? If you're finished, I'll
be glad to introduce you to Oscar Wheeler, up aloft. Good
pilot, if a trifle green by the standards of an old hand like
yourself. Ladies? If you'll excuse us?''

''See there?'' Mrs. Langer, seated on Olivia's left, said.
''Wherever she goes, people take note, don't they?'' Her
sharp eye lit on Olivia for a moment. ''Including some folks,
I daresay, who oughtn't be up quite so late at night.''

Olivia blushed again; but the look on Mrs. Langer's face
was so conspiratorially friendly that she couldn't help grinning sheepishly. ''I . . . I couldn't help myself,'' she said.
''It was all so mysterious. This . . . this Aurora Brand, who
is she?''

The simple question brought a buzz of conflicting answers
from all parts of the table: ''Brand Steamship Line . . . ad-
venturess . . . smartest women I ever . . . shameless . . .''
But balding, moon-faced Arthur Potter, down the table, raised
his strong and confident voice, and his words cut through the
hubbub to Olivia's ears. ''Miss Soames,'' he said, ''you'll
hear a lot about Aurora Brand on the river. If you—''

''Why, you certainly will!'' a female voice down the table
said. ''And precious little of it good, let me tell you.''

''You hush now, Carrie Perkins,'' Mrs. Bertrand said in
that raucous voice of hers. ''She lives high, I'll grant you.
But she has a good name in New Orleans society for all that.
Why, Felicite Desmoulins herself told me that—''

Mr. Potter, solid as a block of granite, his deep voice
carrying through the chatter, ignored them. ''Miss Brand,''
he said imperturbably, ''inherited a failing steamship line
from her father a few years back, Miss Soames. She'd been
in Europe acquiring a finish and taking the waters. She returned to find her pa dead and his assets in doubt. She had

brains and pluck, though, and since that time she's put together an organization of her own—one that's hardly matched among any of the biggest firms on the Bourse—and the line's back in the black again. She's a gallant lady, and she has my own complete admiration, whatever others may say.''

He looked around as he took a sip of coffee; his eyes were cool. ''I'd say envy was a natural reaction among some,'' he said blandly. ''A great beauty, a legendary beauty . . . and proud and smart and independent. If I were twenty years younger myself, you know, I might . . .'' He looked back at Olivia now, and a small smile showed in one corner of his wide mouth. ''She's a queen, my dear. In everything but title. A veritable queen of the river.''

After breakfast Olivia wandered back out onto the boiler deck in the fresh morning air. Dawn came early on the river. Six hours below the point where the two great rivers joined, the sun had risen bright and balmy on the Mississippi, cutting early through the dense fog that had lingered all night on the bottoms. Now the air was sweet and clean. Olivia lingered at the lee rail, her hand on the polished wood, her eyes watching the play of morning sunlight on the waters. Turning her face to the long row of stateroom windows in the main cabin, she wondered idly which of those rooms now held the woman with the red hair.

Behind her, a sudden commotion broke into her reverie. Olivia heard pounding footsteps, voices raised in anger, sounds of a scuffle. She wheeled, and as she did, she saw a woman, well past her first youth but still comely despite her dowdy dress, break free from the grasp of a burly man in traveling dress. She ran toward Olivia, gasping: ''Help . . . help me, please!''

''You!'' the man bellowed, setting out after her. ''You stop right there, you little bitch! Stop or I'll . . .''

The woman flashed past Olivia, heading for the staircase that led down to the hurricane deck below. Olivia shrank back, but as she did, seeing the burly man bearing down on her, she yielded to a mad impulse without thinking. Mindful of the morning sun, she'd brought her parasol with her; now she half dropped, half tossed it into the pursuing man's path.

His foot landed on it and slid. He fell headlong—just as the woman he was pursuing reached the steps, only to run into a party of guests climbing the staircase, blocking her path.

"Please!" the young woman said, looking back to where the heavyset man was struggling to his feet. "Please let me pass."

Olivia watched, wide-eyed. At the head of the party coming up the stairs were the red-haired woman of the previous night, looking even more regal than before, and the handsome, hawk-faced man who had accompanied her aboard. They stopped, and Aurora Brand's hand went to the fugitive's arm. "It's all right," she said. She looked hard at the burly man who stood facing her, his heavy hands clenching and unclenching. "Halsey," she said. "What's all this about?"

"You stay the hell out of this," the heavy man said, his voice a menacing rasp. "This is none of your business."

"Let the girl go, Halsey," Aurora Brand said. "And I'll hear some explanation from you before I debate what's my business or not." She smiled down at the small silver pistol that had suddenly appeared in the steady hand of her partner on the stairs. "Steady as she goes there, Ben."

The hawk-faced man smiled, and his smile was as cold as the Maine snows. "Right you are, ma'am," he said.

Chapter 2

The heavyset man Aurora Brand had called Halsey looked sharply from the gun in Ben Samuels's hand to Samuels's thin-lipped smile, and then to Aurora Brand herself, to the haughtily arched brows below the shock of startling red hair, to the green eyes that regarded him unflinchingly. "Look here," he said in that rasping voice, "the woman works for me. She contracted to—"

"No!" the young woman said. "I mean, I did sign the paper . . . but, ma'am, that doesn't give him the right to take advantage of me, does it?" She held clenched hands before her breast, partly to hide the tear at her bosom. Olivia took note of her now for the first time: she was perhaps thirty-five, very dark, with almost a Gypsy look about her. She's possibly a French or even a Cajun mother, Olivia thought. Her eyes were large and bright and a deep, deep brown, and her careworn face had an appealingly vulnerable look about it. Instinctively Olivia's heart went out to her. Poor thing . . . and with a man like that.

"How about that, Halsey?" Aurora Brand said in a low, thrillingly vibrant voice. There was anger in her eye, but it was a controlled, deadly sort of anger. "You know the laws. An indenture?"

"Yes, damn it," the man Halsey said through clenched teeth. "Signed and sealed. But no sooner than that, she decides she isn't taking orders."

Samuels smiled his thin smile. Olivia caught the touch of humor in his brown eyes. "I understand, Halsey," he said in a voice with a vaguely Eastern accent. "Miss, what kind of orders?'' He caught the discomfort on the woman's face and nodded. "You don't have to answer that."

"Here," Aurora Brand said, putting a hand on the woman's olive-skinned arm. "Don't worry. You're not the first to have had this sort of trouble with Simon Halsey, my dear." She shot Halsey a barbed glance and ignored his low mutter. "Look, my friend here is an attorney. Any contract you've signed recently—it was recently, wasn't it? I thought so—any contract you've got, we can break. You come with me. I'll have someone go for your goods if you like. Ben?"

"I'll send Ragland or Leggett, ma'am," the lawyer said. The pistol in his hand, hardly bigger than a child's toy, still pointed unwaveringly at Halsey's thick middle. "I doubt that even Halsey will refuse the likes of them." He changed his tone. "Halsey? Had enough? Ready to leave? There's a good fellow."

"You! We'll see about this," Halsey growled. "You can't just steal away—"

"No," Samuels said, "but you can. Steal away, I mean. Why don't you do that right now?" He watched amusedly as the thick-set man turned, scowling, and angrily made his way down the row of cabin windows, fists bunched, his rolling gait resembling a sailor's. "Say hello to Rathbone for us," he said in a sardonic half-whisper just as a shrill hoot from the steamer's whistle cut off his words.

Aurora Brand turned to the lawyer. "I was bluffing, Ben," she said, one arm around the shoulders of the now sobbing woman. "You can nullify an indenture, can't you?"

Samuels, his smile turned thoughtful, uncocked the little weapon and pocketed it in his stylishly cut topcoat. "I think so," he said, "given Halsey's record. You'd think he'd have learned to keep his hands off by now."

Then his eye lit on Olivia Soames for the first time. "You, miss," he said. "I suppose we mainly have you to thank for the fact that this young lady is free just now. I saw what you did with the parasol." He bent and picked up the little umbrella, dusting it off with a delicately formed hand, and handed it to her with a courtly flourish.

"Oh," Olivia said, embarrassed, "I didn't—"

"Oh, yes, you did," Aurora Brand said in that rich, low

voice of hers. "I saw it too." Her smile was warm and welcoming. "That was courageous. Most people wouldn't have involved themselves." The dark woman disengaged herself from her protector's arms and tried to pull her torn gown together. "Here," Aurora Brand said. "I can fix that in a moment. Come to my stateroom. I'll find some thread, and then we can discuss your coming to work for me. That is, if you need work."

"Oh, yes, ma'am!" the woman said. "I'd be so obliged to you. I . . . I'm Cassie Quayle. I've got kin in Cincinnati. They'll vouch for me."

"That's all right," Aurora Brand said soothingly. "Don't you worry. You just come along with me. And you, miss?" She looked at Olivia, and Olivia's heart almost stopped. "Would you join us too? That is, if you're not doing something else?"

Doing something else? Olivia caught her breath and nodded. "Y-yes, ma'am. Why, yes. Maybe I can help."

Samuels smiled at her, a kindly, friendly sort of smile. "I'm sure you can, my dear. Miss Brand? I'll go after Ragland. And . . . Miss Quayle? Your cabin number?"

"F-fourteen," Cassie Quayle said, a strange touch of huskiness in her voice. Her broad mouth bore the first traces of a hopeful smile.

A quarter of an hour later Aurora Brand sat sewing by her window, the blinds half drawn. Cassie Quayle was in her shift by the bedside; Olivia, eyes aglow, was perched on the single bed behind Cassie, listening.

Cassie's story was brief and brutal. She'd married a man supposedly of no family or fortune. Only after they'd lived together for a time had she learned that he was previously married and not yet divorced—and that he was the ne'er-do-well son of a family of means in Pittsburgh. The family, learning of his now illicit liaison with Cassie, had bailed him out of the poverty in which he'd been living and thrown Cassie out into the street. She'd been pregnant at the time; the baby had died in childbirth. Her health had been broken down by a year in which, awaiting the child's birth and with neither husband nor visible means of support, she'd lived hand-to-mouth in the bleak Pittsburgh winter. Halsey had offered indenture as a tutor to the children of his boss, Laird Rathbone.

"Rathbone!" Aurora Brand said with a wry smile. "I'd almost rather see you fall into Halsey's hands than into Laird Rathbone's. Consider yourself lucky—" She stopped abruptly, looking at Olivia. "Miss Soames? It seems the name Rathbone registers with you. Do you know the family?"

"No, ma'am," Olivia said. "I just heard people talking at breakfast. He—Mr. Rathbone—he's a business rival of yours?"

"You might say that," Aurora Brand said, biting the thread and holding up the dress. "Here, Miss Quayle . . ."

"Cassie, ma'am. Please." The dark woman reached for the garment and turned her back to put it on.

"Cassie it is. And you, Miss Soames? Is it to be first names with us? Olivia?"

"Yes, ma'am!" Olivia said, trying hard not to grin so obviously, and failing. "I . . . you were talking about Mr. Rathbone."

"Very well. Laird Rathbone came to New Orleans while my father was still alive. He's a parvenu, as they say. No background at all. Not that that should hold anyone down. But Laird had a mind to make a big name for himself, in the fastest sort of way. Money, power—and a good marriage. By whatever means." She sighed, half smiling. "I don't know what New Orleans names will mean to you. You say you've been away since you were a child."

"Yes, ma'am. And . . . well, Papa was never terribly social after Mamma died."

"I see. Well, Rathbone carved his way into a position of power fairly quickly. Some said he cheated at cards. Some pointed to certain questionable stock exchanges on the Bourse, others to some fast-and-loose dealings in fast-turnover commodities such as cotton . . . and stolen slaves." She looked at Olivia curiously. "But wait. I think I know your father slightly. Soames . . . yes. He has the plantation next to Lance Whitmire's? On the river? I see . . . your father doesn't believe in slave labor, does he? And it's been costing him dearly to date, competing with planters who do. A brave thing to do. I can see where you get your courage."

"I . . . I don't know. Is Papa in trouble?"

"I don't think he's prospering. But of course, on the river it doesn't take long to turn a man's luck around. Let's see. Dwight Soames . . . Wyvern. He has Wyvern under sugar, doesn't he? I think I've done business with him. More likely with his overseer. An impressive young man named McClellan, as I remember. But I'm digressing. Rathbone cut a swath through the city, cheating, double-dealing. After a time the only thing he did that was surprising to anyone was his courtship of Allison Pryor. The bigger surprise was when she accepted him."

She smiled. "Probably I ought to explain. Allison Pryor was—is—one of the most wonderful people in the entire Delta. She's close friends with every friend I have. Probably we'd be friends, too, if it weren't for Laird. But he tried to ruin my father, and when he failed, he tried to ruin me. He's *still* trying." She smiled at Olivia conspiratorially. "He isn't succeeding. But the Brand Line would have a much larger percentage of the river traffic today if it weren't for Rathbone. He'd like to put me out of business altogether."

"Goodness. And Halsey—he works for Mr. Rathbone?"

"Yes," Aurora Brand said. "The rivalry is bitter on his side. He wants to control not only the docks—which he does, in part—and much of the crops on the river but the shipping as well. If he isn't successfully opposed, he'll do it too. He's just able enough and rapacious enough." She looked at Cassie Quayle now, buttoning up her blouse. "There!" she said. "Your dress looks as good as ever, Cassie. How'd you like to work for me now?"

"Why, yes, ma'am . . . of course."

"I don't mean in my organization. I mean for me. I need a dresser. A personal maid. Would that be appropriate work for you, do you think?"

Cassie Quayle, eyes wide, smiled hesitantly. "Why, Miss Brand! I . . . I'd love to. I mean, if you wouldn't mind . . ."

"Bosh," Aurora Brand said, pressing her hand impulsively. "It's all right. Look, I'll have you put on the payroll from today—even if it takes Ben a few weeks to break your contract with Halsey. We'll find things for you to wear. You've come to me at just the right time, you know. The social season's already under way—''

She stopped, stood, and looked at Olivia. "My goodness," she said. "I'll bet we're invited to the same party. At Justin Hague's, a week from tomorrow night? Why, yes! I'm sure we'll see each other again . . . soon. Justin and your father are good friends, as I remember, however much they may disagree on the subject of slavery." She took Olivia's hands, and before Olivia could react, Aurora Brand had leaned forward and kissed her cheek impulsively. "So we'll meet again, and soon," the red-haired woman said, smiling. "I'd like that. I like a girl with courage and spirit. You reminded me of myself a few years back. I'm sure we're going to be great friends."

Olivia's heart was pounding wildly. She grinned, brighteyed, abandoning all reserve. "Oh, yes, ma'am! I'd love that! I really would!"

Hands on hips, a scowl disfiguring his already unpleasant features, Simon Halsey stood watching the two roughs Ben Samuels had sent down to retrieve the two wicker hampers that contained all the portable goods Cassie Quayle had accumulated about her in thirty-five years of life. One of the burly men—the larger of the two—caught his eye and winked at him insultingly. Halsey snarled and balled one big fist but made no move to halt their forward progress. "You're done," he said in that harsh bass voice of his. "Now get the hell out of here."

"Yes, Your Worship," the bigger of the two said with a raucous, whiskey-soaked laugh. "Say, easy does it, there, Mack. One false step right now and you'll be up to yer arse in lacy underdrawers."

The smaller man, shouldering his hamper unsteadily, didn't answer until the two were out of earshot of Halsey. Then he stopped and put down his bundle. "Quint," he said, "hold up a minute there, yer drunken bum."

The big man rested his parcel on one thick hip and looked his wiry little companion up and down. "Yer got a hell of a big mouth on yer for such a runt," he said. "Whadder yer want?"

"When we was packin' this 'ere froufrou—I reco'nized one o' them dresses. The red 'un, yer know . . . the one with the—"

"Huh," the big man said. "I be goddamn." He pursed his thick lips over broken teeth. "Yer right," he said. "Wasn't that the one the gal was wearin' when we saw Halsey . . . ?"

The smaller man smiled sourly. "Yer not as dumb as yer look, yer big moose. Look, Samuels says Halsey tried to force the gal, right?"

"Huh. An' we seen him and her back on the docks in Cincinnati, lookin' chummier'n a couple er turtle doves. Sparkin' right out in broad daylight. They was—"

"Right. An' now she says he was tryin' to—"

The big man scowled at him. Then he hoisted the hamper to his broad shoulder and snorted contemptuously. "Aw, yer just tryin' to make too much o' nothin'. What yer need is a drink."

The little man looked sourly at him; then his expression changed, and his good humor came back. "Right yer are. An' do yer know what, yer big ox? I seen where Mike Cassidy stowed his jug last night, at the end o' the watch."

"Yer didn't. But how do we get to 'er in broad daylight?"

"We don't," the little man said, his face wrinkling in a big horse wink. "Too hard. Too dangerous." He belched mildly and shouldered his own load again. "That's why I took the precaution o' stealin' 'er last night. It ain't Four-Star Monongahely, but—"

"Yer little bastard. I got half a mind to carry yer damn hamper for yer."

Chapter 3

In the early afternoon the *Newport* docked at Natchez, and Olivia, standing by the guardrail of the boiler deck in the shadow of the texas, could see the twin towns clearly in the bright midday sun: Natchez-Under-the-Hill, squalid, mean, shabby, a cutthroat's town, and above it the lovely white houses of Natchez-on-Top-of-the-Hill, where for the first time in her epical voyage the girl could see signs of the tropical greenery that lay ahead in the Delta low country: pawpaw, palmetto, and orange trees side by side with lush tropical flowers in full bloom, and everywhere the bright green of lush grass—and all of it backed by the dark line of thick forest that all but encircled the tiny city by the river: the dark forest through which cut the legendary Natchez Trace, a forest highway along which no woman, and no unarmed man, dared venture.

Below Baton Rouge, the country took on an even more familiar look, and Olivia's heart thrilled to see it. It was a world of magnolia trees and hanging moss and wildflowers growing thick and free, a land of spreading live oaks and tropical swelter. And now the levees began to appear: tall, earthen barriers cutting off the great river from the lowlands beyond. It was her home country—green sugarcane country, lush and ripe, and as flat as a painted section of a map. The river was broad and deep here, and the pilot's path was much the easier for it, for all that the Mississippi's lazily winding route to the Gulf more than doubled the as-the-crow-flies distance. It wouldn't be long now, she thought. What would it be like? If . . .

There was a presence at her elbow, one she felt rather than saw clearly. She turned, startled, and saw the tall, patrician, uniformed figure of Captain Crider, master of the *City of Newport*, standing silently beside her. "Oh, Captain . . . I didn't see you come up."

"Sorry," the captain said. "I didn't mean to frighten you. I just wanted to inquire—"

She smiled. "Oh, everything's fine," she said. "It's been a wonderful trip. All the way."

He took off his hat and resettled it on his balding head. "I had my doubts," he said. "About a young lady your age traveling all that way without a chaperone, and me beholden and answerable to your pa." He smiled down at her, though, steady as a rock. "I put the word out that the smallest inconvenience to you at any point along the way and I'd—"

"Thank you for your concern," Olivia said. "But I would hardly have felt safer back in school. I'll tell Papa you minded after me like a baby." She turned back to the rail, watching the tops of a magnificent stand of live oaks pass by, just beyond the levee aport. "Isn't it lovely?" she said. "I'm beginning to feel as though I were home at last. I had no idea how much I'd missed it all."

"Well," the captain said, "I suppose you've got some catching up to do. Old friends to meet again and—"

"Oh, but that's just it. The *look* of the land is familiar, and there'll be Papa and Uncle Dris, but I hardly know anyone. It's been so long. I was hardly more than a baby." She smiled. "Although I must say everyone aboard seems to know *me*. Mrs. Bertrand, Mr. Flythe, Miss Brand . . ."

"Miss Brand? You met Miss Brand?" the captain asked.

"Why, yes. And I'll be seeing her again soon, she says. It seems a Mr. Hague is throwing a party next week, and we're both invited."

Olivia turned and caught the captain's expression for the first time now. Stuffy? Disapproving? No, skeptical. Well, maybe that meant disapproval, after all. She sighed. Controversy seemed to follow Aurora Brand around.

The captain took his leave of her, his manner courtly but a trifle more distant, she thought. She leaned against the port rail, looking out across the river at the tall levees. Why, she thought, do they disapprove of her? Is it because she's strong and independent? Because she doesn't just sit back and let the men run things? Because she has the courage to live her own life, the way a man does, and not ask anybody's permission or leave to do anything?

She sighed. *I wish I could be like her,* she thought. *If only . . .*

At dusk there came the time when the arrangement of lights on the levee showed a familiar configuration, one Olivia had seen before. Her heart started pounding like a steam engine. And now the steam whistles hooted, a pattern of signals any knowledgeable landsman along the river could hear and identify, that any river-bred child could hear no more than once and recognize as the *City of Newport.* The great engines cut and went dead, then started to life again, backing water.

She turned, intending to head for her stateroom and make one last check of her bags, and saw, all of a sudden, the lean, darkly handsome form of Ben Samuels standing not ten feet away. Behind him were two roughly dressed men she recognized as having been among the midnight group that had boarded with Aurora Brand in Cairo. Beside them, her bags and movables were stacked neatly, ready to unload. "Why . . . why, Mr. Samuels," she said. "You didn't have to do that."

"Compliments of Miss Brand," he said in a rich, almost theatrical voice. "She sends her regrets. She'd see you off herself, but she's talking business with a cotton factor in the main cabin. She asked me to deputize for her. I hope you're not disappointed."

"Oh, no," Olivia said, immensely flattered. "And . . . would you thank her for me? She's been so nice."

"She likes you," Samuels said impulsively. "I think you've made a firm friend. Miss Brand follows her instincts, and they seldom lead her astray. You'll find that the friendship of Aurora Brand draws a little water on the river, my dear, especially down here in Delta waters."

"I . . . I'm sure it does. She's a great lady, isn't she?"

Samuels smiled his thin, philosophical smile. His voice was thoughtful. "The greatest of ladies, my dear, for all that you'll hear the opposite from some small-minded people. I owe her everything I have, from my position on the New Orleans bar to my entrée into Delta society. I'd die for her . . . and in that I'm one of many.'' He saw her puzzled glance and laughed quietly. ''To answer a perhaps too personal question in your eyes that you're too well-bred to voice, no, my dear, I'm not in love with her. I'm betrothed to a rather dazzling young lady in St. Louis. But the service of Miss Brand is the one thing in the world that would tear me from her side.'' He smiled confidentially, a twinkle in his dark eyes. ''But now I think we're nearing the dock. And that might well be your father standing there, waiting for you. Mr. Leggett? Mr. Ragland? Time to disembark, I believe.''

Eyes wide, Olivia turned, and saw the dock, the familiar, rickety dock of Radford, the neighboring plantation to her father's. Radford! Of course! Old Mr. Whitmire! But . . . but no. Papa had written her that the old man had passed on. And what was it they'd said at breakfast about young Lance? No, it had been Miss Brand, hadn't it? She'd said there was bad blood between Papa and—

There was Papa himself! Older, grayer, thinner, but recognizably himself and beaming up at her, waving proudly, looking happy, excited, enthusiastic!

On the dock she hugged him close, and he waltzed her around for a few steps, pounding her back, chuckling to himself. ''Olivia, my darling, I'm so happy. At last you've come back.''

''Oh, yes!'' she said, opening her eyes and stepping back to hold him by the arms and look him up and down. ''Yes, and to stay this time, Papa.'' Her heart skipped a beat, seeing him for the first time now. ''Oh, Papa . . . you're so thin. Hasn't Sukey been feeding you properly?''

''Poor Sukey died some time back. I freed the last of her offspring two years ago. They've all gone north. I suppose you've heard. Wyvern isn't doing well. Two straight crops failed, and the bank . . .'' But he drove the sadness from his face now and forced a brave smile. ''I'm fine, my dear. Just a bit older.''

''I'll feed you myself,'' Olivia said. ''If there's one thing a graduate of Mrs. Fitch's can be counted on for, it's cooking.

Papa, I'll put some weight on those skinny bones of yours for you. Just you watch."

Behind her, the steam whistle hooted again. Olivia whirled. Ragland and Leggett had unloaded her baggage and scrambled back aboard. Ben Samuels, lean and debonair, stood at the main deck's rail, watching her as the roustabouts pulled up the gangplank. His face bore a courtly smile; he inclined his head and tipped his hat gallantly at her. She waved, smiling, and her eyes sought the upper decks for some sign of Aurora Brand, but the red-haired woman did not appear.

Olivia looked back at her father, and as she did, she took note of the tall, powerful-looking man standing silently behind him. The big man's head inclined slightly in deference; the eyes—deep set, intelligent—regarded her with interest. "Oh, Olivia," her father said. "This is Mr. McClellan, our overseer. Zachary, this is my daughter Olivia."

"Pleased to meet you, ma'am," the big man said in a voice at once resonant and quiet. "Mr. Soames, I think we might do well to head in. It'll be dark before we're home as it is."

Dwight Soames brushed the gray hair back from his forehead with one palm. It was an old tic Olivia remembered. "Why, right you are. The buggy's waiting, my dear. If you'll just step this way . . ."

Zach McClellan drove, sitting high on the seat before them. She took more than one surreptitious look at his broad, powerful-looking back and shoulders, taking note of his erect carriage and the gentle hand he had on the reins. Her father leaned forward, facing her on the opposite seat, and said in a low voice, "I hired him a couple of years ago when I freed the boys. He's quiet—perhaps too quiet—but a good man, steady and strong. Loyal too. Lance Whitmire tried to hire him away from me some time back, and he said no, and to an offer I couldn't have matched without hardship. Ever since, Lance has had it in for him."

"Papa, you said Wyvern was in trouble."

"Ah," he said, waving the thought away. "Time enough to chatter on about that. The main thing is, you're home." He stopped and sighed. "No. I can't dissemble with you, can

I, my dear? Any more than I could with your mother. You're a lot like her in that sense." His smile was indulgent and loving. "Young Lance . . . I can't get on with him. Never could, even before his father's death. He has strong feelings about . . . about my freeing the boys a couple of years back. Says things about how I'm undermining the system. I can't see how, with him working cheaper labor than I. But that's the way he looks at it. And . . . well, he's doing poorly too. I know some folks down at the bank. They say he's in the same boat I am. Overextended, with two outstanding loans going bad on him. If either of us brings in a good crop this year, he's out of trouble. But one more failed crop for either of us just now . . ."

"Poor Papa," Olivia said. "But I know you'll pull through. You always do."

He tried to smile, but the thought carried him farther afield. "And, of course, there's the matter of the landing. We had rather a terrible row about that this morning, I'm afraid. Very public. Very embarrassing. He was really quite abusive. He's been drinking more and more, and I think he was under the influence when he called me down."

"I don't understand," Olivia said, leaning forward and taking his hand. "Why was he angry with you?"

"Well, you know I'm landlocked here. Always have been. Although it wasn't a problem with Lance's pa. I depend on an easement through Lance's land to get crops to market and to receive supplies by the river. When I ship, the crop's loaded on Lance's own docks, and it's been hauled through his own land, and here we're rivals for what business there is up here, you know. Common law guarantees me the easement, but it doesn't guarantee me Lance's cooperation, you know. And if he needs to ship same time as I do . . ." His final sigh was one of resignation. "I don't really know what I can do about it, you know."

"Well," Olivia said, "we'll talk it out some more later. Right now . . . oh, Papa, it's so good to be home." Her eyes were bright and blue and shone with the unstoppable optimism of youth. Dwight Soames sighed one more time, this time in a mood tempered by his pleasure in seeing her. "And . . . and I understand we're invited to a party next week."

"Party?" Dwight Soames said, blinking. He ran his thin hand through his hair. "I don't remember any—" He stopped. "But of course. At Mr. Hague's. But how did you know, my dear? I don't—"

"Oh. I met Miss Brand on the boat. Aurora Brand. She says she knows you slightly."

"Aurora Brand! Well, how flattering that she'd remember me after several years. But how did you come to—"

"Oh, it's a long story, Papa, and an exciting one. We became fast friends, I think. She says she'll see me again at the party. Perhaps we can chat for a moment."

Dwight Soames smiled mildly at her in the gathering dusk. "My, my," he said in a tired voice. "Your first day back below Memphis in years, and you've already made friends with perhaps the most powerful woman on the river. Olivia, my darling, you amaze me. I'm going to enjoy having you home."

She smiled at him, taking note of the thinness of his face, the careworn look at the corners of his eyes, the general air of great weariness. Well, perhaps he'd been ill. He'd be the type not to tell her for fear of alarming her.

She pursed her lips and looked at him again. Well, there was nothing to do but start taking care of him. It was obvious that nobody had been caring for him all this time, not since old Sukey's death. She'd make that her own special project.

But now, as the last rays of the sun faded, Zach McClellan turned the buggy into the familiar road that led through its overarching avenue of stately live oaks thickly decked with hanging Spanish moss. It was a place where the sun never shone, a place of cool and welcome shade through the hottest summers; that much Olivia remembered from childhood. And at the end of the dark archway warm lights burned, lighting the pillared front of a still gracious, homey-looking Louisiana Creole mansion with slender colonnades supporting a high-pitched, dormered roof. The porch, set above a raised basement and bearing white railings, had an infinitely inviting look to it.

Wyvern!

Chapter 4

As her father's buggy approached the house and Olivia could see it more clearly by the light of the outside torches and the lamps gaily illuminating the vestibule and the open front door, she could already begin to see the signs of decay. The house hadn't been kept up; it needed paint here, plaster there. She started to say something as Zach pulled the buggy up before the steps and stepped down to unload Olivia's luggage before handing her down; but something made her hold her tongue. Surely her father had already taken note of these things. If he had not attended to them—well, there might be various reasons, and perhaps they did not bear discussing before someone she didn't know.

Zach lifted her down easily. She felt the power in the big man's hands—and the gentleness too. She gave him one lingering look as he walked away, but he did not notice.

"I don't know what we can fix up for dinner, my dear," Dwight Soames said. "Red beans and rice, perhaps. I've got out of the habit of doing much in the way of formal cooking."

Well, Olivia thought as she swept in the open door and looked around at further signs of disuse, of lack of maintenance, of downright dirt, *at least I know what I'm going to be busy with for a few days.* She peeped into the kitchen for a moment and winced at the unexpected mess. A large pot sat simmering on the open stove. "All right, Papa. Red beans will be just fine. I'll just put some rice on." She looked around at the pile of dirty dishes. Goodness, she thought. There'll be flies in here tomorrow morning, too thick to talk about it. Perhaps she could come in and do some dishes to-night.

Olivia had intended to get up at dawn on her first full day at Wyvern, but to her chagrin the sun was high and the air was already warm and humid when she awoke. She threw off the cov-erlet and dressed quickly. Oddly enough, her old room was pretty much the way she'd left it. It was far and away the cleanest room in the house; perhaps this was because, unlike the others, it hadn't been used. Other than a good sweeping and dusting, it wouldn't require much work. But the rest of the house!

As she went out into the drawing room, though, she looked toward the front door and suddenly saw Zach McClellan standing there, tall and silent. "Oh," she said, "Mr. Mc-Clellan. You startled me."

"Sorry, ma'am," the overseer said. "I don't mean to bother you, but . . ."

She thought about inviting him in, but something in her, some streak of family pride, made her join him on the porch instead. "Yes?" she said. "I . . . I'm sorry. I meant to get up early today, but . . ."

Her words sounded disgustingly coy, and she wished she could call them back. Of course he'd understand; she needn't comment. She sneaked a look at him and saw his eyes on her, his expression noncommittal. "Mr. Soames had some urgent business," he said. "He asked me to drop by once I had the morning chores in hand and see if you'd like to take a ride around the grounds."

She smiled at him. Yes, she thought. This was one straight-forward person. The standard coquetry women learned down here would pass right by him. "Why, thank you," she said simply. "It's kind of you, and thoughtful of Papa."

"Then I'll bring up the buggy. Or should I saddle the mare?"

"Horses!" she said, charmed by the idea. "Why, I haven't ridden in years. I'll bet this mare you're talking about is the granddaughter of one of my old favorites." She looked down at her simple dress. "I'll change. And thank you for thinking of it."

All the way back into the house she could feel his eyes on

her. But the look in his eyes had been less hungry than curious. He was an odd one, all right, a quiet man who kept to himself. But very much a man for all that.

When Olivia was little, there'd been slaves scurrying about, busy with the chores of a flourishing and affluent plantation. Now, as she rode past the old milk house, where cool cistern water, pumped by hand into long zinc vats, had provided Wyvern's cooling system for its milk crocks, she felt almost as though she were riding through a ghost town or a graveyard. Also echoingly empty were the yards, the outbuildings, the old covered ways that had connected the kitchen below the servants' quarters to the dining room. Dwight had closed the buildings up, and had converted back to regular use the in-house kitchen that had come with the house long before he'd added the outbuildings. Everything had the look of something long forgotten.

"Mr. McClellan," she said, turning the mare into the lane past the long dead garden. "I . . . I have to know. Is Papa going to lose Wyvern?"

"Well, ma'am . . ." he began. He pulled his gelding up alongside her, looked her once in the eye, and set his jaw before speaking. "Ma'am," he said, "I'd rather not be the one who has to tell you, but—well, you're going to own this place someday, if it survives, and I suppose you ought to know."

"Know what?" Olivia said, her eyes on the blighted plants, the unwatered vines. "I gather the place is failing by leaps and bounds. How many people are working the place now?"

"There's me and fifteen Cajuns. Free labor. That's part of the problem, ma'am. Since your pa freed the boys and they took off . . . well, it's been hard meeting the payroll, let me tell you. If it was anyone but the Cajuns, ma'am, they'd have been long gone by now too."

"Cajuns?" she said. "Working a sugar plantation in competition with slave labor right next door?"

"Yes, ma'am," McClellan said quietly. "I tried every other source of labor. No one would work for me. I was ready to toss it up when Mr. Dallas Boyd ran into your pa in the city and offered his help. The Cajuns over across the river in the islands think the world of Mr. Boyd, for all that polite society doesn't seem to know what to think of him."

"Dallas Boyd," she said. "Well, the name rings no bells with me, I'm afraid."

"Oh, no, ma'am. Mr. Boyd didn't come into the area until . . . oh, I'm not sure of the year. But it was after you went off to school. He just sort of turned up, and quite well-to-do. Walked into the city off the boat and deposited quite a healthy sum on credit at Mr. Charpentier's bank. Made no explanations about where he came by it. Some folks don't like that. Some folks like a man to put his pedigree on display right off."

She looked at him, mildly puzzled by the earnestness in his tone. "And if you don't mind my asking, Mr. McClellan, what do *you* think about it?"

The expression in his eyes was once again straightforward, his voice steadfast. "Ma'am, I—and your pa by extension, too—we owe Mr. Boyd everything we've got. I suppose you do too. He stood up like a friend right when everyone else was daring your pa to go under. I'd swim a riverful of gators for him." He paused, perhaps a little embarrassed by his outburst. "Well, I mean . . . anyhow, I sort of figure a man's pedigree is his own business. I'm not too loose-mouthed about my own background, either."

"Oh?" she said. Was he going to leave it there? "I'm sure there's nothing in your own background that won't bear scrutiny," she said courteously.

There was more than a little surprise in the look he shot her now. "You've a delicate way of asking a question, ma'am," he said.

Embarrassed, Olivia stammered, "I—I'm sorry." She fidgeted with the reins, unable to look him in the eye. "I . . . I was prying, wasn't I?"

"It's all right, ma'am," he said. But all the same, he didn't break his reticence. "I'm no river cutthroat or Natchez Trace road agent, if it means anything." They could see the cane fields now, and above them the long levee. "Look," he said. "The crop's good this year. If nothing happens—no acts of God or whatever . . ." She looked at his profiled face now. His expression was a dark and brooding one.

"Or . . . whatever?" she said. "You said that rather strangely, I think."

"It's nothing," he said, looking out over the long rows. "Or maybe it is. I don't know. I—I have this feeling. As if something I don't know about is happening. Some tension building, some problem arising. There's something vaguely wrong." He looked up at the cloud banks to the north of them. "Or maybe I'm just being an old woman, responding to the weather. We're going to have a blow and a big rain. I talked to someone on the boat that brought you. The telegraph says there have been storms to the north. That'll mean high water, and soon."

"Goodness," Olivia said. "A storm? That's some welcome." But the bantering tone failed her, and there was no humor in her words at all. "I . . . I suppose that'll mean everyone will be out minding the levee."

"I suppose so," he said emphatically. "I wouldn't be surprised to hear you had totally forgotten that your head, is . . . hmmm . . . something like thirteen feet below the surface of the Mississippi. And it's low water right now."

She shivered but said nothing, her eyes on his strong profile. "About that other business," he said. "There's somebody—something—that has it in for us here at Wyvern. I don't know who. Your pa made a lot of enemies among the planters who compete with him. They don't like his working his plantation with free labor. Although why that would make anyone want to . . ." He scowled. "There are others. There's young Mr. Whitmire, for one. There are business enemies of your Uncle Driscoll . . ."

"Uncle Dris? Why would that affect my father?"

"Well, when your pa needed a cosigner for the loan two years ago, your uncle went along with him—but at a price. He's now a third partner in the plantation. And he's pressuring your pa to listen to the offer Mr. Rathbone made him last year. Your pa, of course, says no. Puts his foot down. But that doesn't stop your uncle from pestering him."

"But . . . what has been happening here?" Olivia asked. "I don't understand."

"There've been a couple of unexplained fires," Zach McClellan said. "There've been little things. Somebody sawing halfway through the axle on a wagon at night when nobody was looking. I put guards on the place after that one, but things keep happening. His face was troubled as he looked up at the dark clouds again. "Still, if we can just get by this one year and bring this one crop in, there'll be enough to pay off both loans, buy out your uncle, and live for another two years in some sort of decent style."

"The crop—it's that rich?"

"Oh, yes," he said in a confident voice. "Yes, indeed, ma'am. This is rich land. Rich as a man could ask for. And the crop I've got out there—it'd make a man wealthy beyond his wildest expectations. All it would take to bring it in would be"— and unconsciously he ticked the things off on his fingers—"for that rain cloud up there, and a lot of others like it, to break up and blow out to sea; and for the high water coming down the river to be way below expectations; and for there to be no hurricanes, or fires, or tornadoes . . . and," he said, taking off his hat and wiping his brow with the back of one big hand, "for whoever it is to let up on us for long enough to get the cane cut and stacked and loaded on a ship bound for market."

"Goodness. It's a chancy business, isn't it?"

"Certainly is, ma'am." But then he put the questions from him and turned back to her, forcing his features into a matter-of-fact expression. "But, ma'am, you're talking about cleaning up the main house. You'll need help, I think. Maybe I'll ask the Cajuns if any of them has a wife or a girlfriend who can come in and pitch in with you."

"That'd be very kind of you," Olivia said. "If you can find the money to pay them, I could use two girls right now." She sighed. "Of course, I appreciate Papa's conscience telling him to do what he did with the slaves, but I have to admit it's a lot harder than it used to be."

"Not really, ma'am," Zachary McClellan said. "Not in the long run. Some years from now the slavery folks are going to find the sand's run out of their glass. And when that happens, I believe the troubles folks in your pa's position have right now will look like very minor troubles indeed. There's something in the Bible, I think, about sowing the wind and reaping the whirlwind."

Now Olivia caught herself looking at him in outright astonishment, openmouthed. A moralist! A man with a conscience—perhaps with a sense of personal mission! "Mr. McClellan," she said thoughtfully, "you're an unusual person, if you don't mind my saying so. But . . . I suppose the most unusual thing is your sense of loyalty. You've stuck by my father when everyone else deserted him, everyone except blood kin. I want you to know that I appreciate that."

And when she found him turning to look her in the eye, she was amazed at her own boldness in speaking this way to him. Could it be that she, timid, tongue-tied Olivia, was somehow developing poise and self-confidence now that she was back on her home soil and in a situation in which she was not only valued but, as she could clearly see, very much needed? Or was it simply because she was the mistress of the manor and he was the overseer, the underling? Tearing her eyes away, she thought hard and long about that. And try as she might, she could locate in her present impressions no sign of any condescension in her own attitude, or deference in his.

She looked back up at the dark clouds, though, and shifted her weight in the sidesaddle. "You're right," she said. "It feels more and more like rain. Perhaps we ought to get back now. I've got the dining room left to clean and supper to put on." An idea suddenly popped into her mind. "Mr. McClellan, would you be our guest at supper?"

Zach McClellan bit his lip and quickly shook his head. "Thank you, ma'am," he said, "but I think I'd better not. I think my time would best be occupied right now with setting up night watches on the levee. The rain's no more than minutes away, and God alone knows how far upriver the high water is just now." He calmed the skittish gelding under him. "You're in sight of the house, ma'am. Do you suppose you can find your way back by yourself? I apologize for asking, ma'am, but . . ."

Surprisingly, he didn't quite wait for her answer but turned and spurred the pony back down the road, his back straight and stiff. Olivia, startled, sat staring after him until he had disappeared over the rise two hundred yards away.

Chapter 5

The rain began in the middle of the night with a light drizzle that pattered softly on the roof outside Olivia's dormer window. Then it picked up slowly, steadily, and, to her surprise, suddenly turned into a violent thunderstorm, with deafening peals of thunder preceded by wild flashes of light outside the curtained window. After a time she got up and walked to the window to look out and to close the window tight against the wind-driven rain that had already made puddles on her floor.

From the upper window she could see people, by the light of the lightning flashes, going to and fro far out in the fields. She could see the high line of the levee and men wrestling sandbags high onto its already towering surface. Chilled by the very sight, she clasped her arms against her body, hoping against hope that the rain wouldn't bring the kind of damage Zach McClellan had feared. If the levee gave . . .

Then the lightning flashed again: a powerful bolt that broke into pieces, stabbing down from the sky with a dozen mighty arms. And by its light, in the driving rain, she could see her father's frail-looking form riding his stallion slowly across the rain-soaked grounds under the arch of dripping trees. There was a dejected set to his shoulders, and his head hung low under the broad planter's hat he wore.

Poor man, she thought. Poor darling. And she stepped into her slippers and reached for her robe. She'd meet him at the door and help him dry off. She lit a candle and went to the stairs. Yes, she'd make a nice fire and bring towels.

But when she reached the first landing, she looked down

and saw him standing in the door, but looking out, not in. He had his hat off and was mopping his face with the other hand. "Papa!" she said, holding the candle high. "Come in right now. You'll catch your death!"

He turned, and by the candlelight she could see the sag of his fallen features. "Olivia," he said in a hoarse croak. "What are you doing up, my dear? You go right back and . . ."

She tripped down the remaining stairs and set the candle down by the fireplace. "You get out of those wet things right now," she said. "I'll start a fire here, and by the time you're out of those dripping clothes, I'll have you a nice warm spot here to dry off in." She tossed the two towels she'd picked off her bedside table onto a chair before the fireplace.

Dwight just stood looking at her. "The water's high," he said. "Too high. I don't know if it'll hold. Telegraph says there's more coming downriver. And then there's this." There was more than fatigue in his voice. "Well, it's small consolation to know it, I'm sure, but young Lance Whitmire's in an even shakier position than I am, isn't he?" He looked to her upturned face for understanding but found none. "Oh, I suppose you've forgotten the layout here, haven't you? When you left, you were so young. Well, Lance's place is on a point of land, right in the middle of Ackerman's Bend. I'm a little inland. A levee breaking, a cut getting opened in the neck . . . well, Lance'd be in an even worse position than we'd be."

"A cut?" Olivia said, arranging the fat lightwood and striking a lucifer below it. "You'll have to explain these terms, Papa. At school all the other things I had to learn just plain washed my mind clean of everything a Southern girl ought to know."

"Well, the river changes course now and then," he said. "When a bend, a spit of land projecting out into the channel, gets cut into at the neck, the way it might in a real flood, well, the land inside the bend would become an island, pure and simple. The river'd cut right through the neck of land and go its merry way, and what had been good land on this side of the Mississippi would suddenly become bad land on the other, out in the middle of it." He put his hat down at last and wearily struggled out of his heavy coat. As she watched, he started, out of habit, to drop his clothes on the floor, but noting her eyes on him, he retrieved them shame-facedly and draped them over a chair, picking up one of the towels to wipe his face.

"I'm sorry," he said. "I've been alone here so long, I haven't proper manners anymore. I don't go out. I don't in-vite anyone in. I should be ashamed of myself."

"Papa, I'm going to fix all that," she said, fanning the flame and reaching for one of the cut logs to set it firmly atop the firedogs. "I'm going to clean this place up, and I'm going to get you back to seeing folks again. Do you know what? You're going to take me to the party at Mr. Hague's."

"Party?" he said dully. "Oh, no, my dear. Please. I couldn't."

"Oh, yes, you could." She stood and wiped her hands on the other towel. "Now get out of that vest and shirt." She draped the garments one by one over the chair back. "After all, if you don't take me, how am I going to go? No, Papa, you're in some danger of turning into an old recluse here, and I'm not going to let that happen. You just forget about it. We're going to the party, and that's all there is to it."

Dwight stopped undressing. "My goodness," he said. "I can't undress in front of you. Why, you're grown, aren't you?" He was looking at her as if he hadn't clearly seen her before. "Why, here I've been thinking I had my little girl back. And instead you're a grown woman." His smile was wan but it showed his pleasure. "And with ideas of her own, too. Party, indeed. Well, I suppose I've no choice, have I?"

Olivia smiled and went to the garderobe and found an old and tattered man's robe. "Here, this'll have to do," she said. "I'll turn my back if you like, but I'm not budging until you're out of those trousers and into this." She turned to stand before the fire, warming herself.

Thunder boomed outside, and the rain battered the win-dows. "Mr. McClellan showed me around today," she said. "He's a nice man, isn't he? I mean, a good overseer?"

"Wonderful," Dwight said. "If it hadn't been for him and Dallas Boyd . . ."

"That name keeps cropping up," Olivia said. "This Dal-las Boyd, who is he?"

Dwight didn't answer for a moment. Then he said, "Nobody seems to know, quite. He's as charming a rogue as ever breezed into town, and a man of very considerable parts. Around here, you know, if a man has family, he usually takes some pains to let you know who they are. And yet Dallas is patently a man of gentle breeding—he has a finish that few of the local bloods can boast when he cares to display it— but . . ." He sighed. "Well, some folks' taste runs that way, I suppose. He's as much at home roistering with a bunch of lowlifes down on the swamp as he is at a fancy ball. Some say more so. But I think they're just jealous."

"But he's accepted in society here?"

"Of course he is. He plays piquet with the biggest names on the Bourse and takes pains to lose slightly but steadily to the most influential. And to let them know, by the subtlest possible means, that he's losing as a matter of deference, and could, if he chose, clean out half the town with the cards in an evening's play."

"Goodness. It all sounds so strange. I'm going to have to get used to some things here. I'm only a few weeks out of Mrs. Fitch's. These social subtleties are too much for me."

Dwight seemed not to have heard her. His tone had a note of reverie in it. "The curious thing is that he's romanced half the women in town, but never seriously. And yet no one ever takes him to task for trifling with anyone's affections. He does have that kind of charm. Why, he and Aurora Brand . . ."

Olivia half turned to see him belting the robe. "Miss Brand? Was Mr. Boyd involved with her?"

Dwight smiled. "I see Miss Brand interests you. Well, she and Dallas had quite a thing going on for some time. They cut quite a swath through New Orleans. Folks were thinking they'd marry. They'd never seen Dallas get serious with a woman before, and they'd never seen Aurora with a man as strong as herself. Maybe stronger. Who knows? I'd say they were well matched in many ways. But perhaps that's the problem. Both of them are used to the world around them giving way when they come through. Both of them are used to being able to bowl over half the world and charm the rest. And it's a clear case of irresistible force and immovable object." He smiled, and then shuddered visibly as a nearby bolt of lightning lit the room as plain as day and a deafening clap of thunder followed. "Heavens. I suppose I ought to be out there helping Zach with the men."

"They'll do fine without you, Papa," Olivia said. "You were saying that Dallas Boyd and Miss Brand don't get along now?"

"Something happened. One moment folks were thinking wedding bells. The next, why, Dallas had taken off for the East without a moment's notice, standing up Aurora at a ball at Henri Desmoulins's, and nobody heard another word from him for six months. And the next time Aurora saw him—I think it was at a party in the city—why, she cut him dead, as publicly as possible."

"Do you suppose . . . do you think he'll be at Mr. Hague's?"

"Oh, I doubt that," Dwight said. "Heavens, listen to that rain! My stars, I thought I'd had the worst of it, but poor Zach and the boys must be having the devil's own time of it out there."

"Mr. McClellan—Zach—he says he's sending me a girl or two to help with the house."

"Oh? What'll we pay her? Oh, you mean one of the Cajun girls. Well, I suppose you need help. By myself, I've tended to do without . . . and just *look* at the dust and clutter. Oh, all right." He smiled, but there was little of the smile in his eyes. He turned to face the fire and stood warming his hands by the light of the dancing flames. "For all I know, the house may be under water by morning. It'll all be moot. I don't know, my dear. I just don't know. This time we may just not make it. We may just go under. I hate to say it. But if I'm to be truly honest with you, I'd have to say the odds are against me—yes, and young Lance, too; for all his arrogance, he's as frightened as I am and as vulnerable. The odds are terrifying."

Olivia firmed her young jaw and looked him in the eye. "We'll make it, Papa, whatever happens. If we lose the place, well, there'll be other things to do. But we're not going to lose it." Saying it, she wondered at her own resolve and audacity. Was this the same meek little Olivia Soames who had let herself be terrorized by old biddies like Mrs. Langer and Mrs. Bertrand only a few mornings ago?

But looking at the pale, shaken, and surprisingly frail figure Dwight Soames had become in the years she was away, she suddenly saw what was happening to her. He depended on her now, whether or not he was admitting it to himself. And when circumstances conspired to weaken the man of the house, the woman of the house—be she daughter or wife— had to find in herself the strength to take over, to run things, to pull things together. And somehow, somehow she knew that when she reached inside herself for that strength, she'd find it in abundant quantities.

But even as she considered this, a sudden chill of fear ran through Olivia. What if she *wasn't* up to it? What if she couldn't handle the many problems they were facing? Thinking these things, she suddenly wanted, more than ever, to see Aurora Brand again, if only to have one more look at what a strong, resourceful, independent woman could be like. She had *so* much to learn.

Perhaps if the rains had continued, the levee might have given way and ruined both Dwight Soames and Lance Whitmire. But in the night the rains came to an uncertain end, and the levees held. In the morning Olivia woke and looked out her dormer window to see that Wyvern Plantation was soggy but sound.

In mid-morning Zach McClellan rode in in the buggy. With him in the high seat was a dark-featured young woman, thin, intense, with flashing eyes. Despite her dowdy dress, he helped her down as if she were royalty as Olivia watched from the porch.

"Miss Soames," he said, "this is Mrs. Leblond. She's here to help with the house."

Olivia looked the girl over. "I'm pleased to meet you," she said, and then found herself trying to find the French for an introduction as McClellan rode away. *"Je m'appelle Olivia Soames. Voulez-vous . . ."*

The girl shot her an indecipherable glance, in which there was not the slightest deference. "I speak English," she said in a decently bred upriver accent. "A good thing, too. That copybook French works well enough in New Orleans, I suppose, but the men out here speak an older and better kind. They won't understand you at all. Well, maybe I can teach you. In the meantime you'll need someone to translate. Well, nice to know I can be of some use right off.'' She continued to look at Olivia boldly, but there was a hint of friendliness, or at least acceptance, in her unsmiling eyes. "I'm called Inez,'' she said. "Let's go look at the house.''

Olivia stayed a bit off-balance all through that first day. Inez didn't act like a servant at all. She gave about half the orders during the first few hours; she'd ask Olivia what end she wanted to accomplish, think about it for a moment, and then start issuing orders like a field overseer. But there was no disrespect in her manner at all. She was simply efficient, after all, and as the two young women tackled the many chores involved in making the house livable once again, Olivia found herself smiling a secret smile and thanking the good Lord above for sending her another strong woman for a helper. There was much to be learned from Inez Leblond, too, about how to be strong and still be a woman.

At the end of the day Inez looked about her, winced slightly at the dust remaining to be cleaned up and at the windows yet to be washed.

"That's enough for today,'' she said. "We did a good day's work. Tomorrow we'll do more.'' And, giving Olivia that straightforward, straight-in-the-eye look again, she almost smiled for the first time. "You're all right, Olivia. You're made out of the right stuff. One wouldn't know it to look at you.'' She nodded her head curtly and strode out the front door, her dark hair trailing behind her. "I'll see you tomorrow,'' she said.

Chapter 6

The next few days were given over to the hardest labor Olivia had ever done in her young life. Each day she and Inez took on another room of the house, scrubbing the floors right down to the paint, dusting, and washing out curtains. Olivia marveled at Inez's stamina and force of personality as the dark girl attacked the dirt and clutter of the neglected house as if every flaw, every dirt spot, every speck of dust were a personal affront.

For the most part Inez worked silently, and if she spoke at all, it was in curt monosyllables. Every so often they'd stop and rest for the time it took to brew and drink a cup of tea, and then talk became possible. Olivia came to look forward to these breaks in her labors and grew fond of the girl.

Outside, the weather continued to threaten, but the rains had slowed to an occasional shower beneath the leaden skies. The levee had held, and to some extent the affairs of the plantation had gone almost back to normal, although Zach McClellan still posted an overnight watch on the river in case there might be more trouble. Dwight, at Olivia's urging, had taken fabric samples to the city to price material for a party dress for Olivia; she had also insisted he get back to making social contacts with the friends and business associates he'd neglected in the preceding months.

When he returned with the dress material she'd ordered, she and Inez set to work sewing. To Olivia's delight she turned out to be a perfect match for the dressmaker's form her mother had used for years, and this made the assembly of her costume infinitely easier. The pattern she'd chosen was for a floor-length gown of rich brown silk, with chine stripes; the covering basque had a matching fringed trim in pink and brown. The bosom was demure and the sleeves were belled; she'd thought briefly of adding a hoopskirt underneath, but Inez talked her out of it. Instead they sewed casings into her petticoat at intervals and ran canes into the casings to stiffen the fabric. The result was more maneuverable than a hoopskirt would have been—and at a fraction of the expense.

The fashion in hair for this sort of dress was for a braided coronet wound tightly around the head. Here Inez rebelled at fashion. "You've got nice hair, Olivia," she said. "It'd be a shame to do anything with it but to show it off. Here, let me show you."

And, lo and behold, it turned out that Inez's years in the north had been spent as a hairdresser's apprentice. Little by little, as the dark girl worked on her hair, pinning this or that, changing her mind, tucking and twisting, some of her story came out. "My folks were of Spanish blood," she said matter-of-factly. "That doesn't count for much down here anymore, you know. They had ambitions for me. Sent me north to school, got me an education of sorts, an apprenticeship. Then they were wiped out, and times got rough for them. I didn't know. They didn't tell me. My father worked for a man who was selling stolen goods. Papa was caught and tried and hanged. My mother took poison. When the word got out, I tossed up my apprenticeship and came back south, only to find that nobody would speak to me in the circles my folks had traveled in."

"Goodness," Olivia said. "People can be cruel."

"No use crying over that," Inez said. "Now turn the other way. No, hold your head up. There." She pinned Olivia's hair to one side, letting the full length of it hang down over one ear. "That's not bad." She stepped back to look Olivia over. "Well, it's not the fashion in St. Louis just now—or New Orleans, either, for that matter—but perhaps the best thing is to make up your own fashion, if what you want to do is make a splash. That'll look just daring enough to catch the young men's eyes—and just demure enough not to turn their mothers against you."

"I like it," Olivia said, turning her head this way and that, looking at Inez's handiwork in the pier glass. "Inez, when you came home, what did you do?"

"What could I do? I went to work. But the places where they fixed ladies' hair were closed to me. I sold yarn and buttons. I moved on when the owner of the place found out who I was. I worked at a tavern." She caught Olivia's shocked glance and chuckled. "No, it wasn't like that. It was an ordinary over up in Cajun country, in Lafayette. I pick up languages easily. The boys that came in were good-humored, hardworking sorts for the most part, and the ones that weren't, that talked out of turn to me, were pretty quickly put in their place by the others. The life they led—the fishermen and rivermen up there—was attractive, particularly for a no-caste like me. I talked to the cook, learned how to make gumbo, learned how to do a *court bouillon* Cajun style, to make *poutine rapure*, to make *étoufée*. I learned how to play *bourre* and I learned how to say anything in the world I needed to say in Cajun." She smiled her intense smile, her eyes and her mind far away. "It's a strange French. Some of it is boat talk, which is natural for folks who live off the water. Around here, for instance, you got to *amarrer*—moor—your shoelaces, not *nouer* 'em. You don't say, *'Jean va manger,'* or *'Jean mangera.'* You say *'Jean est apres manger.'* "

Her whole tone had softened. Olivia listened, fascinated. "Then one day the boys came in from a cockfight and sat down, and there was this quiet one, strong, with big arms and a bashful-looking smile. And he said, *'Tu parle Cajun?'* And, thanks be to God, I was able to say, *'Oui.'* "

"Oh," Olivia said. "Your . . . your husband?"

"Yes. Jean-Marie. You'll meet him maybe tomorrow. Once we got to know each other, he didn't give a hang who my father was or what he'd done for a living or whether I had any *dot* to bring to a marriage. And he was young and strong and lusty and full of cheer and love, full of life." She smiled, and it made a new woman out of her altogether. "You better hope you get such a man when your time comes, Olivia. He isn't rich, and God knows he isn't likely ever to be. But true is better than rich. Straight is better'n airs. Strong's better'n devious. Just as Cajun is better'n *le francais de Paris.*"

"Inez," Olivia said, unpinning her hair now and shaking

it out before tucking it under a dust cap again, "the thing that happened to your father . . . ?"

"Oh, yes. Could happen to anybody. Just try trusting the wrong man. I later found out my father didn't know the goods were stolen. And the man who did, the man who'd hired him, bribed a judge to let *him* off. Only my father was punished." Her dark eyes flashed. "I'll not forget *his* name soon. A man named Rathbone. Laird Rathbone."

In the afternoon they ran out of thread. Inez set out across the fields for the Cajun settlement in search of some, and Olivia admiringly watched her no-nonsense, almost masculine stride with affection and more than a little envy. What a woman she was—bold, lively, fearless: a perfect mate for the sort of hell-bent-for-leather Cajun her man was said to be.

Olivia was turning back toward the house when she heard hoofbeats on the long approach road that ran down the narrow avenue of live oaks. She whirled and looked. A lone rider was headed her way, at not much less than a full gallop. He rode high in the saddle, with the short *à l'Anglais* stirrup, and his seat was that of a man born to horseback riding. As she watched, he cleared the deep shade and, breaking stride, slowed to take the low fence before the house in a graceful leap. He landed in the little garden Olivia and Inez had planted, the horse's hoofs digging up their tender seedlings and bulbs, and pulled the animal up sharply.

She shot a quick, resentful glance at him, taking in his flushed face, disheveled dress, and unruly hair. He was tall, athletic, and well muscled in the form-fitting trousers men of the planter caste wore that year. His face was puffy, his features indistinct. There was about him the air of an aristocrat who'd run into hard times.

"Where's Dwight, eh?" he said in a slurred voice. "You go right in and tell him to get the hell out here, you hear?" He looked her up and down, taking in her rough-and-ready hairdo and the simple housedress she'd been wearing. "Well, what are you waiting for?" he bellowed, his voice tight with anger. "Move along there, girl."

"Move along, yourself," Olivia said. "What do you want with my father?"

The tall young man swayed visibly in the saddle as he tried to get her more firmly in focus. "Father? Dwight Soames?" He frowned, looking her over again. "Well, I'll be damned. I'd quite forgotten. You'd be his brat, then? Went off to school when I was a tyke, eh? Why, I used to play with you when we were—"

"I remember your name," she said. "You're Lance Whitmire. You'd think I'd remember your manners. Well, perhaps you haven't any. But if you want anything from me, be it information or anything else, you might try going back down the road and starting over again." The words just came rolling out with her anger. She didn't even have time to be appalled at her own brazenness, talking up to a wealthy Delta landowner this way.

Lance Whitmire swung a leg over the saddle and dropped to the ground—a little heavily, she thought. He leaned easily against the horse and then forced himself to stand erect. "My God," he said, "it is a little vixen, isn't it? Talking right up to me as if I were some sort of Johnny-come-lately from upriver." His grin was superior and insulting.

"I didn't tell you you could dismount," she said. "And it certainly seems I have something to say over who I bandy words with around my own place."

"God almighty," he said in that slurred voice, drawling the words out. "And she turned out a real little heartbreaker, didn't she? Not that she won't be sellin' candy at a store in Nyorlins before the month is out, the way her old man's goin' broke by inches. Well, enjoy your high-and-mighty airs, Dark Eyes." He chuckled. "You'll sing a different tune soon enough."

"If you're going to be insulting," she said, "you can leave."

"Leave? Not until I've talked to Dwight." He threw his head back and bellowed at the empty house, "Dwight! Dwight Soames, you come the hell out here and talk to me!"

"He's not here," she said. "Even if he were, he'd certainly have better things to do than talk to a drunken man like yourself. Aren't you ashamed of yourself? Look at you! You can hardly stand up."

"Hah!" the tall young man said. He turned to take the

reins back, jerking the horse around to mounting position. Then, suddenly, he let go of the reins and faced her again. "Drunk, am I? Why, you little snip! Send 'em off to some damned fancy school and all of a sudden they get to puttin' on airs like the duchess of what's-her-name! Drunk, am I?" He looked her up and down again, this time letting lust creep undisguised into his expression. "Well, I'm not too drunk to teach you a lesson or two."

Olivia stood her ground as he took the first two steps toward her; then she backed away, holding her hands protectively before her. "Now you stay where you are," she said. "Don't you come any closer."

"Whitmire!" a voice called out, many yards away. Olivia looked over Lance Whitmire's shoulder to see the tall form of Zach McClellan coming over the fields. By his side was a stockily built young man in rough work dress. "Lance Whitmire!"

The big planter was slow to turn. He took one more step toward Olivia, yelled "Gotcha!" in a voice meant to sound playful, and then turned his head. "McClellan?" he said in a contemptuous voice. "You go pick taters or something. I'm here to see Dwight Soames. You mind your business."

"Anything that happens here is my business," Zach McClellan said. "Miss Soames, Was he bothering you?"

"I . . . no, Mr. McClellan, not really," she replied, noticing the slow-boiling anger in his eyes. "Mr. Whitmire is here to see Papa, and—"

"Bother?" Lance Whitmire said. "Damn right I was botherin' her." He threw his shoulders back and stood tall, as tall as the towering McClellan. "Most likely you would, too, if she'd let a hired hand near her with cow stuff under his nails. What the hell are you goin' to do about it, McClellan? Eh?"

As he spoke, he reached for the saddlebag behind his expensively tooled saddle. As Olivia watched with horror, he drew down a wicked-looking stock whip. "Damn hired help," he said, "talkin' up to people of quality. Workin' free niggers and white trash in good slave-holder country. Most likely stirrin' up trouble with our own blacks, if the truth be known. I told my old man that we ought to run Dwight

Soames out of the parish. I said, " 'Run him out before he carries the damned disease off his own damned no-account hardscrabble property and infects the whole rest of the community.' "

"Whitmire," Zach McClellan said. "You put that thing away. You're on another man's land, and anything I do to you when you're offering violence to me or any other man working Dwight Soames's land is protected by the law." He advanced cautiously, his eyes on Lance Whitmire's ruddy face.

Whitmire's reply was to shake the stock whip out to its full sixteen-foot length. "Hired help!" he said. "Step back, or so help me God, I'll write my name on your bare belly with this thing." For emphasis he gave the whip a jerk backward, and before Olivia could clearly see what he was doing, he had snapped the length of leather forward to knock the hat off Zach McClellan's head with a resounding crack!

"No! No, please!" Olivia said. But as Whitmire withdrew the whip for another lashing blow, something hit him from behind, driving him to his knees. Olivia's hand went to her mouth. On the ground the small, stocky man who'd accompanied Zach McClellan had battered Whitmire into the dirt on his belly; now he jerked Whitmire's hands behind his back and lashed them together with the braided leather strips at the tip of his own stock whip. This done, the broad-shouldered young man pushed Whitmire's face into the dirt— just once, playfully—and stood, leaving the planter lying on his belly in the wreckage of Olivia's little garden.

"Bonjour, m'zelle," he said. "I think you know my wife. I'm Jean-Marie Leblond."

Zach McClellan was helping Whitmire to his feet, turning him around to release his hands. "Good work, Jean-Marie," he said. "Now . . . there we are, Whitmire. I think you've done enough for one day. Why don't you go home and sleep this one off, like a—"

Zach stopped talking as Whitmire turned, and his body whipped into a half crouch, uncoiling. His right fist sank into McClellan's belly, bending the big man almost in half. He followed the blow with another to the back of McClellan's neck; the overseer fell to one knee, trying vainly to grasp at Whitmire's ankles. But the big planter had vaulted into the saddle with a born horseman's grace and moved the animal out of Zach McClellan's reach. He turned to look down at the two men, ignoring Olivia.

"You touch me again, hired help," he said, "and I'll kill you. You're both trash or I'd call you out now. But touch me again and I'll kill you, armed or unarmed. I'll kill you the way you'd kill a rabid dog." He now turned his flushed face, still smeared with the dirt from the ruined garden, to Olivia. "Tell Dwight I want to see him. Tell him to come over to Radford. I won't wait long."

Then he spurred the animal, took the fence again in a graceful leap, and was off down the long avenue of trees at a breakneck clip, sitting high and broad-shouldered in the saddle.

Chapter 7

The men were gone by the time Inez returned, her sewing basket under her arm. "I ran into my husband. He said Whitmire had been here."

"That's an understatement," Olivia said, opening the door to let her in. "He was drunk and violent, and—"

"Yes, I know," Inez said. She set the basket down and looked at Olivia closely. "Come on, now. Let's get back into the dress again and do something about those sleeves. Hmmm. Better put on the petticoats first, just like you'll be wearing it on party night. Otherwise it won't hang right."

Olivia complied silently. Then she said, "Inez, Zach Mc-Clellan just walked away afterward. He didn't even speak to me, as if he were mad at me."

"Well, of course," Inez said. "He was ashamed to have you see him humiliated by Whitmire. Now hold your arms up."

"Humiliated?" Olivia said. "I don't understand. Lance Whitmire struck him a cowardly blow. Zach stood up to him bravely."

"Men don't care a fig about that," Inez said. "It's plain to see you haven't been around 'em much. What matters to him is that, with you watching, he didn't win. He'd like to have beat the daylights out of Whitmire, right there in front of you. Well, I'll have Jean-Marie talk to him. Maybe he can talk sense to him. But I doubt it."

"Your husband . . . I was surprised. He speaks perfect English. I'd half expected—"

"Yes, I know. Well, I've been teaching him, and he's been

47

teaching me." She stepped back and looked at the pinned sleeve, frowned, and stepped forward to rearrange the cloth once more. "He told me about Zach's reaction too. He thought it all funny, actually." She looked Olivia in the eye. "You don't understand, do you? Well, I'll be hanged. You're more of a baby than I thought."

"What do you mean?"

"Why, Zach's taken a shine to you, real strong. And he doesn't dare do anything about it. You're the owner's brat and he's the overseer. Not that that'd make a stroke of difference to anybody with two cents' worth of brains, but—"

"But, Inez, he hardly even knows me."

"That never stopped anybody. Me and my Cajun, we didn't know who each other was when we came together, either. Takes some living together to know that. Takes a lot of loving and fighting and whatever."

Olivia sighed. "Fighting? You argue a lot, then?"

"Argue? I said fight. Why, I tell you we had a real bell ringer a month ago. I hit him over the head with a bottle of *vin rouge*, and he—"

"You didn't!"

Inez laughed heartily, and now Olivia could see for the first time the real beauty of the girl: the fire in her soul, her hunger, her love of life, her spiritedness. Inez brushed the dark hair away from her face with one hand; with her head thrown back like that, Olivia could see the attractive bone structure of her thin face. "Olivia," she said, "you saw that man of mine. You take one look at him and you can see what he's made of, more or less. He has strong feelings, and he's not afraid of showing 'em. Neither am I. People like us are going to do a little fighting now and then."

Her eye caught Olivia's now and held it. "Look. You think this is all talk about somebody else, somebody who isn't like you. You know a little about life, but the hard parts, the parts that call for strong reactions, have passed you by. Well, they won't anymore, my dear. You're out in the real world to stay. And the most important thing you're going to learn is that underneath it all you're just like me. There's a bit of passion in you, too, under those goody-goody ways." She smiled wryly. "Now don't take offense, like a silly little fool. If I couldn't see these things in you, I wouldn't have liked you right off, the way I did." Her hand came up and stroked Olivia's hair in a friendly, affectionate gesture, the way one might pat the cheek of a favorite niece. "Now, there. Let's do that other sleeve. Then we have to iron this nice party dress of yours and we'll be most of the way there." She smiled more gently now. "You're going to look just wonderful. You're going to have the young beaux of the region panting to dance with you. I'll make sure of that."

The rains started again the day before the party at Darrow, Justin Hague's home, slow and steady at first, then turning little by little to a heavy, punishing drizzle, with big drops that pounded on the roof in a steady patter. The rain continued through the night, and the Cajuns, Zach McClellan at their head, manned the levee watch through the evening. Dwight joined them for a time but came in at last looking like a drowned rat, wet and miserable. Olivia got up to fix him cocoa in the chilly dawn. "Papa," she said. "Do you think this will cause the party to be rained out?"

"This?" Dwight said. "No, no. Not unless the river gets out of hand." He felt his unshaven chin with a shaky hand. "No, my dear. Everyone's dog-tired, as I am right now from fighting it all, but by evening they'll all be chipper and full of beans. I wish I could say the same for myself."

She knelt beside him and took his hand in hers. "Papa, don't be that way. I realize you haven't been out to see people in some time. But it's time to change all that. Would you like to see my party dress? I'll put it on for you. Maybe you can tell me how I look."

Dwight Soames's dull eye brightened. "Why, yes, my dear. Please. That'd please me no end."

He was waiting for her, sitting straight and tall, when she came down the stairway, the gown belling out in front of her. She bit her lip, looking at his eyes as he looked her over. "Well, Papa, what do you think? Will I pass muster among these people?"

He smiled and his face changed. Youth crept back into it little by little. Youth and pride and spirit. "Olivia, it's like watching your mother come downstairs, with all her grace and beauty." He stood to welcome her. "You put heart back in me. I . . . I wasn't sure I could face people. I've enemies among them, you know, and I've lost a lot of my self-confidence since the first crop failed. But with someone like you on my arm, I'll walk through that door like Napoleon at the coronation."

Olivia turned this way and that. "Inez is going to fix my hair," she said. "It won't look like this, but you can get the general idea." Her expression revealed a mixture of feelings. There was pride, for one thing. She knew she looked good. But there was also a curious mix of eager anticipation and apprehension. She had never really been presented anywhere, and when she left the area, she'd been little more than a baby. She missed all the gradual introduction to local society that most girls got here, and she'd been pulled out of Mrs. Fitch's before she could be fully tutored in the ways of society, as Baltimore saw them. Well, she could say she was tutored under fire, anyhow. She knew the rules, but she had never tried them out at a real social gathering. She wondered, despite her newly found self-confidence, how she would stand up to the test.

The rain continued through the day, though, and Olivia's doubts about the party increased with it. How were they to get to Darrow, anyhow? The buggy wasn't covered. Obviously they couldn't go in weather like this: they'd get soaked. And she was worried about her father. He'd gone out in mid-afternoon, during a brief break in the drizzle, and hadn't returned. She fidgeted, alone in the house, and then she heard the door open and shut. "Papa?" she said as she left the back room.

But the caller was Inez Leblond. "Hello, Olivia. I'm here to dress you and do your hair. You ready?"

"But Papa . . . the weather . . ."

"Don't worry about it. Zach and your pa, they're fixing things up. Them and that husband of mine. All you and I have to do is put you all together. Don't worry about the rain. We'll get you there dry as a bone. Now, Olivia, let's unpin you and get to work."

• • •

But as the day wore on and the rains did not subside but rather increased, and the roll of thunder could be heard far out over the fields, Olivia began to wonder more and more. Standing before the pier glass while Inez put the last finishing touches of the fourth version of the coiffure they'd tried, she let her uncertainty slip out, in a tone half infected already with defeat. "Goodness, Inez. They'll have to call the party off. Nobody's going out in this. For one thing, the men will all be down by the river . . ."

"Oh, no they won't," Inez said, talking around the hairpins in her mouth. "You can bet your last copper on that. Why, this is an evening the folks around here will talk about for the next six months, maybe longer." She picked two pins out of her mouth and pinned a tress higher. "You picked a good night to make your first presentation in local circles, Olivia. You'll make a nice splash, and the people you'll want to notice will notice, but you won't have to carry the burden of all that attention."

"Why? I don't understand."

"You will. And don't go wondering how you'll get there. Your pa isn't going to take you in any open buggy. Don't you go worrying about that. I heard him talking with Zach. They've gone down to the livery stable—well, I suppose Zach has, anyhow—to rent something decent to take you to Darrow in."

"Well, that's a comfort. But the party. You said—"

"For one thing, leave that alone! How many times do I have to tell you? I can see what'll happen. You'll get to the party, and you'll reach up to pat your hair, and the next thing you know . . ."

"Oh, all right." She examined herself in the mirror again. She had to admit that Inez knew her business, all right. If only she'd had more of a chance. If people wouldn't waste their time looking into other folks' backgrounds, they'd pay good money to have their hair fixed by someone like Inez. "But you said—"

"Well, for one thing, your friend Miss Brand will be there. That always gets 'em out. The men come to look at her, to pay their respects. And virtually every last man jack will do that. The women? Well, some of them go to try to pick flaws.

They won't find 'em. She came into my little button shop once, before I got myself fired. She's quite a girl.''

"But—''

"For another thing, Aurora Brand will be there at the same party with that no-account skunk Rathbone.'' Her voice took on a very sharp edge now as she spoke of him for the second time. "One of the many reasons I admire that lady is how she manages to handle Rathbone. He's broken half the rivals he had on the lower river since he came to town. She just gets stronger and stronger. For another thing—'' She stopped, chuckling to herself.

"Well, don't just stop there,'' Olivia said. "You were going to say . . . ?''

"Well, everybody might get a little surprise tonight. Only some of the folks may be expecting it. I can tell you one thing: I'll bet Miss Brand isn't. I tell you, Olivia, I wish I could be there to see it. But . . .'' She sighed, her mouth set and resigned. "I suppose it's just as well I got cured early of my social notions. I'm likely a lot happier where I am, being what I am, doing what I do.''

Olivia impulsively put one hand on Inez's hand; the dark girl instinctively tried to withdraw it, but then replaced it and squeezed Olivia's fingers back. "Inez,'' Olivia said, "I do want us to be friends. I've never had a friend like you. I like you ever so much.''

"Me, too, honey,'' Inez replied. Her face was sober, unsmiling. "You're worth sixty or seventy of these snooty planters' daughters. You're normal and natural and don't put on fancy airs, and . . . and I wish to God I didn't think that very fact—the fact that makes you worth knowing in the first place—wasn't going to make you some enemies down in this persnickety-mannered place.'' She took Olivia's hand between her own two now, and looked her new friend in the eye. "Look, now, don't let their ways get to you. You promise me that, eh? You stay pretty much the way you are.''

"I'll try,'' Olivia said. "I'll surely try.''

It was getting dark outside when Inez went to the porch and came back, her eyes shining, to announce, "They're coming!'' The rain had settled down to a fine drizzle now,

but neither of them was much fooled. The skies were leaden,
the clouds dark and threatening. There were still low rumbles
of thunder to be heard. Olivia stood at the window and saw
coming up the long avenue of drooping, live oaks a strutting
pair of unfamiliar horses, pulling a stately calash painted
shining black, with a folding top raised high and haughty and
a waterproof storm curtain hanging from it. The curtain
wrapped all around the front, and the driver's hands were
visible through slits left for the reins. Isinglass "lights"—
windows—allowed him to see the path before him, and other
windows to the side gave the passengers a limited view of the
countryside through which they traveled.

"Goodness," Olivia said. "Papa went to some expense!
He shouldn't have."

"Your pa?" Inez said with a snort. "He borrowed the
money from Zach McClellan, most likely. Or Zach paid it
himself. Not that it matters. They both want you to make a
good impression." She snorted again, this time more good-
humoredly. "Look at that, will you?" The calash pulled up
smartly before the steps, and the driver stepped down. "I
thought I recognized those stubby little fingers. Jean-Marie!"

The driver grinned, made a mock flourish. Somehow they'd
found livery the right size for that barrel chest, those heavy
shoulders. He winked conspiratorially at Olivia. *"A votre
service, madame."* He held out his hand for Olivia to step
down to the running board.

Olivia started to comply, seeing her father's dark trousers
inside the conveyance, but Inez turned her around and looked
her up and down. "All right, honey. You look just fine. When
you get there, don't fool with your hair. Go straight to the
ladies' dressing room and touch it up, but not until you've
got yourself a mirror to do it with." Impulsively she leaned
over and kissed Olivia on the cheek. "Now get along! And
have yourself a wonderful time!"

Midway through their journey into the growing darkness,
the patter of rain on the leather roof stopped, and Jean-Marie,
on the seat before them, pulled back the curtains to give
himself a better view. Olivia, sitting alongside Dwight, could

crane her neck and see that they had left the patch of forest and were in open country. Up ahead she saw lights.

"Ah," Dwight said, leaning forward, "there it is."

She sat up very straight and looked, her eyes bright. The big house was lit up as if it were daytime. By the many lights, indoors and out, she could see a noble, squared facade flanked by twin one-story pavilions, its veranda and second-floor gallery framed by four round Ionic columns between two square Doric shafts that supported the massive wooden entablature. The whole was crowned with a parapet breaking over each pillar to a high point in the center. The shutters were wide, showing multiple leaded windows, including those opening onto the gallery and veranda, which were floor-length. The house looked simultaneously brilliant, lavish, and warm and inviting. Darrow!

Chapter 8

Wearing a small smile on his sharp features, Ben Samuels looked out over the small knot of dancers in the middle of the ballroom floor. His head nodded slightly in deference to the decided lilt of the music.

Catherine Hague watched his eyes move around the room, never stopping for long on any pair of dancers. "The rhythm has made its impression upon you, Mr. Samuels," she said. "I'll wager you're something of a dancer yourself, in the proper setting."

Samuels didn't turn; he inclined his head ever so slightly in his hostess's direction. His smile kept the same courtly turn, and the look in his eyes could have been mistaken for a kind one. He had not missed the inadvertent slight, though: "proper setting"? Did she mean some sort of wretched Jewish gathering in the wrong part of town? "You do me too much credit, ma'am," he said affably. "In point of fact, I spent some years studying the violin in my youth. It's an instrument much cultivated among my people. I was admiring the skill of the principal fiddler."

"Oh," Catherine Hague said, "but my husband says you've as light a foot as a hand at fencing."

"I do have some skill with the foil," Samuels admitted. "The fruit of very considerable hard labor at the hands of Monsieur Octave Moreau, whose academy has been so kind as to give me instruction." He turned back to her again, his head still moving lightly in time to the music. "Ah," he said, "Donizetti. *La Fille du Regiment*, if I'm not mistaken."

Justin Hague joined them, his eyes registering pleasure.

"*La Fille* it is, Mr. Samuels. You've a good ear. I purchased the arrangements in the East recently, from a rather shabby young fellow named Foster. They seem quite adequate."

Samuels smiled, his eyes alight. "Not *Stephen* Foster, the minstrel-show man?" His gaze went around the ballroom again. "A young man of considerable talent. I'd love to meet him." He changed the subject. "Well," he said, "I see several colleagues of mine. Mr. Mahaffey, and . . . why, I do believe that's Marc-Antoine Renault." His eyes narrowed.

"*Him,*" Catherine Hague said with obvious distaste. "Justin, I do wish you'd be a trifle more fastidious with your invitations now and then."

"But Monsieur Renault is an attorney of repute," Hague said. "And if I invite his employer, can I . . . ?" He frowned. "I'd rather snub Rathbone, if I had the choice between man and employee. But that would mean snubbing Allison."

"And that would be unthinkable. But, Justin, Monsieur Renault, the whole area knows of his . . . his preferences. Who knows what diseases he may be carrying."

"Oh, come now, my dear," Hague said equably. "Half the respectable men on the Bourse have, if rumor is correct, *maitresses* among the *gens du couleur libres*. Many of the young Negresses and mulattoes among them are gently raised, for all their duskiness. There has never been a question of disease."

Samuels smiled at the two of them. "If the two of you will be so kind as to pardon me for a moment," he said in his smooth voice, "I think I see a young friend of mine, and I think she could use a bit of familiar company."

"Ah, the Soames girl," Hague said. "Lovely. But she appears a bit standoffish."

"She doesn't know us very well down here," Ben Samuels said. "I think she's having an attack of shyness. Perhaps I can stave that off, at least until Miss Brand comes down. The two of them made great friends on the river." A sudden clap of thunder interrupted his speech. "Ah," he said. "The rain's getting worse. Well, let's hope the levee doesn't become flooded." He shrugged and bowed slightly from the waist. Catherine Hague favored him with a broad smile in recognition of his polished manners. He took her hand and kissed the air a quarter of an inch from her fingers before releasing them to move away through the sparse crowd.

"A most remarkable man," Hague said to his wife. His tone was thoughtful. "One sometimes wonders to what heights he might have risen, except for his background. With family, with connections . . ."

"Well, he *does* have good manners. And in general he knows his place. Oh, dear. I hope he hasn't any designs on Dwight's girl."

"Set your mind at ease, my dear," Hague said. "Have you heard me talk of a banker named Mendoza, up in St. Louis? Well, he has a daughter, Sarita—a quite lovely dark little thing, as I remember. The girl and Ben Samuels were betrothed when they were hardly more than children, and word has it that they remain deeply in love. Yes, and whatever you may be thinking, Ben apparently remains quite chaste, avoiding the masked balls and other light amusements. Mendoza has given him a certain number of years to prove his worth in New Orleans, after which he'll be allowed to marry the daughter." He shrugged one shoulder. "I'd say he's proven himself to my way of thinking, given what he and Aurora have done with the shambles Rathbone made of E. P. Brand's business before the old man's death. Samuels and Aurora have built up the Brand Line to the point where it's a definite contender with Laird. And you can bet *he* doesn't like that a bit."

"Oh," his wife said. "Well, maybe the Hebrews drive harder marriage bargains than we do." Her eyes moved from guest to guest. "Come to think of it, I haven't seen Aurora."

"I heard she'd come in," Hague said. "But it's raining pitchforks out there. I suspect she's upstairs freshening up." He looked through the open door to the stairs. "It's remarkable how lovely all the ladies look, considering what they had to go through to get here. See? Why, Felicite Desmoulins's hair must have taken hours to style."

He turned, though, to see his wife's fallen face. He moved quickly to her side, sneaking one arm around her back. "Of course, no one here can compare with yourself, not for so much as a moment."

• • •

"Miss Soames," Ben Samuels said, "how delightful to see you again." He bent over her hand, then straightened to look down into her eyes. "And how lovely you are tonight! I trust you've met everyone by now."

Olivia's smile was all gratitude. "Oh, no," she said. "I . . . well, I may have been presented to a good many of them, but as for remembering names . . ."

"It's all right," he said. "A person of real breeding will introduce himself to you several times until your name and his have registered properly."

"I couldn't even hear some of them. Others I couldn't understand, I think. This Creole French is in some ways harder than the Cajun the boys speak on Wyvern."

"I agree," Samuels said. "Once you've learned the rules of Cajun, it's quite precise. And precision is the one commodity Creole French is most assiduous in avoiding."

"This is a beautiful home," Olivia said, taking the arm he proffered. "It isn't at all like our place."

Ben led her across the hall to the sideboard where black slaves in livery stood waiting to serve them. "Oh, no," he said. "Your place is Old Creole. This is totally atypical. This sort of architecture is more appropriate to—oh, say, tidewater Virginia than to low country like this. The only real justification is that Darrow lies on a rise, on high ground, the way a tidewater house might. You'll note that the wing pavilions repeat the pediment, for instance. That isn't done much here. The columns out front rest on a stylobate, while the locals might put each column on its own pedestal."

"I'm afraid you've just passed me by," Olivia said with a smile. "Mrs. Fitch's School touches on architecture but stops at Latrobe. Baltimore, you know."

"Ah, Baltimore. One of these years the world will just pass it by, and the worst thing is that nobody on Charles Street will have noticed at all." He took two cups of punch from the servant and handed one to Olivia. "Your health, my dear. And . . . welcome to the Delta."

She drank, feeling endlessly grateful for his gallantry, the more so since she knew it carried no designs. "Thank you.

If you don't mind me saying so, you seem to know so very much."

"I don't mind," he said. "I am cursed with an endless curiosity, myself—and it's quite helpful to me as a lawyer. What would you like to know?"

"Well . . . the two girls over there. Who are they? I'm sure I was introduced, but although I came away with the impression that I was meeting important people, I didn't remember any names."

"Ah," Samuels said. "The one on the left is Odile Desmoulins. She's the daughter of the richest cotton factor on the waterfront. There he is over there, and that's his wife, Felicite, with him. I'll be glad to present you if you want."

"No. Please. Tell me about them first."

"They're very big here. You might say Odile was the 'catch' of the season; her mother is one of the social arbiters of the region. And the other girl, that's Avril Charpentier. Her father's the owner of the best bank in New Orleans. Not the largest but the best. He's the portly man by the door. I don't see his wife. She's another of the social lights here. She's a great friend of Miss Brand's, and I owe their friendship for my own currency in this particular society. As for the girls . . . well, Odile is a trifle taken with herself. Not that she hasn't some right to be. But *you* may find her a bit much."

"I see. I thought her a cold one. And the other?"

"Avril Charpentier?" Ben Samuels smiled, and the smile had a bit of warmth about it. "Absolutely charming. If I weren't already betrothed, and if I were five years younger, why, I think I might find myself in conflict with the traditions of my people. It's a matter of honor with us to marry within our own religion, you know." He smiled conspiratorially, letting her in on everything. "You may very well like Avril, unless she quite rightly sees you as the dangerous rival you are. For the hearts of the young men of the Delta, I mean."

"Oh, hush," she said, and put one hand impulsively on his for a moment. "Jewish or not, you've an Irish tongue about you."

"Why Irish? Our own poets invented blarney four thousand years before anyone ever heard of the Irish. But I appreciate the compliment. Have the young men been after you yet?''

''Only the tall one over there,'' Olivia said. ''He's been drinking a bit. I'm not sure I like him.''

Samuels looked where her cup indicated. ''Ah, you wouldn't, I fear. That's Ward Rathbone. Oldest of Laird's three sons and the one most likely to follow in his father's footsteps. The other two boys . . . hmm, I don't see them . . . well, they've perhaps got a bit more of their mother about them, you know. She's an angel. There's no other word to describe her. One of the great ladies of the region. How she came to marry Laird, of all people . . . oh, there she is. The woman by the window. With the maroon dress and the gray streak in her hair.''

''Oh,'' Olivia said. ''She looks sweet. And . . . and somehow . . . I can't think of the word. Regal, perhaps.''

''It's a very good word,'' Ben said. ''I sometimes think we may have Allison Rathbone's very sweetness and beauty to curse for the beastliness Laird has unleashed on this community. If he hadn't fallen deeply in love with her, as deeply as a violent and passionate man like Laird Rathbone can fall in love, if he hadn't looked on her as a sort of queen for whom he had to create a great empire out of nowhere, by whatever means seemed necessary . . .'' He sighed.

''Things aren't always as simple as they look, are they? And this Mr. Rathbone?''

''I've been looking for him,'' Samuels said. ''I don't see him. He's below medium height. Goodness knows where the boys get their height. Perhaps there's some tendency to height among the men of Allison's family. Anyhow, Laird is short-necked, burly, powerful. Dark hair, with muttonchops and a broad face.''

''I've seen him. He has frightening eyes.''

''You've seen him, all right.'' Samuels steered her to the ballroom. ''Now, if the local young bloods aren't going to dance with you, I may have to break my personal code and dance with you myself, although it's not my strong suit. It's called salting the mine, I believe.''

Just then, however, there was a terrific clap of thunder outside, and their eyes went to the vestibule, where the black servant was struggling to hold the door closed. The slave staggered back. In wet, soiled clothes, a thoroughly inebriated Lance Whitmire stood in the doorway, weaving and blinking the water out of his eyes. The slave scrambled off the floor and managed to get the door closed behind him, despite a driving wind that had blown rain onto the oak floor of the mansion. "Dwight Soames," Whitmire said. "Where the hell is Dwight Soames?"

"Step back, my dear," Ben Samuels said, "into the other room. Call Mr. Hague, if you would." He turned to the intruder. "Mr. Whitmire," he said. "Perhaps it might be best if you—"

"Get out of my way, you slimy Christ killer," the planter said. Samuels's eyes narrowed, but he kept his face impassive, even cordial. "Where the hell is Dwight Soames? You get him the hell out here or I'll go in after him. Might be the best thing to do, anyhow. *Hague!* Justin Hague! Where's the high-and-mighty master of this house, anyhow?"

"He's right here, Mr. Whitmire," Justin Hague said. "Please state your business, after which—"

"Business?" The big planter looked his host up and down, his face twisted in a scowl. "Damn right I've got busi—" He belched involuntarily and leaned against the wall with one hand, his wet fingers staining the wallpaper. "I tell you, Hague. You keep the goddamnedest company. Swindlers, kikes, petty trespassers, whores—"

"That'll be enough, Mr. Whitmire," Hague said firmly. "I don't know how your other neighbors have put up with your bad manners and foul breath this long, but I for one have had a bellyful of you. You'll either leave peacefully right now, or I'll have you whipped out the door. And if you ever show your face again on this plantation . . ."

Whitmire pushed himself unsteadily away from the wall and moved indecisively toward Hague. "Look here, you—" Ben Samuels stepped between the two men and held up one cautionary hand. Whitmire stepped back, blinking, trying to get Samuels in focus. "You?" he said. "*You'd* stand up to me, you . . ."

Samuels reached into the umbrella stand and withdrew the long, thin cane he always carried in public. "Mr. Whitmire,'' he said quietly, his voice deadly in the sudden silence, ''you know what this is in my hand. And you know that I'm neither incompetent nor afraid to use it.'' He touched the *colchemarde* with the other hand, just enough to expose perhaps an inch of the length of razor-sharp steel inside the turned oak sheath. ''If I were you, I think I might listen to Mr. Hague.''

Whitmire blinked the lot of them into focus and stepped back, still weaving. One by one the group of faces regarding him became visible, and the sheer weight of the disapproval focused on him by his peers obviously troubled him. With a despairing sneer he firmed his jaw and looked at Samuels with venom in his eyes. ''I'll remember this,'' he said hoarsely. ''You, too, Hague. And wherever Dwight Soames is, he'll answer to me. If not today, then tomorrow, when he hasn't all these protectors and sympathizers around him. Do you hear me?'' He looked daggers at both men, then he turned and lurched heavily into the big door before managing to get it open long enough to slip out into the stormy night outside. The slave closed it quietly behind him, just as another deafening blast of thunder split the air.

Justin Hague stepped forward and took Ben Samuels's arm. ''My deepest apologies, Mr. Samuels,'' he said. ''You shouldn't have had to put up with the likes of that. Not in my house, or anyone's. But thank you. You're a man of rare courage.'' He shook off Ben Samuels's protestations. ''Come, let me draw you a glass of something special. I've been saving this for a particular occasion, for a particular guest—tonight qualifies admirably. Come, sir, I won't take no for an answer.''

The virtual silence around them was broken by a sigh from the women standing in the far doorway. Olivia, standing behind the Charpentiers, craned her neck to look up the long, curving staircase. Hague looked up, as did Ben Samuels, and both men straightened, smiled, and bowed.

Regal, radiantly beautiful, and commanding, Aurora Brand stood at the top of the hall staircase looking down. Her blazing hair, the color of gleaming copper, caught the light of the overhead chandelier. Her eyes were as green as emeralds and shone with a warm glow.

Olivia caught her breath after a moment. And on impulse she looked around her to see the reactions on the many faces that looked up at Aurora Brand. On each she saw a blend of emotions: awe, envy, and admiration . . . except the square, whisker-framed face of Laird Rathbone. His dark eyes blazed with the bright light of hatred.

Chapter 9

Aurora Brand paused at the top of the stairs for no more than a moment, but the effect was striking without being theatrical or studied. Her smile was gracious, warm. Then her hand, small and capable-looking, touched the rail, and, crinoline billowing, she seemed almost to float down the stairs. The enterprising first violin of the ensemble struck up a stately march with a touch of humor; the other instruments took up the tune immediately as Aurora Brand acknowledged the lighthearted compliment with a gracious smile.

Justin Hague, at the bottom of the stairs, took her hand and presented her to the company. "Friends, this is Miss Brand." Aurora Brand's tiny dip of the knee carried the vaguest hint at a curtsy and the saving grace of humor. And now the small string ensemble struck up a gay *valse Viennois*. Still on Hague's arm, Aurora Brand swept into the ballroom of the mansion as one who had come and conquered. And—Olivia's heart skipped a beat here—she caught Olivia's eye for a moment as she passed, and a small conspiratorial smile curved the red lips, and those green eyes took on an added twinkle for a moment.

Olivia pressed her hands together over her young breasts. Her heart was pounding fast. What flair Miss Brand had! And here she'd expected her to wear something daring, something, oh, perhaps a bit on the shocking side. And what had she worn? Something of the most soberly chaste cut, closed to the neck but fetchingly womanly in its very plainness. She was dressed in a gray princess gown, silk with matching gray cords and buttons, and a high white collar of some sheer material. Her hair was adorned only by a single green ribbon that perfectly matched the emerald perfection of those eyes.

Olivia looked down at her own creation on which she and Inez Leblond had labored so hard and long, and felt downright overdressed. Even the presumption of avoiding the crinoline seemed a bit much. She sighed.

A voice at her side broke into her reverie. "Splendid, isn't she? If a bit overdone." She turned her head to see the tall, athletic figure of young Ward Rathbone beside her. His sharp eye went from Aurora Brand to Olivia and stayed there. "I'll wager you're envying her. Well, you needn't. You're quite a picture yourself, if I may say so." His smile was predatory, amoral, and—she found herself admitting, to her horror—rakishly charming in its own way. He held out his hand. "May I have this dance?"

She hesitated for no more than a moment, expecting her nostrils to be assaulted once again by the reek of alcohol; but he had taken some sort of specific for the smell. He stood tall and straight, with a sort of indolent grace that masked underlying power and perhaps even violence. She didn't bother to reflect. "Why, of course."

She found herself being steered gently onto the floor. Ward Rathbone took her hand; his other hand touched her waist; the ensemble shifted into the second number in the *Walzerfolge*, a haunting, lilting tune with a dark yearning under its surface of forced gaiety. Ward Rathbone's commanding hand led her through the steps of the breathtaking new dance at a bold clip that came just short of forcing the already driving tempo. She whirled again and again, feeling light as a feather.

Coming through the room, Aurora Brand, now on Ben Samuels's arm, paused before Allison Rathbone, looking into the woman's clear eyes, marveling at the beauty her oncoming age showed no signs of diminishing. "Good evening, Allison," Aurora Brand said. "You're looking wonderful, as always."

"You always say the right thing, don't you?" Allison Rathbone said, looking her in the eye. "And you never say what you don't mean. I'm flattered." She pressed Aurora Brand's hand, and her smile was gracious and grateful.

The meeting might have ended there, except for the arrival

of Laird Rathbone. "Allison," he said, "may I have a word with you?" The act of breaking in, of pulling his wife away, was so clumsily managed that even Rathbone, normally insensitive to such matters, noticed it. He turned and scowled at Aurora Brand."Oh, good evening." He started to turn away; then he saw Ben Samuels.

"You," he said. "You think you've pulled me off-balance with false quotations, do you?" His look was as cold as the northern snows. "You're going to find yourself sitting on an island in the middle of the river trying that."

"It was a perfectly normal response, Rathbone," Ben Samuels said with a smile. "Perhaps you'll think twice before gunning a stock of ours." He chuckled. "Besides, what false quotations? I put rumors out, not on the Bourse but in the swamp. I figured that with your connections the rumors would get to you as quickly as a rumor that the sun had risen in the west this morning."

Rathbone turned his eyes to Aurora Brand's, ignoring Ben Samuels. "This sounds more like your doing," he said. "You'll pay for this in a dearer coin than you know."

"Laird!" said Allison Rathbone gently, putting one hand on her husband's arm. His expression softened as he acknowledged the touch. "Please . . ."

"Always nice to see you, Allison," Aurora Brand said in the gentlest of voices, allowing Ben Samuels to steer her away gently. "I *thought* that would work," she said, a faintly mischievous smile playing on those red lips.

"It's the Eleventh Commandment here on the River," Samuels said in that mellifluous voice. "Thou canst not cheat an honest man. But it was fun, wasn't it?" He looked out across the dance floor. "Look, it's young Rathbone and our charming friend Miss Soames."

"They look splendid together," Aurora Brand said in a thoughtful voice. "Well, Ward *appears* to be a young woman's dream, I suppose. Until you look him in the eye." She looked at Ben Samuels questioningly. "Young Olivia . . . she does understand about him, I hope?"

Samuels's eyes narrowed. "I had some conversation with her before you came down. I think she has a sharper eye than one might expect. The sharp eye her father could have used, somewhere along the line." He sighed, world-weary. "Well, she may need it. Dwight Soames is in trouble: as much trouble as his hotheaded young neighbor Whitmire. They're both alarmingly overextended."

Aurora looked around. "I don't see Soames."

"You won't for a while. I think he slipped off into the other wing for what I judge to be a rather desperate tête-à-tête with Caswell, the banker—who, rumor has it, is thinking of calling in Dwight's loan."

Aurora Brand's face fell slightly; then she recovered. Her voice was controlled as she spoke. "Ah, poor Olivia. A bad time to be coming into the Delta world for the first time as an adult—and a frightened and vulnerable one, at that. My heart goes out to her."

"It becomes you, my dear. But I wouldn't worry about the girl's ability to handle the facts of life—not emotionally, anyhow. There's real grit there."

"I believe you." Aurora Brand's eye softened as she watched Olivia dance around the room in young Rathbone's arms, all breathless young grace. "But, Ben, please do me the favor of keeping an eye out for her. I mean—"

"I know what you mean," Samuels said. "And I will. I like her myself. I had a younger sister who, if she'd lived, might have turned out rather like her." His smile now masked a private sorrow.

He turned, and Aurora Brand could not read his expression at all. There was a brightness in his eyes and something that, under less rigid control, might appear to be enthusiasm. But his expression changed again, and it was like watching the closing of a great heliotropic flower. "Ben?" she said. "What's the matter?"

He smiled again, his face the same old courtly mask now. He turned her slightly with a light touch of his delicately powerful fencer's hand. "It appears an old friend of ours has arrived," he said. "If, indeed, *friend* is the proper word under the circumstances."

Aurora Brand, her mouth set in a similarly unreadable expression, let no more than the narrowing of her eyes betray the strong emotions she felt as she took in the tall, careless, almost arrogant animal grace of the man who stood just within the vestibule, letting the Hagues' manservant help him out of his dripping greatcoat and take his tall hat and expensive gloves.

"Dallas Boyd," she said. "Well, a bad penny always turns up, doesn't it?"

Olivia also took note of the new arrival just as the dance ended, and Ward Rathbone, with a slight bow, asked his leave and abandoned her to the sidelines. She caught a word or two from others gathered on the edge of the dance floor: "Dallas Boyd . . . nerve of him showing up here like . . ."

Almost shamelessly she found herself staring. Dallas Boyd stood half a head taller than most of the other men, and his carriage was as straight as any man's but without the stiff military posture of young Ward Rathbone, whose only real grace was evident when he took to the dance floor. Instead the grace was that of some great beast of prey: a panther whose muscular strength came not from any set regimen of exercise and self-improvement but rather grew naturally from the normal jungle activities of feeding and hunting . . . and even more base instincts.

He turned, and for a moment Olivia found him looking directly at her, into her eyes. And his smile, already a rakehell's, broadened. He'd caught her staring! She blushed and tried to look away, but he had caught her eye and she could not turn her eyes from his for so much as a moment. There was humor in his smile, a conspiratorial humor that laughed with her, not at her. There was little carnality in it. It was friendly, accepting her and her curiosity and her discomfort with equal aplomb. Then he bowed almost imperceptibly, and—was that a wink of his eye as he turned to look away?

She looked around quickly, hoping no one had noticed. But as she did, she caught the eye—the triumphantly malicious, merrily mocking eye—of Odile Desmoulins, taking in both her covert pleasure and her subsequent discomfiture at having been caught in the act. Olivia turned angrily away. *Damn!* she thought. *Damn, damn, damn!*

Chapter 10

As the back door closed at last behind him, Dwight Soames shook the raindrops off his heavy coat onto the kitchen floor. As he reversed the coat and draped it over his arm, his hand shook. With a grimace he wiped the rain off his face, and he looked at the small belowstairs door that led to the central hall; but he made no move toward the door.

He closed his eyes and leaned back against the wall. *Ruined*, he thought. *I'm ruined.*

Worse, he'd panicked when he got the news. He'd blustered, then begged and pleaded like some craven. Caswell's sharp eye had looked right through him and dismissed him. And the banker had stalked out the door to his waiting rockaway, turning his back on him, Dwight Soames, as one would to a social outcast. He'd followed the banker out into the rain, begging.

Then he'd seen young Whitmire on the front porch, lurching angrily out into the rain. He hadn't had the courage to face him down, either, and he'd wound up slinking around to the back like the coward he undoubtedly was.

He sighed. Cowardice? Perhaps. Perhaps not. Anyone at the party probably would have panicked as he had, faced with the impossible situation he'd landed in. The bank called his loan; Whitmire, drunk, came to humiliate him, to call him out for the bad debtor he was; he learned, from the terrible conversation with Harrison Caswell, just where the real source of his present grief had come from.

Betrayed! he thought. Betrayed, as by a real Judas. What a fool he'd been! Well, there was no use saying you'd never trust anyone again no matter how close; not only was it locking the barn after the horse was gone, it was a vain statement on the face of it. Either you were the sort of damned fool who trusted people or you weren't. And fool he was, once and for all. Fool! Fool, gull and coward!

And now for the first time Soames found himself reaching, with fumbling, rain-chilled fingers, for the little deringer he wore these days in an inside pocket.

No! No, that way out was closed to him because of Olivia. But what could he do? To whom could he turn now that he knew himself to be irrevocably boxed in? Rathbone, who'd made him an insulting offer a month before, undervaluing Wyvern at ten cents on the dollar? He shuddered at the thought. Rathbone would see the defeat in his eye in a moment. The offer that followed would come on the heels of a barrage of brutal insults, and when it did come, it would be half what he'd offered a month before—and less than it would take to settle even the bad debt to Lance Whitmire, much less handle the bank's loan. *No!*

He opened his eyes, and as he did, he caught a glimpse of his own face in a mirror beside the door. The apparition was so startlingly foreign to him that he almost didn't recognize himself. *My God, I look like an old man. A frightened, weak-kneed, shifty-eyed, broken old man.*

He closed his eyes again, then made himself reopen them and look the old man in the eye. *You've got to get hold of yourself. You've got to think of something. You can't go out there looking like this. Not with Olivia looking on and depending on you.*

His hand clenched into a weak fist. "Boyd," he said. His voice was hoarse, rasping, hardly more than a whisper. "Dallas Boyd." Surely Boyd, if he were able, would help. But what sort of collateral could he offer? What sort of promissory note? What sort of . . . ?

God, he thought. Perhaps a drink first. Perhaps a shot of Justin Hague's good 'Nongahely rye would calm his nerves long enough to allow him to think of an answer, to look Boyd in the eye and ask what he had to ask. He forced firmness back into his quaking jaw and straightened his shoulders, wiping the last drops of rain from his face with one hand. He made himself walk through the open door into the narrow space beside the great staircase.

Olivia touched her hair once more with a cautious hand, turning her head this way and that and inspecting her reflection carefully in the pier glass. Well, not perfect, she thought, but it would do. It would have to. She smiled uneasily at herself and made her way out into the second-floor hall. As she did, she saw Ward Rathbone standing at the top of the stairs, looking at her, his eyes cool and appraising.

"Hello," he said. "I was looking for you. I had something to show you."

"Show me?" she said. "What?"

"Come," he said, boldly taking her hand and moving her toward the front of the great house. "It's up this way."

She had it in mind to protest, but the grip on her hand was powerful and imperious. She allowed herself to be steered forward. Only when they reached the long row of floor-length windows that faced the balcony did she pull back on his hand and refuse to go farther. "Stop," she said, "you're hurting my hand."

He let go, turning to look at her, a mocking smile on his arrogant young face. "All right," he said. "But look." He half turned back toward the window and opened one of the glass doors. Past him, through the open door, she could see far away over the fields the long line of lanterns on the levee and the ghostly forms of the men working there, stacking sandbags. The rain had let up slightly, and Olivia saw the scene down by the river through a light drizzle, hardly more than a mist. As she looked, lightning lit up the sky many miles across the river; a great forking blast of it covering half the lower sky. Immediately afterward came the low, faraway rumble of thunder.

He took her hand again, more gently this time, and pulled her toward him, out onto the porch. With an uncharacteristic gallantry he removed his light coat and draped it over her shoulders. "There, now," he said, "isn't that something? Quite a sight for your first visit home in years, isn't it?"

"It's beautiful," she found herself saying. "Frightening too."

"The whole river is frightening," Ward said. "And so is the whole world of people who live on it and off it. That's why I like it so. It's dangerous. Any part of it can kill you, wipe you out, in a moment. That's why it's worth notice in the first place. Nothing you get easy is worth anything at all. Something you fight for . . .''

She looked at his face in profile, looking out over the ghostly scene below, and found herself noting the raw power in his young face, the ruthlessness, the hunger. Why, he's very attractive, she thought with a start. And the thought was in itself a little frightening.

Ward looked back at her and took her hand again. This time, as the half-mocking smile returned to his strong, slightly vulpine face, he used the contact to pull her toward him, and his other hand went to her back, drawing her suddenly to him. He bent, and Olivia felt warm lips on her own, searching, questing.

"N-no!" she said indignantly, pulling herself away. Instinctively her free hand balled into a tiny fist, and she swung at his face—and missed.

"Hah!" Rathbone said, grinning insolently. "I'd have bet anyone a twenty-dollar gold piece you'd do that." He stepped out of range and stood looking at her, arms crossed over his powerful young chest. "You've got spirit. I like that. More than a little passion, too, I'd wager. Well, we'll see. Perhaps there'll come a time when you won't fight me. In the meantime I'll think the better of you for not making it easy." And with the sharp-eyed grin still on his face, he stepped back to the doorway with a tiny, mocking bow and slipped inside the house.

Olivia stood looking after him, one hand to the lips he'd kissed so insultingly, the anger just now beginning to grow in her heart. "Why, you . . ." she said. But the epithet wouldn't come, and her words trailed away. It was a situation totally outside her experience, and she truly did not know what to make of it. She bit her lip and clenched her little fists in delayed rage.

Then—she was never quite sure afterward how it came about—she began picking up bits of a conversation taking place behind a pillar on the porch, beyond the next tall, floor-length window. She started to withdraw and then found herself, for the second time in only a few moments, suddenly obeying an impulse she'd never had before. Instead of withdrawing, she drew nearer the window to hear better.

". . . up here, cool as a cucumber, as if nothing had ever . . ."

"And after all, my darling, what *did* happen? Not very much, when one comes right down to it. Unless you're willing to admit once and for all that you care, that your heart really does flip-flops when I come into the room."

"Conceited, irresponsible . . ."

"Then if you've *not*, as you now insist, committed your heart in any way, and insist upon an independence you value for yourself but profess to detest in me, well, my darling . . ."

"You know good and well what I meant."

"All too well, my dearest, and that's why I reserve the right to remind you from time to time that what's sauce for the goose is, now and forever, indelibly and irremediably sauce for the gander."

Olivia's heart was in her mouth. The woman's voice—it was unmistakably that of Aurora Brand! Tight, controlled, bristling with barely suppressed anger but unquestionably the voice of the woman who'd taken her into her quarters back aboard the *Newport*! And the man? It was a voice she'd never heard before.

"Damn you, Dallas, if you think . . ."

The man's answer was a worldly-wise chuckle rather than words, but Olivia's question had already been answered. The voice—mellow, good-humoredly insouciant, even to the point of theatricality—was that of Dallas Boyd. And from the sound of things, what she was hearing was something very like a lovers' quarrel!

Now she could hear the voices more clearly; they'd apparently turned more in her direction. "But what are we fighting about, my dear, on a night like this? My God, look at it; isn't it beautiful? Look: the spectral line of lamps strung out along the top of the embankment; the strange light in the sky, down on the bottoms, like a will-o'-the-wisp; the—"

A spectacular flash of lightning split the sky in many pieces, followed by an echoing blast of thunder. The man's voice carried to her ear with a poetic lilt, and there was more than a little affection in it, affection addressed to the silent, angry woman beside him. Olivia shivered inside the jacket Rathbone had neglected to take with him and pressed herself flatter against the window. "God!" the man half whispered, his voice husky with desire. "On a night like this—"

"Don't you romance me, damn you! After what you—"

"What I did? What you did? What I promised, and you swore to . . . All that is ancient history, my darling. You know damned good and well that any covenants that spring up between a couple of wild geese like you and me will be written on the wind. They'll have more option clauses than a contract for on-the-margin trading, and they'll be perpetually up for renewal every time the spring breezes blow again, every time the sweet sadness of fall descends once again on the land."

"That's all very poetic, I'm sure. And very practiced. Even the spontaneity has the sound of a speech rehearsed before a mirror. Or perhaps in a bedroom or two, somewhere between here and Savannah or Charleston or—"

"Ah, you do me an injustice, my darling. You—"

"Injustice? You, never!"

Boyd's voice changed, grew sober, intensely serious. "Aurora, my darling, I love you, now and forever. I want to live the rest of my life with you. Will you marry me? I'll get down on one knee."

"Damn you! Marry you? Of all people in the world . . . why, I'd sooner marry Laird Rathbone."

"No you wouldn't," Boyd said, his tone once again good-humoredly cynical. "Besides, he's taken. Ah, look, I've wet the knee of my trousers. Do you think Laird Rathbone, great lover that he undoubtedly is, would do that for you?" He chuckled at the thought. "See? I asked you, as seriously as any man ever asked any woman, to plight your troth with—"

"Serious? You'd mock your mother's funeral with the same careless air."

"My darling, you know me as well as any woman does. And you know as well as I do when I'm being serious. And you know that I was as serious as if I were standing before a firing squad, improvising my last words." His tone took on a note of thoughtfulness, only lightly tinged with mockery. "And come to think of it, there *are* resemblances of a sort between the two situations, aren't there? Picture Dallas Boyd before the guillotine, refusing the mask—"

"You're impossible. Impossible."

"Of course I—" His words broke off abruptly and then he continued. "Aurora," Boyd said in a no-nonsense voice from which all trace of levity had been ruthlessly excised, "look up the river, will you? The light . . . right there . . ."

"Where are you? Oh, yes. Why, it's a side-wheeler. A side-wheeler, here, at a time like this?" Her voice changed, too: it became lower, more businesslike, but with a touch of urgency, of concern. "Dallas! The *Memphis* . . . it was due here within the hour."

"The *Memphis*? That's the flagship of the Brand Line, isn't it? But it's not moving."

Then, as Olivia herself turned to crane her neck and peer up the great river, another of those terrifying bolts of lightning lit the sky and the lands below it, almost as if it were midday. She heard Aurora Brand's voice, low, taut, reflecting the horror she, herself, felt at the scene. "My God! Dallas, the *Memphis*—it's on a snag! It's swung about in the channel! It's going aground! And look at that angle!"

"Jesus!" Dallas Boyd said in a low, tense voice. "The current right there will tear it apart! We'd better get up there damn fast."

"Right!" Aurora Brand said, all business now. "I'll round up the men downstairs. You get outside and see to the—"

"The horses! Right you are!" He threw open the door and broke into a half trot, even before he'd reached the middle of the room. Aurora Brand, moving with as much speed as crinolines would allow, was right behind him.

And outside, the worst had happened. The rain struck up suddenly, even harder than before, driven now by rising winds that howled in the trees beside the house, its drops audibly battering the roof overhead. Olivia shivered inside the borrowed coat and slipped inside, hearing the rising voices downstairs. One of them, louder than the rest, carried all the way to the head of the stairs. "Hurry! There isn't a moment to spare."

Chapter 11

Dallas Boyd hit the front stoop running, hardly pausing, and vaulted into the darkness toward the stables. "Jean-Marie!" he bellowed. "Jean-Marie Leblond!"

The stocky Cajun appeared at his side, his face sober. "You have seen it, too, M'sieu Boyd?"

"Yes. I think it's the *Memphis*. And I don't think we've got long. Quick, we've got to get horses, carriages, whatever . . . we'll need everything we can get our hands on. Even if we do manage to get the people off before something happens, there'll be some injured. If you could get the boys in back to saddle every available nag on the property and have the carriages ready by the time Miss Brand gets everyone out . . ."

"I have already started," Leblond said. "You go get everyone in front. I will have the transport ready." His smile was tight and controlled, the smile of a man of competence. His tone bore the same respect the whole Cajun community bore for Boyd, a friend of the whole tribe of French-Canadian blood and a man with many godchildren among them.

Boyd grinned at him and, one hand raised in an appreciative salute, took off back toward the great house.

There were already men on the porch, struggling into greatcoats. Among them was Ben Samuels, his expression sober and concerned. "Ben," Dallas Boyd said, "the boys will be bringing the horses and carriages up from the back. You parcel out the transportation, will you?"

"Splendid," Samuels said. "No use trying to figure who owns what. I'll just go first come, first served."

Boyd's eyes narrowed, and he grinned lopsidedly. "Good

man. But for God's sake! Where is everybody? There must be a dozen men missing. Justin! Aurora! Get 'em out here!''

But he didn't wait for a reply. He sprang onto the porch and strode through the open door into the hall. Inside, the men of the company were for the most part dressing for the wet outdoors. ''Never mind that,'' Boyd said. ''Carry it over your arm if you need it, but get outside. Please! Lives may be at stake! Aurora, how many aboard, do you think?''

''Perhaps three hundred, if it's full. I have no way of knowing.'' She was wrapping a scarf over her blazing red hair. Boyd was delighted to see that other women showed signs of coming along as well.

''Three hundred!'' someone said. ''My God, if the boat breaks up . . .'' There was a new rush for the front doorway. Boyd, scanning the crowd, was about to turn and leave when his eyes lit on a familiar face. Laird Rathbone, still dressed for indoors, was lighting a cigar unhurriedly from a taper retrieved from above the fireplace.

For a moment Boyd stood speechless, watching him. ''For the love of heaven, man!'' he said at last, his voice tense and unbelieving. ''Aren't you coming with us?''

Rathbone turned, still in no hurry. His eyes mirrored his contempt for the whole proceeding. He puffed the cigar to life before speaking. ''You're asking me to help save a rival firm from receivership?'' he said, his tone balanced precariously between incredulity and insolence. ''You've taken leave of your senses.''

''Rival firm?'' Boyd said. ''There are innocent people on board the boat, Rathbone. Women and children, most likely. People who have no quarrel with you. And you'd sit by and—''

''Rathbone,'' Aurora Brand said, her green eyes full of sparks, ''for the love of God . . .''

The square-faced man puffed and blew a slow smoke ring. ''Miss Brand,'' he said, ''my final offer. Eight hundred thousand for the Brand Line and all its—''

''Eight hundred th—'' Aurora Brand stood with her legs apart, hands on hips. Her head shook from side to side in disbelief. ''You actually have the nerve to make me an offer at a time like this?''

''It's quite generous,'' Rathbone said. ''It's more than your line will be worth after tonight, I'll wager. If you lose a shipload of people and the flagship of your fleet at this juncture—''

"You yellow-bellied bastard!" Boyd said, his big fists balled. "If I didn't have more important things to do just now, so help me God, Rathbone, I'd—"

"You'd do your usual hotheaded foolishness," Rathbone said, staring him down. "You'd call me out, and I'd ignore you. Boyd, the *code duello* is for schoolboys, playing pecking-order games in the schoolyard."

"My God," Boyd said, "I don't believe what I'm hearing. Haven't you any pride, you fat toad?"

"Dallas!" Aurora Brand said sharply. "Later! The boys are out front with some of the carriages. Hurry!"

Boyd shot a glance at her. Her coiffure had slipped, and she had changed her crinolined skirt for a borrowed riding outfit, simple and unaffected. A shining tress of red hair hung low over one of those green eyes. He could virtually feel the tension in her. God, she was beautiful! Particularly at times like these, when she was responding to trouble.

"Right," Boyd said, grinning at her. It was all he could do to restrain himself from taking her in his arms as he passed, but he managed to control himself, and strode briskly out to the porch and the waiting horses.

Dwight Soames peered out into the half darkness, searching for his rented carriage and horses.

"Papa!" a high-pitched voice called out to him, and he looked down to see the face of his daughter looking up at him from the driver's seat of an unfamiliar jump-seat carriage. "Papa! Over here! Quick!"

Dwight stepped down into the mud and made his way unsteadily over to the carriage. "Olivia!" he said. "Surely you know better than to go out in this weather."

"Get in, Papa! You know how to drive one of these things and I don't." Her slim hand took his and helped him onto the high seat. "And don't you dare tell me to go back. With all those people out there on the water, helpless, waiting for the boat to . . .''

Dwight saw the fire in her eyes by the light of the lanterns on the porch. "All right," he said. "But you stick close by me when we arrive. I don't want you doing anything rash." He took the reins and released the brake. Just as he was about to flip the reins and send the animals forward, though, he saw Dallas Boyd striding toward him through the windblown rain.

Boyd raised his hand. "Mr. Soames! I've given away all the horses. Could I get a ride with you?"

"Certainly! Here, up beside . . . oh, yes, Mr. Boyd, this is my daughter, Olivia." Dallas Boyd and Olivia exchanged uneasy smiles. "Perhaps you'd like to drive? I mean, you've a bit of a reputation with horses."

"Thank you," Boyd said. "I'll be glad to. We'll take the high road, the one that runs above the line between your property and young Whitmire's. The levee route will be badly crowded just now."

"I was going to suggest that," Dwight Soames said. "At the top of the hill we may even be able to see the ship for a moment or two. God, what a thing to happen! And on a night like this!"

Boyd turned the animals and urged them forward along the side road. "It's just that that will give us the very small chance we have of rescuing anyone," he said. "The very fact that the river's high, that there are crews out there manning the night watch gives us a ready reserve of strong backs, easily available and able to help out on a moment's notice. I've put out the call to the boys on the levee. I'm sure a high percentage of them will be waiting for us when we get there."

"Mr. Boyd," Olivia said, her voice barely audible above the sounds of the rain and the horses' muted hoofbeats in the slick mud, "is there any chance that—" She stopped, looking at his strong profile in the fading light.

Boyd sighed. "It'll be a lottery at best," he said. "All I can say is that we'll all do our best. We'll be lucky if we can get boats out into the channel in time before the river tears the *Memphis* apart and if there aren't any further on-board complications to deal with." He shrugged, but she could sense no sign of nonchalance in the shrug as they rounded a curve and the last light from the house was blotted out. "Good thing I know this road pretty well," Boyd said. "With unfamiliar horses we could wind up in some trouble if we were . . ."

But now he looked up. "I shouldn't be able to see even this much with the moon half shrouded by the fog like this." He looked up over the rise. "Oh, my God!" he said in a tight voice. He urged the animals forward again, faster. "I do hope to heaven that glow in the sky isn't what I think it is."

But as they rounded the top of the little hill all three of them could see it—and the sight confirmed their worst fears. The stricken vessel now listed hard to port, and from the cabin deck, aft, flames leapt high, illumining a scene of panic. As they watched, a man, trapped aft of the vaulting flames, tried to dive from the lofty deck and into the water below. His body struck the hurricane-deck rail and catapulted from there, arms flailing, into the roiling waters.

"Oh, no," Olivia cried out softly in a broken little voice. "Oh, the poor man."

"God almighty!" Boyd said, clucking savagely at the horses, the reins gripped tightly in his big hands. "Come on there, damn it! Faster!" The animals responded, pulling desperately, but their hoofs slipped in the mud and they made little headway. The rain intensified. "If only the rain would do some good, putting out that fire."

"But won't it?" Olivia asked.

"I doubt it," Boyd said. "Not the way those flames are leaping up like that. My guess is that someone panicked and in his haste knocked over a kerosene lamp. The only real problem with this kind of fire is the way it affects the people on board. They take one look at it up there—imagine, fire on the cabin deck, up where the expensive accommodations are— and they lose their heads. No, my dear, the kind of fire I'm worried about is elsewhere. Anywhere down on the main deck, say." He shuddered. "It's my guess that the *Memphis* is, as usual, carrying some highly combustible cargo."

"Even that," Dwight Soames said, speaking for the first time, "pales beside the matter of what will happen if the engineer's hurt and there's nobody in the boiler room just now. And look. The stack's still belching forth smoke as if the boat were still under a full head of steam."

"God!" Boyd said. "That's bad news indeed. The side-wheel's fouled and can't turn, but the engine's still going. Or is it—"

He never got to finish. There was a flash so bright that it was, for a moment or so, like looking into the direct rays of the sun at midday, and then they heard a sound so loud, it would echo in their ears for the rest of their lives. When the onlookers blinked the white spots out of their eyes, they could see a whole section of the vessel's upper decks had been blown away altogether, and the fire that had sprung up in the wake of the great blast now burned in half a dozen places on the decks of the stricken ship. They could see passengers, their clothing afire, diving from the decks into the water below. The ship now lay at a visibly more acute angle. The light cast by the fire illuminated a wide section of the great river itself, as well the banks along it.

Dwight Soames, sitting beside Dallas Boyd on the high seat of the carriage, stood up precariously, peering through the drizzle. "Oh, my God," he said. "Look. Look over *there*. Look where the bend of the river comes in."

Boyd pulled the horses up short. "That's . . . why, that's on *your* property, isn't it?" he said.

Dwight looked at him, his face set in a stricken look. "No, no," he said. "It's very near the property line. Why, someone's made a cut. A *cut*."

Dallas Boyd looked down at the man-made cleft, into which the fierce waters of the Mississippi were pouring at a frightening pace. "A cut? But that means . . ."

"It means Lance Whitmire's place will be cut off! Once the current gets into a cut like that, there's no way of stopping it. By tomorrow Lance's place will be an island in the middle of the river. The channel will be over here, instead of a mile in that direction." Dwight looked upriver at the burning boat, then at the cut. "But that means Wyvern . . ."

"Wyvern'll be on the river. Papa! You'll be able to load right onto the boat. The riverboats'll be stopping at Wyvern, instead of at Radford!" Olivia looked up at her father, a bright look of hope in her eyes. "Isn't that right?"

"I . . . I don't know," Dwight said. "Perhaps it's too late.

Olivia, the bank called my loan tonight, and I'm extended beyond the possibility of—''

"Called your loan?'' Dallas Boyd said. "Look, Mr. Soames, don't worry about that. Who's your banker?''

"Harrison Caswell,'' Soames said. "But—well, you know him. Once he makes his mind up—''

"Don't worry about that. But, Mr. Soames, every time something like this happens, there's always talk. You and young Whitmire don't get along, do you?''

"N-no,'' Dwight said, sitting down. "Here, maybe we'd better get down to the river. There may be something we can do for those poor devils down there.''

"There are plenty of people to look out for them,'' Boyd said. "Look, I have to say this. I can help you with Caswell. But this business of the cut. . . .''

"I had nothing to do with it!'' Dwight Soames said. "I swear it! I swear it on . . . on whatever you choose.'' He turned to Olivia. "You believe me, don't you?''

"Oh, Papa! Of course!''

"That settles it,'' Boyd said. "I'll take your word, Soames. I have to. But those men of yours. They'll have to have proof of where they were. Whitmire is sure to claim you instigated this.''

"Oh, yes,'' Soames said miserably. "He will. The more so since . . . oh, Olivia, I'd hoped you wouldn't find out about this. But I'm into him, too, and for quite a sum. That's why he's been so difficult lately.''

"Don't worry about that,'' Boyd said. "Does he have a lien on anything of yours?''

"No. Just my signature. But my reputation . . .''

"Hang reputation! That is, if he can't repossess anything of yours. Who's your lawyer?''

"Judd Mahaffey. Why?''

Boyd didn't say anything. His face changed, closed up like a flower. His eyes turned hard, and he turned away to look down the hill at the burning vessel. The set of his mouth was grim. "Come on,'' he said, "let's go down and help those poor devils on the boat.''

Chapter 12

"Here!" Aurora Brand's voice, strong without being shrill, carried easily over the sound of the dull drizzle and the far-away cries of the survivors who'd made it to shore so far. "Over here!"

Standing in the flat-bottomed bateau's squared-off bow, Dwight Soames called back to Olivia, who was astern. "Over that way!" She turned the rudder hard aport as the three Cajun rowers heaved hard on the oars. "Good! Good! Now ship oars! Here he is." He knelt in the bow and reached out his hand. In the water, Zach McClellan, one big hand holding a half-drowned woman under the chin, treaded water and reached out for Dwight's hand. "There, there," Dwight said. "Now hand her to me."

"The current's pulling her away," Zach said, his mouth half full of water. He heaved mightily, and the woman came within Dwight's reach. His hand closed around her open-collared dress, and the fabric tore.

"Try again," Zach said. This time Dwight's hand closed around the woman's wrist; in the struggle, Zach's head went down and he came up spewing muddy river water. "There, you've got her."

Olivia shivered, looking around her. The *Memphis*, a gutted hulk now, still ablaze here and there despite the light rainfall, listed to port at a crazy angle. The river current tugged steadily away at her. There was a great bonfire on the bank now, set by the rescue party. Around it, swathed in borrowed blankets Justin Hague had brought from Darrow, the few ambulatory survivors huddled, trying to get warm.

There were still men in the water, others besides Zach McClellan. Aurora Brand, in the second boat, was directing one of them in the process of bringing in a man who'd apparently broken an arm while leaping from the ruined boat's upper deck. As Olivia watched, she could see Dallas Boyd's head break water beside Aurora Brand's boat. Farther upstream, Ben Samuels and Henri Desmoulins were helping a gaunt survivor into their boat, aided by a man in the water who resembled Jean-Marie Leblond.

Olivia turned her eyes back to her own boat where the woman they'd saved now lay at Dwight Soames's feet. He knelt beside her, covering her with his own already soaked coat. "All right," he said, "let's get her to shore if we can. She's got a bad burn, and she's swallowed a lot of water, but I think she'll make it. Can someone help me bail out this water?"

Olivia let herself sigh with relief. There had been so many others who hadn't made it. She recalled the sight of a man with a horribly burned face; he'd screamed and waved at them as they struggled to reach him, but the current had carried him away, still screaming.

Her face must have mirrored her own terror and sorrow. The boat shifted slightly, and she opened her eyes to see Zach McClellan's big hand on the gunwale as he rested for a moment in the water, looking at her.

"Miss Soames," he said, "it'll be over soon. Don't worry. You've been wonderful." He tried to smile reassuringly, but his own face was a mask of fatigue and disappointment. He took it hard, losing a man, and he'd taken losing a little girl hardest of all. She knew he'd never sleep tonight, that he'd always be blaming himself for letting her go. No matter that it hadn't been his fault, that the spar had hit him broadside, nearly knocking him cold, just as he'd reached the child. He'd be the type to blame himself, to take all the responsibility on his own broad shoulders until he couldn't bear it anymore. She smiled wanly at him, and for a moment their eyes locked.

But then Aurora Brand, tireless and commanding in the bow of the next boat, called out again: "Here's another! Quick! Over here! And there's someone with him!"

• • •

Finally there came a time when a great wrenching sound split the air, and the *Memphis*'s battered hulk broke in half; when the rowers, pulling hard, barely made it away from the derelict in time; when the last searchers failed to bring up any further survivors; and when, at last, the tears streaming down her tired but beautiful face, Aurora Brand called them in to shore.

Olivia, half paralyzed from the cold herself, accepted a blanket from Catherine Hague and allowed herself to be led to the fire. As she passed her father she could see his gray face and the dullness in his eyes. He seemed so pale, so drawn; she longed to reach out to him, but her own fatigue had forced upon her a passivity that made her accept direction from men who'd come with Lance Whitmire, who hadn't been with the rescue party. Olivia looked around her for familiar faces, for reassurance.

Aurora Brand, eyes blazing, her red hair radiant in the light of the leaping flames, said, "Look here! Time enough for this sort of nonsense later. If there's anything to the charges you're throwing around so recklessly, Mr. Whitmire, I'm sure a magistrate will be willing to listen to them. In the meantime we'd all be better occupied trying to remedy things, wouldn't we? Stack sandbags! Try to divert the channel!"

Whitmire turned to her, his face livid with rage and despair. "It's too late for that!" he cried. "The cut's open as far as the first fork in the high road. There's no stopping it now."

"Oh, no," Dwight said. "*That* far?" His eyes searched the crowd around him for Dallas Boyd. "Mr. Boyd! When we saw it earlier, it wasn't that big a cut yet."

"Saw it earlier?" Whitmire said, leaping forward to grasp Dwight Soames by the lapels. "You're admitting to having seen it earlier? And you didn't tell anybody? You didn't send for me?" He threw Soames from him with a roar of disgust.

"But . . . the *Memphis* . . . it drove it from my mind."

Whitmire looked around him. "Well, there he is, boys. I don't know about you, but that cinches it for me." Finding looks of agreement or at least honest doubt on the faces around him, he went on, his voice gathering power. "Soames . . . he owes me money. Lots of it. He knows I need it, and in a hurry. I have outstanding loans, and the bank's after me. And he won't pay up what he owes me. Well, now we know why he feels he doesn't need to pay up. He's been planning this for some time, obviously. Put me out of business and there won't be any need to pay me, for God's sake. And there I'll be, stranded on the far side of the river, on worthless property. My sugar lands are in low pasture. Let water in from the wrong side like this . . . why, it'll leak back and find its way down to—'' He stopped. Hatred blazed from his eyes, hatred and something like triumph. ''For God's sake, you all have lowlands along here, and the only thing that saves it is the levee. How long do you think those levees are going to stand now? Do you think any of your own lowlands will survive this? Why, he's ruined all of us. Moore, you have property downriver. You're wiped out too. Unless you've some investments I don't have. You, too, Veach. You're not ruined, but you'll take a hell of a loss this year too. And who's next? Who knows where the river will cut its new channel now?''

''There's something to what he says,'' a voice said from the back of the crowd. ''If Soames figures on bailing himself out of trouble this way—''

''That's the dirtiest damned thing I ever heard,'' said another man, whose voice Olivia didn't recognize. The crowd had been augmented by many locals who had not been at the party, and apparently many of those who had had left earlier. The individual voices became a low murmur, and one slowly rose in volume and intensity.

''Stop!'' Aurora Brand said. ''You're jumping to conclusions.'' But her words were swept away in the rising clamor. ''Dallas! Ben! Where are you?''

Olivia nervously looked around. Where was her father? She couldn't see him at all, stuck as she was in the middle of an angry crowd of taller men. ''Papa!'' she cried, trying to push her way past the suddenly thick and all but impenetrable wall of flesh that surrounded Dwight Soames. ''Papa, please.'' She tried to push her way in, but a large, powerful man pushed her away none too gently. ''I want my father!'' She moved aside and tried another place. The voices rose again in volume.

The report of the pistol, so close to her ear, startled her almost out of her wits. She stood openmouthed, peering back through the semidarkness. The crowd turned with her, silent now.

Between Olivia and the still glowing fire stood a tall, powerful man, his feet firmly planted a double hand span apart. At first she couldn't see his face. What she could see was the smoking pistol in his hand—a long, deadly weapon the length of a large man's forearm.

"Dallas!" Aurora Brand said, breaking out of the crowd. "I wondered what had happened to you."

"I had to go back to the wagon and get this," he replied. "Ben's coming up with more. Here, get behind me, will you? *Mr. Soames!* Come out here with me, will you, sir? That's right—no, not you!" He spat the words out, his voice edged with anger. When the man who had moved tried to advance again, Boyd fired once more at the man's feet. "There!" he said. "Now, all of you, keep your distance."

"Boyd!" Lance Whitmire said, his bitter young voice carrying easily from the back of the crowd. "You stay out of what doesn't concern you."

"Dwight Soames is a friend of mine. He used to be friends with a lot of you. I'll wager a good number of you owe him favors from way back. What makes the lot of you turn on him all of a sudden, on nothing more than the word of a drunken young fool like Lance Whitmire?"

"Boyd, damn you. . . ."

Dallas ignored him. Instead he half turned his head as Ben Samuels joined him, a short-barreled pistol in one hand, his equally lethal *colchemarde* in the other. "Good to see you," he said. "Aurora! Do me a favor, my dear, and bring the carriage up, will you? I think we'd do best to get out of here. By tomorrow morning these folks—most of them, anyway—will perhaps have come to their senses. I don't know about Whitmire. He'll probably be drunk in a ditch somewhere by dawn."

"Boyd, you'll pay for this!"

"Possibly," Boyd said with an infuriating insouciance. "But not at your hands. *Keep back there!* That's better. Now, the rest of you, I'm probably saving you from doing something you'd regret for the rest of your lives. When you've thought the matter over, you'll likely agree. But for now I think the best thing for me to do is get Mr. Soames out of temptation's way. Along with a number of people here tonight, he performed heroically in a terrible tragedy and saved many lives, often at the risk of his own. Those of you who helped us get the survivors off the *Memphis* will do well to search your memories. If you do, and if you're at all honest with yourselves, you'll call to mind that Dwight Soames has been in the thick of things the entire time. Before that he was with me. Before that he was at a party where perhaps three dozen people will recall having seen him. When could he possibly have had time to open a cut in Whitmire's property?''

''It was that damned overseer of his.''

''Another false assumption,'' Ben Samuels said. ''How many of you worked on the levees in the last twenty-four hours? Ah, quite a number, I see. And that means you know quite well that Mr. McClellan, and virtually every one of the Cajun boys who work with him, has been on watch along the levee most of that time. Ah, yes. I see some recognition of the fact on some of your faces, don't I, now?''

''Boyd,'' Whitmire said, ''you get that Jew-boy lawyer out of here or so help me God I'll—''

Boyd laughed aloud. ''Whitmire, for a dollar I'd turn you loose on my friend Ben here. He'd teach you some manners in a moment or two. He'd write his name on your waistcoat with his sword-cane, he would, and with more fancy flourishes than a monk illuminating a manuscript. But I'm in a good mood, despite the night's work. I'll spare you this once.'' He looked up to see Aurora Brand, her red hair covered by a scarf now, bring the team smartly to a stop and pull her borrowed carriage up behind Dallas Boyd. ''Ah,'' he said. ''I hate to leave the survivors like this, but Justin Hague has a second convoy of carriages coming, and perhaps a doctor with them. Meanwhile, Ben, you stay here with me. No, better: There are a couple of saddled horses over there that we can borrow. We'll stay behind and cover their escape. Aurora, help Mr. Soames up, will you? He appears tired. Well, he's had quite an evening of it, and he's showed a lot more courage and grit than most of these brave-hearted paper tigers here have. He's earned a rest. We'll give him one, once we're out of here. Miss Soames, I gather Mr. McClellan's already out of range?''

''He went with the first group of survivors to the hospital,'' Olivia said.

''Good. Now you . . . up onto the carriage, please. Aurora! Get going there, my dear! I'll join you as soon as we're sure you're all right and safely away.''

Aurora Brand gave him one intense look—Olivia could not read it entirely, but she could see the concern and the yearning in it—and flicked the little buggy whip at the horses. The carriage beneath them darted forward. As the horses drew them away into the darkness Olivia looked back once and saw the two men standing tall and soldier-straight, staring down the wall of angry faces, holding back the lethal tide of hatred.

Chapter 13

A mile down the road, Ben Samuels pulled up sharply, turned his horse, and sat waiting for Boyd to catch up with him. Boyd joined him, looking back once as he came to a halt. "Nobody close behind yet," he said. "Perhaps they had the good sense to take me seriously this time." He turned back to the lawyer. "What's on your mind?"

"The fork's up ahead," Samuels said. "Miss Brand needs you, I think, and so does Dwight Soames. I'd suggest you follow them on out."

"Good advice," Boyd said. "And you?"

"Someone's going to have to get to work immediately on the legal problems involved in all of this. And I mean *all* of it. The wreckage of the *Memphis* will have a terrible impact on the Bourse, I'm afraid. That's in addition to the insurance claims and whatever."

"Right. And that young hothead back there on the bank is sure to be making some crack-brained charges."

"Exactly," Samuels said. "So I'd better get into the city and be prepared for virtually anything."

"Good. Ben, if you were working for anyone but Aurora, I'd hire you away myself. You're a good man in a pinch."

"If I were working for anyone but Miss Brand," the attorney said, "it'd likely be myself. But thanks." He pursed his lips for a moment, considering an afterthought. "Dwight Soames has problems," he said. "Perhaps more than I know about. I saw him in earnest conversation with Harrison Caswell tonight, and Soames was getting the worst of it." He looked at Boyd sharply. "The reason I mention this is that

Miss Brand has taken a friendly interest in Miss Soame's affairs.''

"She would.'' Boyd grinned and looked back down the road again. "Still no sign of any pursuers. Well, they'll be along.'' He turned back to Ben Samuels. "Keep an eye out, however, in case they take the other road up from the river. They'll bear you a little ill will, too, I think.'' His voice changed. "As for the trouble Soames is in, I'm going to talk to Caswell. But Soames's problems . . . as you guessed, there's more to them than meets the eye. Anyone with Judd Mahaffey for an attorney has the kind of trouble money alone won't solve.'' He watched in the moonlight for a response and got none; Samuels's face remained impassive. "Huh. The cat's got your tongue, I see.''

"Lawyers don't talk about lawyers much,'' Ben Samuels explained. "But I share your concern. Soames's troubles aren't all of his own making, I'd wager.'' He tilted his head slightly in the direction they'd come from. "Road's drying. I think I hear them. You'd better get moving.'' He reined his horse and turned it, a thin smile on his face. *"Au revoir.''*

"You too,'' Boyd said, nudging his horse forward. "And Ben—take care, eh?''

With the rains gone, the moon had broken through the drifting clouds and now shone bright and round, perhaps a day short of full. The road, free of overhanging trees now, was clearly visible; Aurora Brand let the horses out a bit, and the carriage picked up speed.

Olivia slipped closer to her father, putting one arm around his back. "Miss Brand,'' she said, "Papa has a bad chill. He's shivering uncontrollably.''

"There's a blanket beneath the seat,'' Aurora Brand said. "I was afraid of this. Your father hasn't been well. I'm sure he's been much too much the gallant to tell you. And to-night—all the exertion, in wet clothing and bad weather . . .'' She let go of the reins with one hand and reached down at her feet. "Here, take this. Tuck it around him. I'll try to get to shelter as soon as possible, but it should be the most secure shelter we can find. I think Lance Whitmire meant business back there.''

"Mr. Boyd and Mr. Samuels were wonderful."

"Oh, yes. Dallas is a good man in a tight situation," Aurora Brand admitted, not entirely grudgingly. "If only . . ."

Olivia watched the red-haired woman's delicate profile: the proud chin, the red lips so grimly set. She loves him, she thought. Why are people so hard on each other? Why do they hold themselves apart from each other when they need each other so?

Aurora Brand turned to smile at her young friend. "You're being very polite by not asking," she said. "Maybe I'll tell you about Dallas and me sometime, when we know each other a little better."

"I didn't mean to sound like I was prying," Olivia said. "But Mr. Boyd—he's such a different sort of man."

"He is that," Aurora admitted. "He's a total change of pace from the average sort of person. He's not the type to ask your leave to do something, whether it's a matter of making a fortune on the Bourse or of—" She cut off the thought and changed tack. "He just goes ahead and does it. This infuriates some people. Others it intrigues." She smiled, and her eyes were far, far away for a moment. "For myself, I'll say that at least I understand it. I'm a little that way myself. I've had to be. When I came back from Europe, my father's business became mine—and it was in pretty bad shape. There wasn't time to pussyfoot around."

"Maybe Mr. Boyd feels the whole of life is like that."

Miss Brand turned again to look at Olivia, and the look in her eyes, visible in the moonlight, was one of respect. "That's well put. I suppose he does. And come to think of it, it's sometimes pretty difficult to come up with an argument against that point of view. I have a feeling you keep your own eyes open."

"I . . . I may have to," Olivia said, hugging her father. "Oh, Miss Brand, he's so ill. If only I could get him to bed soon."

But Aurora put up one slim hand, pursing her lips to indicate the need for silence. "Hark!" she said. "Hoofbeats back there. Olivia, would you look back, please? If that's them coming, I'll protect us." She reached into her carpet-bag and pulled out a small but lethal-looking revolver, holding it lightly in her lap. "If it looks like trouble, I may want you to take the reins."

"There's only one man," Olivia said, craning her neck. "And he's large and—"

Aurora turned her own head then, though, and smiled with relief. "Dallas!" she said, and pulled the horses up short, her hands firmly on the reins.

The pair did not embrace, although something in Aurora Brand's eyes told Olivia the red-haired woman would have liked to do so. The two pairs of eyes locked.

"Aurora," Dallas Boyd said, "Ben's gone to town. Frankly I don't think any of your normal haunts are going to be safe for Mr. Soames just now." He looked past her, his eyes bright and alive. "How is he, incidentally?"

"Not well," Olivia said. "We need to get him indoors. But I don't think I could take him home."

"You're right about that. I'd take him over to a place I know on the islands, but that would take even more time." He thought a moment, then smiled. "Any ideas?"

Aurora Brand looked at him, her face thoughtful. "I did have one thought: They're casting suspicion on Mr. Soames's overseer too. If he wanders into the sort of trap I suspect they'll be setting for him, unsuspecting . . ."

"Right," Boyd said. "I hadn't thought of that. Look, there's only one place fit for lying low for a few days just now. My place."

"In the city? Dallas, have you taken leave of your senses?"

"No, damn it! Bayou Lavache!"

"Bayou Lavache? But, Dallas, if you lead us there, there'll be nobody left to warn young McClellan. And I haven't a hope of being able to find the place myself, even in broad daylight, much less find my way out."

"That's all right. Miss Soames, do you know a Cajun lad who works for your father—short and stocky with unruly hair?"

"Jean-Marie Leblond?" Olivia said. "Why?"

"That's the man. He worked for me before he married the Spanish girl. He knows the way backward and forward. He can also lose a pursuer about as well as anyone I know. And once you're a half mile into the bayous, nobody but a Cajun—or me, perhaps—is ever going to be able to find you. Maybe you can get through to Jean Marie.''

"All right," Aurora said. "And then . . . ?"

"Oh, no. You're coming with me. Ben's going to need you. And the one thing on God's earth that the owner of the Brand Line had better not do just now is disappear for a day or two, whatever the reason. You're going to have to be smack dab in the thick of things, staring down your detractors, brazening it out about the loss of the *Memphis*, reassuring everyone that the accident was a fluke, that the same thing couldn't possibly happen to their Aunt Minnie when she goes upriver to St. Louis to visit—and, above all, extending your tenderest sympathies to the survivors and to the relatives of the dead and missing.''

Miss Brand's face sobered and took on a contemplative cast. "Dallas, you're absolutely right. Thank you for reminding me.'' She put one slim hand on his for a moment, then withdrew it with a start.

Boyd grinned that infuriating grin. "I keep forgetting. You don't like to be in my debt in any way, do you? Well, never mind. The main thing is to get the things done that need to be done. You and I will go in, and on the way warn Mc-Clellan. If Olivia can get her father to Leblond's house, down by the river . . .''

"But I don't know where it is," Olivia said.

"Easy. Take the levee route. It'll be pretty much deserted just now; everyone's gone the other way. When you reach the big bend, take the left fork, and when you've gone about a hundred yards inland, stop and make a sound like a quail, three time. Like this." He pursed his lips and made a cooing sound. "Then pause and do it again. Both Jean-Marie and Inez know the signal.''

"All right," Olivia said. She watched as Aurora Brand, stepping off the high seat onto Boyd's horse, mounted to the saddle behind him—not sidesaddle but the way a man mounted. She took Aurora's place on the driver's seat and held on to the reins.

"Oh," Aurora said, "I almost forgot. Here." She handed over something shiny. Olivia almost recoiled when she felt the cold weight of the shiny pistol but then recovered and took it. "Now, godspeed. We'll be over to see you soon. At the worst, you'll have heard from us, if only by messenger, by tomorrow night." She stretched her hand out again and pressed Olivia's warmly. "Courage! I'm prouder of you than you know. You have enough spirit for three women. Don't you forget that fact for so much as a moment. Whatever happens, you can handle it."

"I couldn't have put it better—or truer—myself," Boyd said. He saluted Olivia, one brave person's tribute to another. Bringing the horse about, he moved swiftly out into the night. Olivia watched the two of them all the way to the dark arch of trees, where they disappeared.

Boyd and Aurora met Justin Hague's caravan a mile or so down the road, cutting off their path. "Justin!" Boyd cried out. "Where's Zach McClellan?"

The big overseer, looking a little the worse for wear in clothing that had, like Boyd's, dried on him, moved out of shadow into view, astride a small paint as rawboned and powerful-looking as himself. "Yes, Mr. Boyd?"

Boyd looked him over. He'll do, he thought, remembering the overseer's tireless service on the river, diving again and again after bodies. "We've got a problem," he said. "Young Whitmire. Someone opened a cut between Dwight Soames's place and his. The river's into it already. If Whitmire can bring in a crop at all this year, it'll rot on docks stranded high and dry." He watched McClellan's eyes. "He's blaming you and Soames for it."

"But that's ridiculous!"

Boyd caught the sincere horror in the big man's eyes and nodded. "That's what I said. But Whitmire's stirring up trouble among the downriver folks. You keep on in that direction, with 'em all worked up like that, and you may just run into a tar party—or worse."

"He means it, Mr. McClellan," Aurora Brand said, her voice low and serious. "They aren't going to be in the mood for stopping for explanations, I'm afraid. I wouldn't wander down that way just now."

McClellan's face grew sober. "But Mr. Soames will need help. Miss Soames too."

So that's the way it is, Boyd thought, smiling. Well, the girl could do a lot worse. So could he. He saw the raw longing in the big man's eyes and wondered if Olivia knew the man's feelings toward her. "She's all right. She's taking Dwight to the Leblonds', down by the river."

"By herself? But the area's all full of strangers just now. People, passersby who got pressed into service to help with the levee . . . Look, I'd better go after 'em. A woman's not safe down there."

"You do that, Mr. McClellan," Aurora said. "Olivia could use a friend right now. She's had a hard night of it, and she'll be cold and tired and perhaps a little frightened. I know in her place I'd be."

"You, ma'am?" McClellan said. "Why, you've been so calm."

"Oh, no," she said, looking him in the eye. "I never had to face anything like this at Olivia's age. But if I had, I think I know how it would have felt. One of the reasons I like her is that we're a lot alike." She paused for the blink of an eye, smiling at Zach McClellan with understanding. "She's quite a girl. She has a lot of courage, but she needs help. She could use somebody to lean on now and then. All of us could." Her smile now took note of Dallas Boyd, whose brow rose skeptically and whose smile was wry. "Go to her. You had the right idea in the first place."

"Yes, ma'am," Zach McClellan said, his face serious. And with a parting salute and a brief nod, he spurred his borrowed horse forward into the trees.

Chapter 14

For the second time in half an hour, the soft sound of a quail's call sounded out in the pines: once, twice, three times. Inez Leblond looked once at the pair by the big fire and reached for her shawl. At the door she said, "Who's there?" Her fingers curled purposefully around the handle of her long fish-skinning knife. She waited. "Who's there?" she said again.

"Ton mari, ma jolie," came the matter-of-fact voice of her husband. "Open the door." She drew the bolt and opened wide to let Jean-Marie inside. "I met Monsieur Boyd on the road, with the lovely Mademoiselle Brand. They told me. How is he?"

"Not good." She motioned him over to the fire. "There's no way you're going to be able to take him across the river on a night like this."

"There is no place else. Perhaps I should take him to the home of Monsieur Whitmire? Ah, yes, that would be *très bon*. I will write a sign and pin it to his shirt: 'Affix rope to neck just so.' "

Inez's eyes flashed. "You'll joke when the devil has you roasting on a spit." His complacent nod and smile only made things worse. "Damn you! Be serious. All right, I'll admit I can't think of a better place to hide him just now. But . . . just look at him, will you? He's in no shape to travel."

Her husband, with a courtly nod to Olivia, approached the bed they'd pulled up close to the now roaring fire. He put one hand under the blankets, his eyes on Dwight Soames's wan face. "He has a fever," he said. "Has he been asleep long?"

"No more than a few minutes," Olivia said. She pulled the covers up close around her father's head. "Jean-Marie, is it as bad as Mr. Boyd said? I mean, would Lance Whitmire hurt us?"

Jean-Marie Leblond nodded solemnly. "Look, he is ruined. *Fini.*" He gestured with his hand, and *pouf*! "He was ruined before the cut, but he does not like to admit that. He wants someone else to take the blame. And he has been drinking. *Mon copain* Achille saw him on the road. Let us hope we do not run into him." He looked at Inez. "I would have to kill him." He shrugged expressively. It was as simple as that. "Now, let us discuss how we are to do this. An open bateau—"

"Jean-Marie! You wouldn't think of—"

"—would be a bad thing, *n'est-ce pas*? So we will take him downriver a mile or so, to the house of Cyprien Thibodeaux, who owes me a favor from some time back. He has a boat that—"

"Good! Good!" Inez hugged him impulsively. "Now you're talking. Olivia, I'll mind your father. You go help get the horses ready. We've got to get out of here in—" She stopped and looked at her husband. "How long have we got?"

Jean-Marie took his shotgun down from the wall. "We should have been away an hour ago," he said simply.

Dawn was breaking when Lance Whitmire, dog-tired and hung over, rode through the trees and saw, framed between arching oaks hung with Spanish moss, the tall columns of Radford—the whitewashed brick walls, the wooden balustrade on the second-floor gallery. He spat viciously onto the road and spurred his mount forward, his eyes on the handsome front of his family's house.

Well, he thought, you're finished, too, aren't you? You'll be sitting high and dry in the middle of a worthless island before the month is out. And somebody else'll own you.

But no. The bank would. They'd try to sell, but who would buy? The property would be worth nothing at all. The crop would rot, even if he could bring any of it in. And much of it would be under water anyway.

He dismounted and, his lip curling in self-loathing and disgust, strode through the open front door. The hallway was full of windblown leaves, from back before the rains; he hadn't had anyone in to clean up in weeks, perhaps months. He could see his own muddy boot prints leading into the library, where the liquor was—what was left of it, anyway. Well, good enough: He'd spent more time in there than he had in his equally filthy bedroom in recent days. What need had he for anything else, with his whole world crumbling around him?

He followed the muddy prints through the doorway to the hutch, kicking aside empty bottles on the unwashed floor. His trembling hand opened the high door to the hutch in the dim light. Why, the thing was empty! Surely there must be . . . But his hand closed on a round bottle, the last of many, and pulled it down.

He wiped his mouth with the back of one hand, feeling the rough stubble on his lips. He raised the bottle to drink from its neck. The raw liquor came out fast and deadly; he coughed but drank again.

The last, he thought. The last liquor, the last everything. There was no more money in the house, no more in the bank. In a week he'd be cadging meals down on the swamp, in New Orleans, or . . .

He drank again, splashing himself in the process. *Oh, that's wonderful. You'll stink of whiskey when you go to the bank today.* But then he stopped himself. Bank? Why go to the bank? The conclusion was a foregone one. He already knew the answer he'd get. Extensions? Forget it. Loans? Help of any kind? With what collateral?

"God *damn*," he said, looking around him. What was there left to sell or pawn? He'd stripped the old house down to the bare walls. Paintings, furniture, wall hangings, his mother's china service and silver, even her jewelry—all of it had been dealt out, one precious artifact at a time, long ago. When had it begun? Probably shortly after the bank had refused to add a personal loan to the already staggering debt he owed them. And what had it all gone for? Whiskey and whores, for the most part. And even that had slipped steadily downhill. He'd begun with expensive high-yallers from the

community of the *gens de couleur libres* down in Rampart
Street, where he'd occasionally run into that high-toned
Frenchy lawyer of Rathbone's. And from the quadroon balls
he'd slipped a little, a bit at a time. Soon he hadn't been
welcome in the off-white society of the Vieux Carré and had
pounded the banquettes until he'd found a "house" to his
liking. From there it had been stair steps, always down.

The same with drink. He'd had the best: imported cognac,
the best wines, the finest West Virginia rye . . . and then the
merchants had started refusing his checks after the bank dis-
honored a few of them. Then he drank cheap stuff from the
wrong side of town, "white lightning" bought from white
trash down by the river, raw and powerful and deadly.

And always the swamp had beckoned. The swamp, where
dozens of floating whorehouses and gin mills lay moored at
the foot of Tchoupitoulas Levee, where you could buy a man's
death with a copper coin, where the women were foul-
mouthed, foul-mannered, and totally lacking in inhibitions of
any sort. Where a man's drink might contain anything from
red pepper to laudanum—and probably would if the host's
palm wasn't kept sufficiently greased. There was brisk traffic
down there in "crimping"—the drugging and kidnapping of
the unwary, who were then sold as unwilling 'fore-the-mast
help on a four-master bound out on the morning tide for
Africa, say, or China, or the Sandwich Islands.

Well, maybe he'd go there when things came to the final
pass. When it was all gone, when . . . but no. It was all gone
now. Why wait? There'd always be a way to live down there.
He still had a quick fist with a deck of cards, and if it came
right down to that, he could always make a living of sorts
crimping, or bashing cruise-rich sailors on the town with a
cosh and taking their money. He snarled at the thought, raised
the bottle again, and drank deeply.

No. There was unfinished business. There was still something to be done. The swamp would wait—at least until he'd
dealt with the likes of Dwight Soames. *Soames!* The name
itself was a stab in his heart. Why, Lance Whitmire wouldn't
be in this state if Soames had paid up what he owed.

The liquor was beginning to take effect. He blinked, trying
to bring the gradually lightening room into focus. Then, with

the bottle dangling from his hand, he lurched back out into the filthy hall and went out the front door. He drank again and looked out into the pale light of the dawn hour.

Gone, gone . . .

Suddenly his gorge rose. He shuddered and drank again. The fiery hatred rose in him once again, rose to conquer his despair and fatigue and, for a moment, drive all thought of either from his mind. "Soames," he said, his voice raspy. "Soames, you son of a bitch. You'll pay for this. Ruining me like this. And . . ." And what? Why, Soames had probably saved himself, in the very act of ruining him, Lance Whitmire! The ships that had once docked on Lance's docks would pass him by and would dock now on land that belonged to Dwight Soames. *He'd* be stranded on an island until the other channel dried up and he was left with an oxbow lake backing his useless land. And Soames? He'd be a stop on the steamer run from New Orleans, from Memphis, from St. Louis!

"Soames," he said aloud. "I'm going to get you for this." But how? What would he do? Beat Soames? Kill him? There was little he could do that wouldn't land him on a scaffold some cold morning down by the river. Kill Soames? Why, the man was better than half dead already. It wouldn't take much. And it'd hardly satisfy the black lust for vengeance that, even this moment, ate away at his guts.

Then a thought came to him, just as he poised the open neck of the bottle before his still thirsty lips, and the thought was so fine that he lowered the bottle, thinking about it. He smiled a slow, malicious smile.

The girl.

Soames's girl. The one who'd come back from the East the other day, the one with the saucy tongue.

Yes, yes. And a pretty little thing, too, dark and shapely, with big eyes. The world could see that Dwight Soames doted on her, that he thought the sun rose and set for his little girl.

What better way to hurt Soames? Hurt him where the hurt would last. And Lance could count on a certain . . . well, a certain reticence when it came to someone filing a complaint. The girl would want to keep it quiet afterward, for the sake of her reputation. And Soames? What could Soames do but call him out—and get killed, legally, in the process?

And yes, she *was* a pretty little thing, wasn't she? No doubt about it. And spirited. She'd struggle a bit. . . .

Whitmire drank again, deeply. But now the strong liquor in the half-empty bottle had the effect of strengthening his will rather than sapping it. He stepped down onto the mostly dry ground before his front steps, the bottle still held loosely in his hand. As the first direct rays of the morning sun broke over the housetop and painted the tops of the oak trees, he sprang into the saddle, drank, and tossed the bottle into the bushes beside his front drive.

"This place of Mr. Boyd's," Olivia said. "Where is it?" She sat in the back of the Leblonds' open wagon, next to her recumbent father, across from Inez.

"Across the river," the girl said. "Bayou Lavache takes off from the Mississippi a little downriver. A lot of it is little islands, grasslands, rich fields. It's not as big or fancy as Teche or Lafourche. But it suits Boyd's purposes, I guess. A man can get lost in there every bit as well as he can in the bigger bayous."

"But how did Mr. Boyd come to such a place? It all seems so odd."

The woman turned her head. "Jean-Marie! Get a move on, there!" she said. Her husband grinned back at her. "Well, Dallas Boyd's an odd sort. But maybe I am too. He . . . why, he's as much at home *chez les Cajuns* as he is at a fancy ball. You should see him at a big *boucherie* dancing the galop, or eating *boudin* or *écrevisse* at a family *veillee*."

"She probably doesn't know any of the terms, *ma jolie*," her husband said.

"Well, she's got an education ahead of her. Don't worry; give her a couple of weeks at Boyd's place and she'll be eating *chaudin* and *fromage de tête de cochon* like an old hand. Yes, and cooking it too. I'll show her."

They passed under low-hanging moss; Jean-Marie ducked low. "Ah," he said. "You, Olivia, you listen to her, then. She's not bad. Not good—one would have to be Cajun-born to be good—but not bad."

"You! You watch out. I'll poison your food."

"You always do," he said. "Look, Cyprien is home. And

he's up. That will make it easier." They looked over the back
of the seat to where he pointed. A heavily built man with
very broad shoulders stood washing his hands at a well pump.
"Cyprien!" Jean-Marie called out, turning the wagon under
the trees and bringing it to a halt. "Quick! We need help!"
His speech went off into rapid-fire Cajun, as impenetrable as
Hottentot. Olivia did not understand another word.

"They'll take care of the boat," Inez said. "Here, help
me with your pa . . . but no. Tell you what. You get down
. . . yes, and . . ." She stood up in the wagon and looked
around. "Best thing might be to carry him aboard, all covered up just like he is. There's a board over in the barn that
ought to do the job, best I can remember; we can lay him on
that, and the men can carry him out. If you could run over
there and bring it back . . . I think it's light enough to carry.
You're stronger than you look, as I remember."

"Oh, yes." Olivia jumped down. "In the barn, you said?"

"Yes. Against the far wall, last time I was here. Hurry!"

Olivia didn't look back, breaking into a trot across the
uneven ground. Her heart pounded with excitement. So much
had happened, just in the last twelve hours alone, that there
had hardly been time to catch her breath. Now they were
taking off into the unknown, into mostly uncharted lands
across the great river, into deep Cajun country where few
outsiders ever penetrated.

She entered the still half-dark barn, blinking to try to get
the interior in focus. A lone horse stood by the door, still
saddled, its coat lathered and uncurried. She ignored it and
went deeper inside. The far wall, Inez had said.

Then the thought hit her. The horse . . . saddled? Lathered, as if it had been running. It seemed odd. She turned,
and then she saw a man step out of the shadows, not an arm's
length from her. Tall, broad-shouldered, powerful-looking.
And smelling powerfully of whiskey. "Lance Whi—" she
said. But his big hand fell across her mouth and cut off the
word, and his other arm pulled her close.

Chapter 15

For the fifth time in as many minutes Inez Leblond put her hand to Dwight Soames's fevered cheeks and head. Was he conscious? She couldn't tell easily. He was so wan, so hot, so dehydrated. If only she could get him to take some nourishment, perhaps a cup of soup.

Biting her lip, she looked up as her husband came in the door of Cyprien Thibodeaux's small, cluttered house. "He's much worse," she said in Cajun. "I don't know if we can risk taking him across the river, even in a covered boat with a cabin."

"We can't risk not taking him," Jean-Marie Leblond said. "Cyprien says he's seen, within the hour, a group of men ride through looking for someone. They were armed. He didn't see young Whitmire, he says—but several of the riders were friends of Whitmire's."

"Ah. That doesn't sound good. They could return at any time."

"No doubt they will. And we don't know where Whitmire himself is. For all we know, he may have organized an entirely separate party." His face changed suddenly, though, and the humor came back into it—a wry, accepting sort of humor. "You know, there is something you and I have forgotten entirely in all this."

She stood and looked at him, pausing to check the sick man's temperature, then frowning at the result. "What's that?"

"You and I . . . we are out of work. Monsieur Soames is out of business, and we are out of work. On the porch at

Monsieur Hague's I heard our patron arguing with the
banker—I forget his name. Pleading with the banker.'' The
corners of his mouth turned down mock tragically, but his
eyes kept their good humor. ''In vain. And now this.'' His
wave of the hand lumped it all together and dismissed it: the
false accusations, the night riders, all of it.

''What difference does it make?'' his wife said matter-of-
factly. ''We haven't been paid in three months, anyhow.''

''Exactly. It doesn't upset me. I was wondering if you—''

''Bah!'' She spat out the words. ''We can live at Boyd's
for a time. We have friends there. The bayou and its tributaries are full of fish, as always. Dallas Boyd, himself, may
have work for us.''

''Certainly. What does it matter?'' He stepped forward and
put his arms around her. ''As long as we have each other.''

She struggled free. ''Now, you! No time for that. Can't
you ever think of anything else?''

''Why should I?'' he said, laughing, reaching for her again.
She scrambled out of his reach, her eyes flashing, but her
mouth curved in a smile she could not drive away. ''It is you
who do it to me. A ravishing vision I cannot resist.''

''Oh, you fool,'' she said, and let him catch up to her this
time. His arms were powerful, his lips demanding. But it
was a game they were playing, one whose main purpose was
to take the sharp edge off the grim situation in which they
found themselves, and both of them knew it. She kissed him
and, her hand curving around his broad back, pinched his
hard bottom. ''There, now. Plenty of time for that later. Now
we've got work to do.'' She slipped free, giving him a little
squeeze as she did, and turned to look at the man on the bed
once again in the thin light of morning. ''We've got to get
him out to the boat.''

An odd look came over her. ''The board. Olivia was bringing the board. I wonder what can have happened to her?''

''Perhaps she couldn't find it,'' he said. ''Where was she
supposed to be looking?''

''The barn,'' his wife said. ''You go have a look.''

''I will.'' He looked at her, unsmiling, and walked out
into the clear morning air. He suddenly stopped dead, looking around him at the loose ring of riders who faced him,

their eyes hard, rifles and shotguns visible above the saddles of each. His hand edged toward his pocket, but he remembered now that he had given Inez the little revolver he'd gotten from Olivia. "*Bonjour*, gentlemen," he said with a forced smile. "What can I do for you?"

He recognized the man who answered: a small landowner named Veach. "We're lookin' for Dwight Soames. You seen him?"

Jean-Marie looked him right in the eye, still smiling. "No, *monsieur*. He seldom comes down this way. He must have gone home."

"Hey, Veach!" one of the riders said. "That's one of Hague's wagons out back, ain't it? What's this hired hand doin' with one o' them? And two of Hague's horses?"

Veach turned his head, looked, then looked back down at Jean-Marie Leblond. "Good question, white trash. You steal 'em? Speak up."

"I borrowed them," Jean-Marie said, praying his wife would stay inside the cabin, praying that Cyprien would remain in the boat and Olivia in the barn. "I was driving a coach for Monsieur Soames, one rented from the livery stable. After the disaster on the river the big coach was taken to carry the survivors. Monsieur Hague loaned me this one to get home in." It sounded plausible enough, he thought. If only Veach agreed.

"Veach," another rider said, "he might be tellin' the truth. I saw a whole train o' coaches headin' for town, carryin' folks from the *Memphis*."

Veach looked Jean-Marie hard in the eye again, his hand tightening on the stock of the big-bore shotgun he carried. "All right," he said, "but you keep an eye out for Soames. He comes this way and you try hidin' him, let me tell you . . ."

"Hide him? Me?" Jean-Marie said with a Gallic shrug. "Why should I?"

A cold bolt of fear ran through him as his eye ranged past Veach into the forest behind him and the other riders. He saw Zach McClellan standing, holding his horse by the bridle, gentling it, watching the riders. Zach! he thought desperately. Go back. Slip back into the trees. Don't let them see you. "I . . . I will not hide him," he said, his eyes narrowed, an ingratiating Latin smile on his face for the first time. He kept his eyes on Veach, but his gesture—one hand raised, seeming to push something away—was for McClellan. "Forget it. I will send a messenger to you."

"You better," Veach said, and turned to·go. With relief Jean-Marie saw McClellan lead the horse back into the oaks. The riders moved away. Jean-Marie stood watching them until they were out of sight. Then he rushed to the clump of trees and saw McClellan move toward him.

"Jean-Marie!" Zach McClellan said. "Have you got them?"

"Yes. The father is inside the house with my wife. *La petite* . . . I was just going to the barn to fetch her when I ran into them. We're going across the river, to Monsieur Boyd's place."

"Good," McClellan said. "I'm coming with you. But I've got to hide this animal. They'll recognize it. I'll go get Olivia. You get Dwight ready. Those boys may·be back." He waited for Jean-Marie's curt nod, then turned and walked his horse toward the barn, silently, like an Indian.

"You get away from me," Olivia said, backing into the darkness, vainly trying to hold the torn cloth over her naked breasts. "I'll scream. I don't care if they come. I . . . I won't let you hurt me again."

"Go ahead and holler," Whitmire said, holding a handkerchief over the torn place on his lip where she'd bitten him in her desperation. "They're my friends, not yours. They'll just help me hold you down. By God, you little bitch! You've bit me right through! I got half a mind to call 'em myself. We'll spread-eagle you on the barn floor and let the boys take turns at you."

Olivia circled, keeping the wreckage of Thibodeaux's ruined hay wagon between them. If she could just get around to the rear . . . She'd seen a pitchfork leaning against the barn wall. Her heart pounded with fear and hatred. She'd kill him before she let him touch her again! She had no qualms about that.

Suddenly, silently, Whitmire lunged forward. His hand caught hers across the broken wagon. She wriggled loose, desperation giving new strength·to her movements; but his hand closed on the cloth she'd been holding to her and pulled at it. She tore herself away, and now the dress came away, and she was naked before him, naked in the chill of morning. She backed away, circling.

Olivia's hand, stretched out behind her, closed around the polished wood handle of the pitchfork, just as he swung around the rear end of the wagon and came at her in a rush. She thrust at him and missed. In a panic now, she ran, still holding the long fork, toward the barn door he'd closed when he'd first surprised her. Keeping an eye on him, she turned her back to the barn door and shoved.

It wouldn't open! It was stuck on something!

Lance Whitmire lunged toward her, cursing. She felt the cold wood of the door against her naked back as she shoved again, and as he bore down on her she raised the pitchfork in her hands, raised it chest high. She'd do anything to keep him away, to keep him from hurting her again.

The shock of his big body, striking home like that, tore the implement from her hands. It knocked the door of the barn slightly ajar. Olivia fell to her knees and scrambled to one side. If she could get to the partly open door, get out into the light again, get to where Jean-Marie and his friend could help her . . .

Then she looked up and saw her enemy stagger backward, his steps fumbling, his hands flailing away, beating at the thing in his chest. She got to her feet, unable to tear her eyes away. In the middle of the barn floor, Lance Whitmire struggled to free himself from the tines of the hayfork, imbedded deep in his chest. But his every motion moved the sharp tines in further and drew from his open lips another groan of pain. His hands tore at the wooden handle. He got his fingers between the tines and pulled.

But now the strength was going out of him. He fell to one knee and cried out again. His suffering was more intense now; his face was twisted in pain, and a thin line of blood ran down his face from one corner of his mouth. He'd impaled himself on the fork, and the weight of his own lunging body had been enough to drive the implement too far into his chest to remove with any ease. Now his own hands were too weak to do the job. "Help," he said in a thin childlike voice. "Help me."

Help you? she thought. She shivered, as much from rage as from the cold. Still shaking, she watched him slowly dissolve into absolute weakness now and, just as slowly, land on both knees. The fork stretched out ahead of him; with a last burst of strength he pulled at the handle with both hands and pulled the wooden shaft out of its metal shank, leaving the fork itself buried in his chest. He fell forward, and the weight of his big body drove the metal tines all the way through him; they protruded now from his back, their tips wet with blood. He did not move again.

Zach McClellan, flinging the barn door wide, found Olivia there, oblivious to the cold and in the aftershock of her violent episode, staring down at the inert form on the earthen floor. Her little body was as nude and as ravishingly lovely as Venus', he thought for the first heartbeat's length. Then he saw the scratches on her bare back and flanks, the beginnings of bruises on her arms; saw the sudden, frenzied shaking of her body as the reality of the attack suddenly hit her.

"Olivia," he said hoarsely. She turned, her face desolate, and ran into his arms.

Standing above the open grave, Inez put her arm around Olivia and squeezed. "Don't think about it," she said. "You did what you had to do. I'd have done it myself." Her face hardened at the thought. "I wish I *had* done it myself. The filthy bastard."

"It's me that feels dirty," Olivia whispered so low, the men couldn't hear it above the sound of their shoveling. "Oh, Inez, I'll never forget what happened."

"Yes, you will," the girl said. "At least you'll forget enough of it to allow you to get on with your life. When you remember the attack, just think of him lying there in that hole, with my husband and Zach shoveling dirt on him." She turned to Olivia. "Look me in the eye now. I tell you, I felt dirtied, too, after I'd been . . . well, I never told you about that. But the same thing happened to me, before I met Jean-Marie. And I didn't get a chance to get back at that man for some time, but I did, after a while. Oh, I didn't kill him. Not that I don't sometimes wish I had. But . . . well, I fixed it so he wouldn't rape any other woman again."

Olivia closed her eyes. "If only it hadn't happened. If only . . ." She drew herself together inside the man's shirt and pants Thibodeaux had given her from his absent son's old clothes. She watched the last clods falling into the grave, her eyes empty of all emotion.

"Look," Inez said. "Nobody but us knows. We all love you and care for you, and we'll all forget. In the meantime everybody'll think Lance just went away. It'd be a natural thing for him to do, anyway. You just try to forget him." She gave Olivia another hug and pulled away. "Jean-Marie!" she said in a stronger voice. "Let's get over the river. Too much happening on this side."

Her husband patted the grave flat. "Cyprien," he said in Cajun, "plant an herb garden here. Who will think to look under watercress or garlic or tarragon, eh?" He turned to his wife. "All right," he said in English. "We'll get Monsieur Soames. You two get onto the boat."

Sails billowing, Thibodeaux's boat tacked its way in dog-leg steps across the great river. Inez Leblond came up on board from the below-decks cabin and stood beside her husband. "Look," she said. "She stands apart from him. She'll hardly speak to him." She spoke in fluent Cajun.

Jean-Marie frowned, watching Olivia and Zach McClellan, each standing by a different rail, both looking back toward the receding eastern shore. The girl hugged herself tensely, and the pair watching her thought they could see her shudder a couple of times. "He doesn't know what to make of it," he said. "Poor devil. And *he* blames himself for not arriving earlier." He sighed. "The ways of love are not easy."

"He's seen her shame," Inez said. "She feels soiled. And although it was his arms she ran into when she was free, she'd like to forget that. She'd like to forget that he knows what happened to her. It doesn't matter to her that it wasn't her fault it happened."

"Women," her husband said. "Who can understand them?" But his face and voice softened, and the words came out in a world-weary sigh. *"Pauvre petite . . ."*

Chapter 16

After a time Olivia came aft, her face somber and disconsolate, and stood beside Inez. "I'll go look after Papa," she said in a voice drained of emotion.

"No," Inez said, putting one hand on the girl's thin shoulder. "I'll handle him. You stay up here. Watch. It's a different world this side of the river. It's a healing place. If anything in the world can make you feel good after what you've been through, coming over here will do it."

Olivia shrank from her touch, drawing even more into herself. "Oh, Inez, I'll never feel good again. I'll never feel the same . . ."

"Not the same, true," the dark girl said, leaning back against the cabin frame to look at her. "When you've run into injustice pure and simple, when someone's abused you beyond all forgiveness, you think the hurt's never going to heal. But the Lavache is a special place. After all, the Cajuns had wounds to heal when they came here, too. Some of 'em worse than yours, dear, whatever you may think at the moment. They'd had fathers, mothers, little children die on 'em—of cold, disease, or just plain terror. They'd been raped and beaten on the ships that took 'em away from Canada. They'd had their babies snatched right out of their arms; some of 'em never saw them again, or knew what had happened to them." She stared Olivia down when the girl turned a resentful eye her way. "What did you think *Le Grand Dérangement* was anyhow, honey lamb? Some sort of picnic in the woods? Countless Acadians were dislocated."

"Oh, Inez, don't talk to me that way. Please." She covered her nose and mouth with her two hands, her big dark eyes still on the girl's face. "Please don't be harsh."

"I don't mean to be hard on you, Olivia, but damn it, you got to let folks help you. You got to let life help you. You let the life up the bayou get to you and it'll work for you. It's a healthy life, lived out under the sun in the open, under God's blue sky. The folks here work hard and play hard, and they eat like kings and queens never ate in the Old Country. You'll be among folks who'll love you and make you well—if you'll let 'em. And they'll show you how to love their country and live off it. They don't fight it, the way the Creoles and Kaintucks do; they work with it. It doesn't make 'em rich for the most part, but that isn't their style, anyhow. They're free folks, and that's more important to 'em."

Inez went on. "You're entering a world where that damn slavery your papa has been fighting his war with, and losing, never really got a toehold. You don't need slaves to run a farm a family can live off comfortably—and big plantations don't work well here, anyhow. The *petits habitants* here don't cotton to the idea of anybody owning anybody anyhow, black or white. That's why they liked your papa: Anybody who'd take the stand he did and stick to it has their sympathy right from the start. Dallas Boyd, too. He's just about the only Kaintuck these folks ever let make his place up Bayou Lavache. When you get to know him a little, you'll understand why. He doesn't come in imposin' any new rules or bringin' in any new manners. He fits in. He doesn't bring anybody in who isn't free like himself, and I mean in mind and spirit as well as body. And he's open and generous with the folks here, sharing their ups and downs like an equal. It doesn't hurt that he talks Cajun better'n I do, either."

Her eyes searched Olivia's face and took note of the change in the girl's expression. The distraction was working: not much, but a little. And that was something. She went on. "You'll see," she said. Smiling, she reached inside the little cabin and pulled out two cane chairs. "Here, sit down," she said, taking one of the seats herself. She eased Olivia down, taking both the girl's hands. "Now, look, we're entering the mouth of Bayou Lavache. Soon we'll dock and change over to a *bateau plat*, maybe, or possibly even a pirogue. This boat's too deep-draft for safe travel. Even a shallow-draft paddlewheel paquebot like the old *Eagle*, which used to work Bayou Lafourche, couldn't make it up here without going aground. They got a saying here that a normal pirogue has to float on dew, but that a boat that can navigate Bayou Lavache has to float on a light rain.''

Olivia's eyes cleared. She looked out over the narrower stream into which they had steered. Across the sluggishly moving water she could see high grass first, then high ground. Oak trees dotted the shores; farther downstream, she could see docks and houses, all bunched near the water. ''It . . . it looks like a town,'' she said. ''I thought . . .''

''Hmm,'' Inez said, still holding her hand. ''I suppose it does. And I suppose the waterfront along here is a sort of community of a kind, one house deep and I don't know how many miles long. I guess it hangs together like a town, in a way. Maybe better. Trouble comes, everybody pitches in.'' She felt Olivia's head lean against her shoulder, and she pulled the girl close, ever so gently. The dark hair fell down over her face. Inez held her close, rocking her softly and beginning to croon, ever so softly, a lilting Cajun lullaby:

> Fais dodo, Minnette,
> Fais dodo, mon piti bebe,
> Quand quinze ans aura passe,
> Minette va so marier.

At the third verse she stopped. She looked up at Zach McClellan, standing above the two of them anxiously. ''Zach,'' she said, ''bring my shawl from below, will you? She finally ran out of steam. Best thing she could do right now would be to get a little sleep.''

The big man brought the woven cloth and wrapped it around the two of them. ''She's so small and frail,'' he said, ''and she's had so much to contend with in the last forty-eight hours. If only there were something I could do, something she'd let me do.''

Inez looked at his two huge, powerful hands, clenching and unclenching impotently. Then she looked up at the sorrow and self-loathing in his face.

"Zach, I'm going to have Jean-Marie give you a talking-to. You're being too hard on yourself. Relax and stick close by. You never know when she's going to need you, when she'll suddenly open up to you and let you know. But for now . . . well, we'll just have to give her a little room to breathe, and be as nice to her as we can." She frowned at the expression on his face. "You must be tired out yourself. Go rest a bit. There's a bed in the cabin next to Dwight's. Lie down and put your feet up. There, now, do as I say. Now!"

She sighed, watching the big man move away—sighed at the fatigue that showed in his every move, at the defeat that marked the hang of his enormous shoulders. Well, perhaps the bayou country had some healing to do in his case as well. Hers, too, as well as this poor child's here. She sighed again and sang softly, her words floating aft on the light bayou breeze:

> Fais dodo, Minette,
> Fais dodo, mon piti bebe . . .

Inez had dozed off for a moment or so herself, Olivia's dark head still cradled on her shoulder. When she was awakened suddenly, she blinked and straightened. The girl stirred beside her.

Jean-Marie shook Inez again. "Come. It's Monsieur Soames." She blinked again, got his face in focus, and read his expression. She tensed immediately. *"Oui,"* her husband said. *"Son coeur . . ."*

"W-what?" Olivia said, coming awake, rubbing her face. Inez had slipped out from beside her and was moving away. She looked up. "Zach," she said, "what's the matter?"

"I went below just now. I think your father's having a heart attack. He spoke to me for a moment before, and . . ."

But Olivia was up and, disregarding all the rules of how to move on board a boat, almost dashed toward the little cabin door nearby. She went down the three steps to the enclosed space in one unsteady bound.

Then she stopped, looking at her friends' somber faces. She watched as Jean-Marie laid his ear to Dwight's chest and held it there. She watched as the stocky Cajun sadly raised his head and shook it slowly from side to side. "I'm sorry," he said simply. "He went so quickly."

Olivia clasped her hands together. *Papa? Gone?* She couldn't believe it. But . . . but it was true. Their faces told her that. *It means I have nothing. Nobody.* Her eyes clouded with tears. She searched the faces before her and then looked at the thin body on the little bed, the closed eyes, the drawn face now at rest, at peace, free of the cares that had haunted him. "B-but . . ."

"Oh, my darling," Inez said, her own eyes wet, her hands outstretched, moving toward her. But the arms that folded around her were those of Zach McClellan—large, strong, comforting. She shuddered for a moment and tried to pull away but then gave way to her own overpowering need to accept comfort. She relaxed in his arms, and he held her to him. Inez hoped this closeness wasn't temporary, that Olivia would need *him* and not merely a pair of strong arms.

Dwight Soames's simple funeral was held under a spreading oak, on the high ground behind the little Cajun church, and the service had been in a language Olivia could not understand. The next day Dallas Boyd arrived unexpectedly, poling his own flat-bottomed pirogue down the sluggish stream, his rangy body standing tall and straight in the shallow-draft boat, a big pistol strapped openly to his belt. He nodded greetings to friends on the bank and tied up his own boat; then he stepped ashore to meet Zach McClellan. "You don't seem glad to see me. What's the matter?"

The Soameses' former overseer got in step with Dallas Boyd, and the two made their way across the unsteady ground toward the low, broad manor house Boyd had built on the island. He briefly explained the terrible things that had happened to his employers since their escape from the tense scene on the banks of the river the night of the *Memphis* disaster. Boyd listened silently, nodding here and there. Then, at the porch of his house, he said, "Zach, you and I need a drink. Why don't you come in with me."

McClellan silently followed him in and watched Boyd walk over to a tall hutch and take down a tall bottle and two glasses.

Then Boyd thought better of the matter. "You mind drinking from the bottle?" he asked.

"Bourbon?" McClellan said. His smile was a sad one but one that had known better times. "Using a glass does seem a sacrilege, sir, doesn't it?" He took the bottle and drank, not deeply, but enough to betray thirst. He handed the bottle back, wiping the neck as he did so. "Your health, sir."

"Not much need of formality between you and me, Zach," Boyd said. "Not after the night the *Memphis* died. It's funny, I think there'll be a bond of sorts between all of us who were there, trying to save whoever we could." He held the bottle up; McClellan shook his head. "And young Olivia. How's she taken all this? Poor child."

"I think she isn't a child anymore. She's had enough happen to her for a dozen girls. But . . ." His words trailed off, and for a moment his mind was far away. Then he came back to himself. "I'll change my mind and take that second drink if you don't mind, sir," he said.

"Here," Boyd said. He watched in silence. After a moment's pause he went on. "Aurora Brand doesn't know about all this, of course, but even so, she told me she wanted the girl to come join her. Work for her, live with her. You understand. Now it seems a better idea than ever. When I go back, I'll take Olivia with me."

"That's a wonderful idea," McClellan said. "Even if . . ." He glanced hungrily at the bottle in his hand, but handed it back. "Here," he said. "It's a fine idea. Keep her busy, occupied. She won't have time to think."

"And not having time to think is a good thing sometimes, isn't it?" Boyd said, corking the bottle and putting it aside. "Zach, you're unemployed, and—well, there's still suspicion of you back across the river. Disproving it might be a bad idea just now; some people are beginning to ask just what happened to young Whitmire, and that's a sleeping dog that I think we'd best let lie."

"Right, sir."

"Yes. Well, you get along with the Cajuns over here. And you're a good hand; I've asked around. I haven't had an overseer so far, but maybe I'd do best to get myself one. One who could act for me in several capacities. You've more than one string to your bow. Like to work for me?''

McClellan looked at him, his eyes dark and sober. ''You've got yourself a man,'' he said. ''What you said about keeping busy . . .''

''Fine.'' Boyd extended a hand, which McClellan took in a grip as firm as his own. ''And, Zach, I don't think I'd bandy this around, but you should know that the *Memphis* was no accident. Neither was the cut in Whitmire's property.''

''I wondered. Before he died, Mr. Soames said two things to me. He said, 'Rathbone. Ask Mahaffey.' ''

''Yes. One reason Olivia's going to work for Aurora is that the girl's been wiped out, even if I paid up Dwight's note for him. He's been sold out, all down the line. By Mahaffey, his lawyer, and by his own brother, Driscoll Soames.''

''God!'' McClellan said, balling his big fists. ''Sold out to whom?''

''Rathbone. I can't prove a thing. Any more than I can prove anything substantial about the *Memphis*. I've got divers going over the wreck, looking for clues the survivors mentioned. I've got people out scouring the woods for someone who'll tell what he knows about the cut. So has Ben Samuels. We'll find something, if there's something to be found.'' He smiled wryly, his eyes hard. ''Meanwhile I need someone around me I can count on in a pinch. A lot depends on that. Not only my own well-being, but Miss Brand's as well and everyone in her entourage.'' He let the statement sink in. ''Aurora's affairs are in deep trouble. Bouncing back from a thing like this—it'll take all the skills and ingenuity she has, and her friends' as well. I think we can count on you.''

He looked at Zach McClellan's clear eyes and at the anger in his face and liked what he saw. ''Just tell me what I can do,'' McClellan said.

''Good. You're on. But, Zach, when you're down-and-out, when things look worst, what do you do? When you're down to your last copper coin?''

McClellan looked at him, fire in his eye. ''Butcher a hog,'' he said, new mettle in his tone. ''Raid the wine cellar. Invite all your friends. Throw a party. They call it priming the pump where I come from.''

Dallas Boyd smiled, a deeply satisfied smile. ''You're a man after my own heart. Well, you're my overseer, aren't you? Haven't we sealed it with a shot of whiskey and shook hands on it? Go give the order. We're going to throw the goddamnedest country Cajun *boucherie* anybody's seen down here since Lafitte beat the British.'' He waited the blink of an eye, then barked, ''Well, get to it, man!''

''Yes, *sir*!'' McClellan said, and went out the door with a new spring in his step, the air of command already beginning to settle on his broad shoulders.

Book Two

Chapter 17

Sitting squarely in his oversize chair, his heavy hands planted on the broad desk before him, Laird Rathbone scowled up at his visitor. "Are you finished, sir?" he said in a rumbling bass tinged with sarcasm.

Driscoll Soames, his face drawn, his eyes blinking uncontrollably, looked down at the financier, opening and closing his mouth but unable to find words for what was in his heart at first. "F-finished?" he said in a hoarse croak. "*Finished*, Mr. Rathbone? Why, yes . . . I suppose you'd call it that." He cleared his throat and continued, but now his words had a curiously hollow sound. "So you've got Wyvern now, in spite of it all. And I . . . I trusted you. You and Mr. Mahaffey."

"What has trust got to do with it, Mr. Soames?" Rathbone said contemptuously. "It was business. No more. Harrison Caswell had some paper to sell, and I bought it. It happened to include the delinquent loan your brother had taken out on his—and your—property. As for Mr. Mahaffey, I have nothing to do with him. I'm sure you recognize that. If he gave you advice that proved in the long run to be against your best interests, that's not my fault." He turned the broad palms of his two hands upward but left them on the desk. "What can I say? If you think your lawyer has been guilty of fraudulent conduct toward you, sue him. Take him to court. But don't blame me for making perfectly normal moves in my own interest, that concern you only peripherally."

"Peripherally?" Driscoll Soames said. "I'm wiped out. Foreclosure means that . . ." He straightened for a moment, and then slumped miserably as the thought hit him. "And I—I sold my brother out on Mahaffey's advice. I pressured him into overextension. The pressure and the shock of failure contributed to his death."

"Your brother died of a bad heart," Rathbone said tonelessly. "He'd been drinking a lot recently, neglecting his health. Everyone in the parish knew that. And his last night was a strenuous one, one that might easily have hastened the death of many a stronger man. I understand your brother was something of a hero the night the *Memphis* burned—to those who conceive of such actions as heroism. He—"

"Dwight was a saint. A brave and honorable man. And, listening to Mahaffey, I played him right into your hands, didn't I?" Driscoll Soames's expression was that of a man looking down into the pit, eyes wide, all his defenses shattered. "And that poor child of his . . . I've sold her out too. Two years ago she had a fortune, a future, a handsome dower to bring to a good marriage. Not now."

"Now she starts out in life where I started in life, Mr. Soames." There was a kind of triumph in Rathbone's tone. He leaned forward, and there was a fiery glint in his eye now. "Nowhere. That's where I began, sir. I have built all this from nothing." He made a sweeping gesture with one heavy hand. "If the girl has something to her, she'll find a way of rising as I rose. I'll think the more of her if she does. But spineless jellyfish like you and that brother of yours, who prate of honor and all the other of the seven deadly abstractions, who inherit power, position, money, and then haven't the strength of mind or character to hold it . . . bah!" He sat back suddenly, his face a mask of contempt and loathing. "That'll be all, sir. I've done with you."

Driscoll Soames leaned forward, his fist clenching and unclenching weakly. "Rathbone," he said, "you haven't heard the last of this. I'll—"

"You'll do nothing," Rathbone said, picking up a paper on his desk and looking at it. "If you're not out of this office and on the stairs by the time I've read this, I'll be forced to call in Mr. Halsey and have you dumped on my front step on three bounces." He looked up. "Did you hear me?" he said forcefully. *"Halsey!"* he called over one shoulder.

Driscoll Soames winced. His back straightened. He looked at Rathbone one last time, then turned and walked slowly and purposefully to the door. "Good day, sir," he said.

Rathbone watched the door close. Then he turned his head. "Renault," he said. "Renault, will you come in here?" The side door to his office opened, and Marc-Antoine Renault, Rathbone's attorney, moved inside, a wry smile on his saturnine face. "Well, there he goes," Rathbone said. "What do you think? Will he face down Mahaffey? Because if he does . . ."

"Never fear." Renault hooked his thumbs in his vest pockets and looked out the window down into Royal Street. "Mahaffey has his, and our, footprints all covered by now. That's what we paid him to do, after all. And . . . *that* gentleman. If I'm any judge, he's on his way to the nearest tavern. Perhaps worse. I've know men in a position not unlike his to drown themselves."

"Or shoot themselves," Rathbone said with a scowl. "I'll have Halsey keep an eye on him."

"No. Unnecessary. The more I think of it, the more sure I am that if he shoots anyone, it'll be himself. Although if he does, it'll be with a gun already purchased. This morning he won't find enough credit in New Orleans to purchase a bullet, much less a weapon." He smiled, not at all sympathetically. "Poor devil."

Rathbone sat back in the big chair and reached for a long cigar from the case beside him, cutting the end with a razor-sharp knife from the desk and taking some time lighting it before blowing a large cloud of blue smoke. "Meanwhile," he said at last, "what have you learned about the Brand woman?"

Renault sat down in the big overstuffed chair by the window, hooking one long leg rakishly over the arm. "Well," he said, "we're keeping the pressure on. Insurance claims are coming in thick and fast. I represent several of the claimants legally, and I'm counseling . . . ah . . . an attitude of intransigent rage wherever I can. But she's taken her case to the newspapers, and I must say she's been quite persuasive. She has a way about her, you know."

"I know, damn your eyes," Rathbone said, puffing angrily

away at the long cheroot. "What I want to know is whether she's going to be able to rebuild. Can't you get a line into the banks? I'd like to know how overextended she is right now."

"As far as I can tell, she's still solvent," the lawyer said, long fingers pressed together before his lean face. "Of course, she's in a position where she has to rebuild, not only quickly but also substantially. The new *Memphis* has to be bigger, more lavish, than the old. And that means, with the present purchasing power of the dollar, much more expensive. It's a matter of saving face."

"I understand, damn it. I'm sure Seth Falkner isn't just sitting around all this time twiddling his thumbs. He'll be on the telegraph wire, tickling his shipyard friends, calling in favors from years back."

"To be sure, Captain Falkner is a major factor in the matter, sir. His reputation is known not only on the river and on its tributaries, but also in the East. People who might not extend credit to Aurora Brand—after all, she's a relative newcomer to the river and the daughter of a man whose bills went unpaid for quite some time."

"These same people will extend credit on the basis of Falkner's reputation as a man of honor," Rathbone said, sitting forward and blowing out small wisps of smoke with every explosive phrase. "Yes, God damn it, I know. Do you know which shipbuilders she's working on?"

"Well, there are the ones in St. Louis and in Carondelet."

"Confound it!" Rathbone said, grinding out the cigar only half smoked. "You know damned good and well she won't be buying from small-time operators. She'll be buying in Pittsburgh, taking advantage of the proximity of the foundries. And if I know Seth Falkner, he'll have designed a few improvements into the engines. It'll be sleek and fast and elegant, if he can raise the money for it."

"And he can. You know that."

"Yes! Yes, damn you! And when it makes its maiden run, it'll steal business from our best ships." Rathbone's big fist came down on the heavy desk with a resounding crash. "If only I could have seduced Falkner away from her service."

"An absolute waste of time, as I told you from the first,"

Renault said, taking out a dainty little knife and paring his nails. "Like all the other men around her, he's more than a little in love with the woman, for all that you couldn't get him to admit the fact at knife point."

"Well, we've got to head them off somehow," Rathbone said. "Falkner—he's more than just a shipping genius. He's another damned Henry Shreve. He knows boat building, engine design, engineering. He'll build speed and power beyond the average into her, and—" He stopped and looked at his attorney with blazing eyes. "God damn you for a whoremongering swine!" he said with sudden, real hatred. "Put away that disgusting knife and that stomach-turning habit. You make me want to heave up my breakfast."

Renault sat up suddenly, his face drained of color, his own eyes hard. "Nobody talks to me that way," he said. "You mind your mouth, Rathbone! I know enough to put you behind bars forty times over, and—"

Rathbone held up one hand. His scowl cooled; and with visible effort he mastered his own black rage. "I . . . I'm sorry," he said. "I've been under pressure with all this. Halsey had to deal with the men who cut into Whitmire's property. They were asking for a bigger payoff. Threatening to tell everything. He had to—"

"Don't tell me any more," Renault said. "That kind of information isn't privileged."

Rathbone ignored him. "And the *Memphis* . . . I'm not sure that wasn't a mistake from the first. Too chancy. If any evidence turns up in the investigation . . ."

"I . . . ah . . . have some contacts," Renault said coldly. "I'll see what I can do. It's a good thing the captain and the key members of the crew went down with the boat." He stopped, looked at Rathbone sharply, and did not continue for a moment. "You'd better not confide any more about *that* sordid little business to me, either, I think." He held one slim hand up. "No. I mean it." His hand sawed the air. "But I do agree. That *Memphis* business may well come back to haunt us all. Imagine: she lays the keel on the finest steamer on the river. And there we are with our own stodgy fleet, and she'll be running rings around us. Whereas if the sinking of the *Memphis* hadn't forced her hand—"

"All right, all right," Rathbone said. "It's obvious what I have to do. I have to find out what she's going to order from the shipwrights and beat her at her own game. I'll put out an order for a new steamship—faster, more lavishly appointed than hers—the moment I find out just what it is she settles upon."

"How are you going to do that?" Renault said. "I mean, in time to steal a march on her? By the time the news leaks out, she'll have the keel laid and the work under way. There'll be no way you can catch up with her. Not and do a better job than Falkner will be doing on his own boat."

Rathbone stood up suddenly and began pacing the floor of his office, hands together behind his broad back. "I'll find out," he said. "Don't you worry. I won't wait for a leak. I've got . . . well, I've got ways."

Renault stared at him. Then his thin face lit up in a sardonic smile. "Well, I'll be damned," he said. "You've got a spy in Aurora's camp, haven't you?"

"Never you mind," Rathbone said. But his tone was one of vindictive triumph. "There are things I don't dare share, even with you. The less people know who it is, the better. If my informant's name is divulged, I'll be ruined."

"All right, all right," Renault said. "Just make sure the information doesn't get delayed along the way. And, Rathbone, I'll accept your apology this time. But watch your tongue. There are certain things I'm temperamentally incapable of taking from anyone."

"I understand, I understand," Rathbone said. "I'm sorry. I'm more distraught than usual. My wife . . . she hasn't been feeling well these last couple of days. You know how that affects me."

Renault's face changed. "I *am* sorry, my friend," he said, stepping forward to put one hand on Rathbone's arm. "I had no idea. I didn't have any notion that Allison was sick. Is it serious?"

Rathbone's face was dark and troubled; Renault was, as always, a little shocked to see the vulnerability that infected Rathbone's manner whenever his wife's name was mentioned. "I—I'm not sure. Dr. Spangler was going to drop by the house this morning. He's been ambivalent about the symptoms so far. We should have some idea in a day or two." He mastered himself, though, and looked Renault in the eye. "You get to work on that investigation now," he said. "The quicker it's over and done with, the better. And I'll keep an ear to the ground about Falkner. He's trouble. Another damned Henry Shreve, always tinkering, always improving things, a little here, a little there." He pounded one big fist into the other palm. "But I'll beat him," he said, as much to himself as to Renault. "Him and her and all of them."

Chapter 18

With his hair in disarray and his face flushed, Ward Rathbone picked himself up off the wooden banquette in front of his father's office building and dusted himself off. He gasped, trying to catch his breath, and stared malevolently at the man he'd collided with, who was picking himself off the elevated walkway and knocking the dust from his own otherwise impeccable clothing with gestures that were at once delicate and efficiently masculine.

A black rage ran through Ward, and it seemed for a split second that he would explode. Damned clumsy outlander! And an English one at that!

He managed to control himself while he brushed himself off and took a moment to size up the man he'd run into as he'd come around the corner. The other man was tall, athletic, and broad-shouldered, with thick, powerful-looking forearms, for all his dainty ways. Now, brushing off his tall hat, he briefly showed his face in profile. He had curly, unruly hair that fell over his forehead; cool, observant eyes and a straight nose in a long, horsey, but pleasant face; and a mouth capable of expressing both humor and grit. Ward's attention turned again to the hands, though: the hands of a cultured man and a competent one. Most likely a horseman's, a swordsman's, a . . .

"I *do* beg your pardon," the man said now, turning to Ward unhurriedly. "Clumsy of me."

"I . . . it's quite all right," Ward said, dusting off his sleeves. "I must not have been watching where I was going." His face did not change; no smile appeared in his eyes.

He was obviously trying to control his rage. He nodded and walked away but not without first taking note of the expensive carpetbag the newcomer carried. New in town, he thought. English. Have to look out for him. Then he opened his father's downstairs door and took the stairs up two at a time.

The newcomer squinted up in the afternoon sun at the lettering above the door: RATHBONE BUILDING. He smiled mildly; idly he moved to the plaque beside the handle and read off the list of upstairs businesses: Rathbone Enterprises; Rathbone Steamship Line; Rathbone Investments; Rathbone Properties. His smile became a wry one, full of understanding. He turned to see, standing next to him, a well-dressed gentleman of mature years, ruddy-faced and gray-bearded. The gentleman wore the clothing of a successful tradesman, but the sunburned face and hands were those of an outdoorsman, and the stance was . . . what? A sailor's? "I was reflecting," the Englishman said, "on the curious ubiquity of the name Rathbone around here."

"Hah," the seaman said. "He'd have his brand on the dirt in the middle of the street if you'd let him." He chuckled. "I gather you're new here, sir, or you'd know that was Rathbone's brat you just ran into." The bearded man looked him up and down. "Young Ward's a bit of a hothead and fancies himself something of a duelist. He's shot men for doing less than run into him on the street. His father spends a pretty penny every year quieting the scandals the boy starts up."

"It seems I've been spared that fate," the Englishman said. He changed hands on the bag and extended a big hand, which the bearded man took. "My name's Endicott, sir. And you're quite right, I am new here."

"Falkner," the other man said. "Captain Seth Falkner, sir. Welcome to New Orleans. I gather you've arranged housing—"

"Well, yes. I'm booked at the St. Louis Hotel, but I thought I'd walk rather than take the carriage. See a bit more, you know . . ."

"That you will, sir. And the St. Louis is just down the way: the monstrosity with the dome. You've made quite a good choice. One of the few kitchens in the city equipped to

serve both American and Creole food." He smiled and turned
in the direction of the hotel. "I'm going that way myself.
Perhaps you'd like to join me for a noonday drink? The free
lunch counter at the St. Louis is famous hereabouts."

"Splendid," Basil Endicott said. "I'd be delighted. And . . .
you said 'Creole' food? I'm sorry, I'm new here, but . . ."

"Ah," his host said, setting off down the long banquette.
"Then you have yet to make the acquaintance of gumbo.
You've quite an experience ahead of you, I believe." There
was a twinkle in his eye as he said it. "Of course, some
newcomers to the city find it a trifle authoritative. 'Hot' is
the word, sir. I warn you: If you quail at spicy food, you will
not ingratiate yourself with the locals."

"Spicy?" Basil Endicott said. "You are speaking to a man
to whom a ten-boy Bombay curry is mother's milk. Lead on,
captain. I'm your man."

Upstairs Ward Rathbone confronted his father. "I don't
care!" he said. "If you want me to earn my keep, you've got
to give me something more responsible to do! I'm twenty-
three, Father! It's time you let me into the business. Other
men my age—"

"God damn it, don't bother me!" Laird Rathbone said.
"All right, I'll forget the fines. I'll forget the clothing bills.
I'll help you square things with the man whose arm you
broke. But if I'm to take you into the business and give you
responsibilities, you damn well have to change your ways. I
can't have a representative of Rathbone Enterprises going
around getting involved in brawls and duels."

"I've heard your opinions of duels, Father, and if you don't
care about your reputation, I care about mine. But I see what
you're getting at. I'll keep my temper." The phrase triggered
a memory: he'd backed away from one of his notorious rages
downstairs just now. Why? What had there been in the Englishman's manner to make him, Ward Rathbone, step back?

"You'll do more than that. You'll stop your damned trifling
around with high yallers down at the quadroon balls. Renault
saw you last week."

"He's a fine one to talk," Ward said hotly.

"That's no affair of yours. Look, I'm going to marry you

well in this town to someone of substance. And when I do, I'll be goddamned if I'm going to have someone's father coming to me and saying you've given his precious daughter a disease you've picked up at the Bals du Cordon Bleu. Do you understand?''

"Well . . . yes. But—''

"No buts. You mind your step. And in the meantime I'll be thinking of where I could get the best use of you in this organization.'' His father scowled and took down another monstrous cigar. He stood, the cigar in one hand, the little knife in the other. "Have you been home yet? Your mother . . .''

"No, sir,'' Ward said. "Todd's with her. Alex is painting in the park.'' His lip curled at the word: *painting.* "Wasn't the doctor supposed to come in?''

"Yes,'' his father said. He put down the cigar and knife. "I'd better get home. I want to hear what Spangler has to say. Frankly, I'm more than a little worried. I've never seen her like this. No energy, no strength at all. Why, the woman's never been ill three days running in all the years we've been together.'' He bit his thick lip. "This isn't like her.''

Ward started to speak, to steer the conversation back to the subject; but something in his father's expression stopped him. *Why, he's really worried. Really concerned. He really loves her. And he's afraid she's going to die. And what would happen if she did?*

But then the haunted look left Laird Rathbone's face and he again wore his familiar expression of malevolent vigilance. "Come on,'' his father said. "Come back to the house with me. We'll talk more after I've had some conversation with Spangler.''

Ward lagged behind him at the top of the stairs, though. He shook his head as if in disbelief. His father had a vulnerable side? The one man in the world in whom he'd never found a weak spot? The one man he'd met who was harder than himself?

Captain Falkner carefully arranged the accoutrements of Basil Endicott's introduction to Creole cooking on the bar before him. The glass of good 'Nongely rye; the larger glass of good river water, its bottom already stained by the sediment; the bowl of steaming, piquant gumbo; the silver spoon. A small crowd had already begun to gather around them at the hotel bar, and the barkeep stood back, polishing a glass, his face noncommittal but his eyes betraying the same sense of fun that could be openly found in the faces of the onlookers. At the back of the gathering Basil could hear bets being offered and taken.

"A word about what you're eating," Captain Falkner said, the twinkle still in his eye. "You'll never believe me, but this dish began as bouillabaisse of a sort." He registered recognition of Basil's raised brow and went on. "The Creoles found they'd have to do without *rascassé*, for instance, or eel or lobster. But crabs were easy to come by in Lake Pontchartrain, and there were plenty of oysters, shrimp, snapper, and pompano in the Gulf. Then the Acadians—the Cajuns— showed them they didn't need fish at all: they could get by with crabs and shrimp. Then the Indians added *filé* powder— that's ground sassafras leaves—and the blacks added okra. And the Spanish, who were still around at the time, added peppers."

Endicott sniffed delicately. "I thought I smelled pepper in there. Bangalore chiles, then? Something like that?"

"Avery Island peppers." Falkner signaled the bartender. "John, would you be so kind as to bring a little plate of red peppers? And perhaps a few of the yellow jalapeños as well? Thank you."

"Good, good," Basil said. "And is that a bottle of hot sauce I see down there?" He smiled at the grinning faces around him, his face all innocence. The bets were raised audibly, back in the growing crowd. "I always like to be prepared," Endicott said.

He bent and dipped the spoon and ate, delicately at first. He raised his head and looked around with a thoughtful expression on his face. "*In*teresting," he said. He ate again, more heartily this time. And now, even this far into the meal, the spectators could see the cold sweat breaking out on the Britisher's forehead. He reached for the glass of rye, drained it, signaled hastily for more.

"My word," he said. "That's quite different. I've never had anything like that before." He smiled, perhaps a little unsteadily, at the wolfish grins around him, at Seth Falkner's microscopic smile. And reached for the pepper sauce.

"Look out there," someone said beside him. "Somebody stop him. He's going to hurt himself."

"Oh, good heavens, no," Basil Endicott said. "Just raising the stakes a trifle." He opened the narrow-necked bottle, doused the stew liberally, then stirred it in and doused again. Then, as a sigh of disbelief rose from the crowd, he reached into the shallow plate beside his stew plate and picked up a handful of peppers—whole ones with the seeds still in, both yellow and red—and threw them into the steaming bowl. "There," he said. His face was red, his temples drenched with sweat; but his smile was appreciative. "Splendid stuff. Marvelous stuff. How this would go over at an officers' mess!" He ate, drank, ate again—and, almost as an afterthought, reached once again for the hot-sauce bottle and emptied it into the bowl, stirring briskly, signaling for more rye. "The bottle, if you please," he said. "This is a proper one-bottle dish, you know." He smiled delightedly at the ring of utterly incredulous faces around him, poising the spoon for another assault on the deadly bowl. Then, the mischievous smile playing on his pleasant, horse-faced features, he raised the glass of rye in salute. He winked at Falkner, who sat beside him on the high stool, his face fixed in a poker player's mask. "Here's looking up your bloody kilt, sir," he said, and drank thirstily.

"By God," someone said at the rear of the crowd, breaking into the respectful hush. "He looks like a dude, but that don't mean much, I'd say. He's a man, he is."

Seth Falkner smiled and raised his own glass, saluting his new acquaintance for the first time. "That he is, sir. Your health, Mr. Endicott."

When the crowd had broken up, Basil Endicott sat back on the high seat, fanning his suddenly ruddy face with one hand. "By George," he said. "I wouldn't have admitted it before witnesses, but that *was* a trifle hot."

"A trifle?" Seth Falkner said with a chuckle. "By the time you'd finished doctoring it, that mixture could have been used to clean out an oven. You've made your mark in the city already, sir. They'll be talking about this on the Bourse for days, gossiping like a bunch of old women. But it's the kind of mark it doesn't hurt one to make, I'd say. People hereabouts in this polyglot society don't agree on much besides the dismal institution of slavery''—he made a wry face—''but one of the things they do agree on is that a man of quality—a woman, too, I suppose—won't back away from a challenge, no matter what it is.''

"That was my understanding," Endicott said. "Of course, it's not a point of view the locals invented. In my family one gets it in the mother's milk, hones it in public school, and polishes it in the military. And black-sheep remittance man that I am, I am my father's son. And if his normal Anglo-Irish stubbornness weren't enough, my mother's dower included a dash of Gascon blood, brought over by some chap on the Conqueror's boat.''

"Endicott, eh?" Falkner said, his eyebrow raised. "The family name rings a bell somewhere."

"It might. My august father is the Earl of Westmarch, and one of my ancestors took a terrible drubbing from your first president during your revolution." He sighed, poured a last shot of rye from the bottle, and drank. "We never cut much of a figure in uniform, I'm afraid—although I'm the only one of us who ever got around to admitting the fact. We're tactical thinkers in a world in which strategists rise. No patience for that sort of thing. Defect of character.''

"I'm sure you wrong yourself," Falkner said. "Mr. Endicott, I've a business meeting in an hour or so. If you'd be so kind as to wait for me during an hour of business talk, I'd be proud to show you a bit of the city. I know it fairly well, I think, although lately I spend a lot of my time upriver in St. Louis or on the river.''

Basil Endicott smiled. "How very generous of you," he said. "I'd be delighted to accept. I'm afraid I don't know a soul in the city. Or—well, it's quite likely I don't. Used to know a girl in Europe who came from here. Dazzling creature but a little much for the likes of me. My tastes run to the lighter sort, you know, and this one was—well, a fascinating woman. Brilliant. Spoke several languages. Marvelous mind. Well, I suppose she's some staggeringly rich planter's wife by now with a load of brats . . . but no, she'd be bored with that."

Seth Falkner took a gold watch from his vest pocket and opened it. "Just in time to get there," he said. "Don't forget your bag."

Chapter 19

Aurora Brand took the swatches from Olivia's hand and crossed her palatial office to stand beside the open window, looking down on the busy thoroughfare of Royal Street. She held first one cloth, then another, up to the light. "This is quite nice," she said. "And this—this is *very* lovely." Her tone was less that of mistress speaking to servant than that of friend speaking to friend. "You've done well, Olivia. You, too, Cassie." She turned, still holding one of the pieces of cloth. "I'm satisfied. From now on I'll leave this in your hands. You're now my official cloth buyers." Her smile was warm and approving. "Oh, by the way, did either of you hear from Mr. Boyd?"

"Yes, ma'am," Cassie Quayle said. "He said he'll be a little late. He has business at the bank."

"At the bank?" Aurora repeated, an ironic smile on her full lips. "More likely a game of piquet with Jules Charpentier and his cronies, if I know him. But let it pass. The men will be here in a few minutes—the rest of them, anyhow. And I'm sure all the business talk will bore both of you. Why don't you take an hour or so off? Go down and amuse yourselves in the street, perhaps? There's a vendor down in Bienville Street who sells the most ravishing *oreilles de cochon*, if you've a taste for pastries today."

Olivia turned to Cassie Quayle with delight, and the girl said, "Oh, no, ma'am. If you don't mind, I'll just stay outside in the reception room." Olivia frowned. This was unusual behavior; ordinarily Cassie's sweet tooth ruled her, heart and soul.

"All right," Aurora Brand said. "You, Olivia?"

"Yes, ma'am," the girl said. "Can I get anything for you?"

"Well, if you do run into the vendor I mentioned, you might have him . . . But just listen to me. If I listened to my instincts all the time, I'd be fat as a pig. Tell you what, darling. Buy a dozen pastries for the table. He'll throw in one extra for lagniappe. I'll take that one."

"Yes, ma'am," Olivia said. She turned to the girl beside her. "Cassie, you're sure you don't want to—"

"No, no. You go along without me. I'll stay here."

Olivia hesitated, watching Aurora Brand, who was still holding the cloth samples, go off into the adjoining room. "I know why you're staying," she said in a teasing, half-conspiratorial whisper. "Arthur Gilliam's coming—Miss Brand's accountant. And everybody knows he's stuck on you."

Cassie Quayle flushed. "That hasn't got anything to do with it," she said. "And it's none of your business, anyway. I don't care a fig for Arthur Gilliam, and I don't care in the slightest what he thinks about everything or anything." There was more than annoyance in her voice, though. What was it, guilt? Resentment? "You go *on* now."

"All right," Olivia said. "But I tell you, Cassie, if I had a handsome young man—smart and good-hearted and with a future—hanging around me giving me that puppy-dog look the way Arthur does to you, I wouldn't play it quite so uppity and hard to get, for fear I'd drive him away. I'd figure out some way of letting him know, just once in a while, that I knew he was alive."

As she spoke, she thought briefly of Zach McClellan. Her heart beat a little faster, but then another darker thought slipped into her heart, as easily and as deadly as a knife. She remembered Lance Whitmire and the fear she had felt, at least once daily, ever since that horrible day. Fear and loathing.

"You mind your own business!" Cassie said in an angry whisper. "You want Miss Brand to hear you?"

• • •

Olivia passed several men on her way down Royal Street toward Bienville, their various paths converging on Aurora Brand's office building. Seth Falkner, gray-bearded and sun-burned, arm in arm with a tall, handsome man dressed in fashionable but slightly foreign-looking clothing, waved jovially to her as the foreigner tipped his hat. Arthur Gilliam passed her, smiling his shy, boyish smile. Ben Samuels, turned out dressed to the nines as usual and looking like French royalty, a watchful if benevolent smile on his handsome hawklike features, bowed to her and, with Continental panache, kissed her hand. And Dallas Boyd, coming out of a dignified, sumptuous housefront on the corner of the street, waving good-bye to his friends Charpentier and Desmoulins and crossing the dried surface of Royal Street, heading for his bank, dodged the landaus and rockaways and cabriolets that clogged the busy thoroughfare.

Seth Falkner paused at the top of the stairs, looking at the hat rack. "Ah," he said, "Gilliam's here, I see. And that'd be Ben Samuels's cloak. No sign of Boyd so far." He checked his watch. "Damnation, I'm late. Mr. Endicott, if you could amuse yourself for a bit . . ."

"Oh, quite," Basil Endicott said, sitting down in one of the reception-room chairs and crossing his long legs. His eyes scanned the room, coming to rest on the name painted in dignified gold letters on the frosted-glass door. "I'll be right here," he said, his friendly expression relaxing into the same devil-may-care smile it had worn during his epic confrontation with the Creole gumbo. "Anytime you're ready."

Then his eyes turned to the dark, nervous-looking young woman who moved from table to table in the little room, dusting things that didn't need dusting, straightening antimacassars that didn't need straightening. The door closed behind Seth Falkner, and the girl hovered near it. Then she noticed Endicott looking at her; blushing, she turned away, dusting all the more furiously.

"Ben," Aurora Brand said, "what's the latest on the court?" She sat back against the edge of her big desk, her slim hands resting on the tabletop beside her hips.

"Bad news, I'm afraid," the attorney said, opening his briefcase. Like her, he stood as he reached inside the case for his papers. Seth Falkner sat in the big armchair facing her desk; Arthur Gilliam sat in a straight-backed chair beside him, a heavy paper envelope in his lap. "The claimant is petitioning the judge to enjoin us from indulging in any river trade whatsoever until a complete investigation has been made." He frowned, looking up at her. "I'll be quite frank. I haven't the smallest idea how this development managed to get past me. I thought I'd closed off all their avenues of exploration in the matter, as I believe I told you two days ago."

"So," Aurora said, clutching one small fist inside the other, "we've been outflanked again. I don't know how many times that's happened so far in this case. Don't tell me, let me guess: The claimant you're talking about—"

"Just so happens to be represented in the matter by Rathbone's lawyer." Ben's smile was hardly a smile at all; it was the wry, humorless grimace of a man struggling with many frustrations. "Renault has, I'm afraid, beat me again—for the moment. I wish I knew how. It's almost as though he were able to read my mind, to look over my shoulder and see what I was going to do and anticipate my actions."

"Isn't there anything we can do?" Aurora said.

"I've already responded," Samuels replied. "But we'll lose a couple of days of river traffic before a decision can be reached. Traffic, I mean, here in New Orleans. He hasn't jurisdiction over upriver traffic."

Aurora shook her head. "Too bad. Arthur, how does that leave us? Do we have enough in the way of receivables?"

Arthur Gilliam, his open, vulnerable young face turned up to her, said, "I think we can go six months on what we have. Our credit's good most places. People are used to the notion of our having a good, steady flow of cash, and I've held to the habit of paying all essential bills early. People will carry us for a time just on the basis of that."

"Good," Aurora said. "Now, Seth, I think you said you had received some correspondence from Ormsby and Flint in Pittsburgh about the new *Memphis*."

"Yes, ma'am," Seth Falkner said. He reached inside his heavy coat and withdrew a large brown-paper envelope. "I think you'll like its lines. There are other features too." The other men rose and gathered around the desk as he spread open the plans.

"It's lovely," Aurora said. "Beautiful. But looks aren't my pressing concern. What about the power plant?"

"Look," Falkner said. "It has a Tom Copeland engine developed from the Evans pattern. Engines, forty inches in diameter, with a ten-foot stroke. Six boilers, forty-two inches in diameter, thirty-two feet long."

"Good heavens," Ben Samuels said. "You're talking about a real behemoth."

"Right you are, Ben," Captain Falkner said. "Four flues in each boiler, see; paddlewheels thirty-five feet in diameter with eighteen-foot paddles, a three-foot dip . . ."

"Good heavens," Ben Samuels said again. "It'll be the only river steamer in the Port of New Orleans that'll need a turning basin."

"No, no," Falkner said with a chuckle. "I've seen the prototype, or something very like it, in the yards in Pittsburgh on my last trip East. This thing will float on the ghost of a dew. And, Miss Brand, Ormsby wants to make us a snag boat. I have the plans here. Double-hulled with a big windlass up for'ard . . . it's a real tooth puller. Let me show it—"

Aurora Brand stepped back and looked at him. "A snag boat? But, Seth, we'll be overextending ourselves as it is. The new *Memphis* is going to cost me everything but my—"

"No, no," Falkner said. "It's an experimental model. And . . . well, Ormsby owes me something. There was a time when I loaned him five hundred dollars out of my savings, when he had a note due and no money to pay it with. He'll let us have it at cost, just to test it. And I think we can arrange favorable credit terms on the package, given George Ormsby's debt to me and your own respectable credit record. That is," he said, turning his head slightly in Ben Samuels's way, "if we aren't held up more than a couple of days by this injunction thing."

"We won't be," Ben Samuels said. "I can promise you that. I do wish I knew what was happening here—how Renault is able to anticipate my moves. But I'll stop him yet. Next time I won't tell anyone what I'm doing—even you, ma'am—until it's done. Then, if he still outflanks me, I'll know he's going to a conjure woman down near Congo Square and getting some . . . ah . . . expert advice.''

''That I can assure you he isn't,'' Aurora Brand said. ''Not from Marie Laveau, at any rate. I know Marie, as well as any white woman knows anyone down in that part of town. She owes *me* a favor or two, now that I think of it.'' She chuckled softly, and the men's heads turned to see her smile. ''You don't suppose if I went to her place down on St. Ann Street and bought a *gris-gris* to use on Rathbone . . .''

Falkner and the accountant laughed. Ben Samuels limited himself to a wry smile. ''Look,'' he said, ''I can use all the help I can get. Belt *and* braces, you know. If someone can do me up a *gris-gris* that will stop Rathbone, I'll do down on Congo Square and do the *danse Calinda* until dawn. God knows nothing else has stopped Rathbone so far, or done much more than slow his pace. If voodoo can do it, I'm your man.''

''Well, we'll wait a bit on that,'' Aurora Brand said. ''If you gentlemen would be so kind as to leave me your reports, I'll have a look at them tonight. Meanwhile it's too nice a day to spend indoors. I've a mind to take Olivia shopping. There's a dance at the Charpentiers' next month, and she'll need a new outfit. So will I, as a matter of fact. I intend to indulge myself this once. I can afford to, can't I, Arthur?''

''Ma'am, you know that even if you couldn't, I'd figure out a way for you to afford it.'' Arthur Gilliam's smile was eager, ingratiating.

Aurora pressed his hand impulsively. ''I'm a lucky woman to command such loyalty,'' she said. But then she looked around her. ''There's one face missing. The piquet game must have gone on a bit longer than anticipated. Well, never mind. Thank you all for coming, and for your good work.'' She smiled: Arthur Gilliam's mind was already a million miles away, for all his devotion to her. With the door open wide now, she could see young Gilliam already in eager but shy conversation with the somber-faced Cassie Quayle, out in the anteroom. Behind them a tall, well-dressed man stood, hat in hand. There was something familiar about his stance.

''Now, ma'am, if you please,'' Seth Falkner was saying,

making way for her progress across the room, "there's someone out here I'd like you to meet. A gentleman from England
whom I met today. I think you'll like him. He . . ."

But Aurora had gone ahead of him and now stood just
inside the reception room, one hand over her heart, her eyes
wide, her mouth wide open. "Why, if I didn't know better,
I'd swear it was—"

"Oh, but it is, Aurora, my dear," Basil Endicott said with
a tiny bow and a good-humored smile. "You didn't think
you'd got rid of me as easily as all that, did you?" The bantering, self-deprecating tone barely concealed a real affection, coupled with respect.

"Basil! Basil, darling!" Aurora Brand said, rushing into
the long arms he held wide for her. She hugged him mightily
and, rising on tiptoes, pulled his face down for an impulsive
kiss. "Seth!" she said when the embrace broke. "Seth, do
you know who this is? Why, we knew each other in France!
Basil was engaged to my best friend in Paris. Not that I can
imagine him ever going through with it, with her or any other
woman. He'll die a bachelor, and he'll break hearts around
half the civilized world when he does."

"Not yours, I'm sure," Basil Endicott said, kissing her
forehead and stepping back, the comic smile still on his face.
"The last time I saw you, I believe you upended an entire
vase of roses on my head, water and all. And all *over* a jacket
given to me by the Countess of—ah, but I promised not to
tell about that, I think. She'd be furious if it ever got out."
He thought about the matter for a blink of an eye and said,
"And *he'd* cut out my tripes."

"Come," Aurora said with a laugh that was at once infinitely appealing and totally unaffected. "Let's let bygones be
bygones. Where are you staying? The St. Charles?"

"The St. Louis, I believe," Basil Endicott said. "I say,
Aurora, you will have dinner with me tonight, won't you?
I—" He stopped, his face falling, and faced Seth Falkner.
"I mean, Captain Falkner and I were going to dinner, and
we—"

"No, no," Seth Falkner said. "I'd no idea you two were
old friends. You go ahead and renew acquaintances. You'll
do that the better without me. Mr. Endicott, 'well met' is the

term, I believe." He extended a hand. "And . . . lunch tomorrow, perhaps? The St. Louis bar, noon?"

"Agreed," Basil said, taking his hand. "Splendid. And thank you." He turned back to Aurora. "I was just talking about you when we came up. Then I saw your name on the door. I couldn't believe it was you."

The voices blurred into an incomprehensible murmur in the murky acoustics of the stairwell. Dallas Boyd stood on the third step, looking up into Aurora Brand's reception room, watching her embrace and then kiss the tall stranger—kiss him with an unfeigned warmth. Boyd's eyes narrowed, and his bare hand tightened around the white glove clutched in it. So *that* was why she'd been so cold the night before, so distant. So that was why she was back to insisting on her need for "independence." Well, he thought, sauce for the goose, sauce for the gander. He grinned a sardonic grin and turned sharply on one well-shod heel. He was out on the banquette below in two angry bounds.

Chapter 20

Olivia blushed and tried to turn away, but the clear eyes that had caught hers held them. She bit her lip and forced herself to look at him squarely, to stare him down, if he could be stared down. But when she then tried to pull away once more, she found she could not. She dropped her eyes instead.

"Miss Soames," he said, bowing with a mock flourish, the sardonic grin on his young face. She looked back at him angrily. "Or I suppose I can call a woman I've kissed Olivia?" Ward Rathbone's manner was all mock courtesy.

"I . . . I should think you'd have better taste than to address me at all," she said coldly. But she couldn't look him in the eye, for all her resolve to do so. Again, she tried to look away, down the long row of French Market stalls, the odd mix of purchasing gentry and slave-labor vendors; but even here she dropped her eyes.

"Taste?" Ward Rathbone said. "Oh, I see. A thousand apologies. I have been a disgusting boor." He bowed even more deeply this time, and the gesture made sport of itself, of himself, of the whole book of Low Country manners—but not, somehow, Olivia. She realized this with some surprise, and the fact drew her eyes up to his again. When she did, she saw him smiling down at her from his commanding height; but somehow this time the smile was an ingratiating one. "I *was* horrible, wasn't I?" he said. "I really am sorry. I shouldn't drink. It brings out a side of me that's likely better repressed. Well, you see before you a reformed man. My father's orders. I've given my word." He held up one hand in a gesture that hovered between sincerity and irony. "In exchange for certain considerations . . ."

"I'm happy for you," she said. "Now, if you'll please excuse me . . ."

"Oh, please," he said, his tone changing. She looked up at him, startled to hear any hint of vulnerability in his ordinarily arrogant young voice. "Please let me make amends. I really am sorry, you know. It's a lovely day. You still have some shopping to do, I think. May I carry your basket for you?"

She looked up into his eyes, still puzzled. And found herself, to her amazement, agreeing. She handed him the wicker basket, her heart silently assenting. "I . . . I'm mostly done," she said. "But . . ." The words trailed off. She couldn't think of anything to say.

"Here," he said, steering her gently down the long aisle. "What have you got there? Pigs' ears? Come, the real bargains are over here. But no, the best stuff is outside, on the street. May I?" He didn't wait for an answer. The gentle pressure on the back of her arm moved her easily out the side door of the building onto the banquette.

Again, the mixed smells were ravishing—every kind of fresh-cooked pastry, cake, pie, and, above all, the smell of the fresh sea air just beyond the quais at the Dumaine Street wharf. "Oh, goodness," she said, looking around her at the confusing mix of stalls, open-air stands, hearing the polyglot cries of the vendors, black, white, Indian. "I don't know where to start."

"Try over here," Ward Rathbone said, leading her to an ancient black crone. "Best *calas* in town. It's a rice fritter. But the selling point is the street cry. Listen." He put one finger over his lips, smiling. Olivia, peering through the crowd at the old woman, listened.

> Belles calas, belles calas—Aaaaaa!
> Madame, mo gaignin calas,
> Mo guaranti vous ye bons,
> Si vous pas gaignin l'argent,
> Goutez c'est la meme chose. . . .

And sure enough, the crone held out a little tray of samples, which the people in the front reached for hungrily. "Free samples," Ward said. "She's the slave of one of the planters across the river. She's licensed. She must bring in several thousand a year just from her stall alone. Try one, they're quite good."

"No thank you," Olivia said. "But why out here? Wouldn't she bring in more money indoors?"

"Not necessarily. Besides, the fee's more. Inside, you pay for your concession. Out here there's just the license fee and *'Calas tous chauds, Madame . . .'* Besides, it's the older tradition. And traditions count for a lot here. The indoor market has been here since the Spanish days—1791, I think—but the outdoor market has been here since . . . who knows? When the first explorers approached the mouth of the river, they found the Choctaw squatting here selling herbs and sassafras leaves, not a dozen steps from here. They still do. Look over there. The Green Sass Man. The one with the champagne basket balanced on his head."

He steered her again gently down the street. "Look there. Yam cakes—*pam patat*. And that one's selling potato bread." He sang along lightly with the vendor's street cry:

> Pain patatte, madame,
> Achetez pain patatte. . . .

"And look," he said. "Over there. The one with the little triangle he's beating on. The Candy Man. Caraway comfits, the best you ever tasted. My mother used to bring us down here when I was a child. And there's the Waffle Man. And see the old mammy with the kerchief? *'Belles pralines . . .'*"

"It's fascinating," Olivia said. She looked at him now, his young face flushed with pleasure as he strolled easily through the crowd beside her. "And you—you love it, don't you?"

"It's my city," he said, looking around him at the stately buildings on the Vieux Carré, at the Market, at the tall masts of the ships at anchor, showing above the warehouses on the wharf. "There's no other like it. And, by God, it'll be mine one of these years. I intend to own as much of it as I can get my hands on—and to rule what I can't own." He smiled with the bald-faced hunger that lay upon him, admitting it, accepting it, even glorying in it. And when he turned, he found her eyes on him. "Ah," he said, "one isn't supposed to be that open about it, eh? The usual sort of hypocrisy is better—more genteel. Well, let them have their gentility. While the rest of 'em are minding their manners I'll be buying up everything they own, until I'm master of the city."

"Your ambition's impressive, I'm sure," she said.

"But you don't approve," he said, smiling. "Or you think that you're not supposed to approve, so you try not to. But the truth is—and if you'd search your heart, you'd have to admit it—that small ambitions breed small respect. For every trace of humility you found in me, I'd find in you a corresponding trace of contempt."

"That sounds like something you learned from your father," Olivia said, and suddenly wished she hadn't said it. It was unfair, wasn't it? Surely Ward shouldn't have to pay for his father's boorishness. "I . . . I'm sorry," she said. "That was a personal remark I'd no right to make."

"It's all right," Ward said, his eyes steady, his face unsmiling. "I stand on my father's shoulders, but that doesn't make me bigger than he is. I'm not ashamed of him. I'm rather proud of him, for all the things the 'genteel' types say." His lip curled with contempt at the word. "And for your information, I did learn it from my father. That, and all the other things he taught me, will make me master of the city one day. Just watch me."

He stood now, facing her, hands on hips in a defiant attitude, a cold smile playing on his thin lips. "You think you don't approve," he said. "You think you don't like that. But in your heart of hearts you respect it. And you're an honest enough sort to come around to admitting it someday. That's why I like you. That—and the fact that you're more like me than you think you are. It's just that it comes out different in a woman. Unless," he said as an afterthought, his smile taking on a new irony, "she happens to be an Aurora Brand." His keen eye searched hers. "I see a reaction in you, but I can't read it. Is *that* one of your ambitions? To be another Aurora Brand?"

He chuckled, but his eye sobered, and his smile went away.

And Olivia, silent, wondered if the new light in his eyes wasn't one of increased respect.

Thin, intense, absorbed, Alex Rathbone, youngest of the Rathbone sons, stood tall as a crane in the warm light of the sun room of his father's house, frowning at the canvas before him. He scratched his nose, and a dab of oil paint appeared on the end of it, left there by his paint-stained finger. "The highlight," he said, annoyed. "I can't get it just so. . . ."

"Hush," his brother Todd said. "I can't hear what they're saying." He pressed closer to the barely open door that led to the hall. "But Father . . . he looks upset. He doesn't look like himself. I've never seen him quite this way."

"Anything," his brother said, his brush poised over the palette, his eyes still focused on the patch of painted green leaves, "so long as it isn't one of his rages. I'm going to move out one of these days. I swear I am. I don't have to take that anymore. I have some money. Grandfather left me some. I can live on that."

"Poor Father," Todd said. His face fell; he looked back at his brother, the painting on the easel, and the potted plant on the stand. "Nobody understands him. Not you, not Ward, not anybody. Only me—and Mother. And with Mother ill like this . . ."

"Poor Todd," his younger brother said, licking the tip of his brush. "You might turn out to be somebody someday, if you ever get over that badly misguided case of hero worship you have for that cannibal we have for a father. My God, it's like dying of unrequited love for a bayou gator. Or a snapping turtle. Or a razorback boar."

"That's just what I mean." Todd's eyes revealed his pain. His open young face turned toward his brother, a half smile, beseeching, understanding, invading the worried cast of his features. "If you'd only try to see what his problems are and what he's going through . . . but no. All you can ever think of is yourself. Really, Alex, he loves you. Everything he does is for us and for Mother."

"Oh, come on," his brother said. "Try that line of fiddle-faddle on someone who hasn't felt the weight of his fist as often as you and I have." He turned in his brother's direction now, and his voice was flat and unsympathetic. "What use is it telling me about Father's vulnerabilities when he never shows them to me? What use is it pointing out to me qualities in him which he takes such pains to hide in my presence? All I know, or care about, in people is the face they show me. Otherwise—"

"Shhh!" Todd said suddenly, turning back to the door. "They're talking again. Dr. Spangler's leaving. Father's following him to the door."

"Tell him to follow the good doctor *out* the door," Alex said, mixing pigments on his palette. "And then put the both of them on a boat to the Sandwich Islands. One-way."

Dr. Spangler paused at the front door and turned back to Laird Rathbone. When he did, he was shocked to see the change in the burly financier. The broad face was sullen; the eyes registered hurt and fear and despair. "Mr. Rathbone," he said, "I could be wrong. No doctor is perfect. If it would set your mind at ease at all, I'd advise you to seek a second opinion in a matter of such urgency."

"But . . . this is what you think?" Rathbone said, his voice husky. All the confidence seemed to have drained from him. "Your considered opinion? You'd stake your reputation on it?"

"Mr. Rathbone," the doctor said, "if I could say something that would give you hope, you know I would. If I could tell you something that would allay your fears, I'd do so without a moment's hesitation. You know that. But Mrs. Rathbone—"

"Please," Rathbone said, his voice breaking. "Not so loud, please. She might hear you."

"Oh," the doctor said. He stepped back and looked hard at Laird Rathbone for a moment. "You realize, of course, that she knows. She's known for quite some time."

"Knows?" Rathbone said. "What do you mean?"

"She knows she's dying, Mr. Rathbone. She was the one who told *me*. And once I'd examined her, I knew that she knew exactly what she was talking about. Your wife, Mr. Rathbone, is a kind of lay saint in this community, and a woman of surpassing intelligence and understanding. She has nursed the ill of this city for many years. I don't know how many of my own patients over the years have gone to their rewards peacefully because of a month or two of the tenderest, most self-sacrificing care by Allison Rathbone, who took time from you, her family, her own concerns, to help friends in distress. She is a bright and observant person, and she recognizes by now certain symptoms as readily as I might— I or the most accomplished or experienced physician in New York or London.''

"She . . . knows?'' Rathbone said in a small voice. "And she didn't tell me?''

"I followed her wishes in the matter as long as I could, sir. She swore me to silence—until the turning point came, when you absolutely had to be told. But there comes a time when the pretense has to stop, when affairs have to be put in order. Now I can no longer obey her wishes.'' He put one consoling hand on Rathbone's arm; the financier shook it off with a weak gesture. "If it helps you to know it, sir, her mind's at ease. She's at peace with her God, gallant creature that she is. And her love and concern for you and her sons, sir, if I may say so, is one of the most touching things I ever . . .''

Rathbone turned away, his eyes glassy, his knees suddenly weak. "Allison,'' he said in a voice hardly more than a broken whisper. "Allison.''

Chapter 21

Alex looked up from the canvas. His eyes narrowed; he lowered brush and palette and turned to face his brother. "What's the matter, Todd?" he said. A little concern had crept into the general coldness of his speech.

"Alex, I heard what the doctor said." Todd Rathbone, his eyes registering his shock and pain, leaned back against the now shut door as if all the wind had gone out of him. "Alex, he says Mother's dying. Dying! But . . ."

Alex Rathbone sighed and carefully put the tools of his art down. "You mean, you didn't know?" he said in a voice both sympathetic and a little incredulous. "You've been fooling yourself, the way Father has?" He moved forward to put his hands on his brother's shoulders. "Poor Todd. One would think you were the youngest son, not me. And all because of your attachment to your illusions."

"But Mother dead?" his brother said. "I can't believe it. She was just—"

"Todd. Mother told me last week. But I'd guessed it, a little before that. There was something in her manner. She could see I recognized it, although I didn't know what the reason was. I just knew something was wrong—terribly, terminally wrong." Under his hands his brother's shoulders shook; Todd was crying, sobbing silently. "Poor Todd. You're not ready for this, any more than Father is. It'll probably be no consolation or help to you at all, but I do know what you're going through. In my own way I have already gone through the same thing myself."

"She . . . she was always so strong, so . . ."

"Yes," his brother said. "Wonderful, strong, accepting, forgiving Mother. She was always going to last forever. If one of us ever hurt himself, she'd always be right there to help. No matter how unrealistic all *that* was. We were all of us raised to the notion that there were two things we'd always, always be able to count on, no matter if all the stars fell out of the sky and all the wells ran dry: Father's money and power, and Mother's love." He tried to look his brother in the eye, but Todd, still weeping, wouldn't look up. "Well, all things come to an end, and that's the long and short of it. Even—"

"But, Alex . . ."

Alex looked at his brother now and, sighing, faced the fact that the last thing in the world Todd needed to hear now was common sense. "Here," he said, embracing him, patting him consolingly on the back. "Here, there, old feller. It's all right now. . . ." But he closed his eyes, and a bleak feeling crept into his own heart even as he spoke.

It was some minutes before Laird Rathbone dared approach his wife's door. It wouldn't do to show her how shattered he was, he thought. He had to get hold of himself, compose himself. But how? The news had hit him like a bolt of lightning, and the devastation it wrought reached into every part of his being.

Now he stood at the foot of the stairs, afraid to take that first step. Afraid to learn from her own lips the confirmation of the things the doctor had told him only moments before. Afraid to face her. He wrung his heavy hands, looking wildly around the great hall of his home for some source of consolation, of distraction.

A tall hutch stood at the entrance to the dining room. On a sudden impulse Rathbone lurched toward it and threw the doors wide to reveal a long row of bottles of high-priced liquor, imported at great cost from England and the East. Rathbone, who never drank (drunkenness meant loss of control), reached for a squat bottle of rare French brandy and drew the cork, drinking deeply from the bottle.

The harsh draft brought a fit of coughing and spluttering. He wiped his mouth with the back of his hand and drank—

again too deeply. This time he mastered himself, and the raw liquid, thrown down like water, burned his throat; but he firmed his jaw and made himself endure the discomfort in silence.

Allison.

He looked at the bottle in his hand, and his instinctive loathing for intoxicants returned. He set the bottle down roughly; let someone else come behind him and cork it and put it away. What were house slaves for, anyhow? And his eyes went once again to the long curving staircase, elegant and graceful, leading up in a swooping spiral to . . .

"Oh, God," he said. "What am I going to do?" He buried his face in his hands. "What in heaven's name . . . ?"

Ward, coming in through the sun room, threw his outer coat on the love seat and stopped for a moment before the easel on which Alex's still life stood. His younger brother, poised with palette and brush in hand, stared at him coldly. "Well?" Alex said in a tone heavy with sarcasm. "I gather I'm about to receive some informed criticism. Am I going to hang in the Louvre, Ward? Do I have talent? Promise? Competence? Or should I chuck it all up and take a nice job hustling gilt-edged stocks on the Bourse? Or trading able-bodied Mandinka niggers on the slave market?"

"The shadow at the bottom of the vase—my God, where did you dream up that color? It looks like dog vomit." Ward's tone was only bantering, not vicious; Alex smiled with tempered hostility. "Where's Father?" Ward said, yawning.

"I'd stay away from him just now," his brother said. "He's just learned about Mother. He's pretty broken up. Although the sight of Father unhinged and no longer in perfect control of everything on God's earth; it might be worth a peek. But don't ask him any questions because you won't get any answers. He won't be listening to you."

"Learned about Mother?" Ward said, taking an apple from a bowl and biting into it. "Learned what about Mother?"

"Why, that she's dying, of course." Alex raised the implements of his avocation again and pretended to mix colors; but he was watching his brother out of the corner of his eye.

"Dying?" Ward said. The apple, poised for another bite,

lowered. Ward's face lost all trace of expression. "Are you sure?" He frowned. "But of course you're sure. You like to say things to shock people, but you seldom say untrue ones."

"The true ones get stronger responses," Alex said, looking at him. "Well, brother? I gather this is news to you. I'm curious about your response. No tears? No weeping and wailing and gnashing of teeth?" The younger man's tone was a mixture of incredulity and cynicism. "No beating of the bosom? Well, I say well and good. You'd make a terrible actor anyhow."

"You . . . you say it's really hurt him?" Ward said, a thoughtful look on his face. "He's broken up about it?"

Alex turned slightly to face him, the sarcasm back in his voice full strength. "Oh, for Christ's sake, Ward. You know how something like that would hit him. He thinks he's been doing it all for her all these years—all the grabbing and stealing and cutting of throats. He has this picture of himself all built up in his head as a man who does what he does out of love: building an empire for his princess in the tower."

"Hmm," Ward said, putting the half-eaten apple down carelessly. "This *will* put him out of commission. It will. He'll be in no shape to do business for weeks and weeks—more, if she dies. And just when he needs to be right in the thick of things, pulling all the strings. Putting pressure on the Brand woman." His eyes grew bright. "Now, ordinarily he'd delegate most of it to Renault and Halsey. But if I step in just now, if I show him I've 'reformed' and am ready to take a bigger hand in the business . . ."

"By God," his brother said, a slow smile creeping onto his face. "You *are* one of the seven wonders of the world. By Christ Jesus alive, Ward, I've never seen your like in all my born days." He whistled softly. "What a family. More pure entertainment than a season of minstrel shows. And here I am, right in the middle of it. Hell"—he chuckled sourly—"I'm part of it. I'm probably just as entertaining as any of you, with my artistic pretensions and my asinine insistence on acting as though I were above it all. Yas-*suh*, Mistuh Intuhlocutah. Ol' Tambo's one o' the end men, after all, no better than any of them."

"Now," Ward said, ignoring him, "what'd be the best

place to really show off in a hurry? Increasing revenues? Showing my business sense? Hmm . . . perhaps the rentals on the south bank of the river. Yes . . . the rentals in Algiers. He hasn't paid much attention to those properties lately. If I were to take them over and increase the yield as quickly as I think I can—even if it means mass evictions . . .''

Alex rolled his eyes heavenward. ''So what matter if Mistuh Bones is sick tonight? The understudy is right there in the wings, ready to go on like an old trouper. Junius Brutus Booth, move over. Make room for young Joe Jefferson.'' He daubed angrily at the canvas, his face a mask of bitterness and self-loathing. ''And the curious thing is, the only *real* one of us is dying upstairs. And there isn't any understudy for her. There never was.''

He shot a quick glance at his brother now, though, and stopped again. Ward's face was beginning to take on a curiously mixed expression. ''She . . . she *is* dying, then. Mother? Mother dying?'' Ward said in a dry, flat voice. A fleeting moment of vulnerability passed across his face, as it had passed across those of his father and brothers. There was a difference, though. In Ward's case, recovery was immediate and almost complete.

God, Alex thought, suppressing a shudder. He's just like him. But a second even more unsettling thought followed in the wake of the first and shocked even him, the cynical one. *No,* he said silently to himself. He's worse. He's Father—but without that touch of vulnerability that Mother always brought out in the old man. He's even harder. And there isn't any Achilles heel there to stop him.

Now the shudder broke itself loose and shook him to the core. Evil days were ahead. That was for sure.

''Why, Laird,'' Allison Rathbone said weakly from the bed. ''I do believe you've been drinking.'' Her reproach was gentle and unassertive as always, but even so, it had the effect of shaking him, filling him with shame. ''That's unusual, my dear. I don't really remember the last time you—'' She saw the look in his eyes now, though, and her words broke off. Compassion and love transfigured her drawn but still lovely face. "Come," she said. "Sit by me, won't you, my darling? Right here."

"Allison," Rathbone said. He tried to speak again but couldn't. She took his heavy hand in her two small ones and held it to her. His broad shoulders shook with silent sobbing. When he spoke again, his voice was a husky half whisper. "I can't seem to say what I want to," he said.

"Spangler," she said. "He told you?"

"Yes," Rathbone said. His hand, ordinarily so hard, so strong, lay inert in hers. "I . . . I can't—"

"Don't try," she said in a voice of infinite gentleness. "Not just now. Not until you're ready. All in good time, my dearest. Just . . . just sit here with me a bit, will you, please? You have no idea how comforting it is just to have your company just now. No more. Just having you beside me."

"Oh, God," Rathbone said softly.

Coming back up Royal Street, Olivia spotted a familiar face across the street: Arthur Gilliam, Aurora Brand's young bookkeeper, walking slowly, disconsolately, along the wooden banquette. His face bore such a somber, woebegone look that she almost broke stride to turn back to the corner and cross the street to speak to him. But she hesitated—and the hesitation was enough to dampen the impulse.

Poor man, she thought. But no, poor boy is more like it. He hardly had the experience of a full-grown man from all she, Olivia, could tell, and Cassie Quayle's coldness, her distant attitude toward him, seemed to hurt him as they might not have hurt a more worldly person. Look at him now. She rebuffed him again, and he looks as though his poor heart could break in a million pieces. She'd have to remember that. Men were often as soft, as easily hurt, inside as women were. Perhaps some of them were more so. And poor Arthur—he had *such* a hopeless case on Cassie.

Why wouldn't the girl give him a tumble? Heaven knew poor Arthur was handsome enough—and, as Aurora Brand's money manager, brilliant and accomplished at his trade, he certainly had a bright enough future ahead of him.

She sighed. One just never knew what was going to engage—or fail to engage—another person's feelings. Taste was just one of those imponderables a person couldn't really discuss. Cassie just didn't love the man; obviously it was as simple as that. But what a pity. He *was* such a nice young fellow.

Chapter 22

Aurora Brand's lips curved into a haunting smile as she read the letter through again, but there was no smile in the green eyes that she turned up to Cassie Quayle, standing beside her mistress's chair, the comb and brush still in her hands. Instead there was a great sadness, one that made the mock smile all the more poignant.

"Ma'am?" said Cassie Quayle. "Something's wrong?"

Aurora Brand turned to look at herself in the pier glass. Her eyes searched the eyes in the mirror. No, she thought. You don't know all the answers yet, do you? Perhaps you never will. And now . . .

Had she lost him, then? She looked down at the letter in her lap again, at the simple emotionless words.

> Madam:
>   Circumstances tear me from your no doubt desirable side. My apologies. I would not leave just now if I thought my presence and my resources irreplaceable. I do so, however, in confidence that my action in no way impoverishes you and, in fact, removes one more obstacle to the independence you cherish so highly. Good fortune to all your enterprises.
>
> Yours,
D.

That was all—all except for the scrawled postscript at the bottom of the page. "In case of real need, a note to McClellan, Bayou Lavache, will reach me in due time."

She sighed and looked up again to see Cassie Quayle's mirror image standing at the shoulder of the sitting woman in the glass opposite her, looking at her mistress. "Dallas," she said in a weary voice. "He's pulled out—just when I needed him most. And the perplexing thing is that I have the strangest feeling I caused it. But I haven't any idea how." She sighed. "If I knew . . ."

"Men," Cassie Quayle said. Aurora looked up to see the look of anger and resentment on the girl's face.

Aurora Brand put one hand on Cassie's arm for a moment. "No," she said firmly. "It isn't their fault. They're the way they are, and it's up to us to learn to deal with that—just as it's up to them to learn to deal with our ways. It's no good complaining that their minds don't follow every vagary, every whim, of our own. I've hurt him somehow, and it's up to me to find out what's the matter—and to do something about it. That is, if . . ."

"*If* you want him back," the girl said, her voice full of bitterness all of a sudden. "*I'd* be figuring out how I could get by without him."

Aurora's eyes once again sought her own in the pier glass. She sighed once more, and this sigh was from the bottom of her heart. "No," she said. "Not this soon, anyhow. You don't know Dallas. Of all the men in the world . . ." She shook her head. "He's infuriating. Just get the tone of the letter, will you?" She handed the missive to her dresser. "Insulting. Hoity-toity. But . . . hurt. Hurt badly, and by me. But how? How?"

She stared at the lovely face in the mirror. "And the worst thing is, the thing that tears me up the worst, Cassie, is the postscript. Because I know, as sure as I know the sun'll come up in the east tomorrow, that if I really were in trouble, the kind of thing that's really serious, and if I did send a note to Zach . . . well, Dallas'd be there. And he'd stick by me through the hottest fires of hell, even if he were still mad at me. He might be too angry to speak to me, but he'd be right there at my shoulder, and he wouldn't be gone until the trouble had passed."

"He's gone now," Cassie Quayle said, a trace of venom in her voice. "And you need him."

"That's just it," Aurora said. "That's what I can't understand. But no. Perhaps I do, a little. Somehow he doesn't perceive the present trouble as something I can't handle without his help. Somehow I've given him the feeling that I don't need him." Her face grew suddenly serious. "There *was* that argument we had the night before the meeting he missed. But he wouldn't have taken offense anew just at that. We always argue along those lines. It had to be something new. But what?"

"They'll all let you down," Cassie Quayle said in a low voice full of deep-seated resentment. "All of 'em."

Aurora looked up, and caught the girl's eye, startled by the sour and vengeful tone of her words. But a second shock followed the first: the look on Cassie Quayle's face reflected not only hatred, anger, and hurt suffered at another's hands, but also a thorough and violent self-loathing.

She sighed a third time. "Let's do my hair, if you will," she said. "As for the other thing—well, I don't know the answer. I wish I did. But when I find it, Cassie, I think it won't be in Dallas or in any other man. It'll be in myself." Her lovely lips set in a somber, self-aware smile. "In the end we're all alone, with all our problems and our joys. It's rare enough that we can share any of them with another human being for a while. And if the person we share them with leaves us—why, we drove him away somehow. And it's a problem we have to solve alone."

"Yes, ma'am," Cassie Quayle said, her voice as lonely and bitter as ever. "You'll find no disagreement from me on that."

After doing her mistress's hair Cassie Quayle put away her equipment and went to her room to change. She put on a drab dress and covered it with a dark cloak. Then she changed her shoes, putting on heavy walking shoes. She slipped into the kitchen and spoke to Augusta, Aurora Brand's black freewoman cook. "I won't be here for dinner," she said.

"Oh?" the cook said. "You goin' out with that nice Gilliam boy?"

"No," Cassie said. "I—"

"Land sakes. You gonna wind up an old maid, honey."

"He didn't ask me. And I'd appreciate it if you'd mind your own—"

"Whether I minds my own business or not ain't gonna change things none. You gonna win' up one disappointed old lady, settin' in a col' an' empty room somewhere ten'in' to your knittin'. Ain' much comfort in that, girl.'' The cook stirred her pot fiercely, huffing and puffing all the while. "Nice boy like that . . .''

Cassie shot her an angry glance and went out, buttoning the cloak around her neck. When she reached the street, her steps lengthened as her speed increased.

The stigma, if stigma there was, of being a second son—a ne'er-do-well second son, not viewed in the family as quite presentable—and a remittance man sat lightly on Basil Endicott's shoulders. The parental interdiction lay by now across the entire British Empire, but the land of his ancestors had always had little appeal for Basil, with his randy ways, and he had long since worn out his welcome in many places he didn't really belong in, anyway. France and Germany had proven far more hospitable to a rogue of his stamp over the years, and now America was beginning to assume a most favored position in his hierarchy of affections. America in general—and in particular the multifaceted river society he was beginning to learn about, one level at a time.

On the first day of his visit, thanks to Aurora Brand, he had ridden the supposed cachet of his family connection into an invitation to tomorrow's party at the home of the influential cotton factor, Desmoulins. Now, as if to balance his social calendar, he strolled Tchoupitoulas Levee, having left Aurora off at her hotel. Ah, Sailortown! And what next? A drink, perhaps a girl, perhaps a fight of some sort, and perhaps—no, more than perhaps. Most certainly a game of chance.

For some reason Fiddler's Green, anywhere in the world, had always had the most irresistible attraction for him. Perhaps at first it had been no more than the smell of the sea; now it was, as well, all the other colors and smells and flavors of the Ropewalk, or Shit Street, or whatever the locals cared to call the sailor quarter. It was a delicious stew of

smells and sounds and sights. To the sea reek were added,
here on the swamp, the smells of rum, hides, musk, bones,
saltpeter, tobacco, oil, guano, and pitchpine—yes, and the
wonders of Creole cookery: stews foul with *filé* powder, rank
with peppers; fish and crab and crawfish. And the sounds:
curses, screams of rage, the wheedling entreaties of the
whores from their windows above the water, and, in a dozen
languages, the songs and shanties of the sea:

> As I was a-walkin' down Pensacola shore,
> I went in a grog-shop to pass me an hour,
> An' I sat there a-smokin' and drinkin' me glass,
> An' feelin' the starn of a young Injun lass.

There was something about it that sang in his blood, something comforting, as sweet as the sounds of home. Small
wonder, too, with the blood of a dozen of the blackest pirates
in English history running through his veins (for all that they
called themselves "privateers" at the time, and sailed under
British letters-of-marque against the treasure ships of the
Spanish Main). Yes, here was the place for him. Just listen:

> Oh, Rosie, she's the gal for me,
> Away you Rosie, walkalong!
> She hangs around on the big levee,
> Walk along me Rosie!

By the time two hours had passed, he had made the acquaintance of three swamp taverns, each tougher than the
last, and had tried sample drafts of such liquid refreshments
as Milk Whiskey, Hoosier Grog, Old Levee Tanglefoot, and—
boldest drink of all—Tarantula Juice, a powerful concoction
the barkeep swore was brewed by mixing in a hogshead two
quarts of alcohol, some burned peaches, a plug of tobacco,
and five gallons of river water, thick with sediment. And he
had bought drinks for sailors, beachcombers, roustabouts,
cotton hoosiers, flatboatmen, pimps, and sneaking damned
crimps who wouldn't look him in the eye. Now he had his
game going in a corner, and there was a growing pile of
money before him, and he was just on the verge of raising

someone, just for the hell of it, on nothing more than two pair, kings high, when a fragment of bar conversation came through a sudden and uncharacteristic lull in the general noise.

"Don't mean it! God a'mighty, they hang folks for that."

"Told me just like you're standin' here. Torched the *Memphis*, just like you'd burn weeds in a field. An' forgit about the 'angin'. 'E's livin' off a string o' whores now down on Gaff Tops'l Street in Valparaiso. I 'ad it from a chum that saw 'im in Vallipo, drinkin' *anisado* in a fandango house. I tell yer, 'Alsey pays well—particular f'r a chap 'at can keep 'is mouth shut."

Basil sat up, eyes sharp and observant. He looked at his cards, then let his glance steal to the men at the bar. Then he turned his cards down and said, "Too rich for my blood, boys." He scraped his earnings off the tabletop and left a handsome tip for the slavey who worked the tables. "Got to piss," he said. "Little trip to the lee rail, if you don't mind." But when he left the table, it was not to the pissing rail that he wended his way; it was to the bar. *Halsey!* he thought. But that was the name of the chap Aurora had said this Rathbone cove employed as a sort of first mate, wasn't it? His interest piqued, he elbowed his way to the bar and signaled for the tavern keeper. "Here!" he said. "Drinks all around." He turned to the man who had been speaking earlier. "Was that a Cockney accent I heard just now, my friend?" He slurred his words deliberately. "Always good for a drink, hearing a voice from home. . . ."

No more than a block down the levee, Simon Halsey stood on a dock talking to three roughs, crimps who worked the swamp on a series of lucrative shipping-company contracts to provide cheap, even free, labor for outbound merchantmen: sailors—and other derelicts—who could be drugged and sold like slabs of salt pork to the ships as unwilling 'fore-the-mast seamen. He looked to the right and left, making sure no idle ears overheard, and then spoke. "China-bound, you say? Good work! On what ship?"

"The *Island Princess*, out of Liverpool," the fat crimp said. "With special orders for our pal Captain McGuinness.

No liberty anywhere. Under lock and key in port. No chance at all of any of 'em payin' off with the jib downhaul.''

"Fine," Halsey said. "And . . . he understands? I mean, about making sure they never get back to the States alive?''

"Righto," the skinny one said, spitting tobacco juice over the side into the river. "Part their hair with a belaying pin first. Send 'em to keep company with the fishies. We got an understandin' with the good cap'n.''

"Good, good," Halsey said. He caught the half-skeptical looks on their faces. "No, no," he said. "You're safe with me. You keep your end of the bargain and I'll keep mine. *Those* scum couldn't keep their scissor-bills shut. Somebody heard one of them bragging about opening a cut above the point at Radford Plantation.''

The three looked at one another, and when they looked back at Halsey, it was with complete understanding. "Damn fools," the fat crimp said. "You can count on us. And Mr. Halsey—the money . . .''

"Ask Henry Forbush, at Sloames Hall. Upstairs, second door on the right. He's got orders to pay you in gold, just as we agreed." He frowned and looked around him again. "Now get on with you. Wouldn't do for us to be seen together.''

The three nodded and left. Halsey, his teeth set in a fierce grin, turned and walked briskly out to the hut on the end of the dock, throwing the door open. "Well?" he said to the woman sitting on the bed. "Aren't you going to come greet me?''

The woman did not rise. She glared at him with hatred. "You go to hell," she said. "And shut the door. People can see in.''

Halsey walked over to her and hauled her roughly to her feet. His embrace was equally ungentle. "Oh, come on," he said. "Give us a little kiss, there, Cass.''

"Let go of me, damn you!" said Cassie Quayle, struggling. "Just let me go!''

Chapter 23

"All right, damn it," Halsey said. He released her, stepped back, and reached for the row of green bottles on the shelf behind him. "Getting damned uppity there, girl. You're beginning to forget, a little at a time. You think just because the Brand woman likes you, you've got a job there forever. You'll come to find that isn't true, not once she's found out about—"

"Please!" Cassie Quayle said, burying her face in her hands. "It's hard enough as it is, with her trusting me like that. Don't remind me—"

"All right, all right," Halsey said again. He popped the bottle's cork and tipped the bottle up to drink deeply. Then he sat down in the straight-backed chair opposite her, the bottle still in his hand. "Tell me what you've found out, then. You ought to be good for something."

Cassie Quayle sat heavily on the bed, as if all the strength had gone out of her legs. "Simon, I feel bad about this. I can't recall many things in my life I've felt worse about. She treats me like—"

"Look," Halsey said, leaning forward to spear the air with an accusatory forefinger. "You can forget about that right now. You start getting a queasy stomach now, and I've got some papers in my safe the authorities will find very interesting. And it's my word against yours, Cass, don't you forget that. Only you don't have any manumission papers to show because there weren't any, ever. And I *do* have a certified fair copy of a bill of sale showing you were sold to

Elijah Bonham, of Hanan's Bluff, Mississippi, when you were four years old, and . . .''

She put her hands over her ears. Halsey, in a moment of sudden rage, put the bottle down and came at her like an attack dog, tearing her hands away. ''Damn you!'' he said. ''Putting on airs like a white woman, after all this time! Don't you know what'll happen when Bonham's heirs find you? Particularly if you're passing? Passing for white? Do you know what the legal penalty is for that? Even if all Bonham's heirs are dead, and nobody gives a goddamn whatever happens to his slaves. Do you know?''

''Simon, I don't care anymore. I swear, if God would strike me dead this moment, I'd consider it a blessing. You can do as you like.'' She sat inert and drained on the bed before him. ''If they make a slave out of me again, I'll kill myself. But I can't go on—''

Halsey's hand went down and clutched her roughly by the hair. He pulled her face up to face his. ''You're bluffing, goddamn it, and you know it!'' He hauled her to her feet again and shook her by the hair.

''Simon! Stop it! I mean it!''

''The hell you do!'' Halsey said. ''Well, let me tell you. You know that little file of letters that you used to keep in that little carpetbag of yours? Eh? You know the one, don't you, Cassie? Don't you?''

''L-letters?'' she said, real terror in her eyes for the first time. ''I—I don't know what you're talking about.''

He shook her violently by the hair again and then threw her bodily, one-handed, against the wall. ''Don't *know*?'' he said. ''The ones from your son? Up in Ohio? The one who doesn't know he's one-eighth nigger? Who thinks his ma is a white lady just like anybody else? Well, what do you think the headmaster of that boys' school Aurora Brand's money is paying for would think if he knew he was not only a darky but, under slave-state law, a—''

''No! No!'' she said. ''Simon! You didn't! You didn't read—''

''Read? *Read?*'' He chuckled humorlessly. ''You haven't counted 'em lately, have you, Cass? Well, I'll tell you. Back in Cincinnati, remember? I held your bag for you while you went into the sewing shop to get a paper of needles to do some sewing on the trip. And while I was waiting—''

''No, Simon!''

''While I waited, Cass, I looked over the little packet of letters. Some of 'em were so good, I took the liberty of taking 'em along with me. They're in my safe right now. Six of the best. All of 'em with return addresses and plenty of identifying material on both ends. Little Philip doesn't know anything, does he? What sort of effect do you think it'd have on a boy coming out into the world, suddenly finding out he's not only dark meat but—technically, at least—a runaway slave? He'd—''

''Simon! Simon, no! No, please! I'll do whatever you want.'' She collapsed onto the bed now, her face a pale mask, drained of blood. Her eyes, when she looked up at him, were those of a person whose last hope had deserted her. ''Only, just don't—''

''That's more like it,'' Halsey said with satisfaction, sitting back down on the straight-backed chair. The green bottle had never left his free hand; now he drank, slowly, savoring the raw taste of the liquor as it went down his throat. ''Now,'' he said, ''what happened at the meeting?''

''N-not much,'' she said in a lifeless voice. ''I—I couldn't hear all of it. There was someone else in the room with me. He kept me from being able to stick close to the door. I'm sorry, Simon. I . . . I couldn't help it.''

''Don't waste time telling me what you didn't hear. Tell me what you did.''

''All right,'' she said. ''For one thing, they know there's a spy in the organization. They don't know who. And Ben Samuels is getting cagey. There are things he won't discuss with anyone but Aurora Brand—alone. And . . .''

''They suspect something, eh?'' Halsey said. ''Well, keep your fanny covered. Go on.''

''I . . . I did get something on the plans for the new *Memphis*, Simon. Not much, but I—''

Halsey rocked forward on the seat again. ''What's that?'' he said eagerly. ''The new *Memphis*? Out with it, now.''

Cassie Quayle sighed and shrugged. ''I'll tell you what I did hear, what I can remember of it. First, is there a firm that builds ships called Something and Flint? In Pittsburgh? I didn't get the first word.''

"Ormsby and Flint?'' Halsey said. The woman nodded listlessly. "For the love of Christ, woman, the Brand Line's broke! There's no way in the world she can get sufficient credit just now to get Ormsby and Flint, the most expensive firm in the East, to even lay the keel on—''

"It's Seth Falkner,'' she said, and he looked at her more attentively now. "Ormsby—that's the word?—Ormsby owes Captain Falkner a favor. A big one. Seth's calling it in. And they're cooperating, I think. To the extent of sending him preliminary plans and specifications. And . . . Simon. From the way they were talking, it's going to be a big, lavish ship. Let's see what I can remember. A Tom Copeland engine . . . engines forty inches in diameter with a ten-foot stroke. Six boilers . . . a thirty-five-foot paddlewheel, eighteen feet across.''

"God almighty,'' Halsey said. He drank again and put the bottle down to stare at her, his hands in his lap. "That's a hell of a big boat. How the devil is she going to pay for it?''

"It's . . . it's . . . well, there's more. Ormsby wants to build her a snag boat, and it's part of the payback on the debt he owes Falkner. Two hulls with a big windlass—''

"My God,'' Halsey said. His next thought was: *I'd better get this to Rathbone immediately.* But then a second thought followed the first, and he held up his hand. "Hold it up right there,'' he said. "I'm thinking.''

Rathbone? What good would Rathbone be right now, with his coming apart the way he was? When he'd gone by Rathbone's house an hour before, it had been as though the man had taken leave of his senses altogether. He'd been weak, shaken, vague—a pale shadow of the old Laird Rathbone at best. Who'd have thought that hearing about his wife's imminent death would wreak such changes in him?

No, he needed to do something himself. And quickly. He needed to step in and take over, before Aurora Brand stole a march on him. For this he needed the authority. Time to get back to Rathbone's, talk him into giving him, Halsey, a freer hand in Rathbone's business dealings. It was time to see if a copy of the Ormsby and Flint plans could be stolen or copied—and fast. It was time to put double pressure on Aurora Brand's lines of credit. It was time to order a new flagship of the fleet, something that would compete successfully with the new *Memphis*.

He frowned. It was also time to do something—he couldn't think of what, at the moment—to tie up the Brand Line financially. But how? He needed a way to get a line into Aurora Brand's books.

He stopped right there and smiled slowly. He looked at Cassie Quayle. "You said last time . . . there's this boy-wonder bookkeeper of hers? What's his name?"

"Arthur Gilliam. Why?" Life came back into her eye. That, and a new pain and fear that had not been there before.

"You said he's taken a shine to you—but you brushed him off."

"I . . . yes, I did. He's just a boy. Emotionally, anyhow. Simon, I don't have the heart to let him get himself all involved."

"Cass," he said with a deadly, threatening mock patience, "you'll have the heart to do whatever I tell you to. Or that young-un of yours will get a letter. And so will the headmaster of that school of his in Ohio. And so will the police constable of the town where he—"

"Simon. *Please*. I . . . what do you want me to do?" Her eyes sought his, beseeching. "Do you want me to play up to Arthur? Is that it? I'll do it, if that's what you want. But what then? What earthly good will it do for me to string along a nice boy like that? And break his heart?"

"The hell with his heart," Halsey said. He reached for the bottle again and gestured with it, underscoring his words. "What we've got to do is get a line into Aurora Brand's books. It's the only way to find out, once and for all, where she's vulnerable. If what you say is right, and they have a suspicion that they're being infiltrated, spied upon—well, you'll have to keep your rear end down on all the other fronts. Do everything you can to divert attention from yourself. Forget about listening in on any other conversations. Put 'em back off their guard again. Convince 'em that the last person in the world who could be interested in Aurora Brand's business is her dresser, who sticks to her pincushion and thimble and minds her own damn business. But while you're doing that . . .''

She sighed, and the life had gone out of her voice again when she spoke. "Play up to poor Arthur. And get him off *his* guard, poor dear, and I suppose steal and copy the key to his office, and then some night when I've got him all tied up, you or one of your friends can slip in." She sighed disconsolately. "All right, Simon," she said in a tone that, for the first time, conveyed a trace of the intense self-loathing she felt. "What else must I do? You might as well give it all to me right now."

Halsey didn't speak for a moment. He smiled viciously, drank, and looked her up and down, all submissive and tamed, the way he liked women to be around him. He put the bottle down. "Take off that damn dress," he said.

Ward Rathbone looked down at his father in the overstuffed chair and once again marveled at the changes one event could bring about in a man as strong, as commanding, as powerful as Laird Rathbone had been. His eye once again went to the brandy bottle at his father's elbow, to the half-empty glass in the heavy hand. "You won't be sorry you did this, Father," he said. "I promise you that."

Laird looked up at his tall young son, saw the coldly confident look in his eye. "The leopard changes his spots," he said dully. "Well, we'll see. I've . . . I've been doing some reading lately. The sort of thing I neglected on the way here. To . . . this." His eye and hand conspired to indicate the mansion, its lavish furnishings, and all he owned and controlled—and to dismiss it as little more than chaff. "I've been reading Shakespeare. Who would have thought it would make such sense? I always thought poetry was for the weak, the womanly. And yet when I read it now—"

"Excuse me, Father, I've got to go. But rest assured: The more responsibility you put in my hands now, the more I'll work to live up to it. And, Father, the fooling around with women—that'll stop too. As a matter of fact, I've given some thought to what you told me about settling down. I've got an invitation to a little soiree at the Desmoulins' house tomorrow night."

"Yes. I know. We . . . I sent regrets."

"Of course. But, well, I'm going. I've been thinking. An alliance of our family with theirs . . ."

Rathbone looked up dully. "Odile? Is that the name? You could do worse. And she's attractive enough. But . . . I'm sure Henri Desmoulins would never go along with such a thing."

"Sure he would," Ward said confidently. "I'm going to do a campaign on him too. Once I've begun my campaign on her. I've got it all planned. Father, imagine how proud Mother will be—"

As soon as he spoke that last sentence, Ward wished he could call the words back. His father's face, which had showed signs of minimal alertness and attention a moment before, lapsed with a great suddenness into the same mask of pain and confusion it had worn before. "Father," Ward said, "I'm sorry. I wasn't thinking. I didn't mean to hurt you." He tried to put a hand on his father's shoulder, but Laird, locked into his own grief, pulled away. Ward withdrew his hand, almost angrily, as if he'd touched a red-hot stove. "Father . . ." he began again. But there was no talking with Laird Rathbone now. He stepped back, looked at his father hard, and withdrew silently. The older man betrayed no knowledge of his leaving.

After a time Laird Rathbone looked around him and found himself alone. He scowled, drank from the brandy glass, put it down. Then he reached for the leather-bound volume of Shakespeare beside him on the floor. It opened in his hand to the ribbon that marked his place. Holding the book in his lap, he slumped down and read from the play called *The Second Part of King Henry IV*.

> God knows, my son,
> By what by-paths and indirect crook'd ways
> I met this crown; and I myself know well
> How troublesome it sat upon my head:
> To thee it shall descend with better quiet,
> Better opinion, better confirmation;
> For all the soil of the achievement goes

With me into the earth. It seem'd in me
But as an honour snatch'd with boisterous hand;
And I had many living to upbraid
My gain of it by their assistances;
Which daily grew to quarrel and to bloodshed,
Wounding supposed peace: all these bold fears
Thou seest with peril I have answered;
For all my reign hath been but as a scene
Acting that argument . . .

Rathbone let the book fall lightly into his lap and sighed
heavily. It was curious: With life leaving Allison upstairs little by little, he could feel his own life, his own power and
vigor, seeping away, unmanning him. Would it return after
her death? He didn't think so.

He thought now of Ward, of the apparent change in him.
A second Prince Hal? he thought. A change of heart? An
abrupt about-face this late in his young life? Well, perhaps;
of his sons the boy was the only one with the right spirit,
fierce and relentless and without fear. Todd was a typical
second son, soft and fair-minded and contemplative, a mother's boy. Alex? He'd never understood the boy from the first.
He was sure he never would. But Ward? He had the true hard,
acquisitive, combative streak in him. A leader. If he *could*
turn over a new leaf, get serious about life . . .

But then the thought of his wife upstairs, dying by bits,
struck him again with unbelievable force, shaking him to the
core with grief. As his eyes blurred with tears, he sought
help in the still-open book in his lap. His eye picked out, at
random, a line from the same speech, Bolingbroke's on his
deathbed:

How I came by the crown, O God forgive . . .

Chapter 24

The weather, even after dark, had remained warm and balmy, yet Cassie Quayle, slipping stealthily through the streets, shivered inside her heavy cloak, clutching it tightly to her. The day's experience had been a bone-chilling one, one she would never forget—or forgive.

She paused at a street corner, peeking out from behind a tall brick warehouse into the street ahead. Good enough; the street seemed empty, at least. She took a deep breath and hurried forward, hugging the wall, her soft shoes silent on the cypress banquette beneath them.

Soon the more civilized areas of town became visible down the street, areas policed by *gendarmes* and thus safe for her to walk alone in. She increased her speed, heading for the torchlit pool of light at the first corner.

As fear left her, it was replaced by a dizzying mix of emotions, all of them hateful and degrading. Guilt, self-loathing, shame. Then, in a sudden flash, came white-hot hatred. *Damn* Halsey! She wished she'd killed him.

Under the lamp now, she slowed her pace for the first time. Another thought ran through her confused mind, and her heart sank. Philip! He'd found out about Philip! And this very fact was a potent weapon he could use against her at any opportunity, and one against which she had no defenses at all. *Oh, God!*

Her lips curved in a bitter smile. God? What God? If there was one thing that her life—her whole life, from the moment of her conception—proved without the smallest possibility of doubt, it was surely that there was no God, that the whole concept of religion was a vile and brutal fraud designed to keep the maximum distance between the haves and the have-nots. What a swinish and hateful type of fakery that removed all possibility of happiness on earth on the one hand and held out vain promises of improvement in some never-never land beyond the skies . . .

Look at her, for instance. Born a slave, sold a slave, torn from her parents . . . then sent unexpectedly into apparent freedom by the Underground Railroad after her master's death—but without manumission. In the years that followed her shipment north, she'd been taken in by one foster family after another and in general abused by all of them. Even raped by one of them.

She smiled a wry smile and increased her pace as she crossed the broad and littered street. Well, out of *that* wretched little episode had come one good thing, anyway: Philip. And her love—her fierce, protective, all-encompassing love—for her boy child, with his dark and delicate good looks. This alone had saved her. It had made her independent-minded, self-reliant, tough, and resilient. The struggle to protect the boy from the pain and shame of her own youth, to educate him, to give him chances she'd never had: these concerns had sustained her through a series of grubby employments in which she'd done virtually every kind of work short of outright prostitution. And some of the working conditions in those early years had flirted dangerously with even this distinction, she thought now in disgust. She'd resigned herself to the notion that she would have to be separated from the boy for long periods of time while his education progressed, and although the distance from him tore at her heart constantly, she'd told herself that it was all worth it, the pain and the fatigue and the loneliness . . . all worth it if she could make a better life for her little son.

Little? He was fifteen going on sixteen now. Almost a man. And from his last letters he was doing well in school and full of pride in his achievements. Nearly ready to go forth into the world and compete as a man, a free man, without entanglements, taints, or—

She stopped in the street, her hand pressed to her heart. A sob tore itself from her, shamed, angry, self-despising. "Oh,

God!'' she said, ignoring her own apostasy of a moment before.

Now her whole house of cards was being torn down, one card at a time. How cruel life was! Just when it had begun to look as though she and her son might have some sort of chance in life, the worst had happened. Philip had stood on the very threshold of a better life, with graduation imminent—graduation with honors—from the expensive little academy, with excellent prospects for financial aid in furthering his education from one of the rich men who had endowed the little school and who took an interest in ''developing the talents and minds of the unfortunate.'' And what would happen if Halsey wrote to the school? What if he wrote to Philip himself, who had no knowledge of the taint in his blood, of the terrible fate that might await him if he ever wandered south into the slave-state territory to which his mother's relentless destiny had led her?

She shuddered at the thought. As the bitterness rose in her by leaps and bounds she thought, *The only thing I can do to forestall this is to betray, to ruin, the only real benefactress I've ever had.*

If only Halsey had never been born! But no—it would have been some other grasping, exploiting, manipulative swine, pushing her this way and that, bullying her, forcing his vile sexuality on her, beating her when she complained or failed to respond. Men were that way.

If only Halsey were dead!

She couldn't think about that. It would be the worst thing she could possibly do. He'd told her, ''Don't get ideas. You try having someone stick a knife in me, girl, and there's a packet of papers in the safe—letters, the whole thing—with instructions to Renault to mail 'em to certain addresses if anything should happen to me.''

Oh! It was too cruel! Too hard! And the worst part about it was that she was alone, utterly alone, in all this. She could tell nobody, confide in nobody, ask for help from nobody. Not even from Aurora Brand. How could she ask for help from the person she was betraying?

And now—perhaps worst of all to date, though she was sure even worse was to come—she had to ruin poor Arthur

Gilliam. Lead him on, seduce him, pump him, betray him, and break his heart. The poor boy was so trusting, so vulnerable, so very much in her hands to do anything she wanted to do with him.

That was the worst thing so far. Yes. Because—and this was one of the reasons she'd felt an attraction for Arthur, and one of the reasons why she had fought so desperately against giving in to that attraction—Arthur bore a startling resemblance to Philip. He was what Philip would look like in ten years—if he managed somehow to retain something of Arthur's present innocence and boyish, uncorrupted charm. And there was a way in which her loathing for the present occupation—the seduction and corruption of Arthur Gilliam—touched upon not only the mock incestuous aspects of their proposed union but upon the symbolic corruption, the profaning, of her love for her only child.

But now the self-loathing in her was almost too much to bear—now she had to go through with the scheme. The odds against her were too much, as they always had been, from the moment of her conception.

At the top of the stairs Rathbone stopped Marie, his wife's personal slave, at the door and took the platter from her hand. "I'll take it in, Marie," he said. "You go down and help Cudjo with the silver." His tone, as it often was these days, was one of unaccustomed gentleness; its very novelty was enough to frighten the girl, more accustomed to rages and curses from Rathbone. She half curtsied, the way Allison had taught her in her childhood, and beat a hasty retreat. Rathbone paused at the door, thought of knocking, and then opened the door instead.

Allison's eyes opened as he entered. She smiled wanly. "Laird . . ." she said in the thin voice that was the most she could manage now.

"Time for your medicine," he said. He put the platter down with its bottle and spoon, and sat down in the chair beside her. He'd intended to keep a poker face, to betray no sign of his own distress, but the sight of her there, so weak, so helpless, broke his resolve, as it always did. He stifled a sob and reached for the spoon with a shaking hand. In a moment he'd mastered himself, and he poured the spoonful of painkiller and managed to get it to her lips without spilling it.

Then he sat watching her as the laudanum quickly took hold, and the look of pain on her lovely face was replaced by the near habitual look of half-intoxicated peace that she wore almost all the time now under sedation. "Laird," she said, "hold my hand. Please."

He took her small hand in his large one and forced himself to look directly into her large and liquid eyes. "Are you feeling better now?" he said. "Perhaps a little?"

She smiled, and something in him was hurt worse by the sweetness of her smile than by any overt evidence of pain. He suddenly let out a heartbroken sob. "I . . . I'm sorry," he said, weeping openly. "I . . . I've been sitting thinking. From the moment I met you, my whole life changed. Before you I was nothing. Everything I did since then—everything— it was all to impress you. To make you notice me, care for me, love me. I clawed my way to the top . . . over one ruined competitor, one dead body, after another, and . . ."

"Oh, Laird," she said. "Didn't you know? Didn't you ever know? I didn't need any of that. I'd have lived with you in a shack in the bayous. I loved you, my darling, from the very first. Didn't you know that?"

Rathbone stared at her, his eyes showing his shock. "I . . . I knew who I was. A parvenu from the wrong side of society. You were a princess on a cloud, in a high tower. I never believed you'd care for me. Not unless I moved mountains to make my mark in the world. And I never thought anything I did, or could do, would be enough. I felt I had to win you every day. All . . . all for you."

"Laird. Laird, my one and only love." She turned her head toward him now, and her voice, even under sedation, carried a tone of such sincerity and passion that he looked at her, openmouthed, his eyes wide. "There never was another man in my mind from the first. You didn't have to do anything to impress me. I tried to tell you. Many times. But you'd never hear me. And perhaps . . . perhaps it was all for the best, as far as I was concerned, anyhow, my dearest.

After all, what woman could possibly resist the chance to have always, at her beck and call, a knight in armor.''

''A knight in tarnished armor,'' he said. ''The things I did in the service of my dream of impressing you, making you at last respect me and love me.''

Allison smiled. ''I knew,'' she said, ''and I didn't care. Whatever you did, out in that other world of business and men's affairs, I didn't consider it my bailiwick. I didn't want to know about it. I kept it outside my doors. Inside, what I had was what I'd always wanted: a gallant and caring lover, one who never once showed me the face he showed the world. A man who was always gentle and attentive and loving with me. That was all I ever cared about, Laird. I hope you know that. And . . .''

''Yes? Yes, Allison?''

''I want you to keep this in your heart forever, Laird, after I'm gone, as well as now. I have no regrets. Not for anything. The things I needed in life—the life you gave me provided all of them. No regrets.'' She squeezed his hand weakly; it drew a fresh sob from his throat, and he bowed his head. ''Laird,'' she said softly but insistently. ''It has been a good life for me. It has. I want you to know that. You have to believe me.''

Laird Rathbone raised his head, stared at her, his eyes puzzled, his face fallen. Then it had been all in vain. All of it, beyond the shelter his efforts could give her. He needn't have done the things he'd done. The rapacity, the single-minded and poisonous ambition; the cheating, the chicanery, the lying; the vicious assaults on friend and foe alike, on anyone who stood in his way; the double-dealing, the character assassination, the murders.

He covered his face with his hands. ''Allison,'' he said in a broken voice, ''too much has happened. I'm a different man than I was when I met you. And now . . .''

''Different?'' she said. ''Not to me, my darling. Your devotion and love have remained exactly the same all these years.''

But for the first time he didn't seem to be listening. ''Now,'' he said, ''I . . . I don't know who I am. I find myself questioning everything I ever stood for. Everything I ever believed in. Everything I ever—''

"No, no," she said. "That's not true. You believed in me, my darling. And the whole point of your little speech just now was that you haven't stopped believing in me. Have you? Have you, my dearest?"

Rathbone looked at her through eyes brimming with hot tears. "No," he said hesitantly. Then his confidence returned for a moment, "Oh, *no*." He put one hand on her thin wrist. "Never! But—"

"But you're losing me now. My dearest, that happens to everyone, doesn't it? It happens to people who've never had a fraction of the happiness we've known together. Tell me, Laird, have *you* any regrets? Other than the fact that it's coming to an end, as all things do?"

He stared. Her voice was slurred with the aftereffects of the powerful drug he'd given her, but her mind seemed even more lucid than before. Now, more than ever, he felt in his heart the same strong surge of love, the same burning passion, that had animated him back in the first days he'd known her and courted her. He smiled now, a small smile through the tears he no longer bothered to hide. "No," he said in a stronger, more resolute voice. "No regrets. Allison, I sent Marie down. I won't need her now. Not here. The person to look after you is me. I'm replacing her in this. I want to spend these last days—" His voice broke and he couldn't continue. But the look in his eye was that of a man who'd learned his own mind at last.

She pressed his hand, even more weakly than before. "But, Laird. Your business . . .''

"Halsey can handle it," he said. "And Ward, I suppose. Perhaps it's the boy's turn. I've got a more important use for my time. Nothing else matters. Nothing."

Chapter 25

A small frown settled on Aurora Brand's lovely features as she looked abstractedly at her image in the dressing-table mirror. A light breeze drifted through the half-open window; shivering in the chill of morning, she pulled her wrap closer about her and slipped her bare feet into felt slippers. She leaned forward as she continued to study her image in the glass. Was that a wrinkle in the corner of one eye?

She heard a light knock on the door. "Yes?" she said, drawing back.

"Olivia, ma'am" came a voice from beyond the door, "with the morning coffee."

"Oh," Aurora said. "Come in, dear." The girl entered with a tray in her hand. "You can put it over there on the bedside table. And, Olivia . . ."

"Yes, ma'am?"

"Oh, come now. We're alone. Just us two girls. You can drop the *ma'am*, I think." She smiled. "Why don't you pour both of us a cup and come talk to me?"

Olivia stared and hesitated. But then she recovered, and, perhaps a little nervously, did as she'd been asked. She approached the dressing table, carrying two brimming cups of the strong, chicory-flavored New Orleans roast. "Here you are, ma'am," she said, and then smiled at her own little gaffe. "I mean . . . Oh, I almost forgot. There was this note, slipped under the door. It seems to have been there through most of the night, at least. It was wet with dew."

Aurora took a sip of coffee before opening the letter. Then she read it quickly and put it down. "My word," she said.

"Basil certainly gets around quickly. Pardon me, I mean Basil Endicott, the Englishman who—"

"I know," Olivia said. "I saw him yesterday."

"Basil has only been here a day or two. He must have gone out pub-crawling after he left me off. Already he claims to have some information for us about . . . ah . . . 'important matters,' " she said, reading from the note in her hand. "He wants me to meet him and Seth at the St. Louis Hotel at noon." She frowned again at the face in the mirror. "Oh, dear. That means doing my hair twice today. And you've got your own to do, if you're going with me to the Desmoulins'. Well, perhaps we can press Cassie into service."

"Oh, no," Olivia said. "I can manage. Really I can."

"Well, whatever you think," Aurora said. "Drink your coffee, dear. It's better hot."

Olivia complied, her eyes on her mistress. Then she put the cup and saucer down. "Miss Brand—"

"Aurora. Please."

"Yes, ma'am." She flushed and went on. "Has Mr. Boyd left town?"

"I'm afraid so, dear," Aurora said with a sigh. "I suppose that means I'm in pretty good shape where the present crisis is concerned. Dallas has an almost infallible knack for knowing when a person really needs him—and when she doesn't." A wave of emotion passed over her lovely face, and she brushed a wisp of flame-colored hair away from her temple. "I'm speaking of only one kind of need, of course. The other way a woman can need a man . . . Well, that's another matter." Her sigh was even larger this time.

Olivia stared. Aurora Brand had never taken her into her confidence this way before. "Ma'am," she said, "do you love him?"

Aurora turned that beautiful face toward her young friend. "That's quite a question," she said.

"Oh, I didn't mean to pry. Forgive me, please."

"No, no. I'm not chiding you. We're friends. You have a right to ask, when we're here talking woman talk. Love Dallas? Good heavens, what a thought! Might as well ask if I love the wind or the rain. Or the river, for that matter. The word *love* has never come up, except as banter, as teasing."

Her face was quite serious now. "Dallas and I . . . what we have, when the engine's running, my dear . . . well, it may well be something stronger than the thing most people call love. There are times when I hate him. Really *hate* him, mind you—the way you'd hate the worst enemy you ever had. Because someone who's under your skin as completely as he's under mine . . . why, you're vulnerable to him. He can sting you, hurt you—and in ways a lesser person might never be able to. You think Laird Rathbone's an enemy of mine? Or Simon Halsey? Good heavens, dear, they can't hurt me. They can put me out of business, perhaps, but they can't hurt me. Not really. But a friend, a person whose attachment to you is deeper than that of a friend . . ."

"I think I understand. On the island, Zach McClellan . . . I think he had a thing for me. Poor dear, I think I was all wrapped up in myself, and I must have hurt him. But—"

"You have a little piece of it," Aurora Brand said. "Oh, Olivia, I think I've hurt Dallas somehow. The same way. And I haven't any idea how. We had a little tiff at dinner the night before, to be sure, but it has to be more than that." She sighed. "There are times I almost wish he had a bit of Basil in him."

"Mr. Endicott? But I thought you said—"

"Oh, there's nothing between Basil and me. We had a brief fling way back, just long enough for him to realize, at the same time I did, that we were like oil and water—a bad mix. The things a man and woman give each other—we don't get them from each other at all. Which doesn't stop us at all from being friends. Perhaps you'll have men friends like that, as you begin to circulate. I'd treasure them. They provide a fresh view of things, one that even the best of woman friends can't provide. Besides, even when there isn't the smallest real attraction between you, conversation with a man always has a slight edge to it that conversation with a woman doesn't have—even nice girl talk like this. I think you know what I mean."

"I guess so," Olivia said. "I ran into Ward Rathbone in the street the other day. I couldn't possibly love him, ever. I'm not sure I even like him. But there's something in the air, a kind of electricity, when I talk with him."

Aurora looked at her and did not speak for a moment. "I can see where Ward might be quite attractive," she said in a measured manner. "But, Olivia, I'd have restraint, if you know what I'm saying."

"Oh, yes, ma'am," the girl said, blushing. "It's just that—well, there's so much force in him. Like Mr. Boyd. Only with Ward, it's all out of control."

"God help us all if Ward Rathbone ever gets himself under control," Aurora said. "He'll surpass his father in every way. He'll make Laird look like St. Nick." She frowned, thinking. "Come to think of it . . ."

"Yes, ma'am?"

"Laird's never had but the one weakness. Allison. If ever a man was a woman's slave, it was him, but she's such a wonderful person, she'd never exploit it. She's been his one Achilles' heel. But," she said, looking Olivia in the eye, "we've never found one for Ward. He's got all his father's intelligence, rapacity, and cold-bloodedness, but, to my eye, at least, hardly a trace of the one humanizing element Laird always had, from the first moment someone introduced him to Allison Pryor."

"But I said I wasn't interested in Ward. I don't understand."

"Oh, this isn't about you. I was just thinking—what would the Rathbone empire be like with Ward running it and not his father? If something happened to Laird?" She shivered, perhaps from the open window, perhaps not. "God, what a thought. Heaven help New Orleans. Heaven help the whole Mississippi Valley."

"But what about the others? I thought I heard Mr. Rathbone had two other boys."

"He does. I don't know them well myself, only what others tell me. Everyone seems to like Todd, for all that he has a terrible case of hero worship for his father. Perhaps he doesn't know what Laird is up to, the way Ward undoubtedly does. It's natural for a boy to feel that way about a successful father, though. Perhaps he'll grow out of it. But I don't see him challenging Ward's rights under the rules of primogeniture. You'd like him, I think. He has a nice little smile anyhow. He has more than a trace of Allison in him."

"Oh. And the other son?"

"Alex? Now him I don't know at all. But he has the most amazing reputation in some of the circles I don't always travel in here. He's the youngest but in some ways seems the oldest, from what friends say."

"What do they say?"

Aurora smiled. "They say, for one thing, that he's a genius. An artist, and a fine one. Why, did you know he'd already exhibited once or twice before he turned fourteen? By now he's quite well known in art circles, they tell me. But under a pseudonym. Laird never would have stood for his showing under his own name. To this day not many people in the city or elsewhere know who the mysterious Mr. Peter Lightfoot is, whose pictures hang in several aristocratic salons here and in a surprising number of homes upriver and in the East. There's a rumor that he's had at least a couple of foreign sales. I heard there's a collector in Paris who buys his work."

"And yet . . . he's the youngest? But Ward's only—"

"That's the amazing part. Alex is nineteen, but he paints with the confidence of a master. People tell me he's a very old nineteen in other ways too. If I believed all the rumors I heard, well . . . He's supposed to be keeping a mistress. On what he makes as a painter, without his father or mother knowing a thing about it."

"Goodness! What a family."

"They are that. But, Olivia, I heard from Felicite Desmoulins that Laird has canceled out tonight. He can't come to the party. Apparently Allison's ill."

Olivia's face fell. Then, seeing she'd betrayed her interest, she blushed. "Then none of the Rathbones will be there?"

"Oh, no," Aurora said with a chuckle. "Ward sent a runner to confirm his attendance." Her chuckle turned into a laugh. "Don't worry, Olivia. This is New Orleans, not an upriver ball at an isolated country house like Darrow. You won't have any trouble finding young men to ask you to dance here. You'll be hoarse by the evening's end, as a matter of fact, just from saying 'no, I'm already taken.' "

• • •

At lunch Basil Endicott, despite his usual immaculate British turnout, looked like a man who'd undergone the ravages of some deadly disease. "Coffee, please, and quickly," he told the black waiter almost as soon as he'd been seated. "I feel like someone whose tongue has been painted with tar."

"Good heavens, Basil," Aurora Brand said. "And you did this to yourself after leaving me off? What in heaven's name were you up to?" She thought a moment and added, "But no. Perhaps I'd better not know."

Seth Falkner's smile was knowing but unobtrusive. "I think our friend Mr. Endicott has made the acquaintance of the Tchoupitoulas Levee."

"Oh, God, don't mention it," Basil said, grimacing. "I've tasted some vile concoctions before in my young life, but . . ." He shuddered. "The morning after is worse than the drink."

"What were you drinking?" Falkner asked. "Tarantula Juice?"

"Oh, good heavens, no. That's not bad, actually. A bit strong. The thing I finished up with—the thing that finished *me*—came from under the counter. The dregs of fifty previous drinks of all kinds, all mixed together. I believe I saw the man adding laudanum." He made a bad face. "Or perhaps it was paregoric. I wouldn't be at all surprised." He frowned, and then changed the subject. "No matter. Let me tell you what I overheard before things started getting a bit vague." He reached with a trembling hand for the cup of coffee the servant handed him and drank uneasily. Then, quickly, efficiently, he told them of the conversations he'd had with the men in the tavern. "And the damnable thing about it," he said at least, "is that we can't prove a bloody thing."

"He's right," Seth Falkner said. "Even if those two could be coaxed into court, no magistrate would accept such testimony."

"That's all right," Aurora said. "At least we know what we're up against. We know what Rathbone and Halsey will stop at. Nothing."

For the third time Cassie Quayle strolled slowly past Arthur Gilliam's open door in the Brand Line offices on Royal Street, again carrying a trivial burden—a file folder, perhaps, or a stack of papers—that didn't need carrying to any destination. Each time she had felt his eyes on her, following her every movement, hungry, yearning. She responded by putting the smallest amount of decidedly unladylike sinuousness into her walk as she passed.

And hated herself for doing so. *God,* she thought, *you've stooped pretty low before this, Cassie, but this is rock bottom.* But what else could she do? It was either do as Halsey had said—seduce young Gilliam, draw him out, get him away from the office so that Halsey could get in—or lose everything she had in life.

But it was no good telling herself for the thousandth time that there were extenuating circumstances. It did nothing whatsoever to palliate the feeling of fierce, emetic self-loathing that ran through her every time she let herself think of what she was about to do. If anything, it convinced her more and more of her own worthlessness. After all, if she was someone who mattered, wouldn't she have an alternative by now? Wouldn't she have acquired a protector from Halsey, perhaps, or maybe gotten something on *him* that she could use to force a standoff?

But she was in his hands entirely. There was nothing she could do. It was that or . . . *Philip,* she thought. *I can't let him do anything to hurt you.*

Now, however, Arthur Gilliam had slipped out from behind his big desk and stood in the doorway, looking at her, that shy, half-frightened smile on his unlined young face. "I . . . uh, good morning, Miss Quayle," he said.

Cassie swallowed the vile taste in her throat and forced herself to smile at him, to look him in the eye, to speak in a voice as sweetly ingenuous as a schoolgirl's. "Yes, Mr. Gilliam?" she said, turning to face him and catching his eye. "Did you want to talk to me?" she said in a voice full of open invitation.

Chapter 26

The afternoon light, harsh and direct, streamed through the overhead skylight in Ben Samuels's tastefully appointed office and fell full on the ruddy, sweating faces of his two visitors. Hulking, bearlike Quint Ragland fidgeted and shaded his bloodshot eyes with a hamlike hand more notable for its scars than for its grace. "Christ Jesus, Ben," he said. "I shoulda stayed in bed today."

"Obviously," the attorney said, sitting lightly on the edge of his desk. He turned to Mack Leggett, Ragland's inseparable crony, half his size and, from the looks of things, suffering twice his pain. "My apologies for getting the two of you out. But something's come up. Fortunately the solution may involve a bit of the hair of the dog . . ."

"Oh, Christ," Leggett said. "Oh, suffering Christ on the cross, Ben." The face he made, Samuels thought, would make a good model for a gargoyle on some cathedral somewhere. "I'll never drink again, so help me God."

"Arrr, shut up," the big man at his left said. "Yer little bastard. I'll pay yer six bits for every sober breath yer draw after sundown." He kicked his partner in the leg but softly, a gesture of crude affection. "Ah, Ben, yer might's well give it to us right off, no matter now bad it is. The waitin's as bad as the hearin'."

Samuels offered a case of cigars, smiled wryly at the sour faces, and busied himself with lighting one of his own, long and slender. "All right," he said. "A friend of Miss Brand's—an old friend from Europe—went pub-crawling in the swamp last night and heard a few things." Swiftly and

187

succinctly he passed along what Basil Endicott had learned from the men in the tavern the night before. As he did, the dulled faces of the pair perked up; the bloodshot eyes narrowed; the hands of the two roughs clenched and unclenched. At the end Ben paused and looked at the two of them. "You can see what we're up against, I think."

"The sons of bitches!" Mack Leggett said, sitting up, his face a mask of cold rage. "We had pals on the *Memphis*. And yer say Halsey just up and murdered 'em, just like that?"

"That's our only lead so far," Samuels said, drawing on the cigar. "You can imagine—we need more. And it's worse than that. It seems Halsey has a spy in our camp somewhere. Someone's been leaking information to him. Maybe you could find out something about that." He blew blue smoke up at the skylight, watching the sun play with it. "Discreetly, of course."

Leggett looked at Quint Ragland. "Halsey knows us," he said. "We ain't about to get close to 'im ourselves, Quint. What do yer think?"

"I'll cut 'is tripes out," the big man said. The slow anger in him rose visibly as the two of them watched. "I'll kill 'im. So help me . . ."

"No, no," Samuels said, holding up a slender hand. "You'd slow Rathbone down that way, perhaps—but for no more than a month or two. By the end of that time he will have gone upriver and found someone even worse than Halsey. The best thing we can do is to try to make sure nothing like this happens again." He shifted his body on his desktop perch. "I was angry, too, when I heard of this an hour ago. I had notions of taking it to the courts. But you can be sure Rathbone's got his—uh—posterior covered. It'd just be a big waste of all our time, and of Miss Brand's money. We're better occupied with trying to outflank Rathbone just now— by putting him out of business if we can."

"Rathbone's got boats o' his own," Leggett said, his voice taut, his mouth curving in a sour grin.

"No!" Samuels said firmly, getting his drift immediately. "There's been enough sabotage. And whenever something like this happens, innocent people get hurt. No, that's out."

"So what'd me and Mack ought to do?" Ragland said.

Samuels gestured with the cigar. "Keep your ears and eyes open. And quietly, discreetly, now . . ."

"Mum's the word."

"All right. Quietly, now, see what you can learn about all this. And see if we can't do a little spying on our own. I'm sure you must know some reliable boys down on the levees, on the docks. People who'd be glad to pass on what they hear in exchange for a picayune or two, to do what they can to get a bit closer to Halsey than you two can. And report to us." He reached for the little leather bag atop his desk and tossed it lightly into Ragland's lap. The big men hefted it and raised one scarred brow at its weight. "There's money in this. Spend it how you may—as long as you get results. But buy loyalty while you buy information. I don't want any double agents in this."

"I got yer," the giant said in a harsh voice. "Anybody gets caught burnin' the candle both ways winds up teachin' card tricks to the fishies." He weighed the purse again. "We'll make this go a ways." He scowled and stood up unsteadily. "Arrrrh, Christ," he said, holding one hand to his sweating temple. "Rum for me tonight, Mack. No more o' that painter's piss at the House o' All Nations."

Leggett pulled himself up a little at a time, his grimace an index of his pain. He finally pushed himself erect, his hands on the chair back. "Rum it is, Quint." He sighed. "And don't yer worry, Ben. We'll get wot yer need."

"I'm sure I can count on you," Samuels said.

Aurora Brand, her slim feet in their soft leather boots, as nimble as a dancer's, threaded her way through the tangle of carriages on Royal Street, pausing to let a graceful jump-seat barouche pass, pulled by a handsome pair of geldings. The driver saluted her gallantly as he passed.

Safe on the banquette again, she paused once more. And now the dark feeling went through her again, poisoning her heart, depressing her. She closed her eyes for a moment and reminded herself again: *Smile. Don't let your sadness show. For God's sake, don't let it show.*

She resumed her homeward pace, more slowly this time. Her mind raced wildly in circles, trying to find a chink in the dark wall of sadness and despair that had risen around her heart. Sadness, despair, and loneliness.

Why should she suddenly feel this pain, this fear, this loss? Was it because Basil's sudden appearance out of nowhere had reminded her of the swift passing of the years since she'd seen him last? Of the fact that in those years, neither she nor Basil had ever found safe harbor for their hearts—found someone to love and love them back, to make commitments to for the rest of their lives?

Perhaps that was it. Because, looking at Basil, one could see that the bloom of youth had definitely passed. The boyish charm had begun slowly, almost imperceptibly, to fade. Worse, it seemed mildly inappropriate. After all, the kind of charm a man displayed in the first carefree years of his majority was out of place in an older man. There was no mistaking it. One could not go on, year after year, living a careless and improvident life while most men around him were finding anchors, finding stability, finding commitment.

In Basil's uneasy aging she had found unsettling images of her own. Here the same years had passed for her, too—and what had she to show for them? The Brand Line? Her position in New Orleans and on the river? These to be sure, but were they enough? Or were they perhaps hardly more than the empty accomplishments a distracted and lonely woman erected around herself to hide the desolation in her own heart?

Oh, Dallas, she suddenly thought. If only . . .

She bit her lip and forced the smile back onto her lovely face. There was no use in thinking along those lines, was there? He was gone. And she had no idea where he was, and although she knew good and well that she could reach him in case of a real emergency, sending a message to him now, in the absence of a good reason, would amount to begging. And that was one thing she'd never do, not in a million years, and least of all to Dallas Boyd.

Damn, damn, damn, she thought. How had it come to this? How had she come around to this state of desperate vulnerability, where one man's defection could hurt her this way? Where the loss of one man, in a city where she was the center of attention at every social gathering, where she knew

herself the envy of every woman in the parish, could reduce
her to—

She stopped, a sour taste in her mouth. Envy? Envy her?
Did they now, indeed? Did the women around her, safely and
comfortably married, with men who came home every night
and loved them devotedly, with children to tend and care
for—did they envy her? Or did they pity her? Did they perhaps say to themselves, "Poor woman. Pretty enough, perhaps. Rich and powerful. But what comfort are these things
in a cold, empty bed, in a house with no little ones to love
her and depend on her? Isn't the poor thing lonely?"

Aurora firmed her jaw and made herself hold her head up,
made herself smile graciously and nod as she passed Etienne
LeBeau and his tall, horse-faced wife, Helene, out for an
afternoon stroll. *Look at them,* she thought. *Helene is plain
and half a head too big. Etienne is a mild and mediocre sort,
with little backbone or push about him. He'll never amount
to a hill of beans.*

But she admitted to herself with a sigh that they were
happy. Happy as she was not. They had each found something in their marriage that made them happy. Helene's joy
in having found a man she could manipulate was evident,
and Etienne adored her as though she was Cleopatra of Egypt
rather than a bride her father hadn't been able to give away
until she was nearly twenty-seven. There was a peaceful con-
tentment about them that might well last until old age. What
more could a person want, really, than a situation in life that
gave comfort, sustenance, stability, support? What more
could a person want than love?

And yet . . .

Oh, come, now, she told herself. *You know what and who
you are. And you know good and well that what would content a woman like Helene would bore you stiff. Subordinate
the rest of your life to the managing, the manipulation, of a
man stupider than yourself? Never.*

But what about an equal? A partner? A man she could
respect? A man whose strength and intellect she could rely
upon? A man with whom she could feel proud, independent,
strong, and protected. Ah, if only she could find such a man.

Dallas! she thought again and wept inside. Why did they

always have to quarrel? Why couldn't either of them ever lay down their damned foolish pride, their stiff-necked self-reliance? Why couldn't they simply reach out to each other when they felt the need, the way couples the world over had done since the dawn of time?

Oh, there was no doubt about it. He was as bad about this as she was. Look at him now. Traipsing off at a time like this, just when she needed him and wanted him, getting his feelings hurt as if he were some freckle-faced schoolboy. Taking off for the far country over nothing more serious than—

She frowned. This line of thought was sophistry, self-serving and futile sophistry. That was the sort of argument a person worked up to shore up her own bruised ego by pulling down the other person's. He hadn't acted any more foolish than she had. Look at her, the night of the party at Darrow, the night the *Memphis* had gone down. Snapping at him like some little fool of a shopgirl. And what had he done afterward, after she'd treated him so badly? He'd come to her side when the tragedy occurred and stuck by her with a bravery and fidelity that would have done credit to a knight in silver armor, offering her—unquestioningly, without thinking—a loyalty few wives ever found in the men they'd elected to spend the rest of their lives with. He had also offered his own powerful protection against any danger, any threat. That and his own strong right arm, sheltering her against the winds and the cold.

Oh, God, she thought. *I'm a fool. A damned stupid, proud fool. I've lost something that most women never have the faintest hope of finding in the first place. And all because of my own wicked and futile pride.*

She came almost to a stop in the middle of the uncrowded walkway. The thought ran through her like an icy wind: *Is it all worth it? What have you got? And when you're old and gray, when youth and beauty have faded, what will it all buy, this life you've sacrificed love and comfort for? What will you have to look back on? With no man of your own? With no child of your own?*

Ah, God, she thought. *A child? Me, with a child?*

Even as she dismissed the thought angrily, resentfully, indignantly, a shiver passed through her and shook her to the core. There was a strange feeling in her breasts and loins. A feeling not overtly sexual but not much removed from it. A child inside her? A child to bear, in a gory and painful ritual that would tear her body apart and bring her, in a moment, more pain than a woman ever had to bear short of death?

Suddenly her body ached to feel a tiny body pressed close to her own, needing her, wanting her, reaching for the milk in her own breasts, depending upon her.

A child of her own. A child to love and care for. A child to pass along her possessions to. A child to inherit the Brand Line and all she owned and had worked for and fought for. Was it so farfetched, then? Was it so foreign to her life, her dreams, her hopes?

And what would she have to give up for this?

And was it worth it?

Chapter 27

Marc-Antoine Renault, his leonine features dark with half-suppressed anger, scowled at his visitor. "Well, Halsey?" he said. "What business have you with me?" He slipped his big railroad watch out of his vest pocket, opened it, and looked at it. "Come on, out with it, please," he said irritably. "I have an appointment."

Simon Halsey stood across the room from him, big hands on heavy hips. His expression was one of cool insolence. "It can wait," he said contemptuously. "Or, most likely, *she* can wait. Don't play uppity on me, nigger lover."

Renault's hand tightened on the pair of gloves it held. "You watch your tongue, you guttersnipe! Or I'll—"

"You'll nothing," Halsey said. "You won't call me out because I'm not a gent in your eyes. And if we fight, it won't be by any gentleman's code. I'll haul you out in the street by the scruff of the neck, in your drawers and fresh out of some high-yaller's bed, and gut you like a fish. And you know it. So mind your mouth with me, paper shuffler, or I'll come over there and pull your whiskers for you."

Halsey didn't wait for an answer. Instead he threw a rolled sheaf of papers on the lawyer's desk. "Here," he said. "You were questioning whether I had any authority to act in Rathbone's name. Here's his letter, signed by him, directing you to follow my instructions." He almost snarled his next words. "Go on, goddamm it. Read it. Satisfy yourself."

Renault glanced over the document. "It's not in Rathbone's hand," he said.

"It doesn't matter. I wrote it for him—and he signed it.

Are you going to contest the signature? Because it'll mean going over there, and you know what he's like just now." Halsey stared at him as he read the letter again. "Read it carefully now."

"I did," Renault said after a moment's pause. "There are questions. The Algiers properties and the . . ."

"He's handing them over to the tad. You know, Ward."

"Ward? But—"

"Yes, I know," Halsey said impatiently. "But the boy got to him before I could. It doesn't matter. He can't do much harm across the river. Now, let's get down to business. Do you have anything to report? If you do, tell me. I'll boil it down for Rathbone tonight."

"Ah. Of course. Rathbone wouldn't be going to Henri's party." The attorney sat back down heavily in his overstuffed chair. "All right," he said. "There's good news. Six of the best local Brand Line accounts have transferred to us. Three cotton factors, a sugar account, and—"

"Good, good. Details later. That's very good. The Brand woman is going to have a hell of a time with the bills next month. If we keep the pressure on—" He stopped in mid-sentence, then said, "Go on."

"Very well. I have a letter from the governor. He's considering mandatory inspections of equipment."

"I knew about that. That's no victory. The sword cuts both ways. It'll tie us up too."

"I have a line into the inspector. Oh, by the way, I've got an itemized bill for just such matters as that." He made a small face of distaste. "Bribes, if you will. I was waiting for authorization from Rathbone. I suppose I can get it from you."

"All right, all right. So the inspectors will go easy on us and come down on the Brand Line like avenging angels. Good, good. What about the upriver accounts?"

"She's losing trade there too. Not quite as quickly. I necessarily exercise less control there than here. But I have people working on the matter—spreading accusations, innuendos, libel—in Memphis and St. Louis. I haven't heard from the people in Cairo and Natchez."

"Forget Cairo. She's too well connected there. But she's

vulnerable in Natchez. We can ace her out there if we try
hard enough. Tell your man in Natchez to put the pressure
on and keep it on.''

"Right," Renault said. "That's all I have for now. Now,
if you'll excuse me?'' His tone was acid, malevolent. "I do
have an appointment with a client."

Halsey smiled slowly, insultingly, as he picked the dis-
carded papers off the desk and stowed them in an inside
pocket of his coat. "Client, eh?" The inflection he gave the
word was full of nuance, none of it flattering. He chuckled
to himself as he went out the door. "Client," he said. "I'll
have to remember that."

"I have to go," Cassie Quayle said. "Really I do. Miss
Brand . . ."

Arthur Gilliam sat opposite her on the long couch, barefoot, wearing rumpled pants and a half-unbuttoned shirt. He
looked at the young woman across from him, all soft curves
and lovely olive skin; she sat in a pose unconsciously erotic,
as ravishingly beautiful as an artist's model's. Her delicate,
dark-tipped breasts softly hung down. He could see the sweet
curve of her naked hip, the dark patch of hair between the
legs she'd parted for him with such delectable abandon. "Oh,
Cassie," he said. "I'm so happy. I can't believe this is really
happening to me."

He reached hungrily for her, but she slipped away and
stood before him, hands on those wide and womanly hips,
gorgeously naked before him. "Now, none of that," she
said. "You get me all heated up again and I'll never get
dressed. And then when Miss Brand needs me . . ."

The sight of her, standing there like that, sent a shiver of
delight through him. "God," he said. "I never imagined . . ."
He swallowed and started again. "Cassie, I can't wait to be
with you again. Tonight?"

She shook her head and reached for her chemise and her
dress. As she did, she turned, and Arthur sighed at the sheer
animal grace of her movements, the beauty of legs and flanks
and strong, sensual buttocks. "Not tonight," she said. "Tonight I've got to go to a party with Miss Brand and do her
hair and all. Maybe later. Maybe later in the week."

"Later?" Arthur said. "But . . ." He sighed again, this time in frustration. He watched her slip the chemise down over her head, her back to him. It hung on her hips, leaving her bottom bare. His loins stirred again at the sight. "Oh, Cassie," he said. "I can't wait. If you—"

"Now, now," she said. She turned to face him, and the chemise covered only the top half of her. His eyes went immediately to the dark patch of hair; she smiled as she saw this and, teasingly, half covered her lap with a coy hand. "There, now," she said. "Don't you go getting greedy." She pulled the chemise down to cover herself, her eyes still on his face. Then she walked over to him, into his open arms. "You can wait a day or two, can't you? After all, you waited all this time."

"Cassie," he said, still sitting, his face pressed close to her breasts. "I tried again and again to approach you. But you always stayed so cool and aloof. And now—it's all so sudden. I don't know how to handle it. So much happening so quickly. So . . ."

He could feel her fingers in his hair now, caressing the back of his head, slowly, softly. "I—I didn't know," she said. "I had no idea you found me attractive."

He heard her words, and suddenly they sounded false and—professional? He didn't believe her for so much as a moment. And the thought went through him like a knife: Why lie to him? Why, now that they'd . . . ?

But he gave himself over to his joy and dismissed the thought from his mind. His hands ran over the soft skin of her back. After a moment he ran them up under the chemise, the better to feel the silken smoothness of her, warm and naked and yielding under the thin cloth.

"Let me have one of your ties," Ward Rathbone said. He watched his brother brush his hair, and the impatience swept through him like a fever. "Oh, come on, goddamm it, Todd. You've plenty to spare. You never go out. Stop your preening and—"

"Go ahead and take one," Todd said, his eyes still on the face in the glass. "Leave the red one for me." He carefully brushed the thick hair away from his forehead. "Ward," he said, "did you know that Alex has a mistress?" He turned to look at his brother. "No, I'm not joking. It's true."

Ward, tie in hand, paused as if caught in a daguerreotype. "You're not serious. Alex? Alex keeping a nigger woman? Down in the *quartier . . .*"

"No!" Todd said. "Not a black. As a matter of fact, it's a married woman. The wife of one of Father's business associates. I'm almost afraid to tell you who."

"Why, the little bastard! And him the quiet one. I was beginning to wonder if he had any interest in the ladies at all. Someone's wife, you say?" He chuckled and began tying the borrowed tie. "Well, good for him. He can have my place in the swordsmen's lineup. I've reformed, just in time for him. He can have my old castoffs." He grinned again, derisively. "Unless old, timid Todd wants to try."

"Reformed?" his brother said. "What do you mean?"

"I talked to Father," Ward said. "He's taking me into the business. On condition, of course, that I mend my ways and do something about my reputation in society. So I suppose it's no more trips down to the—"

"Ward!"

"You watch me. Tonight I'm going to make a play for the Desmoulins girl that'll look like Washington at Yorktown. She won't know what hit her. Old stuck-up, high-and-mighty Odile Desmoulins." He stood behind his brother's chair and looked over his shoulder at his own fingers, tying the tie. "Too bad about the little Soames girl. I think I could have had that if I'd persisted. But I'll give her the air, pretty as you please. She hasn't a penny." A stray thought occurred to him. "Unless *you* want her," he said. "God knows she's pretty enough. Better company than Odile by far, as a matter of fact. And a hotter piece in potential, too, if I'm any judge." He sighed. "Well, that'll have to remain a matter for speculation. Unless *you* want her," he said once again. He turned again. "Not too bad an idea at that. She's got a bit of spirit about her."

Todd stared at his face in the mirror, his mouth hanging open. "Ward," he said. "You didn't . . . ? I mean, the girl—"

"Bed her? Oh, no. It never got that far. Not that I considered the matter a closed book by any means, of course. A little more effort and . . ." He made a mock sigh this time. "Well, it's moot now. I'd make a play for her myself if I were you. Could do worse, you know. Even if she's penniless." He dismissed the matter. "Me, I'm going for the money and the position. The Desmoulins girl. Start at the top. If the old man says no, I try elsewhere. Go right down the book of the twenty top families in the parish. Then if nothing works there, I start on the next ten." He smiled a crooked smile at his reflection. "I suppose it's all for the best. A man could come down with a nice dose of the Spanish Onion, going the way I've been going. I've been damned lucky."

"I don't even know the girl," Ward said.

"Who? Oh, you mean Olivia Soames. I'll point her out to you tonight. She'd be a better catch than Odile by far if she had any money, any family." He chuckled again. "Imagine. Alex. Little Alex. I'll wager she dotes on him. Feeds him cookies in bed afterward. You're sure you can't say who?"

"I know better than to trust you. I . . . I caught them at it. She invited me inside to talk to them. I had to promise I wouldn't say. Ward, there was a painting half finished by the bedside. It was of her . . . naked. And she didn't even mind me seeing it."

"Painting, eh? That means the honorable husband is out of town, and has been for a fortnight or more. Alex doesn't work quickly." He grinned lewdly. "Not on canvas, anyhow. Hmmm. Who among Father's crowd has been out of town for . . ."

"Oh, I wish I hadn't told you."

"Don't worry. Keeping my own counsel is part of my present plan. I've reformed. Don't ask me about my plans and I won't tell you any lies." He smiled indulgently at his brother. "I will tell you this: I'm managing Father's tenancies and rentals south of the river now."

"Ward!"

"Since last week. And I can tell you there are ways of increasing the yield. Although it's going to mean some controversy."

"Controversy? I don't understand."

"It's going to mean turning some unproductive people out

into the street to make way for people you can make an honest living from. It's going to mean changing crops on some properties. Some people aren't going to like that.''

''But will Father approve?''

''What does he care? As long as the revenues increase. Besides, Todd, he's pretty much out if it now. He can't think of anything but Mother. He waits on her hand and foot, like some nigger nurse. Have you seen him?''

''Y-yes,'' Todd said unsteadily. ''Ward, have you been in to see her today? She looks terrible. She's going fast. I don't think she'll—'' He gulped, stopped. He could not continue. ''Oh, Ward,'' he said thickly at last, ''she's so frail. Father says he can't get her to eat anything. She—'' But this time he couldn't recover quickly enough. He wiped his eyes. ''Ward . . .''

His brother looked at him, his expression a mixture of compassion and contempt. ''Don't think about it too hard,'' he said. ''She's had a good life all in all. Come on. We'll go to the ball tonight, and you'll forget all about it. Live, Todd, live! You're only young once.''

Todd watched his brother go a moment later, envying his resilience, his boisterousness, his air of jaunty panache. And for a moment he wished he were more like Ward—strong, uncaring, less easily hurt by life . . . but then the moment passed. He blinked. A tear rolled slowly down his cheek. He sat staring at his mirrored reflection, morose and silent, for quite a long time.

Chapter 28

"Six of them," Ben Samuels said quietly. His face was drawn, his tone tight and controlled. He shuffled the letters once again, scanning them in the dim light, reading the signatures. They read much the same, almost as if a single voice had dictated them. "Six in one day, and three of them from the biggest accounts we had."

"It's . . . it's terrible news to have to bring," Arthur Gilliam said, wringing his hands nervously. "I stopped by the office, and the letters were stuck in the mail slot, and I . . . well, I don't know why. But I had this funny feeling of urgency. I felt somehow that they had to be opened right away."

"You continue to follow your hunches," Ben said. "It was a good one. Miss Brand will have to hear about this immediately. Although I'll tell you frankly, Arthur, I hate being the one to tell her." He looked up from the papers at young Gilliam, seeing the air of worry in his face. Worry, yes, but something else as well. There was something new—a new strength and authority.

He dismissed the thought, though, and kept his mind on the business at hand. "Tell me," he said. "How do we stand on the quarterly projections? You don't have to give me any details—I have to get over to Desmoulins's, anyhow, and I'm already late—just the overall picture."

Gilliam thought a moment. "I've been turning it over and over in my mind all the way here," he said. "It's been driving me crazy, as a matter of fact. I almost let myself get run down by a wagon in the street, thinking about it. Ben, we

201

have a pair of enormous loan payments due in a month and a half. And there's the—''

''Just one question. Can we make it?''

''With present assets and with projected revenue?'' The bookkeeper frowned. ''No. I don't see how. And, Ben, any relief we get has to come right now. We have to get rock-solid guarantees of new revenue sources immediately or I can't get even an extension on one of the loans. The banker is George Presnell in St. Louis, and—''

''And he's tight as a drumhead, and the last time he granted an extension was when Andy Jackson was in knee breeches. I know. I know.'' He sighed, and his anger was apparent. ''Well, thank you for getting the news to me quickly, Arthur. I'll break it to Miss Brand as gently as I can.'' He looked the younger man in the eye and decided to change the subject. ''You're looking fit and chipper these days, incidentally. Getting a bit more color in your face. Losing that bookkeeper's pallor. Are you getting out into the world a bit more? Or . . . but that's a personal question, isn't it? Forgive me. I had no right.''

''Oh, no,'' Gilliam said. ''It's just that . . . well, I . . .'' He started to say something else, then thought about it. His face fell; his open, trusting expression closed up tightly. ''It's nothing,'' he said. ''I . . . changed my diet.''

Ben Samuels smiled. A gallant lie, he thought. Well, the boy was learning. Time for him to have a social experience. Long overdue, as a matter of fact. ''Never mind,'' he said. ''I spoke out of line. But now I think I'm way late for the evening at Desmoulins's. I'd better be going. If anything new comes up, good or bad, you know where to find me. And I want to hear it right off, as quickly as I can. I can count on your staying on top of the situation and keeping me posted, right?''

''Right,'' Gilliam said, and he almost said something else. But he thought better of it, and his face darkened as he visibly suppressed further comment.

The string quartet had retired to belowstairs for a break in the dancing, and a pianist the host had hired in the middle of a failed tour was playing pleasant conversation music from

Central Europe: mazurkas, schottisches, ländler, kuyawiaks, minuets. Olivia stood by the slightly open window, sipping punch and watching the passing parade. From time to time her eyes went again to the scene in the far corner of the room, where Ward Rathbone stood in earnest conversation with Odile Desmoulins, his handsome face animated, his manner almost professionally ingratiating. How, as he looked over Odile's shoulder and saw Olivia watching, he grinned and winked one eye before turning back to his conversation.

Olivia turned away, her face burning. The nerve of him! She sipped punch from the little glass in her hand, but her hand shook and spilled a little of it on her new gown and she had to brush it off quickly to prevent staining.

In a moment her anger returned. He'd been toying with her, no more. Trifling with her, until a more likely prospect presented herself! She flushed with suppressed rage and turned her face to the wall to hide her discomfiture from the crowd. No, she thought, this would never do. She'd really do best to go upstairs to the powder room until she could control herself.

She turned now, though, and when she did, she found herself looking into the eyes of a new arrival: a well-built, youthfully handsome young man with brown hair and a shy but clear-eyed smile. He was smartly dressed, even expensively, but there was something tentative and unconfident about his manner.

"Pardon me," he said in a quiet voice. "I . . . I don't think we've met before. If I might present myself . . ." He smiled bashfully again and said, "I'm Todd Rathbone."

She looked him over. Rathbone! This must be the middle son she'd heard of. What had she heard about him? Well, whatever it was, it couldn't have been bad. She looked in his eyes and sensed there was something missing that his brother had in profusion—and Olivia abruptly concluded that it was a quality she could do well without. "How do you do?" she said. "I'm Olivia Soames."

"I . . . I know," the young man said. "I mean, I asked someone. I . . . I usually know everyone here, and I hadn't seen you before. I know I'm being much too forward, but—" He gulped, faltering.

Olivia decided to put him at his ease. "I don't think so," she said graciously. "I'm working with Miss Brand. I've been away in the East to school. I don't know many people here yet. I suppose I'm here mainly because Miss Brand was invited."

"Oh, I can't imagine that," he said gallantly. "I'm sure that before you know it you'll be perfectly at home in the life of the city."

"You're too kind," Olivia said. She looked into his eyes again and decided to encourage him. The pianist finished his piece, stood to acknowledge sparse applause, and retired. The quartet came out, instruments in hand, and seated themselves. Olivia looked around. At the door, Ben Samuels, his face grave and serious, handed his coat to the black slave, liveried and dignified, who had earlier greeted her at the door. His eyes scanned the room, looking for someone, and he found Aurora Brand; he moved forward through the crowd, pausing no more than a moment to acknowledge greetings from friends among the guests at the party. His eyes remained on Aurora Brand, his expression solemn and disturbed.

The music began just then, with a rousing flourish from the strings. "Miss Soames," the young man at her side said softly, "might I have this dance, please?"

Aurora Brand excused herself and made her way with Ben Samuels to the veranda outside. "What is it, Ben?" she said. "You look terrible. It must be really bad news you have for me."

"It is," Samuels said. "We got simultaneous letters from six of our biggest accounts today—canceling their contracts. Do you know the clause in the standard contract that provides . . ."

"Ah," she said. "The safety thing, isn't it?" He nodded. "Ben, can they do that without warning?"

"I'm not sure," Samuels said. "I'll be at work on that bright and early tomorrow morning. But in the meantime we won't be getting any business from them. Those are big accounts. Hammer and Strauss. Cartmill Sugar. John Biggs. The Fairbairn Plantation. Marchand Frères. Harrison and—"

"Oh," Aurora Brand said, her face falling. "Not the Marchands. Oh, Ben . . . and Peter Fairbairn?"

"Yes," Samuels said. "And—well, you know what the effect of these defections is likely to be. There'll be more. And soon. When people like those leave us, and for stated cause . . ."

"Oh, God," Aurora Brand said. "We're . . . I'm ruined, Ben. I'm out of business."

Ben Samuels uncharacteristically reached out and took her hand. "No!" he said in a vehement whisper. "Don't think that for so much as a moment." He squeezed her hand so hard, she looked up into his eyes—and she suddenly realized the depth of the lawyer's feeling for her, suppressed and diverted though it had been and remained to this day. "We're not licked yet, Aurora. Just you watch. In the morning I'm going to court. I'll challenge the cancellations. I don't think they can make the escape clause stick. I'll tie them up. And I'll have Seth get on the wire and stir up the waters. Look, clear your mind of all this for now and you'll realize what I'm saying. In the morning you'll think of a dozen things to do, even though not one of them occurs to you now." He squeezed her hand once again and held it lightly. His voice was tense and emphatic. "We're not licked. We're not. Now get that out of you mind. There are plenty of cards left in the deck, and I intend to play every one."

"All right," Aurora said in a small voice. "But, Ben, how could this happen? I thought Rathbone was out of commission, what with Allison's illness and all."

"It's Halsey's work," the lawyer said. "It appears he has limited power of attorney for Rathbone. Although my informants say young Rathbone has the properties south of the river now." He shuddered. "Mainly tenants. God help every one of them. There have already been two evictions, I hear. The word is, the boy has a hard streak in him that makes his father look like so much pudding." He sighed. "No. It's Halsey. Working through Renault. I should have seen it coming. And there's a definite new pattern to it. Halsey has reserves of subtlety that Laird never bothered with." He shook his head. "Although I wonder how the boy managed to get the Algiers properties away from him. I'd have pegged Halsey to grab control of the whole package.''

''Ward's inside romancing Henri's daughter. Can you imagine it?'' Aurora Brand thought about the matter for a moment, then put one slim hand to her heart. ''Oh, my God. Ward is moving in. Can you imagine a combine between Henri and the Rathbones?''

Ben Samuels shuddered visibly in the light washing through the veranda windows. ''Terrible,'' he said. ''Desmoulins dotes on his daughter too. He could be fooled by young Ward for a time, I think.'' He bit his thin lips and thought about the matter. ''I can't see Halsey standing still for a move by Ward, however, no matter how ambitious and strong-willed the boy is.''

''There'll be a power struggle,'' Miss Brand agreed. ''But, Ben . . . it'll all be academic, as far as we're concerned. By the time all this has happened, we'll be out of business. If Halsey can turn the defection of these six firms into—''

''Don't say that!'' Samuels said fiercely. ''Don't even think it. Not for so much as a moment!''

But even as he left her off at the door to the Desmoulins town house, to return inside and circulate among the guests, the sinking feeling of despair gripped Aurora's heart with an icy hand. It was the death blow, the coup de grace to all she'd worked so hard to build, the killing stroke to end all her dreams. If this first raft of defections were followed, as it was sure to do, by others, she'd be ruined quickly.

She turned away from the door and clenched her hands, shutting her eyes tightly as if to shut out all the evil Rathbone—and now his second in command—had brought into her life. *No!* No, she wouldn't let them do this to her! She'd fight them to the last!

But then mocking thoughts came back to her: *Don't you see they've got you boxed in? You're through. You might as well toss in the towel. Send a message to Rathbone now, while you can, and see what can be salvaged of the offer he made you earlier, the night the* Memphis *went down.*

''Ah! *Mademoiselle* Brand! There you are.''

The voice cut startlingly into her consciousness and brought her back to herself. She tensed, then she forced her taut nerves to return to normal. Only when she was sure of herself did she turn and face the speaker—her host, Henri Desmoulins. "Yes?" she said, her smile unreadable once more.

"I have been looking for you," Desmoulins said with an easy and unforced warmth. "It seems an old friend of yours is visiting in the city and has been asking for you."

"An old friend?" she repeated, keeping the mask of polite interest, forcing the friendly smile to hide the chaos and emptiness in her heart.

"Why, yes," Desmoulins said, beaming, stepping aside to usher forward a tall, spare, Byronically handsome man whose dark curly hair now bore dashing streaks of gray. Aurora looked up, startled, into dark and haunted eyes that bore hypnotically down into her own. "Down from Natchez, I believe. Mr. Allan MacMaster."

Now the tall man was bending gallantly over her hand, and she could feel the touch of his lips on her fingers. "Aurora," he said. "It's been such a long time."

Chapter 29

Desmoulins looked at the two of them and smiled. "Please excuse me," he said. "My wife is signaling to me. I seem to have forgotten something." He looked once, briefly and sympathetically, into Aurora Brand's eyes and withdrew, leaving them on the veranda together.

Aurora patted her hair with one hand and avoided Allan MacMaster's eyes. "Allan," she said. "What has it been, three years?"

"Three and a half," MacMaster said. "God, let me look at you." He took her two hands in his and stepped back to look her up and down. "You haven't aged a day," he said warmly. "My God, my God . . . look at you. There's nobody in the world like you." His voice changed, sobered slightly. "There never was, Aurora. Never. I suppose I can't ask you to believe that. Not now, anyway."

She looked up into his eyes again. This time she could see something there—sadness? Seriousness, perhaps, that had not been there before? "Allan," she said softly, "it *is* good to see you again. I wouldn't have predicted it. I would have thought the best thing would have been to forget and not go stirring up old memories." She stopped and looked him in the eye. Their eyes caught, locked, held. "Something's happened to you, Allan," she said. "You've been hurt somehow. There's something in your eyes . . . it's not age. It's something else."

MacMaster smiled, but this only intensified the impression his eyes had made. "Same old Aurora. You never miss a nuance, and you always speak your mind. God! You haven't any idea how I've missed talking to a woman who gives straight answers.'' He sighed and squeezed her hands, then let go of them. ''No, that's not quite what I wanted to say. What I've missed was you.''

But here his voice broke off in something like a sob, and he turned his face away, but not before she could see its handsome features twist in a grimace of pain. ''What am I saying? Here I am a . . . a married man, talking to you as if nothing had changed.''

He could say no more for a moment. Aurora caught the sound of grief in his voice and stepped forward to stand beside him, taking his hand between hers. ''Allan,'' she said, ''I heard you'd married. People told me afterward. But I was too busy to inquire further. Perhaps it wasn't just being busy. Perhaps I wanted to wash my mind clean, to avoid thinking. It doesn't pay to dwell on things sometimes.''

MacMaster turned back to her again, and the eyes that looked down into her own were tortured, anguished. ''Then . . . then it wasn't easy for you, either?'' he said in a hoarse voice.

''Easy?'' she said. ''Allan, if I hadn't had my work to fall back on—punishing, grueling, backbreaking, around-the-clock work, rebuilding the Brand Line from the shambles Father left it in . . .'' She smiled, but she was on the verge of tears. Suddenly her heart went out to him; obviously he was in anguish. ''Allan,'' she said simply. ''What happened? I mean, after we broke off?''

He didn't say anything for a moment. Then, silently, gravely, he led her by the hand to the edge of the veranda and stood beside her before the railing, his hands on the polished wood. ''Well, I suppose I don't have to tell you what was running through my mind when I went back to Natchez. You can imagine the rationalizations I worked up for my actions. I suppose''—here he chuckled but with little humor—''you must have been doing much the same thing. I told myself my work was all that mattered, that if you had really loved me you would have dropped your own concerns to join me, to come help me hack a great plantation out of the jungle and build a great fortune. Your refusal to do so meant—'' He broke off, unable to finish. ''You might know about this sort of self-serving, self-deluding nonsense.''

''I do know,'' Aurora said softly, ''how well I know. Thank you for understanding what I had to do, though. You always had such a special understanding.'' Her voice took on an added warmth. ''You always could see into a woman's heart.'' She squeezed his hand, but there was no answering pressure from his own hand, inert in hers. ''Maybe as a man you wouldn't take that statement as the compliment it was intended to be, but—''

''No, no,'' MacMaster said. ''I understand. And thank you. But let me continue. Damned fool that I was, I let myself get off into a veritable orgy of self-pity. All the while, as I poured all my energy into work, my heart was breaking. It never occurred to me that you must have been going through the same thing. Not until later—much later. Then it was too late.''

Aurora slipped her hand under his arm, hugging his big bicep to her breast, drawing herself closer to him. ''Go on,'' she said.

''I didn't understand. The more I suppressed my need for love—my need for you—the more powerful it became. There wasn't enough work, not in Natchez or in the whole world, for me to work off my loss. I punished myself, working, driving my blacks to work—twelve, fourteen hours a day. I nearly killed the poor devils. I didn't notice. All I could think was: Get the forest cleared . . . lay out the grounds . . . get as much land under cotton as you can as quickly as possible . . .'' He paused. ''And then my health broke down. I wound up flat on my back in a hospital, raving with fever. I suppose I was ripe for anything that might happen. Anything—or anyone.'' He sighed deeply and despairingly.

''Yes?'' she said. ''What happened, Allan?''

''Then,'' he said, ''I met Celeste. She was young, but not too young. She attached herself to me . . . and she had that uncanny instinct women have for knowing just what a man thinks he wants. In my case it was a need for someone who would subordinate herself to my needs, my concerns . . .'' He shuddered with something like self-loathing, his handsome face twisting with shame. ''You'll note I said 'thinks he wants.' Ah, if only a man knew his own mind when he needed to. If only . . .'' He shook his head violently.

"You see," he said, "I was sitting there waiting for someone like her to come along. Whatever little she got from me in those days, God alone knows. I certainly wasn't in a giving frame of mind. But then, perhaps she was already unbalanced back then. Perhaps it was only my own self-absorption that kept me from seeing it. And maybe she was simply managing to hold herself together until we could be married.''

"Oh, Allan," Aurora said. "What happened?''

He looked down at her for the first time during his tortured monologue. "If she'd had any family left to warn me, maybe the situation would have turned out differently. But she didn't. She was new to the city, as I was, and we had only each other. All I know is that there were precious few signs beforehand—right up to the first of her attacks. We weathered the first two with medical help. But the third . . .'' He turned away, his mouth a bitter slash across his gaunt face. His profile was a portrait in desolation and wounded pride. "Oh, God. She's mad. Mad as a March hare. She's in a home in Vicksburg, under twenty-four-hour care. I go up to see her once a month, but it's as if it isn't really her there at all.''

Aurora released his arm and stepped back a little to look at him, at his erect stance, stiff with grief and pride; at his finely cut features, set in their mask of suffering. Then, however, he shook himself, as if releasing some intolerable burden. He forced a smile onto his face—a smile that aimed at tolerance for life's vicissitudes, at gentle self-mockery, and missed only by the distance between tranquility and horror. "Listen to me," he said. "My God, you'd think nobody else in the world ever had problems. Well, one learns to live with them.'' She could see him forcing the strength back into his tall, gaunt body, forcing the gaiety she'd once known back into the hollow-cheeked face. Suddenly a pang of something new, something poignant and tender, shot through her, and she took his hand again.

"Allan," she said, "I'd forgotten how much I cared for you back then. Seeing you again now . . . oh, you bring something into my life just now that I need ever so badly.''

"Aurora," he said, "I'm tied to a wretched madwoman,

a woman who fouls her bedclothes, who hardly knows light from dark anymore. I can't act. I can't put her away. You can't divorce a maniac. What can I do?''

Aurora stepped into his arms, suddenly feeling the strength in them as they went around her, holding her tight. She nestled her cheek comfortingly against his chest. ''Allan,'' she said. ''Allan, it isn't important just now. Oh, my dear, it's so good to see you again.'' She thought for a moment and then looked up into his eyes. ''You're down from Natchez,'' she said. ''For how long?''

''I'd intended to stay a week, no longer,'' he said. ''But seeing you like this . . . Aurora, I'd better cancel plans to return for a while or go back immediately. I . . . I couldn't stay and not see you.''

''Stay,'' she said. ''Stay for a time. We need each other right now.'' Abandoning all caution, she raised her lips passionately for his kiss.

Ben Samuels, chancing to look out of a window onto the broad veranda, saw their embrace. He smiled his microscopic smile, gracious and unreadable, and moved through the crowd to where the quartet was winding up the coda of the string of waltzes. Standing just below the musicians' elevated stand, he listened, his head swaying lightly in time to the music. His host caught his eye and moved closer. ''Ah, Monsieur Samuels,'' Henri Desmoulins said. ''You listen and do not dance.''

''I never dance,'' Ben said, his eyes on the first violinist, ''least of all in the presence of musicians of such transcendent eloquence. *Mes compliments, monsieur.*''

''I don't understand,'' Desmoulins said. ''Not dance?''

''It would be sacrilege for a music lover such as myself to dance, rather than listen, to the music of such an ensemble. Ah, listen,'' he said, a beatific smile passing over his hawk-like features. ''If I could play the violin like that, I would abandon all my other pursuits, even if it beggared me in the process.''

''Hmmm,'' Desmoulins said, listening. The musicians took the last repeat and played the long, lilting line of the music, carrying thrillingly through the crowded hall despite the general chatter. ''It is unusually good, but—''

"Can it be," Ben Samuels said, "that you do not recall the names of these four geniuses? That you do not recall having engaged the Marchesi Quartet? Whose principal violinist is the renowned Ettore Marchesi, pupil of Spohr, formerly principal second of the Genoa Opera orchestra?" He smiled indulgently. "Surely the press of business has driven it from your mind. I beg you to allow me to introduce you after the music comes to an end."

"Introduce me? To a common fiddler? I—"

"Never. Not on your very valuable and distinguished life, Monsieur. Marchesi is the most uncommon of fiddlers. He's a genius whose name shines throughout Europe, the spiritual heir of Paganini, of Schuppanzigh. He's a man who, on an occasion in London, when I was in attendance, played in such a manner as to—" He stopped, his face falling. "My word, sir," he said. "For a moment there I thought I saw a most incongruous sight, out among the dancers. But no. My eyes must be failing. Is your daughter, sir, dancing with the son of Laird Rathbone? Impossible. Forgive me, sir. Forgive even the ghost of the thought."

Desmoulins turned and scanned the crowd. "Rathbone? Rathbone's son? Where?" His face turned solemn, even angry, at the thought. "Odile? Where is Odile? If that little snip . . ."

Samuels watched him go just as the music ended. He caught the eye of Marchesi, bowed appreciatively, and led the applause enthusiastically. Out of the corner of his eye he could see Aurora Brand and the tall man he'd seen on the veranda with her making their way toward him through the crowd. He was about to approach the violinist when he heard a voice at his elbow. "Ah, Samuels," the voice said, "thinking of taking the fiddle up again? It might be a good idea at that, under the circumstances."

He whirled. Marc-Antoine Renault's sardonic smile greeted him; there was a look of victory in the attorney's cold eyes. "Ah," he said, looking Renault in the eye and smiling, "if only I could. But I have too much to do in my present trade." He bowed slightly, deprecatingly. "I take it I have you mainly to thank for that."

"*Touché*," Renault said. "But seriously, Samuels, isn't it

time to toss in the sponge? It seems undeniable that Mademoiselle Brand has, this time, come to the end of her bag of tricks. Isn't it time to give serious consideration to the offer my principal is prepared to make for what remains of the Brand Line?''

Ben Samuels, however, looked over Renault's shoulder and shrugged. ''Why not ask her yourself?'' he said. ''Here she is.'' He smiled and bowed, this time without a trace of mockery. ''Miss Brand, *Monsieur* Renault is prepared to offer us some table scraps for the Brand Line.''

''Offer?'' Aurora said, eyes flashing. ''Tell Laird he couldn't buy a stove-in bateau with the Brand Line mark on it for all his earnings for the rest of his life. Or is it Halsey you're working for now? Or is it the boy, Ward?''

Renault's thin smile grew even more deadly. ''Prate on,'' he said. ''You're through. Your six biggest accounts came over to us today. Others in Memphis, St. Louis, and Natchez will be quick to follow. Once the desertions begin—''

''Desertions?'' Allan MacMaster said. ''I don't understand. And what's this about Natchez?''

''This is Rathbone's lawyer,'' Aurora explained. ''You know, the man I mentioned earlier. He's spreading lies and vicious rumors about the Brand Line. We've lost some business.''

''You've gained some,'' MacMaster corrected her. ''Aurora, I'm not only a planter, I'm a broker. The biggest in Natchez, if I do say so myself, for all that the last merger is so new, the ink's still wet. Forget about losing Natchez,'' he said, the authority beginning to come back into his voice again. He looked Renault dead in the eye as he spoke. ''I forgot to tell you, me dear, why I was in New Orleans in the first place. I'm here to book shipping for virtually every major planter in Mississippi.'' He smiled, and the smile now was one of triumph. ''So what if you've lost six accounts? I'm booking for twenty. Lose sugar, gain cotton. It's where the money is, anyway.''

Aurora's sparkling eyes went from MacMaster to Ben Samuels and back again. ''Ben!'' she said. ''We're out of shoal water! We're going to make it!''

Chapter 30

In the morning Cassie Quayle passed Olivia on the way back from Aurora Brand's sleeping quarters. "Cassie," Olivia said, "did Miss Brand bring the gentleman home with her?" Her whisper was conspiratorially soft but carried a note of concern.

"Yes. Don't bother her. The door was open a crack. What I heard . . . well, I wouldn't bother her before noon at least." She turned to go but felt Olivia's hand on her arm. "I heard something else," she added as an afterthought. "You might be interested. This MacMaster fellow—he's rich. And he's bailing out the Brand Line. He's delivering a bunch of fat new contracts, probably in the next couple of days." There was a victorious glint in her dark eye as she said this. "That ought to make her easier to live with."

"She's always easy to live with," Olivia said reprovingly. "But what good news! How nice that she's found someone . . . even if it's only for a while. She's been so lonely, so hurt, since Mr. Boyd left."

"Hmmm," Cassie said. "The words *lonely* and *hurt* don't immediately come to mind when you think of Aurora Brand, do they? But you're right. She's human, just like anyone else." Her face twisted into a frown. "Men!" she said, almost spitting the word out. She shook her head, dismissing the subject. "I . . . I have to go out. Would you cover for me, please? If she needs me, tell her I'm shopping. Anything." She pressed Olivia's hand. "You'll do that for me, won't you, Olivia?"

• • •

In the big room to the rear, the light streaming through the open window woke Aurora gently. The satin sheets caressed her naked body as she stretched languorously. Her hand reached out and felt the warmth of the indentation in the sheets next to her; then she touched her own aroused body, running her soft palms and fingertips up and down her torso, remembering. . . .

Now the sounds and smells of the city in the streets below filtered through to her heightened consciousness: the smells of chicory coffee brewing and fresh baguettes baking, drifted on soft air already perfumed with the delicious scents of a thousand varieties of tropical flowers.

Aurora also became more aware of the music of the streets: the creak of wagons and carriages; the soft clip-clop of horses' hooves; the achingly sad cries of the vendors in lilting Creole French; and the mockingbird's hundred songs from the tops of the trees; and, far in the distance, the shrill hoots of the whistles of incoming steamers.

She stretched again, and ran fingers through her red hair. As a sleepy smile played on her lips, she sat up, letting the covers fall away from her perfectly formed breasts.

"Allan?" she said, her voice still musky with love and sleep. "Allan, are you there?"

As she shook the fiery radiance of her hair down around her shoulders she saw him coming: barefoot, bare-chested, wearing only the form-fitting trousers he'd worn the night before, bearing a silver tray with a pot of freshly brewed coffee, fragrant and steaming, and two tiny porcelain cups. His hair was tousled as hers; his eyes were dark and brooding; the lines of his craggy face severe.

"Here, my darling," he said. "Your morning demitasse." He set the tray down on the bedside table and leaned forward to plant a hot kiss on the sensitive spot where her neck and shoulder joined. "God," he said, "you're even lovelier than I remembered. How could I ever have left you?"

She drew him down to her lips, feeling the welcome touch of his big lean body against her own sensitized skin. "Hush," she said. "Past is past. Hush now."

"Ah, yes," he said, and the dark suffering came back into

his eyes again. "There's only now, isn't there? For God knows the future is as bleak as ever."

"Hush," she said again. "Don't spoil a lovely time by expecting it to be more than it can be. It's enough to have you here with me now, when I need you so." She took his big hand and held it to her lips. "Allan, Allan . . . let's take things a day at a time, my dearest."

"Ah, Aurora . . . I'm here for a couple of weeks, no more. I have to be back in Natchez on the fourteenth. If only—"

"It's all right," she said, her hand caressing his broad chest. "I have things to do too. I'll be up and down the river for the next few months. The Memphis and St. Louis offices need attention, and there's the building and launching of the new *Memphis* to see to." She smiled. "Thanks to you, my darling, we'll be able to do all these things, and without fear that we're overextending ourselves. And we'll be able to see each other now and then. I'll keep in close touch with your Natchez office via the telegraph." She hugged him happily. "And when we can arrange it, we can slip away for a few days. I have a secret place inland that I get away to perhaps once a year. Only one other person has been there with me. There's a cabin in an oak grove on a rise, with a freshwater lake below. I own six miles of posted land around it. In the morning you can get out of bed after a night of love and run naked down the hill, nice and early while the dew's still on the grass, and dive into the water, then dry out in the bright sunshine and make love again there above the pool, like Adam and Eve."

"Aurora," he said in a husky voice, pulling her to him, his arms comforting, his lips warm and demanding.

"You're lying to me, you little bitch!" Simon Halsey said, his rough hands bruising Cassie's upper arms as he shook her violently. "Damn you! Damn you to hell!"

She wrenched herself free and went to the dirty mirror to inspect her face. A thin line of blood ran down from her nose; she wiped it off with one hand. "Simon, you hurt me! I'm going to have a bruise, right up where it shows! I'll be lucky if I don't wind up with a black eye!"

He grabbed her by the hair and spun her around. "You'll

be lucky if that's all you get from me, damn you! I ought to break your neck, coming her to tell me a cock-and-bull story like that.''

"No!" she cried, pushing at his chest. "No, it's true! I swear! I heard them this morning."

He let her go suddenly, to drop on the floor at his feet. "You did, eh? What did he say? And what made you believe him?"

"Simon," she said, struggling to her feet unsteadily, "please don't hurt me again. I'm going to have a hard enough time explaining this as it is. If you—"

"Damn it! Just tell me."

"I . . . I told you most of it. This MacMaster fellow is someone she used to know. Sounds like they had an affair back when she first came to New Orleans. Since they broke up, he's got rich up in Natchez. He's not only big in cotton, he brokers shipping for his neighbors. They trust him, he says. He always gets them a good rate and guarantees delivery. He's avoided the Brand Line until now because he couldn't face Miss Brand. But now . . ."

"Damn. Damn. Yes, I remember the name. I had it on the list. I was going up to Natchez to talk to him personally, to see if we couldn't entice him over to . . ." He grimaced angrily. "Go on."

"Well, he has twenty or so clients. And he's delivering the whole package to Aurora Brand. And—"

"Damn! Damn!" Halsey pounded one fist into the other palm. "We had them boxed in. *Boxed in!* In another month . . ."

His eye fell on the dark girl before him. "What are you smiling for, goddamn you? By Christ, I'll teach you to smile, you little—"

Alex Rathbone let himself in the front door without ringing the bell and strode wearily to the sun room, where he sat down heavily and let his big portfolio slip to the floor. He looked morosely at the drawings leaking out of the untied bottom of the folder; then he bent over to pick one of them from the pile and lay it out on the floor before his feet. He scowled at this with a growing anger.

"Not bad, Alex," a voice said at his elbow. The young

man did not look up and did not answer for a moment. "Very good, as a matter of fact."

"Oh, stop it," the artist said. "Anyone who isn't as wall-eyed as a flounder can see that the leg's out of drawing." He looked up at his brother Todd. "When did you start developing an eye for art?" he asked irritably. "Last time I heard, you could barely tell a daffodil from a milch cow." He scowled again at the drawing at his feet. "Although the way I'm drawing these days, you could be excused for having problems with anything that comes off *my* fist." He snarled and closed his eyes. "God! How wretched! I'm losing my touch altogether." He sat up and reached for his watch. "Where's Ward? And Father?"

"They're in the office with Mr. Renault," Todd said. "Or rather Ward is. They're waiting for Father. I don't think he has come down yet."

Alex wasn't listening, though. "Look at that!" he said in disgust, squinting one-eyed at the drawing on the floor. "Just look at that, will you? Put a crayon in the paw of a Barbary ape and look what happens!" He shook his head. "That settles it. One of these days I'm leaving. I'm leaving this whole damn place. The ambience here is horrid. And Christ, Todd, the woman—she's a vampire, sucking the life out of me. Since I've been with her I haven't had the talent of a—" He abruptly broke off the sentence and kicked the drawing to one side. "No, no," he said. "There's no good in staying here. Once Mother's gone, I'm taking off."

"But, Alex, where to? Where could you go that would be better for you than New Orleans right now?"

Alex looked his brother in the eye and sighed. "Anywhere!" he said. "Anywhere at all. Paris, Rome, London . . . my annuity isn't much, perhaps, but it ought to be enough to allow me to live where I can work in peace. Somewhere where I'm not Laird Rathbone's son, where I can make a name of my own, without having to live down the one I was born with. And, Todd, there are reasons for wanting to try Paris. Don't tell anyone, but I'm already hanging there, in a couple of homes. Influential people, you know—people who could help me get a toehold in the art market there." He waved away his brother's questions. "No, no—not under this name. Another. I can't tell you who just now. But when I go to Paris, I will have a small name of sorts. What do I care what they call me, eh? As long as the check cashes, as long as it buys food and shelter and canvases, right?''

Alex looked at his brother's wide-eyed face and scowled once more. "Oh, what's the use?" he said. "You'll never understand." He rose, and, leaving the half-opened portfolio on the floor, stalked out.

Todd looked after Alex for a moment, then he returned to the hall outside the downstairs office. He'd intended to knock, to go in and ask if he could bring Ward and the lawyer some lemonade, or some other refreshments but the door still stood ajar a bit, and the voices inside were audible. Despite himself he found himself stopping and listening, without announcing his presence. After a moment or two he moved behind the half-open door, where he could not be seen either from the room or from the hall.

Inside, Ward paced, his voice ringing with an authority new to it: ''. . . bungled everything, once and for all, god-dammit. Haven't you any idea what this will do to my father when he learns of it? When he put the authority in your hands and Halsey's, he had the Brand woman right where he wanted her. All you had to do was hold things where they were and she was a goner. Now look what—''

"Hold your tongue!" Renault broke in angrily. "I'll listen to outbursts of anger from your father and hold my temper because we've been business associates for a long time, but I'll be damned if I'll stand still for a tirade like this from a young snip like you!''

"Hah!" Ward said defiantly. "You'll dare to speak up to my father because you think you've got something on him. But you haven't got anything on me. And when I take over the running of this firm, you'll either talk out of the other side of you face or—''

"You?" Renault's scorn virtually dripped from the word. "You? Take over the running of this enterprise?''

"Just watch me, hearse chaser. The time's not far off, let me tell you. Now that you and Halsey have fumbled things as badly as this, when all you had to do was follow through with already laid plans, to stay on top of the Natchez situation.''

Todd, listening behind the door, felt as much as heard the new presence, and knew in a flash who it was. He flattened himself against the wall as his father, moving into the hallway with the heavy gait of an old man, opened the door and stepped inside.

"Father," Ward said, "I wanted to talk to you. This paper shuffler and that damned fool Halsey have snarled things up for us just when we had the Brand woman outflanked, snookered, ready for the kill. I ask you, Father—"

"Don't listen to him, Rathbone," the lawyer said. "It's true there's a problem of sorts, but nothing that can't be dealt with if we just lower our voices for a moment and start thinking things out."

"Problem?" Laird Rathbone said. His voice had a strangely remote quality about it, as of a man who had been to the edge of the world and seen for a moment into the other side. "What could these things matter?" His tone dismissed the both of them utterly. He said in a voice filled with an altogether unaccustomed gentleness, "Ward . . . Marc-Antoine . . ." He tried to speak but could not. Todd, behind the door, could hear the clink of glass against glass as his father poured from the crystal flask of brandy that now stood beside his desk in a room from which liquor had once been banned altogether.

There was a moment's shocked pause. Then Todd heard his father say in that same quiet voice, "Ward, your mother . . . she passed away a few moments ago, in my arms. Just slipped away, as if into a soothing sleep."

Todd was shocked at the sob that tore itself from his own throat. He had thought himself primed and braced for the moment when it came; he'd said his good-byes to his mother a dozen times and more, and watched her quietly turn her face away from life, preparing herself for the eventual end. It was not for Allison Rathbone that his eyes burned, that the wild emotions surged in his heart, that the half-spoken words died a-borning in his choked-up throat.

No. It was for his father. His father, who alone among

them had carried his vulnerability into the death room, right up to the last moment, when the woman who meant everything to him had finally flown free of his nets and left him so utterly, desolately alone. *Poor Father!* he thought, the emotions roiling in his heart. *What can I give him? What can I do for him? How can I show him that I love him? That I care? How can I help?*

Book Three

Chapter 31

Months later and miles upriver, Basil Endicott sat at a round table in a waterfront gambling hall in Natchez-Under-the-Hill, staring with watery, blinking eyes down at his cards, his long face taking on an almost comic look of perplexity. "My word," he said. "With the hands I've been drawing, *this* is a most unusual occurrence." He folded the pasteboards into his palm and stared down at the piled chips before him. His mouth twisted down, twisted up, pursed, and then twisted down again.

He looked up, around the table, at the ring of faces with their various expressions, and saw, once again, the tall man looking at him with some interest. There was no readable expression on the big man's face at all: curiosity, perhaps, but no more.

Basil looked at the fat man across from him again, then looked down at his hand once more, fanning the cards a quarter of an inch at a time.

"You opened," the fat man said. "Your bet." *His* expression wasn't hard to read. There was suspicion, outright dislike, perhaps even a xenophobic disapproval of all things foreign in the too small eyes. "Come on, goddammit. We don't have all day."

Basil smiled mildly and looked around the circle of faces again. "I'm dry," he said. "If the porter could bring a glass of—"

"Goddammit, bet," the fat man said, thick lips twisting around the stub of the half-smoked cigar in his mouth. "Fish or cut bait."

Basil shot him a bland glance. Then, one eyebrow raised quizzically, he appealed to the men around the table. "I say," he said, "the game's difficult enough as it is without a row. Is this customary here?" He nodded at his adversary across the table. "House rules? That sort of thing?"

The tall man two seats to his left put his hand palm down. "I'm folding, anyway," he said affably. "Will whiskey do you?" he said to Basil, rising and pushing his chair back.

"Admirably," Basil said. "Thank you." He turned back to the business at hand. "Openers check." He put his hand down, looking the fat man in the eye, his expression still bland. All hands remaining checked to the fat man. He looked at his cards, stared Basil in the eye, and shoved a pile of chips across the green table. "Two hundred," he said. "Two hundred to the dealer." The look in his eye was now venomous.

The tall man returned, putting a small glass of brown fluid at Basil's elbow. "Thank you," Basil said, and sipped half of it. He watched two players fold; the bet was to him. He looked at the fat man and smiled a small smile. "Very well," he said, leaving his cards down and reaching for the mixed pile of chips and bills before him. He shoved the chips across, counting them as he did. Then he counted out a dozen of the large bills before him and shoved those across into the center of the table. "See two hundred," he said, "and raise . . . ah . . . twenty-six hundred."

There was an audible gasp from around the table, not so much from the players as from the noncombatants gathered behind the chairs. Basil looked up at the shocked faces and once again found himself looking into the amused, tolerant, distant eyes of the man who'd brought him the whiskey.

The fat man scowled, looked at his hand, looked at his stack, and fidgeted. Then, realizing he'd all but committed himself already, he counted out the huge sum with trembling hands. "C-call," he said. "Call the raise."

Basil put his free hand over his lips, shrugged, and slowly put his cards down one by one. Five diamonds—four, five, six, seven, eight. He looked around at the stunned faces, shrugged again, and moved to rake in the pot, his left hand reaching far out over the table.

The fat man moved fast—faster than one would have imagined him able to move. Something metallic gleamed in the pudgy hand as it swept out and down. Basil tried to retrieve his own hand and arm, but it was too late. Something hard slammed into his hand, and a sharp pain ran up his arm. He blinked and looked at the table where a nine-inch Bowie knife pinned his left hand to the oak tabletop. As he moved, he could see blood welling up around the deep cut. "Good . . . good heavens," he said.

The fat man let go of the knife and stepped back, as if only now realizing what he had done. The knife stood upright in the middle of the table, in the mixed pot of bills and chips, Basil's hand skewered on its razor-sharp blade. "Damned bottom-dealing son of a bitch," the fat man said, stepping back, his right hand near his vest pocket.

"Here," Basil said, "if someone would please help me get this thing free . . ." He sat up, trying to keep his moves gentle ones. "N-nothing broken, I think. I believe it passed between the fingerbones, but by God, it hurts!"

The big man and another of the players freed him in a moment, not without pain. Basil accepted a clean handkerchief from the big man beside him and wrapped his hand, instantly staining the white cloth dark red. His face, in the dim light of the saloon's back room, seemed drawn, drained of blood. His unhurt hand shook as he reached for the half-empty whiskey glass beside his chair. "Please," he said, "if someone could get me another, I'd be much obliged."

"Sure," one of the players said. "Drink the first one now, though." He turned to head for the bar, but something in Basil's stance stopped him.

"I say," Basil said to no one in particular. "I'm not familiar with local protocol." His voice was dull, dead. "But where I come from, this sort of thing is usually called for in such circumstances." He smiled wanly and threw the remains of his drink across the table into the fat man's face.

The idle chatter suddenly became absolute silence. "Leave the money on the table," the fat man said. "I'm the aggrieved party, and I say it's pistols on the Vidalia bar. Dawn will do. It's not much more than half an hour, anyway. Plenty of time to row across."

The big man stepped forward. "Look here," he said, "this man's losing blood as it is. You can't be serious. Give it a day or so." His eyes narrowed, and his voice had an unmistakable note of authority behind it.

"No!" the fat man said. "And if anyone touches the pot before I'm back from across the river, I'll see him, too, within the hour. Does everyone get my meaning?"

Basil bit his lip against the pain and against the shock that was just now beginning to settle in. He shivered uncontrollably, then he got hold of himself and straightened his back. But his voice was the voice of a sick man as he said hoarsely, "Dawn it is, then." With trembling hand he rewrapped his dripping wound. "You, sir," he said to the tall man beside him, not looking up, "might I ask you to second me in this? I know it's an imposition, but I don't think I can row just now. And I'll have to borrow a weapon from someone, I'm afraid."

The big man did not speak for a moment. Then he grinned. "You're all right, Englishman," he said. "And you're on." He looked across the table at the fat man. "That's all, isn't it?" he said, the grin still on his face. "I don't think we need further formalities. Not under the Hill, anyway. We'll see you across the river in an hour. And if you don't mind my saying so, sir, I admire your courage."

"Courage?" the fat man said, the scowl back on his heavy face now.

"Why, yes," the big man said. "Picking pistols, I mean, when you present fifty times as large a target. If our friend here manages to miss you, it'll be because he aimed behind him."

The fat man's eyes narrowed, but he let the insult pass. He turned on one heel smartly as he headed for the doorway and the docks.

Suddenly Basil was seized with a fit of uncontrollable shivering. The big man sat him down gently and called for a blanket. "Look here," he said, "you're in no shape to fight. Besides, did you know who that was, my Sassenach friend? It was Bert Dowling."

Basil looked up, his eyes glazed. "Bert who? My friend,

I've only been on the river a year or so, and this is my first
trip to Natchez. If the name's familiar to you . . ."

Someone came up just then and handed Basil a brimming
tumbler of whiskey. "Bert Dowling," he said, "only the best
shot south of Moline. He killed Gaylord Holt on the same
bar a year ago. Blew out his left eye, cool as they come.
Drink up, friend. You've got a nice morning's work ahead of
you."

The big man rowed, the heavy muscles of his shoulders
bunching and relaxing, his face showing no sign of effort.
He looked past the wan face of the wounded man and the
gambler who'd come along for moral support at the tall bluff
above the squalid docks of Natchez-Under-the-Hill; at the
stately homes above, the hellholes of Silver Street below.
Then he looked back in the pale light at the sick man in the
stern, shivering under the blanket. "Charlie," he said to the
gambler huddled beside the wounded Basil. "The more I
think about this, the less I like it." They hit the current and
he caught crabs for a stroke or two; he swore lustily. "He's
not fit to fight. Anybody can see that."

"No—no," Basil said. "Please. Don't interfere. I've dealt
with questions of honor b—before . . . in w—worse circumstances than these."

But his face betrayed him, even in the dim backlighting of
the Southern dawn. They could see him shaking with chill,
could see his struggle to stay erect, awake. "Damn it," the
man called Charlie said, "you're right. He's out on his feet.
Matter of fact, I'm not sure I'd trust him on his feet. I'm for
callin' things off once we're over on the bar."

Basil sat up, clutching the blanket tightly around him.
"No!" he said. "Confound it, I won't have it." He bran-
dished the horse pistol the big man had loaned him. "Can't
have people going around nailing a man's hand to the table."

The big man glanced around, then turned the nose of the
bateau a trifle downstream and began rowing steadily again.
"Reminds me," he said. "Have you got the bleeding stopped
yet? Charlie, have a look at that."

"I can't," Charlie said. "Not without unwrapping it. And
I don't dast do that right now. No, the more I think about it,

the more I think we ought to be rowin' back to Natchez, 'stead o' headin' across the river to let this pore devil freeze to death on the bar. Take him to see the croaker instead, get that cut closed up. Gonna take stitches as it is.''

"Nonsense," Basil said, stiffening a bit. "Be good as new. Only time to teach this chap a lesson or two, then plenty of time for doctoring." He weaved as he spoke; Charlie handed him the brown bottle of rye again, and he took a stiff drink, shuddering at the end of it. "Fit as a f—fiddle."

They faced off at opposite ends of a sandbar, their trouser legs wet to the knees from wading to their rendezvous. The others stood on the main bar, high and dry. The fat man stood at ease, his pistol dangling from one hand carelessly. Across from him, Basil Endicott, weaving slightly, held his borrowed gun unsteadily in both hands. The seconds shook their heads at one another; expressions on both sides of the argument were equally grave.

"I don't like this," Charlie whispered to the tall man. "Look at him."

The big man smiled, but his expression remained serious. "I know," he said. "Still . . . look at him. I like him, damned fool Englishman that he is. He can barely stand up. He's shaking like a leaf. I had to show him how to thumb-bust the pistol. But I think if you or I had tried to stop him from coming over, he'd have put a bullet in us too quick to talk about it." There was a note of admiration in his voice. "But enough. I'd better get on with it." He stepped forward, speaking in a loud voice. "All right," he said. "At the count of three, turn and fire. One shot only. One . . . two . . . *three*!"

Lightning-fast, the fat man turned and fired. But Basil Endicott, dizzy from loss of blood, wavered; the round creased his cheek, leaving a line of fresh blood across his face. Basil staggered, recovered, raised the revolver in one shaky hand. Bert Dowling, the fat man, turned sideways to present less of a target but stood unflinching, waiting for the shot that could, in steadier hands, end his life.

The Englishman shook violently under a sudden chill, then bent over, half hugging his bleeding hand. Finally he straightened with visible effort. "The . . . the second button on the waistcoat," he said. "The brass one." He raised the revolver with one hand, and the expression on his face was a ghastly thing to behold. All eyes went to the fat man's face; there was a stoic acceptance there. He stood, grimly awaiting the end.

Basil Endicott aimed and fired.

The fat man wavered, fell heavily to one side, rolled over onto his back slowly, and did not move.

Then, like a puppet whose strings had been cut, Basil Endicott, too, pitched forward on his face.

Hurriedly the seconds splashed into the brackish water, making it to the bar in a dozen noisy strides. None too gentle hands turned the fat man over onto his back.

There wasn't a mark on him.

The second button on his waistcoat was missing.

"For the love of God," one of the seconds said. "Shot away clean as a pin. And Bert, he's fainted dead away."

"So has this one," the big man said, bending to take the inert Englishman in his arms. "Here, somebody. Help me get him to the boat. He's losing blood fast."

Chapter 32

Somehow the two seconds got Basil Endicott back across the river again and up the embankment to the home of a doctor in Natchez-on-Top-of-the-Hill. The big man banged lustily on the door until the doctor appeared at the door, foul-tempered and wearing his nightshirt; it took the discreet flashing of a sizable wad of bank notes before the door swung wide and Basil, shivering and in deep shock, could be helped inside.

An hour passed, and the big man sat patiently in the doctor's parlor, reading dog-eared Eastern women's magazines. The other second had been sent after the now undisputed pot from the disputed poker game. After a time the big man reached inside his broadcloth coat for a silvery flask and drank. As he did, the inner door opened and the doctor, looking disheveled and irritable, scowled down at him. "Here, damn your eyes," the physician said, "give me that."

The big man, smiling mildly, handed it over. "All in a good cause. I'll go out and get him better whiskey if you like."

"This'll do," the doctor said, and upended the flask, drinking deeply. In the end he shook the flask upside down, half sneering at the one or two drops that fell to stain his carpet. "Only fair," he said. "Your patient finished a pint of my best while I was sewing him up." He handed the flask back and pulled an oblong piece of paper out of his pocket to squint at it. "Paid me with a check on a New York bank," he said sourly. "Is it any good?"

The big man examined the paper. "I haven't any idea. He

looks solvent enough." Then a thought occurred to him. "Don't worry. I forgot. There's someone on the way up from Silver Street with something like five thousand dollars of his. That ought to cover a little minor surgery—and perhaps an hour or two of rest time in your downstairs office here, eh?" He grinned that maddening grin again; the doctor shot him an angry look. "Hey," the big man said, "if there's any problem, send the bill to me. Here's my card. I'm not totally unknown in these parts."

The doctor frowned at the card. "I suppose not. All right, but get him out by noon, will you? I've got house calls for an hour, but I've got people coming in here through the afternoon." He looked the tall man over and walked out. After a moment or two the big man opened the door and went in. The patient, propped up on a double bed with his boots off, his left hand thickly bandaged, turned his head to look at him. "Well," the visitor said, "I suppose it's none of my damned business asking where you learned to shoot like that under pressure."

"I don't mind," Basil said. "Wouldn't do you a bloody bit of good, though. Younger sons and remittance men don't have to learn. Either it comes with the position or you don't live past twenty. I take it the good doctor is elsewhere."

"House calls," the big man said, grinning. "Why?"

"When he opened that cabinet over there, I saw another bottle of something. I think he didn't want me to notice. If you'd be so kind . . ."

"Sure," the other man said, his grin broadening. "The old bastard. Telling me he was all out." He retrieved the bottle. "Ah," he said, "Tennessee sour mash. Splendid stuff. Here. I think you'll like it." He handed it over; Basil uncorked it and drank deeply. "Hmmm. You can drink too. One sips that, usually. Like brandy."

Basil handed it back, wincing. "Sipping doesn't do much when the hand is throbbing like this. I hate pain. I can rise to an occasion when I have to. But afterward I'm a frightful coward." He looked quizzically at the big man. "I keep trying to place you. I don't think we've met before, though." He waited out the pregnant pause, then added gently, "My name's Basil Endicott. I didn't get the name."

The big man drank, then passed the bottle over again. "I didn't give it," he said. "I'm Dallas Boyd."

An hour passed. The bottle's contents diminished steadily. Basil was sitting up now, his legs dangling over the bed's edge. "Extraordinary mix-up," he said. "Imagine anyone thinking anything like that. Me and Aurora?" He shuddered and sipped from the bottle. "I can hardly imagine a worse fate for either of us. She'd shoot me inside a week, if by that time I hadn't poisoned her." He paused with the bottle halfway to his lips. "Oh, splendid woman, of course. And a good friend. But, you know a dead eye isn't the only thing that comes in the blood for a ticket-of-leave man, Boyd. There's also the taste for low life. In my case it takes the form of an irresistible attraction to women another man might find intolerably frivolous. Stupid, even. And a strong-willed, intelligent woman like Aurora? God save me!" He drank, this time more deeply, and passed the bottle to Dallas Boyd. "But you've been gone a year? And all because of—"

"No, no," Boyd said. "Not entirely. Although that was part of it. I had some business reverses. I went to California to recoup them." He grinned. "I never struck gold, but the man next to me did. It took me all of three months to find his weakness. Faro, piquet, poker, three-card monte—he was invulnerable to all of them. In the end it was his vanity, after all. He thought that just because a horse was his, it could run." He handed the bottle back. "Here. You need this worse than I do. I gather a hollow leg is another one of the family heirlooms."

"A family curse," Basil said. "Costs me a small fortune every year." He didn't drink, though, but sat holding the bottle and looking at Boyd. "I know you by repute, you know. And, Boyd, I think you've no idea of the depth of her feeling for you." He looked Dallas in the eye. "She's here just now, you know," he said. "In Natchez. Although you're going to hate me for telling you."

"Hate you?" Boyd said guardedly. "Why?"

"In your absence, in her loneliness, she drifted off into an affair with another chap."

"Well," Boyd said a little too quickly, "I don't own her. She's a free woman." He looked hard at the Englishman now. "Did you expect me to rush out and shoot someone? It wouldn't work, anyway. Not with a woman like Aurora Brand." He looked down at the bottle in Basil's hand and reached for it. "Who was it?"

"Chap named MacMaster. Married. Insane wife. Can't divorce her or remarry. Lonely, driven sort. Rather liked him, you know. But I don't think she would have slipped into this thing in the first place if MacMaster'd been free to marry. I think she'd have shied away. Better sense, you know, than to commit herself deeply on the bounce that way. And too much pride."

Boyd drank, then wiped his lips. "Pride," he said. "That's our problem, both of us. That and the damn-fool independence that's got us where we are in the first place. It's a curious thing, Endicott. I'd never have thought I could talk about her this way with anybody."

"It's the whiskey," Basil said, reaching for the bottle again. "Excellent stuff, by the way. Tennessee, you said?"

In the end they jury-rigged a sling for Basil's hand and set out on foot up State Street, past Lawyers' Row and the courthouse, toward Basil's hotel. The pace was slow, easygoing, as if Boyd were in no hurry to have the conversation end.

"You say Rathbone's wife died?" Boyd said. "But what happened then? She was the only thing keeping Laird from outright piracy all that time. He must be the great buccaneer of the world by now."

"One would think so," Basil said, "but in point of fact, Rathbone seems to have disappeared back East. His affairs are in the hands of a chap named Halsey—"

"God almighty!"

"Yes, and his eldest son, Ward, who seems to be turning into everything the old man ever was, minus the minimally civilizing influence of Mrs. Rathbone to temper his steel for him, has taken charge of part of the business. He's cut a bloody swath through the area south of the river, where Rathbone held immense properties but had done little with them. Young Ward has evicted tenants by the hundreds."

"Yes, yes. I think my own overseer wrote me something about that but didn't include the details. The Cajun tenants he dispossessed turned up in Bayou Lavache. We found work for as many as we could. Go on, please.''

"Certainly. Halsey, too, turns out to be a vicious and un-principled competitor, particularly since the contracts MacMaster delivered last year bailed out Aurora. It's been nip and tuck ever since, and Ben Samuels thinks Halsey has somehow planted a spy inside the Brand Line, but she has no idea who it could be. Security is very, very tight just now; the new *Memphis* is due in shortly from Pittsburgh, and Ben fears an attempt at sabotage.''

"That would be in character. But Laird? Where is he?''

"Nobody quite knows. Nobody outside his own organi-zation. I think you know something of his attachment to his wife. Her death shook him up rather badly. People who knew him said he aged twenty years in the month or so around her death. He took ship for the East soon afterward.''

"In the East, eh?'' Boyd said. The two slowed to watch a blond girl pass in street dress. "I wish more of the locals would do that. Go to the East, I mean, and get some notion of the crisis this area has facing it in the next few years. Everyone down here seems to think the present situation can last forever, and that all you have to do to deal with the abolitionists in the North is to blow a lot of empty rhetorical fiddle-faddle at them. It's a lot more serious than that.''

"Is it?'' Basil said. "I don't pretend to understand your politics here. I never quite understood ours, either.''

"Well, it boils down to this: Northerners were the traders in slaves and we were the users. I say 'we' generally, al-though I'm a dissenter myself and not popular for that reason. In the beginning, everyone involved made money off this dis-mal trade. Then the trade itself was disbanded, as was new importation. This left only half of the country profiting from the institution, and at the other half's expense. The abolition-ist fervor is the temperance fervor of the dried-up ex-drunk.''

"God spare me.''

"Exactly. Add to this the problem that half the country operates with cheap labor, the other half without. That can't go on forever. So far they've been fighting it out mainly on the floor of Congress and in the territories—Kansas, in par-ticular. But one of these days it'll come to bloodshed. When it does, God help the people down here. They'll find themselves being asked to fight to the death for an institution that has crippled them, held them down.''

"Crippled? Held down? I don't understand. I thought slave labor was supposed to be an advantage.''

"So it seems—to the North. Down here it perpetuates a feudal society and helps keep the lower classes—the lower-class whites, mind you—in their places. It keeps the power permanently in the hands of the only people who can afford to own slaves. And outside of cutthroats like Rathbone, who rise by sheer criminality, the system keeps any new blood from entering the power elite. That isn't healthy. All of the slaves—all of them—belong to seven percent of the Southern population. That means ninety-three percent of the people stand to benefit not at all from the institution, and what would otherwise be some sort of middle class is disenfranchised by slave labor. I tell you, Endicott, if these people down here ever get to understanding—really understanding—the events of 1848 in Europe, they'll wind up rising in a revolt that will make that look like a mild argument.''

"Now I'm hopelessly lost.''

"Well, look. What's the best way of heading off a revolution, my friend? Start a war. Keeps idle hands busy, you know.'' There was pain in the cynical smile on Boyd's face as Basil, perplexed, looked his way for a moment. "Start a war. Tell the poor bastards who are going to have to fight it that they're defending their homes, their way of life, and don't let on for a moment that what you're really doing is muddying up the issues, keeping the dissidents busy fighting someone else so they won't have time to think of fighting you, and, worst of all, well . . . you break the back of the revolt before it's begun by simply killing off the brightest and best young men in the society. Men who'd otherwise be leading the fight to break up the big combines, abolish slavery, restructure the society. Yes, war's the best answer. Up to now there have been conflicts that would naturally bleed off discontent and weed out the restless young. Wars with Indians. With Mexico. Filibustering expeditions like Lopez's in Cuba and Walker's in Nicaragua. But in the next few years they're not going to be enough. Just you watch. There'll be war. And it won't

be started by the North, for all the blather the abolition crowd
puts out. It'll be started down here. By one of 'us.' "

"Horrible," Basil said. "And what will you do when it
breaks out?"

Boyd didn't answer for a moment. "I . . . I don't know.
I've been puzzling over that one for quite a while. I've no
affection for the system here, God knows. Not enough to
make me fight to defend it. As a matter of fact, if a revolution
were to occur, I think I'd probably wind up on the barricades,
trying to overthrow the very system that I'd employed on the
way up, before things got frozen into this feudal cast. But if
war came, right or wrong, I'd have to think that in deserting
the area in protest against a war I didn't believe in, I'd be
deserting my friends, my neighbors. Oh, I don't mean these
damned silly New Orleans society types. I mean the little
people on whose shoulders the burden of the war will be
borne. The Cajuns in my parish. The little shopkeepers and
tradesmen in the country towns. The—" He stopped, sighed.
"Well, I'm boring you. It's not your fight. I'll leave you
here. It's been pleasant. I like you. You're quite mad, of
course, but you're my kind of mad. And there's a bit of grit
about you."

"It's in my blood," Basil said, holding out his good hand.
"Ticket of leave, you know. Well met, Boyd. I'll tell Aurora
I saw you."

"No," Dallas Boyd said, looking him in the eye, his face
serious. "I think I'd rather you didn't. It would just complicate things." He shook hands, his grip firm and resolute.
"Good-bye, Endicott. Good luck."

He turned on one heel smartly and marched away with
military precision, head held high. Basil looked after him all
the way down the street, until he turned into a side street.
He smiled. *"Au revoir,"* he said softly.

Chapter 33

Allan MacMaster was through the door and out in the road beside the big rockaway almost before it pulled gently to a halt. He held the door wide and with the other hand guided Aurora Brand down to the ground. "There," he said, looking down from the top of the bluff to the docks below. "No sign of anything yet."

"I heard it," she said. "I tell you, I heard it. I know the whistle and bell of every packet that works the Lower Mississippi and half the ones that work above Cairo. You'll be seeing it in a moment or two, coming around the bend up the way." She smiled and took his hand. "Allan," she said, "it's not too late to change your mind. Come with me. Take the trip down to the city on the boat. We'll at least have another day together—and another night."

MacMaster's face darkened. "I—I can't, Aurora. We've been over that. I told you what she was like, last time I went to see her. She's improving. She was lucid the whole time. No matter that she hardly remembers a thing that's happened during the whole last year. Aurora, I can't leave her. Not just now. It's not that I love her. I don't. Not that way. But if I pull out on her just now, when there's a chance of her recovering . . ." He took her hand between his, and she was astonished to feel his big hands tremble with some incomprehensible emotion. "Aurora, if she recovers, fully and completely, then I can think of—well, of you, my dearest." He bit his lip. "But this way . . ."

"Oh, Allan, I do understand," Aurora said. "I wouldn't have you do anything else. Really I wouldn't. It's all of a piece with your nature, never to do the unfair thing.'' She suddenly drew him to her, burying her face for a moment in the ruffles on his white shirt. ''It'll be lonely without you. It will, my dear.''

MacMaster looked over her shoulder across the great river to the lowlands beyond. ''Aurora,'' he said, ''it's all I can do to hold firm to my convictions as it is. Don't make it harder for me. If we could—''

But as he spoke, the shrill hoot of a steamship whistle broke into his words, and in the far distance they could hear the distinctive pattern of a steamer bell, ringing joyously in a complex rhythm. ''Aurora,'' he said. ''Is that it?''

She pulled away and eagerly looked upriver. As she did, around the bend came a stately white packet, its twin stacks protruding proudly above a complex system of decks, its great wheels churning powerfully. High above its decks, the pilot-house jutted delicately above the texas. There was an addition MacMaster had never seen before: an additional deck between the main and boiler decks. The whole, lofty and unspeakably lovely, floated high in the shallow river, like a leaf skimming the meniscus on a forest pool. ''My God,'' MacMaster said. ''A triple-decker! That's the most beautiful thing I ever saw on river water.''

Aurora, beaming, made a tiny curtsy of acknowledgment. ''The *Memphis*,'' she said proudly, her heart beating fast.

Basil Endicott, his hand bandaged and in a sling, was waiting for her at the dock. With him was Ben Samuels, looking every bit as proud as Aurora Brand herself. Basil's long face bore a thunderstuck expression as the giant vessel bore down on them. ''My God, Aurora,'' he said. ''The thing beggars description. It makes the summer residences of half the royalty in Europe look like tenant cottages.''

''You should see the inside of it,'' Ben said. ''If it lives up to the advance description . . .''

''It will,'' Aurora said excitedly. ''Basil, what happened to you?''

''Oh, this?'' Basil Endicott said. ''Drunken manicurist. Poor woman had the shakes worse than anything I've ever seen. A proper case for the Temperance League, if you ask me.''

Ben Samuels's hawk face settled into a frown that somehow didn't manage to match the twinkle in his eye. ''That's the tale he's telling now,'' he said. ''Half an hour ago it was a runaway Boston chaise that ran over his hand just as he was bending to pick up a wallet someone had dropped in the street. Heaven alone knows what the story'll be by the time we get to New Orleans.''

''I won't ask,'' Aurora said, beaming at the great edifice floating so gracefully downstream toward them in that brief pause between the cutoff of the great engines and their reversal to brake for docking. ''Oh, Ben, isn't it lovely?''

Todd Rathbone and the telegraph boy caught up with Olivia at virtually the same time as she turned the corner into Royal Street, just in front of Aurora Brand's New Orleans offices. ''Olivia!'' Todd said. She stopped, hesitated, and smiled perplexedly. She accepted the telegram before turning to him. She stood, holding the envelope in her hand, her eyes on Todd's flushed face.

''Hello, Todd,'' she said. ''What brings you to town?''

''I just heard,'' he said breathlessly. ''Father's coming back. We got a letter from his yesterday. I . . .'' He looked down at the envelope in her hand. ''But I think you want to open that first. Don't let me stop you.''

She smiled. ''Thank you.'' She opened the paper and read swiftly. ''Oh, my goodness,'' she said. ''I've got my work cut out for me. Miss Brand will be here by nightfall. And I've still got the papers to talk to.'' She smiled at him. ''It's the *Memphis*. It's passed Natchez, and Miss Brand is coming down with her. And, oh, Todd, I've got to get back to work. I'm sorry.''

''Oh, it's all right,'' he said. ''I . . . I've got things to do myself. I want to surprise Father when he comes back. I . . . well, I'll see you later, Olivia,'' he said shyly. She started to turn away but saw the boyish smile on his young face and weakened.

''Good-bye, Todd,'' she said. ''It's nice to see you. Perhaps we can talk later sometime, when we're not so busy.''

She felt an inexplicable tug at her heart in noting the gratitude in his clear young eyes as he smiled again and turned to go.

At the top of the stairs Olivia called out, "Cassie? Cassie, are you there?"

There was no answer for a moment, then Arthur Gilliam came out of his office, his face morose and drawn. "Oh," he said haltingly. "Cassie has gone out. I don't know where. She never tells me."

Poor Arthur, she thought, looking into his haunted eyes. What was wrong? Love requited was supposed to make a man happy, not miserable. But look at him! He'd lost weight; his habitual expression now was one of anguish. "Well, I'm sure she'll be back," she said lamely. "But, Arthur, this telegram came in just now." She passed it over and watched him skim it, holding it in a hand that shook like a drug addict's. "Isn't it exciting? The *Memphis*! It'll be here by dusk." She put her hand over her mouth suddenly. "Oh, my goodness! I have two newspapers to deliver the fliers to yet, and look at the time!"

"No, no," he said nervously. "I sent them all along already. I didn't know you were supposed to do it. It's all taken care of."

"Arthur," she said, "thank you. You've made my day. Is there something wrong? You look terrible. Is there—pardon me for asking, I know it's none of my business—is there something . . . between you and Cassie?"

His eyes, haunted, pained, sought hers, and for one moment she thought he was going to speak, to blurt something out. But then, with visible effort, he got control of himself again, and Olivia saw his face close up against her like some sort of night-blooming flower at the first touch of the morning sunlight. "N—no," he lied. "No, it's nothing like that. I . . . I just haven't been feeling well."

But as he excused himself and went back into his little office, his thin shoulders bent, as if bearing the whole weight of the world on them, she didn't believe him for so much as a moment. Poor man. Poor dear. What could be eating away at him like that? And such a sweet boy, really. Was there some sort of cruel streak in Cassie that she couldn't see? Was she the sort who had to hurt the person she loved?

Olivia pondered this as she went in to straighten up and dust Aurora Brand's already near immaculate office. Perhaps that was it. There had been a change in Cassie since she and Arthur had come together, that was for sure. But it hadn't been the same sort of change that had taken place in poor Arthur. Quite the opposite: Cassie had grown harder, more defensive, more secretive. As if anyone couldn't tell in a glance that the two of them were lovers . . .

Lovers. The word stopped her dead. She thought about it. The whole thought of physical love—of sex—continued to frighten her after the terrible day and night in which Lance Whitmire had—

She shuddered. She couldn't think of it. Couldn't let her mind dwell on something like that. It wasn't that way between men and women, she knew. Not if they loved each other. There would be tenderness and caring and gentleness . . . yes, and passion, too, she somehow knew, although this was a quantity so far unknown to her by direct experience. She'd picked up just enough from talking to Cassie, to Aurora Brand, to Inez Leblond.

Inez! She smiled suddenly, thinking of the first real friend she'd made after coming South again. Suddenly she found herself wanting to see the Spanish girl again, to talk with her and pour out her heart to her. Olivia could always say what she felt to Inez, and she'd give a straight answer. No matter what the problem was, she always seemed to understand and to have good and welcome advice to give.

Yes. Inez. And that nice, outgoing, good-humored Cajun husband of hers, strong and happy-go-lucky, the equal of any man he met and the master of any challenge that life cared to throw at him. Inez's words came back to Olivia now, as clearly as if she'd spoken them only a moment before: "He didn't give a hang who my father was or what he'd done for a living or whether I had any dot to bring to a marriage. He was young and strong and lusty and full of cheer and love, full of life."

Olivia, remembering, sighed. When she closed her eyes, she could see Inez's thin, intense face before her. "You better hope you get such a man when your time comes, Olivia. He isn't rich, and God knows he isn't likely ever to be. But true is better than rich. Straight is better'n airs. Strong's better'n devious. Just as Cajun is better'n *le francais de Paris.*''

Olivia kept her eyes closed and sighed again. She thought of the two men in her life, the men who wanted her. There was Todd Rathbone—young, untried, full of a boyish charm, and not at all threatening in the way a man tended to be with a girl, the way his brother Ward had seemed before he'd dropped her like a hot rock to concentrate on Odile Desmoulins. And then there was Zach McClellan.

Zach. What was he? He was solidity, strength, quiet competence. *Not* exciting, or was that merely the fact that he was poor, that he had little but himself to bring to a girl? But he was threatening. Very threatening. And all because of the powerful sexual need she knew he had for her. And now, thinking of him, she could feel a shiver of apprehension run through her. Zach's arms would be strong—too strong. He'd be in control, not her. And somehow she didn't want to lose control. She wanted to be the one who decided things. Would she be able to do so with Zach? Or would his own powerful animal attraction—yes, and the immense strength of his mighty hands—would these prove too much for her in the end? She shuddered and thrust the thought away from her. No! No! She wanted to stay in control of things! She'd never give it over to a man again, ever!

Arthur Gilliam, coming out of his office, saw Olivia standing there, eyes closed, the play of changing emotions reflected on her lovely young face. He thought of going to her, of offering comfort, and then talked himself out of it.

He shook his head miserably. Why couldn't he fall in love with someone like Olivia, simple and straightforward and uncomplicated? Why did he have to fall for a woman who had it in her to break his heart?

He looked at the girl, standing slim and straight. Pretty as a picture in a book. But not the girl for him. It had nothing to do with looks. Cassie, if you were to analyze her, she was . . . why, a little coarse, really. Her ways were so very far removed from the days of innocence, of purity. Even her behavior in bed tended sometimes to shock him, even as he was caught up in the mood of sheer animal lust she generated when the spirit was upon her.

It didn't matter. It didn't matter a damn. He loved Cassie, coarse or not. His flesh cried out to hers. There was hardly a moment of the day when he didn't feel some sort of sexual need of her, and even when they were together, when she was deliciously naked before him, her eyes full of passion and her bed manners ravishingly uninhibited, he was thinking ahead to ways to prolong the moment, to make sure it would not go away too soon.

If only she would marry him!

His face twisted with pain. God! God! If only she'd been honest with him! If only he'd never learned what he'd learned! If only he could go back to that puzzled and disturbed innocence he'd known before he'd followed her that night! If only he could erase his foolish action, go back to the status quo, before he'd yielded to curiosity and spied on her!

Chapter 34

The conversation—if it could be called that—was conducted entirely in French. English was good enough for general use, in a city in which the old Creole influence was definitely on the wane; but in the household of a man like Henri Desmoulins family matters were discussed (or shouted) in the old language, fluid, expressive, even deadly when required.

"Please, Henri," his wife said for perhaps the tenth time. "I'm sure it isn't as bad as you say. Surely there must be an explanation."

"Bad?" The banker's eyes rolled heavenward, and his fat hands once again rolled into fists. "Good God, Felicite! Not as bad as . . . Tell me, how could it be worse? Eh? Tell me that. Oh, it *is* possible. She could have dallied with some drunken hoosier down on the Tchoupitoulas levee. She could have opened a bordello right in the middle of the city, trumpeting the name of Desmoulins far and wide. She could have gotten herself *enceinte* at the tender hands of some Negro in the middle of Congo Square, with the whole world watching. She could have been arrested by the gendarmes while doing the Danse Bamboula stark naked in front of a hundred blacks at one of the soirees presided over by Marie Laveau. She could have—"

"Papa! Please!" The girl wrung her hands angrily, desperately. "Please! The neighbors will hear! The—"

"Let them hear!" the banker said, pacing angrily back and forth before the open window. "Assuredly they will hear quickly enough. Why make them wait? Why put them to the expense of buying a newspaper when they can learn firsthand

246

from the aggrieved father that the offspring of Monsieur Desmoulins, of the Banque de Nouvelle-Orleans, has soiled her
reputation and her father's and mother's by getting herself in
a family way at the hands of the most thorough swine ever
to pollute the air of the unfortunate parish afflicted by him?
At the hands of a parvenu, a guttersnipe, an adventurer, a
cutpurse, a—"

"*Please*, Henri!" His wife hurriedly closed the window
and drew the curtain. "If you will not spare Odile, please,
for the love of heaven, think of my convenience and your
own. If you would only calm down for a moment—"

"Calm down? Calm down! I tell you, woman, if the boy's
father were here rather than gallivanting about the world, God
knows where, I would go to his house this moment and demand satisfaction! Not that it would do any good, I'm sure.
Rathbone has refused challenges, as only a man totally lacking in honor could do, too many times to make me think that
his sense of manhood can be restored at this late date. But at
the very least one might thrash him until he could not stand,
or—"

"Henry! Calm down, please!"

"Silence, woman! And get this—this shameless slut upstairs, and keep her there until I can think what to do. God
in heaven! Keep her under lock and key before she strips
naked and goes gallivanting down the streets of the city to
parade her shame and my misfortune before every friend and
enemy I have before—"

"Henri! Your heart!"

On the levee a celebration was in full swing. A gaily uniformed brass band was playing spirited jigs and reels with
deafening volume, and dancers in costume were capering on
the adjacent docks. A large crowd had gathered, but only
selected people—dignitaries, the city fathers, and certain large
shippers—were being allowed aboard the great steamship,
Memphis, to be given the grand tour in an atmosphere of
suitable pomp.

Standing on the deck, watching the dancers, Olivia could
look up and see Aurora Brand standing slim and straight and
queenly on the texas deck, talking to the mayor of the city.

Olivia thought Miss Brand had never looked more regally beautiful than now, speaking with animation and authority from her own deck, mistress of the great *Memphis* and the equal of anyone, man or woman, fit to be allowed aboard the shining vessel.

She'd had her own private tour, of course—she and Arthur, with only Miss Brand and Ben Samuels and Captain Falkner to guide them. It had been a special honor, one she'd never forget, and typical of the loyalty and consideration Miss Brand always showed to those near and dear to her. A pity poor Arthur, claiming illness, had begged off halfway through the tour and left the boat! He *did* look terrible: sunken eyes, drawn face, shaking hands.

"Olivia!" a voice cried out behind her. "Hey, Olivia Soames!" She turned unhurriedly, trying to place the familiar, high-pitched voice. Suddenly her heart beat fast with delight as she saw Inez Leblond, dark, thin, a happy grin on her face, bearing down on her to throw herself into her arms, squeezing her so hard that she couldn't get her breath for a moment.

Inez let her go, then stepped back, her hands on Olivia's shoulders. "Let me look at you. Well, well! Look at this! You're not the same girl at all, are you? Jean-Marie! Come here and look at this girl, will you? She's filled out a bit. Grown a little in the bosom, have you? My God, she's growing up. Next thing you know . . ."

But then the broad-shouldered little Cajun behind her caught up with them and was hugging Olivia as if she were family. *"Dieu!"* he said. "She *is* beautiful! Inez, go away. I will take up with this one. I will—"

"Vache!" the dark girl said, a wicked smile on her face. She turned back to Olivia. "We heard about the new boat. We thought it was a good excuse for coming to town to see you."

"How wonderful," Olivia said, scarcely able to contain her joy. "I'll show you the town. And . . ." Something made her look past them, to scan the docks. "Who else came with you?" she said. "Anyone I know?"

"Just us," Inez said. She looked at her husband. "Ah,"

she said, "I win my bet, Jean-Marie. You have to clean the fish all next month. Don't forget. I won't let you, anyway."

"I don't understand," Olivia said, looking from one to the other. "A bet? What about?"

"Why, whether or not you'd be asking about Zach," Inez said. "Don't try to fool me. That was who you were looking for, wasn't it? Well, get it out, girl, and don't try to beat about the bush with the likes of me." She looked in Olivia's eyes and read there something she'd expected to see. "Ah," she said knowingly. "Well, he did ask to be remembered to you. He'd have come himself if it hadn't been for Mr. Boyd coming back. Plenty to do just now. Always is, when Dallas Boyd's back in the parish." She smiled. "Zach's doing real well, honey. Boyd likes him. Trusts him. Best damn overseer he ever had, he said."

"I'm glad for him," Olivia said.

"Is that all?" Inez Leblond said irreverently. "Is that all you can say? My God, Olivia. What a stick of wood you can be sometimes."

Cassie Quayle paused in the doorway. "I was looking for Simon Halsey," she said warily.

"It's all right," Marc-Antoine Renault said. "He . . . ah . . . deputized me to act for him today. Come in, Miss Quayle. Or is it Mrs.? May I call you Cassie? I think we ought to get better acquainted. I—"

"I don't think so," the girl said, tight-lipped. She turned to go.

"Wait," the lawyer said. "You know, Halsey has told me everything." She paused in the doorway, looked at him over her shoulder with sudden hatred and turned slowly. "Everything," he repeated with a slow and insinuating emphasis. "The son up north . . . everything. I repeat: You and I ought to become better acquainted."

She came in and closed the door behind her. Her eyes blazed with bitterness and hatred. "So that's it?" she said in a low, controlled voice. "I'm to be passed on to you, too, am I? And you're interested for your usual reasons? And you like the touch of the tar brush a little too much for propriety, don't you, Renault? Can't get it up with white women, the way I hear it, and prefer to deal with women you can feel superior to, eh?''

Renault showed no feelings of shame at all. "One man's taste is not the next man's," he said blandly. His smile was snakelike. He moved toward her, not without a certain grace in the doing. "Come," he said. "I find you quite lovely. Particularly in this light, with those blue highlights in that marvelous hair."

She didn't move. She crossed her arms over her breasts. "Condescending bastard. Nigger lover. If only you knew what we think of you. All of us. Including your last three mistresses. Why, one of them told me you couldn't even—"

His hand, long and slender, lashed out and struck her in the face, hard. "Shut up!" he said in a voice made all the more deadly by its softness. "Don't you *ever* speak to me that way. Never!" He struck her again. Her hands went up, protecting her face; he grasped her by the hair and threw her heavily against the nearby wall. "Nigger slut! You mind your damned insolent tongue when you speak to me! You hear?" The hand whipped out again, backhanding her across the mouth. "You hear?"

Arthur Gilliam arrived just as Cassie came out of Halsey's rented office on the docks. Standing out of the lights, in the shadow of a warehouse, he watched the girl walk slowly, dejectedly, down the long catwalk to the shore. He had never seen anyone look so beaten, so defeated, so shamed. He ached to run to her, to comfort her, but something held him back.

Then what he was waiting for happened. He saw the door open again and Marc-Antoine Renault emerge, looking cautiously to and fro under the dim light of the lantern above the door. The lawyer's thin hand went up and turned off the lantern. Only then did he venture forth along the walkway, one barely visible hand running carefully along the rail.

Arthur's heart beat fast. It was true! It was true! She *had* been meeting with Rathbone's people! And betraying Miss Brand!

He leaned back against the warehouse wall, his face in his hands. *That* was why she had been sleeping with him. She'd been using him, using him and his helpless love for her to learn more about the workings of the Brand Line so that she could leak them out to Rathbone's people. And the "love" she'd shown him, the supposed passion she'd displayed, it was all a sham. He'd been a blind, stupid, infatuated pawn in her hands. In the grip of his mindless bondage to her he'd betrayed Miss Brand as well, however inadvertently. Good God!

He could no longer control himself. The sobs shook his gaunt body; he bent over, face in hands, and wept inconsolably. How could she? How could she have done it to him? Knowing his inexperience in matters of love, his helplessness in the face of the first real passion he'd ever felt, ever allowed himself to consummate?

Her voice, low and flat, interrupted his anguished thoughts. "Arthur?" she said. In a flash he straightened up and looked at her in horror. Framed in the lamplight, she stood looking at him in the shadows. "That is you, isn't it, Arthur?" She sighed. "Well, it had to come sooner or later." Her voice was tired, dry, empty of all feeling. She moved toward him and put one hand on his arm. He shook loose violently.

She stepped back. "I understand," she said. "I'd feel the same way myself. You feel I've betrayed you completely. I've profaned the feelings you have for me. I've . . ." She sighed and let her shoulders droop. "Well, I know it won't do any good to tell you I love you, Arthur, will it?" He didn't—couldn't—answer. He couldn't look at her. His hands covered his face again as he sobbed silently.

She shook her head. "I didn't at first," she said in that flat voice. "At first I couldn't feel anything but shame, shame at what I was being forced to do, spying on Miss Brand, using you to do it, faking feelings I didn't feel."

"P-please," he said miserably. "Please . . ."

"Oh, no," she said. "I don't mean to hurt you. But at first all I could feel was the shame. There wasn't any room for any other feeling. That and hatred of Simon, and what he had made of me with his threats and beatings and blackmail. And now—now Renault too. I've been passed down to him. And he likes to beat women as well. Arthur? Will you look at me, Arthur?'' She stepped back into the light and held the hair back from her face.

He looked up in horror. One of her battered eyes was swollen half shut; there was a dried line of blood that ran down from one nostril, down the puffy lips to her chin. ''C-Cassie,'' he said. ''Oh, my God.''

''That's Renault,'' she said. ''He's a fool. When Simon beats me, he takes pains to see that it doesn't show. Nights after something like that, my dear, I keep the lights turned low when you and I are together and make sure I'm gone by the first light.'' The voice was still flat and lifeless. ''I suppose I ought to make all that past tense,'' she said, ''because it's all over now, isn't it?'' She smiled bitterly through her bruises. ''Well, for the record, Arthur, I *did* come to love you. And I *did* come to feel the passion I'd been faking before. Eventually any woman would come to love you, I think. And if it hadn't been for all this hatefulness, I'd have been perfectly happy to spend my life with you.'' She sighed, shook her head, and turned away from the light. ''But—well, things were the way they were,'' she said. ''I guess I'm glad in a way that it's all coming out now. Really I am. At last I can be straight with you. Or . . . or can I, Arthur?'' She looked into his eyes now, hard. ''Or don't you want to hear?''

''Cassie,'' he said hoarsely. ''Oh, my God.'' He reached out one trembling hand. ''My God.''

''Come,'' she said, taking his hand. ''Come walk with me, Arthur. I have a story to tell you. And this time I'll hold back nothing. You're stronger—stronger than you think you are. I think you can take it.''

''Cassie, I didn't know. I didn't mean—''

''Hush now. Hush, my dear. Just hold my hand and walk with me. And listen. I have to say it. I *have* to. There can't be any more dishonesty, any more holding back. We have so little time left together.''

Chapter 35

Late the same night Ben Samuels, a dark coat covering his peacock finery, climbed the stairs of a rickety, decaying wooden structure on Iberville Street, down near the river. At the top of the stairs he knocked—once, twice. Then a pause and another knock.

The door cracked open; a thin line of light appeared. A body blocked the doorway. "Who's there?" a rough voice said. "Oh. Oh, it's you, sir." The chain was loosed and the door opened, but not before the lantern that had provided the only interior light had been half covered.

Samuels watched as the speaker uncovered the lantern again. "Well, Mack?" he said. "Where's Ragland? I expected to find him here too." He took a chair behind the round oak table and sat down after taking off his coat and draping it casually over the square chair back.

Mack Leggett sat down opposite him, waving a bottle of liquor. "You'll have some, sir? No? Well, sir, here's lookin' at yer." He tipped up the bottle and drank. "Quint's followin' up a lead, sir. Truth is, sir, he's over in Algiers workin' for Rathbone's brat, sir. Neither of us could go to work direckly for Halsey, if yer get my meanin'. But the Rathbone cub don't know us from Mary an' Joseph."

"Good, good," Samuels said. "I gather you've got a line into Halsey's camp by now?"

"Yes, sir. Not as good as we'd like. But puttin' two an' two together, sir—me an' Quint, that is—I can tell yer there's trouble brewin' between Halsey an' Rathbone's whelp."

Samuels took a long cigar out of his vest, cut it, and lit it.

He blew a thin cloud of blue smoke upward in the flickering light. "I anticipated that," he said. "But there's more, isn' there?"

"Yes, sir. Quint thinks the puppy is plannin' somethin' Somethin' damn big. He don't know what just yet, but it': somethin' nobody but a Rathbone tad would think up. A rea bastard, Quint says he is. Quint can hardly look hisself in the eye, doin' what he done for the tad over acrost the river."

"I understand. There'll be a bonus if you turn up anything I can't keep you from having to go through all this, Mack but I can buy you what will help you forget it."

Leggett tipped the bottle at him with a broken-toothed grin "Right, sir. But Quint says he thinks the two of 'em, Halsey and the boy, they're fixin' to try to put each other outer busi ness. I wouldn't put it past the sprout to cut some poor bas tard's tripes out for him and make it look like Halsey done it."

Samuels gestured with the cigar. "Well," he said, "keep on top of things and keep me posted daily if you can. By messenger, if you can find a reliable one. I've just had word that Rathbone—Laird, the old man—is headed back for town. As you can imagine, that's a new wild card in the deck, and it makes all of us nervous. See what you can find out, without being too conspicuous about it." He rose. "And the moment you hear anything—about Rathbone's whereabouts or what he's up to, anything at all—get the word to me immediately.""

"Right, sir. Too quick to talk about it."

Aurora Brand had slept on the *Memphis* that night, in her private cabin. In the morning, after coffee in the main cabin with Seth Falkner, she stepped out on the main deck and looked down to the dock, to see Olivia standing talking to a dark-haired couple at the foot of the gangplank. She leaned over the rail and called out: "Olivia! Come on up!"

As the three boarded, Ben Samuels, as impeccably dressed as ever, came out of the office. "You asked me to remind you," he said. "The French consul will be here in ten minutes for the grand tour. That coincides with the visit, I believe, of the mayor of St. Louis. Might as well kill two birds with one stone."

The three appeared at the top of the stairway now, and
Aurora smiled at them. "Ben," she said. "The French consul and the mayor of St. Louis can wait, I think. Could you
take them in for coffee while I show our friends around?"
She held out hands to Olivia's companions. "I remember
you," she told Jean-Marie Leblond. "I owe you for what you
did for Olivia, the night of the old *Memphis* explosion." She
turned to his wife and said, "You must be Olivia's friend,
Inez. I'm so happy to meet you. Any good friend of Olivia's
is a friend of mine."

The tour they took was a necessarily short one but unhur-
ried; Aurora took pains to make Olivia's friends feel at home
aboard the glittering vessel. They visited the pilothouse, a
lacy gazebo housing the top few degrees of a vast wooden
wheel twice a man's height, and Olivia was thrilled to hear
the pilot's apprentice tell of Aurora Brand—"the best gosh-
darned pilot on the river, ma'am, when she's in touch with
it"—acting as her own steersman below Natchez in the *Memphis*'s maiden voyage a day before. Then they looked into the
palatial main cabin, with its stained-glass windows, intricate
scrollwork, white columns connected with lacy arches, and
Brussels carpeting; at the end of the promenade a huge mirror
created the illusion of a room double its already impressive
length.

The cabins themselves were trimmed expensively with wal-
nut or rosewood and were elaborately furnished; one even
housed a grand piano. As they turned to go, Olivia cleared
her throat discreetly. "Ma'am," she said, "your visitors must
be waiting."

"It's all right," Aurora said. "They'll keep. Incidentally,
I expected to see your friend McClellan. Didn't he come?"

"Oh, no," Inez said. "Mr. Boyd had some pretty pressing
things to do when he got back—" She stopped and looked at
Olivia helplessly. "Listen to me," she said wryly. "Me and
my big mouth . . ."

"It's all right," Aurora said. "I knew Dallas was back and
lying low for now. I take some pains to keep myself informed. I know about his little adventure in Natchez, with
Basil too." She smiled wryly at Olivia. "Basil never could

fool me for long. You should have heard the absurd storie
he told me, explaining the wound on his hand.''

Thus she passed off the subject lightly. But Olivia ha
caught the look in her eye, and so had Inez. Behind her slir
back, as they descended to the boiler deck, the two ex
changed glances.

''*Pauvre petite,*'' Jean-Marie half whispered, mouthing th
words almost silently.

Back in the *quartier*, Cassie Quayle sat down opposite th
lovely, exquisitely dressed young octoroon woman and lifte
her veil with both hands. ''Here,'' she said. ''This is wha
he did to me last night.'' One eye was closed; her face nov
bore visible bruises and scratches all over. Her one good ey
blazed with a dull, aching hatred. ''I'm sure,'' she said bit
terly, ''that this sort of thing is not news to you.''

''No,'' Agnes Maritain said coolly, ''only I didn't know
he'd broadened his tastes in such matters to white women
Ordinarily . . .''

''I'm not white,'' Cassie said. ''I'm . . . I'm passing.
have a son up north who doesn't know. I thought I coul
protect him, but I can't. Halsey knows, and now Renault. It'
been a stick to beat me with, when beatings didn't work.'
She half smiled, bitterly, but her battered lips didn't coop
erate. The smile was a travesty. ''I suppose it's what I get fo
trying to be what I'm not. But I'd hoped that my son—''

''You hush!'' Agnes Maritain said, her brown, almos
black, eyes bright with an angry fire. ''You hush now. Don'
you ever go blaming yourself. That's what they want. It takes
the guilt off them. You know what I mean?'' She paused fo
a moment to let what she'd said sink in. Then she called ove
her shoulder: ''Achille! Achille, come here!''

Cassie looked up to see a huge, powerfully built half-caste
male appear in the doorway, all but filling it. Agnes didn'
wait for his answer. ''You heard what she said?'' Her voice
was icy with rage. ''You see her?''

''I see her,'' the big man said in a rumbling bass. ''So?''

''So . . .'' Cassie sighed tiredly. She hadn't slept that nigh
after telling Arthur the whole story and watching his broker
reactions. ''I . . . I saved my money. I was going to send i

o my son. But now it may be better to spend it trying to
make sure a certain telegram doesn't get sent. If Philip finds
out who he is just now—"

"I understand," the big man said, his deep voice almost
silky now. "And save your money." He looked at Agnes
Maritain, nodded, and looked back at Cassie's battered face.
"I'd rot ten thousand years in hell for taking money for something like that." He stepped forward and laid one huge hand
ever so gently on the dark girl's shoulder; Agnes Maritain
laid her smooth cheek against the tanned hand affectionately.
"After what he did to this girl, and now you . . ."

Agnes Maritain looked up at him. "You're sure?" she said.
"It's time for that?"

"No," the mulatto said in that frightening voice, so deadly,
so gentle. "The time was when he was in his cradle. But we
can't wait longer. He has to go now. No later." He turned to
Cassie again. "Keep your money. Save it in a sock for your
boy. Guard it with your life."

"You're going to . . . to kill him?" Cassie said, her expression unreadable.

"With these hands," the big man said softly. "As quietly
as I can manage it. And as slowly." He looked at the black-
haired woman who now held his big brown hand. "And once
I'm done, I'll sleep better than I have in years—since I met
Agnes, here, and she told me."

"Goodness," Cassie said. She looked at the other woman
in horror. "How long has Renault . . . ?"

The octoroon woman didn't answer for a moment. Cassie
tried to gauge her age. Twenty-eight, perhaps? Thirty? "He
paid the nuns at the orphanage for me," she said in a flat,
dull voice. "He told them he and his sister wanted to raise
me, to be responsible for me. It sounded legitimate enough.
People have done that before with the *gens du couleur*. It
sounds philanthropic. But the moment I was away from the
orphanage, he set me up here, with a nanny to watch after
me and keep me coiffured, well dressed, ready for him. He
has visited me promptly every Tuesday and Friday ever since.
The only thing that has changed has been the increasingly
bizarre means that had to be employed to combat his first
sporadic, then almost complete, impotence."

"A . . . a nanny, you say?" Cassie croaked in a voice hoarse with unshed tears. "My God, how old were you when he set you up, Agnes?"

"Why, thirteen," she said, her voice cool and calm, a voice from beyond the grave and all forgiveness. "He liked them young in those days. When I met Achille here. . . ." She sighed. "We would have liked to have had a child, once Renault was disposed of. But three weeks before my fourteenth birthday Renault brought me a disease. It turned out to be the most effective form of birth control this side of death. Achille is cheated. So am I, I suppose." She kissed the big brown hand as it tightened up involuntarily. "But . . . no. I could have been cheated worse. I might never have met Achille."

"He dies," the big brown man said softly. "He dies tonight."

Aurora Brand stepped into the big C-spring coach facing Ben Samuels after calling up to the driver and telling him her destination. She settled herself into the cushions and opened her briefcase. "Not a bad day's business, I'd say," she said, smiling down at the papers in her lap. "One or two more like this and we're within a couple of leagues of landing in the black."

The coach picked up speed as traffic thinned, jouncing lightly over the rutted street. Ben laced his thin fingers together and looked at her. "Yes," he said. "Cross a few fingers. Incidentally, have you seen Arthur Gilliam today?"

"Yes. I sent him home. He looked terrible. He must be coming down with something."

"Yes," Samuels said, "but nothing physical. Something's bothering him, eating away at him. I'll ask him point-blank in a day or so." He looked out of the window, started, and in a flash stuck his head out to call out to the driver. "Driver! Stop here, please!" He was out on the street and through the narrow door before the coach had come to a complete stop.

Aurora let the papers fall into her lap. She stared after him, one beautifully arched brow higher than the other, her lovely lips pursed. "Ben?" she said. "Ben, are you there?"

But now Samuels was climbing back into the coach and

bellowing an order to the driver. "Driver! Back to the docks! Quickly, man, quickly!" He sat down, winded, a sheaf of crumpled papers in his hand, and looked at her, gasping for breath. "I . . . I saw some urchin with a stack of handbills," he said. "By chance I caught a word or two . . . it couldn't wait. But see for yourself." He handed one of the papers across.

Aurora read it openmouthed.

NEW ORLEANS,
NATCHEZ AND VICKSBURG PACKET.
STEAMER ANDREW JACKSON.
Captain Jacob Cutler, Master.

Length of Hull,	307 feet
Width of Beam,	44 feet
Depth of Hold,	10 feet
Diameter of Wheel,	44 feet
Length of Bucket,	16 feet

Eight Boilers, 34 feet.
40 inches diameter and 2 Flues.
Two 34-inch Cylinders, 10-feet Stroke.
Extreme Height, 119 feet, six inches.
Capacity for 5,500 bales cotton.

Aurora looked up. "But the *Andrew Jackson*, is docking today. I read it in the paper. It sounds like a magnificent boat. Whose is it?"

"You're slipping," Ben Samuels said, white-faced with shock. "Or you're forgetting your ancient history. There was a *Jackson* before—back in your father's time. It burned. The owner's firm retains the right to the name. My God, my God. And it's docking today, you say?"

"Yes," Aurora said, remembering. "Yes. It had slipped my mind. Rathbone's back with his new flagship. The answer to the *Memphis*."

Chapter 36

"You can't mean it," Todd Rathbone said, straightening his tie and giving himself a final once-over in the pier glass. "You're not going? Why, it'll be the biggest event in town in ages. And Father . . ."

"Father doesn't need me or my approval," Ward said. "Not just now, anyway. He'll be in his glory. He'll have upstaged Aurora Brand, made a triumphant return, and impressed everybody south of Vicksburg all in one day. Nothing you or I can do will detract from that." He brushed lint off his coat and prepared to go. "Besides, I'm busy today. I'll see him later and congratulate him. You can handle the felicitations today. All right?"

Todd looked at his brother. Ward was thinner, more intense—"Drawn fine," as his mother used to say. It was as if he'd been tested in some sort of flame, one that had burned away all the baby fat and had taken all trace of youthful softness and vulnerability with it. "W—ward," he said timidly, "when Father finds out . . . I mean, about Odile."

Ward turned savagely to him and almost spat out his words. "Mind your own goddamned business. I'll take care of that when the time comes. Do you hear? You just tend to your knitting—or whatever you do with your time." He turned on one heel and strode to the doorway. Todd could hear his heels pounding on the stairs as he went down.

Passing the parlor, Ward stopped dead and looked the visitor up and down with angry eyes. "What are you doing in here?'' he said in a brutal tone. "Who in hell's name let you in? By God, I'll have his hide!''

The farmer, dressed in his shabby Sunday go-to-meetin' best and holding his shapeless hat in his two hands, could barely get his words out at first because he was stammering. Then he tried again. "I . . . I beg your pardon, Mr. Rathbone, but Mr. Mercer said, over at the office in Algiers—''

"I know what the goddamned hell Mercer said,'' Ward said brusquely. "I told him to say it. I told him to tell you you're out, Paxton, at the end of the month. If I could legally put you out before that, you can bet your greasy little soul I'd have done that.''

"But, sir . . .''

"There aren't any buts. There isn't any appeal. Do you get that? I told you to increase the yield on the property in question or I'd find someone who would. You've had your year. Are you going to stand there and seriously try to tell me—''

"Well, no, sir. I can't. You know that. But havin' us out just now, with my wife expectin' and two of my young-uns ailin' . . .''

"Tell it to someone else. Tell it to the circuit rider next time he comes by your house to preach hellfire and damnation at you and eat you out of house and home. But don't waste it on me. I'm not the proper audience.'' The glint in his eye was cold and deadly. Paxton, the farmer in charge of Tract Sixteen, shrank back before the sheer insensate cruelty of it. "That's all, Paxton. Do you hear? If you're not off the grounds in one minute, so help me God, I'll have you removed bodily.'' He reached for the umbrella stand and took out a stout walking stick. "Or maybe I'll not call for help. It'd be a distinct pleasure to handle that particular chore myself if you . . .''

But with one last anguished glance backward, Paxton was already beating a hasty retreat.

"My God,'' Aurora Brand said in a half whisper meant for Ben Samuels's ear alone. "It's . . . it's magnificent.''

"So it is,'' Samuels said, looking from one end to the other of the gorgeous vessel. "If it were anyone but Rathbone putting up the money, I'd say he beggared himself paying for it." He sighed and took a long, slim cigar out of a vest pocket. "You'll forgive me for smoking, ma'am? The distraction would come in handy just now, I think."

"Oh, yes," Aurora said. "Look, there's Seth. And that's Captain Cutler he's talking to." She waved the two nearer and watched them walk slowly toward her along the dock. "Perhaps we can learn a thing or two from a moment's chat with him."

Seth Falkner attended to the introductions with economy. "Jake's an old friend of mine, ma'am, from my first days on the river. He's been working the upper reaches so long, I'd near forgotten him altogether. But if I'd known he was at liberty and willing to work Gulf waters, I'd have hired him in a moment."

"Captain Falkner is too kind," Cutler said. "Tell me, ma'am—if it's not impertinent to ask—did you really pilot the *Memphis* down from Natchez?"

"Why, yes, I did," Aurora said, noting the skepticism in the old captain's eye. "I remembered what I learned from the first days when I was rebuilding the line my father left me. I couldn't afford to hire any more personnel, so I had to learn a lot of the jobs myself, both aboard and on dry land."

"Ah, yes," the captain said. "And coming down, ma'am, if I might ask, how did you make the crossing in the shoal water below Island Forty-three? It's just a point of record, ma'am, but . . ."

Aurora thought a moment; then she smiled knowingly. "Shoal water, Captain? Our leadsmen found water fit to float a saltwater vessel below Island Forty-three. Quarter less three, and we weren't drawing nine."

Captain Cutler wasn't about to let it go that easily, for all the slowly dawning understanding in his brown eyes. "But the bluff reef opposite—"

"Bluff reef, Captain? Where? Crossing below Island Forty-three, you go inside the first snag above the point. As I recall, you go outside the next one, start out from the lower end of the wood yard, make a square crossing, and—"

"Ah, yes. Yes, I'd forgotten."

"Had you, now, Captain?" She smiled that beguiling smile

of hers, the one that said she knew she was being sold. "Bluff reef indeed. There was a wind reef, to be sure, but the worst apprentice on the river could run it with a bucket on his head, Captain. There's no bottom at all on that crossing. You couldn't find bottom there with a church steeple."

The captain smiled and tipped his hat gallantly. "My compliments, ma'am. And if I may say so, ma'am, if you ever get tired of running a steamship line . . . well, there'll always be a place for you in *my* pilothouse." He nodded his head to the others. "Gentlemen, it's been my pleasure."

Aurora winked at Seth Falkner. "What did you learn?" she said. "I gather you've been given the tour."

"Ah, yes," Falkner said, digging his pipe out of his side pocket. "Frankly, ma'am, it's quite a vessel. Perhaps the equal of the *Memphis* itself. Perhaps even . . ." He fiddled with a penknife and cleaned the pipe as he spoke. "Rathbone's making grandiose claims about the speed of the *Jackson*. Jake says he's bought space in the papers. I wouldn't be surprised to see him issue some sort of challenge."

"Challenge?" Ben Samuels said. "What do you mean?"

"He means Rathbone will claim he has the fastest vessel on the river," Aurora said soberly. "And he'll dare any and all other lines to match her, here to Natchez or Memphis or wherever."

"To St. Louis, ma'am," Seth Falkner said soberly. "All the way. Rathbone means to lay down the gauntlet, not only to you but to every steamship owner south of the Keokuk locks. And I have to say this: From what Jake told me, he'll run the knickers off ninety percent of the boats on the river."

"I don't doubt it, Seth," Aurora said, her voice quite serious. "But is the *Memphis* truly the fastest?"

Falkner, hesitated, lighting his pipe. "Who knows, ma'am?" he said. "But I'll tell you, anybody who could beat the *Jackson*, given what I see of her and what Jake tells me . . . why, that someone would right nigh *own* the river south of St. Louis. Own it, I say."

Marc-Antoine Renault, weaving slightly, stood before the large, graceful oak door to the suite of rooms he'd rented so many years before, fumbling in his pocket for keys. In the dim light he couldn't tell one key from the next on his crowded key ring.

"Goddamned worthless nigger bastards," he muttered under his breath. "Can't count on a one of 'em, whether it's lighting a room properly or . . ."

He found the key now and stepped back to get a better look at the keyhole. The key wavered teasingly before his bleary eyes. He cursed softly and tried to get his eyes in focus. Perhaps, he thought for a moment, perhaps he shouldn't have stopped for drinks. Or perhaps not quite so many of them. But it was getting harder and harder to face Agnes without something strong to drink beforehand. She never said anything, of course—she wouldn't dare—but that look in her eyes . . . it was unmanning him more and more these days. And it was difficult enough beforehand without . . .

There! The key went into the lock and turned over the tumblers. He opened the door and stepped into half darkness. Darkness! "Agnes?" he said in an irritable voice. "Agnes, are you there? Why isn't this light on?" He stepped into the room, and, swearing lightly, reached into his vest for the little container of lucifers he always carried.

The door suddenly slammed behind him. "Goddammit!" he said, and moved toward the door. He couldn't even find the lamp without the little light that had come through the open door.

The first touch on his shoulders was gentle. The two huge hands descended, almost caressing him. Then, unhurriedly, they moved to his neck. First there was no pressure, then gentle pressure, then heavier pressure.

And then there was pain, pain beyond anything he'd ever felt before. Renault tried to cry out, but somehow he couldn't seem to get any air. He clawed ineffectually at the powerful hands, hands that were inexorably easing him down from the near darkness of the room into a greater darkness, one in which the pain would be no more.

"Quickly," Achille said, "we haven't much time. The ship leaves in an hour." He dragged Renault's body into the other room and spoke from there. "Agnes," he said, "the things I took from his pocket, have you looked at them?"

"Yes, Achille," the girl said. "And there's a great deal of money there, Achille. Too much to count just now. But—"

"It's all right. Slip it into the secret pocket of my coat. And the jewels, they'll go in the false bottom of your bag. Mind you, they have to stay out of sight all the way to Valparaiso. You don't dare trust a man on board. And while I can protect you on land, on shipboard it's another story. We have to look, you know, only moderately prosperous. If they even suspect we have this much on us . . ."

"I understand." She sighed and looked at the half-closed door that barred him from her. "Achille, if I could help you—"

"No, no," he said, coming back out again. "Don't look. You won't like what you see. Even if it *is* Renault." He looked at the two bags beside her. "All right. You've got everything?"

"Yes, my darling. I've got you. What else would I need?"

Halsey pounded on the door. "Renault!" he said. "Goddammit, open up. You were due in my office at nine tonight. I need your signature on some papers that . . ."

Then, somehow, it occurred to him for the first time to try the door. Miraculously it opened easily under his hand. He stepped cautiously inside, looking around. So this was how a nigger lover kept his high-yaller whore! God, it was better than he, Halsey, had ever lived in his life. Look at that chandelier! Look at those pictures on the wall!

"Renault!" he said. "Get your ass out here! Kick the little chippie out of bed and struggle into your drawers. Rathbone's back, and we've got some explaining to do about a couple of things. You, too, shyster. If he finds out what you did about that Barbour and McCann contract . . ."

He couldn't wait any longer. With an angry sneer on his face he strode forward into the next room, shoving open the half-open door. "Goddammit, Renault—" He stopped and looked up.

Renault's body, inert, hung from a clothing hanger on the wall. His shirt and stock were open. There were horrible bruises on his bare neck. His face was a horrid sight, bloated, twisted. His tongue protruded grotesquely. His eyes were wide open, as if in his last moments he had looked into hell itself.

"Oh, my God," Halsey said. "My God."

Cassie Quayle walked with small, quick steps down the long boardwalk. At the end she turned and walked up the rickety outside stairs of the building that stood on tall stilts at the water's edge. She knocked on the door at the top of the stairs.

"Who's there?" a voice said through the door that was suddenly opened a crack.

"I . . . I was sent by a friend, Tom Sharp. He said to use his name."

The door opened and the man inside stepped back to let her by. For one quick moment she caught sight of his face in the dim light, scarred and unshaven, and steeled herself against the self-loathing she felt for what she had to ask this man to do. "Tom Sharp, eh?" the man said. He shut the door behind her and looked her up and down. "What do you need from me, girl? Speak up now."

"I—I need a man killed. Quickly. No questions."

"Killed, eh?" His grin was terrible, worse than his scowl. "And this is somethin' Tom Sharp says you can find here, eh? You wouldn't be from the police, would you?" He reached out and took her roughly by the arm. "Speak up, there, girl."

"No!" she said, twisting free. "Look, it's a matter of pressing importance. If this man isn't dead by . . . my God, it has to be as fast as possible, before he can . . ." She swallowed and went on. "I'll pay you whatever you ask. I've got some money saved."

"Money?" he said, looking her over again, appraising her like so much horseflesh. "Well, money has its uses. But there are other things a girl like you might have to trade."

She looked him in the eye and winced, but she firmed her back, pursed her lips, and made the choice. "All right," she said. "But afterward, it's urgent that this man—"

"It'll wait *that* long," he said with a low and unpleasant

laugh, taking a bottle from the shelf beside him and pulling the cork. "Meanwhile, girlie, maybe a little payment on account, eh? And then you can tell me the details?" He drank, then put the bottle down. "Here, now. Let me help you out of that coat."

Chapter 37

The first rays of dawn found Cassie walking slowly homeward, her eyes on the ground before her plodding feet. Ordinarily, in an after-hours situation like this, she'd be traveling in the night streets with the utmost circumspection, hugging the walls, looking out into every street before venturing forth along one of them, as cautious as a mouse in the field. But now . . . now she moved like a person sleepwalking, oblivious to her surroundings.

The deed was done. She'd set in motion all that it would take to end things once and for all. Her own life was over, wasted, thrown away.

She half shrugged; the impotence and despair in her heart was now just a dull ache instead of sharp pain. Had she ever had so much as the ghost of a chance to make it in this world? Or had the cards been stacked from the beginning? Well, perhaps it didn't matter. It certainly wasn't worth bandying about now, now that it was all over. The main thing was to make sure Halsey didn't have the time—or decide to take the time—to go through with this threat to send the telegram to Philip and to Philip's headmaster at school. If she could head off these disasters, prevent them from happening, perhaps the terrible events of yesterday and today would not have been in vain.

Of today! She shuddered, thinking of it. Today was, if anything, worse than the day before. At least she hadn't had to watch the death of Renault. And afterward, Achille, meeting her at the docks before boarding with Agnes for South America and the Cape, had spared her the details like the strong and protective man he was, telling her only, "The deed's done, Cassie. Now do your best to forget about it. *We* intend to."

Oh, if she only could talk herself into believing that was possible! But she knew it wouldn't be. She knew she'd carry the horror and the guilt to her death, just as she'd carry her past and present shame. All the better, then, if death came soon. There wasn't much left to live for. If she could protect Philip from knowing the truth, from the terrible consequences of having others learn about it, too . . . well, that would be something. She could die easily after that.

Suddenly, for no apparent reason, she found herself thinking about Arthur Gilliam. And while the first reaction to the thought was a pang, a sharp stab of guilt for her deception of him, her two-faced assault on poor Arthur's innocent and trusting nature, there was a sudden and surprising undertone there of—of what? Of some new emotion she could not put a name to.

Arthur . . .

Now the nameless emotion turned to sadness: an aching, forlorn, heart-tearing longing. *Arthur!* If only things had been different! If only there'd been some sort of woebegone chance for them, no matter how slim, no matter how long the odds.

To her surprise Arthur, innocent when she'd met him, had proven a surprisingly apt pupil in the arts of love: lusty and robust, for all his skinny arms and chest. He was warm and comforting when that was what she'd needed, and gallant and strong.

Yes, *strong*! The thought came to her as a bit of a surprise now. The truth was, despite her continual and burgeoning guilt over her many betrayals of him, hadn't she in fact leaned upon him the whole time? Hadn't she drawn from Arthur's selfless and adoring love the strength to get by all this time, to get up each day and fight whatever sort of battle she could against the horror and degradation of her life? The strength she'd tried to pass along in her letters to Philip in this last year—where else could she have found that but in Arthur's arms?

She stopped now, leaned back against the wall of a warehouse, put her hands over her face, and wept like a child, inconsolably, from the very depths of her being.

Simon Halsey reached for the bottle beside him. His hand clumsily knocked it aside, spilling it onto the sawdust floor. "G-goddamn," he said in a thick voice. "Here! More!" he cried at the tavern keeper. "Bring more!" He fumbled in his vest, extracted a coin or two, dropped them on the table. "Don't worry 'bout money . . . bring more."

The tavern keeper turned up at his side, holding a second— or fourth? fifth?—bottle in his hand, looking down at Halsey with a skeptical eye. "Are you sure about this?" he said. "Frankly, friend, you look like a man who could use a good night's sleep. You've put away enough for a dozen stevedores already."

"Give it here," Halsey said in a voice meant to be threatening but one that reflected his extreme fatigue. "Goddamn insolence. Take money. Here." He reached out, snagged the bottle, tore it free. The tavern keeper hesitated for a moment, then he scooped up the coins and moved away. Halsey was the only customer left, other than a drunken tar sleeping it off in the far corner. Ordinarily it might be a time for clearing the hall, but the cut of Halsey's clothing tended to suggest a man of means, a man who might have powerful friends. He pondered the matter, polishing a glass idly, and decided to give Halsey one more bottle when he finished this one.

At the table Halsey drank morosely, hands shaking so badly that he could not manage a glass more than half full. "Has to be," he said to himself in a low voice. "Has to be Rathbone's cub. And I'd be next, wouldn't I? Next in line. The boy's made up his mind. He's goin' to move in on the old man . . . knows the old man can't run it all anymore."

Yes, he'd be next. But how? Surely the cub would know he was no match for him, for Simon Halsey. No, it wouldn't be any sort of direct confrontation. Matter of fact, he hadn't done anything like that with Renault, had he? No, sir. Renault's neck had been broken by a pair of hands the size of . . .

He drank again and spat up the drink, suddenly feeling the imagined pressure of those huge hands—whose?—on his own neck, feeling the pressure, feeling the . . . *"Ahhh!"* he said in a half whisper, clutching his neck. And again came the sudden spasm of fear: icy, paralyzing fear.

How? Who? When would death come? Where would it find him? What sort of assassins would the boy have waiting for him around some corner?

He sat up, putting the glass down with a trembling hand, and forced his eyes into focus. "You," he said to the tavern keeper. "Come here." He gestured, once, twice. "Damn it, I said come here."

The tavern keeper reached below the bar for his bung starter, then he looked at Halsey and thought better of it. "What do you want?" he asked cautiously. "I can hear you from here."

Halsey swiveled around, facing him. "All right," he said in a hoarse croak. "I need a couple of men. Good rough customers who can handle themselves in a fight. I'll pay good money."

The man looked at him, at his clothes. He thought for a moment and apparently made up his mind. "I might know someone," he said. "How long you need 'em?"

"Long's it takes," Halsey said. "But need 'em . . . God, I need 'em right now. Somebody layin' for me. You understand? Can't go home." He belched softly, wiped his bleary eyes. "Need somebody can handle a gun. Whatever."

"Now?" the barkeep said. "You need 'em right now?"

"You heard me," Halsey said. His tone had gained some strength with his decision. His hand no longer shook on the whiskey glass.

Arthur Gilliam stood in the doorway, blinking the sleep out of his eyes. "C-Cassie," he said. He looked at her battered face under the makeup and winced. "Oh, Cassie . . . what's happened to you?" He looked around, at the long, rickety staircase that led up the side of his house to his little room, at the empty streets below. "What have they done to you.?"

"Arthur," she said, "just let me in. And . . . and hold me. Please. Hold me."

• • •

Ward Rathbone let himself in and, shoes in hand, tiptoed softly toward the stairs. With the other hand he rubbed the sleepiness out of his eyes and yawned cavernously.

"Well?" a familiar voice boomed from the parlor. "Is this the way you mend your ways? Is this the way you show me you're going to settle down and stop acting like a colt in heat?"

Ward turned, one stockinged foot already on the first step. "Father," he said. "I didn't want to wake you up. I . . ."

"Oh, come now," his father said, his voice heavy with sarcasm. "Don't try that one on me. Not again."

Ward looked at his father and saw with a shock that the Laird Rathbone who had come back from the East was a different man: thinner, more drawn, older. Much older than the one year he'd been gone. There were great circles under his eyes, and the formerly square face, with its bulging jowls under the sideburns, was now an angular one in which you could see the bones. And the lines. And the effect of a year's suffering. "Father," he said. "I . . . I meant to come back for the landing. People told me it was a great success."

"So it was," Laird told his son. "With you or without you. While you were off cavorting in some parlorhouse . . ."

Ward stepped down onto the floor and threw his shoes angrily onto the carpet between them. "All right, now, god-dammit!" he said. "That's quite enough of that. I haven't been off in any whorehouse, and you know it. You—"

"Don't you speak up to me, you puppy!" Rathbone said, stepping forward, clenching his fists threateningly. But Ward looked in his eye now and saw that the old fire was gone. And the expensive clothes hung on his father's reduced frame and didn't fit him well at all anymore.

Ward shook his head. "You know what I *have* been doing?" he said in an acid tone. "I've been tending to business. And let me tell you, if anyone else besides me had been doing that, the family business wouldn't be in the shape it's in. But Halsey's let the Brand woman steal a march on him right and left, let her rebuild her damned business while he looked on, unable to think of anything to do to stop her. And Renault can't be pried away from his nigger wenches down in the *quartier*—and *you've* been off God alone knows where, building yourself expensive toys. And I've been left here to hold together the remnants of what was once an empire. And *this* is the thanks I get for it! Someone calling me out, shouting at me as if I were some sort of catchpenny chicken stealer, calling me names—''

"Eh?" Rathbone said, taken aback by his son's new aggressiveness. "Well, explain yourself. What have you been up to? Coming in like this in the middle of the night, what am I to think?''

Ward looked him up and down, the rage boiling in his heart. "I'm to make accounting in the middle of the night, then, as you put it? I'm to 'explain' myself, am I?'' He sneered, shaking his head angrily. "I'll be damned if I will. For the record, I've been in Algiers, tending to your damned business. As for what I've done with it, ask your goddamned accountants. Ask them on company time so it won't cost you extra money. But if you're used to thinking of me as the sort of stinking lick-spittle who'll stand here and let you curse him out the way you've been doing just now—well, you may have a surprise or two coming.''

"Surprise, eh? What kind of surprise?''

"You'll find that I may, dear Father, have just begun to find myself, as you used to put it. I may be just beginning to show the world what kind of aptitude I have for business. They'll tell you I'm a little on the rapacious side. I think that's the word they're using these days, or maybe they've changed to *bloodthirsty* or some such rodomontade. It doesn't matter a damn to me. But the same people will admit to you that I'm doing well for myself. *And* for you, let me remind you.''

Laird Rathbone stared narrow-eyed at his son. He didn't say anything for a moment, watching as Ward reached down and picked up his shoes. "Go on," he said.

"All right." Ward's tone was far from contrite. There was instead a kind of cocky arrogance in it, daring his father to disapprove. "Every other aspect of your business but the trickle you put in my hands last year—*every* other one— they've all lost ground. You've lost ground in the shipping business, in the cartage business''—he ticked them off on his fingers—''in import-export, in your land speculation, and in your rentals north of the river. All of it. If you don't believe me, check up on it. Give the books a good going over now that you're back.''

Now the triumph—and the malice—could be seen plainly on his young face. "But in Algiers," he said in a voice thick with emphasis, "everything you put into *my* hands has appreciated in value, in productivity, in everything. I've doubled the crop yield in some places. And I've as much as trebled the cash yield in the rental properties.'' He fairly spat the words out in icy, controlled rage. "Look it up. And then see if you have the nerve to pull another of these tirades on me without first bothering to find out what the hell you're talking about. As for where I've been, coming in at an hour like this''—his sneer was as expressive as his acid tone—''why, Father, dear, I've been in Algiers. Making money. M-O-N-E-Y. Which is what we're supposed to be in business to do, in case you've forgotten that in the last year.''

Rathbone stared openmouthed at him as he stalked up the stairs, not looking back, his strong young back straight and his head held high.

Chapter 38

After his son had gone, Laird Rathbone, a thoughtful look on his now gaunt face, shook his head once and looked down the hall at the closed door of his home office. His hands suffered the nervous tic they'd taken on in his year away, his thumbs and forefingers rubbing together as if rolling a small ball of lint back and forth between his fingers. He pursed his lips and nodded, then walked slowly toward the office.

Inside, he lit twin lamps above his desk and looked at the neatly kept room, with the big ledgers stacked on the walls. Under his command the firm's bookkeepers had maintained two identical sets of books on all his far-flung enterprises, keeping even the home copy rigidly up-to-date. He looked up and found the two ledgers that showed the activities of the firm in the year he'd just passed in the East. Opening the first of the two, he sat down at the big desk, opening the pages and reaching for a pair of small, metal-rimmed spectacles he'd taken to using for close work in recent days.

As he read, he looked once or twice up at the row of cut-glass bottles on the shelf and shook his head. No: there'd been enough of that in those terrible first days after Allison's death. Now, more than ever, it was time for clarity of mind. Particularly if there were any truth to what the boy had been saying.

Two hours sufficed to acquaint him with the pattern of his firm's enterprises in the months following his trip East. By the time Marie, his wife's old slave, brought coffee in to him on a silver platter, Rathbone knew what had been happening while he was gone.

He poured his own coffee into a tiny demitasse, relishing once again, after so many months away from it, the strong, half-burned, chicory-tinged smell of French-roast coffee. Then, cup in hand, he leaned back in his big chair and stared down at the open ledger.

Everything Ward had said was substantially true. Renault and Halsey had relaxed their grasp on things in the time he was away. They'd actually lost money in some areas, just as Ward had implied. Worse, they'd let up in their campaign to keep Aurora Brand off-balance and under attack; she had indeed "stolen a march" on the Rathbone fleet, just as Ward had said she had.

Well, it was time to shake things up. He'd have both of them in and take the hide off them. He'd have to give some thought to ways of regaining lost ground with the Brand woman. Damn her! She'd taken the edge off his trip back with that big steamer of hers.

He thought about his son now. The damned insolent puppy! But Rathbone had taken to examining his feelings in recent months, ruthlessly excising all traces of sophistry, demanding of himself an honesty with himself that was as bracing as a cold bath. He had to admit a certain new respect for the boy. He was beginning to show some spirit at last. And—even better—he was beginning to apply himself. He'd done great things with the Algiers properties, although none of them were precisely calculated to make the Rathbone name a by-word for Christian charity and tolerance. Quite the opposite, Rathbone reflected now, sipping his coffee, a hard smile playing on his thick lips. Ward was perhaps as widely hated south of the river as his father had ever been north of it.

He examined his feelings again. Ward was his father's son to be sure, but there was a cold, hard edge to him that Rathbone, even taking the most uncharitable view of himself, could not find in his own personality. Had it indeed ever been there? Well, perhaps. But there'd always been Allison to civilize him, humanize him, take the sharp edges off him. And Ward? Who was there to tame that savage heart?

He wondered idly about the progress of Ward's promised campaign for the heart of the Desmoulins girl. Then he dropped it. Time for that later.

Well, the record was there. The boy hadn't been lying. His were the only enterprises in the firm's care that had not only failed to show losses but actually had prospered. If anything, Ward's seemingly boastful account of his activities had erred on the conservative side. The boy's aptitude for business affairs approached genius.

Rathbone frowned. There was a cocky and thoughtless side to him still, one that was going to land him in trouble in the future if nothing was done to check it. He had the same old tendency to dissipate his energy in displays of temper, for all the fact that these were, he admitted now, a trifle more controlled than they had been before.

Well, he'd roast the hides off both Halsey and Renault and set both of them firmly back on the path. And he'd put a little more power in Ward's hands—but not too much. Not yet. And he'd keep an eye on the boy, watch for signs of that headlong and heedless streak in him. Laird would stay in control now that he'd come back to take over the helm.

Helm. He frowned. The damned Brand woman again—playing to the crowd with a stunt like piloting the *Memphis* down from Natchez like that. The newspapers would be full of it. It would impress the shippers.

He reached out and took down a sheet of fine, hand-laid paper and pulled the inkwell to him, noting with pleasure that the house slaves had kept the well filled and the pen clean in all the months he'd been gone, as if waiting for him to come back on the bridge.

Bridge. His own words conspired to turn his thoughts back to the essentials. And what was the essential thing now? To renew the attack on the damned Brand woman, with her shiny new boat and her gaudy new campaign to take business from his own firm, to assert with such boldness her claim to this ridiculous title the men of the Bourse, of the river and maritime communities, were beginning to bestow upon her. Queen indeed! Queen of the—

A timid knock at the door interrupted his thoughts. "Yes?" he said, the old arrogance back in his voice again.

His son Todd opened the door and stuck his head in. "Father?" he said. "I wondered if that was you. You're up early. I . . . I wondered if . . ."

Rathbone glared at his second son, trying to stifle the feeling of disgust that always overcame him whenever he saw that abjectly adoring look of puppy love on the boy's face. If only the boy had a little of Ward's hardness, his independence! But he couldn't do anything about that now. The boy was the way he was. Laird sighed. "Come in," he said, letting the half glasses fall down onto his nose.

"Father, is there anything I could do for you?" the boy said. "I mean, your coffee's cold. I'll—"

"No, no," Rathbone said. "The coffee's fine. Pour yourself a cup if you like. There *is* something you could do, I think." He handed over the piece of paper, pushed the inkwell across the table toward his son. "My eyes aren't what they were," he said. "I'd like to dictate a letter to the newspaper. If you'd be so kind . . ."

Todd leapt at the chance, almost spilling the ink in the well in the process. He sat down and said eagerly, "Yes, Father?" He dipped the pen and held it poised above the paper.

Rathbone looked at him. "Well, perhaps you could help me with the phrasing," he said. "What I want to do is issue a challenge."

"A challenge?" Todd said, open-eyed. "You mean, like a duel?"

"No, no," Rathbone said impatiently but not unduly harshly. "A race. A packet race on the Mississippi, from New Orleans to St. Louis. A race involving the *Jackson* and any vessel on the river whose owner thinks he can match it. The terms to be—"

"But, Father. There's only one boat on the river that stands the smallest chance of—" He stopped. "I see. The challenge is to sound like an open one. But who is it to be aimed at?"

"At Aurora Brand. At the *Memphis*. And if I know her, she won't stand a chance of being able to resist such a challenge. Jake tells me she and Seth Falkner are going around claiming that thing will outrun anyone on the water. Well, it's time to make the dear lady put up or shut up. And when I've run her into the ground once and for all . . ."

"But, Father, *can* the *Jackson* take her? I mean—"

Rathbone looked at his son, his face showing his sudden self-doubt. "I don't know. But I tell you that if we *did* take her, Aurora Brand would be finished on the river. Just as she'd be finished if she didn't take the challenge.''

"I see," his son said. There was the germ of a thought lambent on his untried young face: something new, something he hadn't quite thought out yet. "This is important, isn't it? I mean, *really* important. Supremacy on the river would put the Rathbone boats back in the top spot when it came to shipping, passenger carrying, everything.''

"It would work much like that," Rathbone said. "Are you ready to start? Dip the pen again; it'll be dry by now.''

"Yes, sir!" the boy said enthusiastically.

Arthur Gilliam woke with a start and reached for Cassie. The bed beside him was empty. He felt beneath the covers; there was no body warmth left there. She had gone—and quite some time before. "Cassie!" he cried out, leaping naked out of bed and looking into the other room. There was no sign of her. "Oh, my God," he said, and reached for his drawers and shirt.

Struggling into his clothes, he stopped suddenly as he spotted a white piece of paper on the little breakfast table in the next room, folded, awaiting him. He reached for it and saw with a sinking heart the single word: Arthur.

Sitting on the bed less than half dressed, he blinked, rubbed sleep from his eyes, and tried to read her hurried handwriting.

Arthur, my darling,
I have to go. You know what it is that I have to do— and before he can get the chance to ruin everything for me and for P. I wish to God it had been different for you and me. Please believe that I loved you and that I love you now at the end. More than I ever loved anyone, my dearest, except perhaps for P. Until you, I had no one but him, and now I owe it to him to protect him from

The letter didn't break off there, but she'd apparently been weeping as she wrote, and her tears had blotted the last line so that he could read no more of it, could barely make out the scrawled signature at the bottom. "Oh, my God," Arthur said. "God in heaven."

What could he do? How could he stop her if he had no idea where she'd gone, or even when, for that matter? "C-Cassie," he said brokenly.

The night before had been so poignant, so sweet, and now he knew why. It had been the last night they would ever know together. She'd known that beforehand, and she'd done her best to make the few hours they'd had together as beautiful a farewell as she could make them. And how exquisite these paltry moments had been! And how painfully few, particularly now that the last of them was gone.

He knew, of course, what she had done. She'd gone after Halsey—the man who'd blackmailed her, beaten her, raped and brutalized her. She'd gone after him with the idea of killing him, hopefully before Halsey could carry out his threats to send the telegram that would forever ruin the life of her son up north.

But where could Arthur go? He didn't even know Halsey's address. Moreover, she'd told him Halsey wasn't likely to be there, anyway. Alerted to the danger to himself by the death of Renault, killed by the big half-caste she'd told him about, Halsey would be holed up somewhere. Most likely down in the swamp, in that hideous rabbit warren of gambling hells, whorehouses, crimps' dens, and smugglers' hangouts. And he'd be armed, that was for sure, and most likely surrounded by bodyguards who—

"Cassie," Arthur said despairingly, struggling hurriedly into his clothes. "If you'd only waited for me."

What could he do now? What chance did Cassie stand of getting close enough to Halsey to carry out her plan? Why, he'd see in a moment what she was up to. She *never* sought out Halsey herself; she only turned up according to pre-arranged plans or came when he summoned her. If she were to show up now, unannounced, Halsey'd suspect . . . Arthur bit his lip and fretted; then he thought at last of the little pistol he'd taken to keeping under his mattress. He reached for it frantically and sobbed when he found it was still there. He withdrew it and clutched it in his hand, weeping and trembling with fear and foreboding. If she'd only taken it with her . . .

He dropped the little gun on the bed now, though, and buttoned his shirt hastily. He knew now what he had to do, although he hadn't the faintest idea of how he'd go about doing it. He'd find her. He'd have to—and fast, before she had a chance to get through to Halsey alone. With him there, at least, there would be the two of them against that sadistic devil. They would come a little closer, anyway, to evening the odds. If there was any way that he, Arthur, could rid her life of Simon Halsey and his brutality and his threats once and for all, he'd do it and be glad, whatever the consequences.

Somehow the knowledge of what he had to do—there were no other possible alternatives—had something of a soothing effect. The thought gave him purpose and undid the unmanning effects of indecision and doubt. He'd found the woman he loved. He must protect her at all costs.

He struggled into his big coat and buttoned it against the morning fog. Now, with a steadier hand, he picked the little pistol off the bed and stowed it in a side pocket.

Chapter 39

"You boys wait out here," Simon Halsey said. "I won't be long." He stepped up and pounded on the big door of Rathbone's house. When the slave let him in, he paced impatiently in the big hall before the servant, standing near the door to Rathbone's office, motioned for him to enter.

Inside, he registered shock at the sight of Rathbone. The weight had fallen off his body and his clothing hung awkwardly on him. His cheeks were sunken, his eyes hollow. The stamp of protracted suffering was everywhere to be found on the man's face and body—and in the nervous tic he had developed, thumbs and forefingers rubbing compulsively one against the other. Only the eyes were the same. Or were they? The old fire was gone, but there was in its place a basilisk chill that reminded Halsey once and for all that Rathbone was still a dangerous man—very dangerous.

"Renault's dead," Halsey said without prelude. "Somebody murdered him, down in Niggertown."

Rathbone's eyes flashed, and for a moment there was a bit of the old fire there, after all. "Dead? At whose hands? Are you sure? He didn't choose to—"

"To kill himself? Not likely. He was choked to death by a pair of hands." He held up his own and looked down at them for a moment. "I wear a big pair of gloves," he said. "The hands that killed Renault were twice the size of mine. And when he'd done with him, he hung him up to dry from a coat hook, pretty as you please."

"I see. This was in the *quartier*, you say? Down in high-yellow country?"

"Yes. The rooms where he's been keeping that nigger girl, the one with the hair. You've seen her."

"Yes." Rathbone swiveled in the chair, his lips pursed. "Well, it was bound to happen. That's a good part of town to stay away from. Renault was one of these people who think they're going to live forever. Because he kept his dueling tools in good shape, he thought he couldn't be killed. And when the time came, there wasn't any 'honor' about the affair at all." All his parvenu contempt for the codes gentlemen lived by came out in the scorn he put into the word *honor*.

He turned quickly back to Halsey. "And you?" he said. "I suppose you've faced up to the possibility that the same person or persons who ordered Renault's killing might also have plans for you?"

"I've considered it," Halsey said. "Of course, it could have been one of the free-nigger bucks down that way. Renault made enemies the way you make money."

"Hmm," Rathbone said. "That reminds me. If Renault were alive, I'd be calling him in just as I called you. I've been looking at the books. Both of you—you've let things go to hell in a handbasket since I've been away."

Halsey tried to pass it off. "Well, of course there are the normal ups and downs of business," he said, "but if you average it out—"

Rathbone's fist came down on the desk with a solid bang. "Goddammit, don't tell me about your average this and average that! You've let things slide. You've actually lost money in some areas. *Lost money!*" His voice now took on a little of its old lion's-roar quality, gathering power word by word. "Worse—you've let the Brand slut get away! We had her in our pocket, and she got clean away! Now she's taking business away from us! Taking business over to the Brand Line, which was on the verge of bankruptcy one year ago today, do you hear?"

"Look," Halsey said through clenched teeth, "if you look at the books carefully, you'll see there's a pattern of—"

"I don't want to hear about any goddamned patterns! I don't want to hear any goddamned bookkeeper talk, sniveling rodomontade about averages, obfuscation about patterns . . ." He stood up and leaned across to look Halsey in the eye, his gaze as deadly as ever. "All I want to hear from you is that business gets better, not worse, and that the Brand woman is on the way out! Do you hear me? I want her bankrupt. I want her taking out advertisements in the paper, putting her wardrobe and furniture up for sale. I want her to be a charity case, living on the dole. I want her out in the street. I want her in penury. I want her begging for a situation in a parlorhouse. Do you hear? *I don't want any excuses!*" The last words came out in single syllables, like repeated punches from his balled fist, and he punctuated each syllable with a heavy blow on the table.

"I get you," Halsey said, his voice subdued but the controlled rage evident in each word. "What else?"

"What else?" Rathbone's rage was a near match for one of his old tirades. "I gave my son the properties south of the river to manage, mainly to get him out of my hair. I thought low-yield properties like those would also prove to be low risk. I mainly thought it was safe to assign this business to him because he couldn't easily get in trouble. And what do I find? In the year he's had them, he's outperformed you—yes, you and the, ah, dear departed—every way around. He's made money. He's turned desert into garden. While you and Renault have been sitting around resting on your laurels, Ward has been building that worthless land into a little empire of his own. By God, I'm of half a mind to let him loose on the portion of my business you two have been neglecting so shamefully! I'm of half a mind to let the boy give you a lesson or two in the management of business."

"Now look here—"

"*You* look here," Rathbone said, his voice low and poisonous. He reached down and tossed over the paper Todd had written out for him. "I'm reduced to stupid and wasteful expedients like *these* to regain the attention of the shipping and passenger trade that the Brand bitch has been siphoning away in the year I've been away. A *race!*" The word came out etched in acid. "A stupid, meaningless steamboat race upriver, for no other purpose than to demonstrate the superiority of our line. I shouldn't have to be doing that, do you hear? She should have been out of business by now! In receivership! Her goods evicted into the street!"

Halsey skimmed the note. "This is going into the papers today?" he said. "But what if she refuses the challenge?"

"She won't. And if she takes it, I'll win. You'll see to that. Or, so help me God, Halsey—"

"She'll lose," Halsey said hastily. "Count on that. One way or the other."

Standing at two widely separated vantage points, Rathbone's two older sons listened to their father's booming voice as the conversation progressed. When Halsey finally stormed out of the office and walked briskly to the door the slave held open for him, Todd Rathbone, below stairs where he'd gone in search of a glass of milk, thought to himself: *A race! A real old-fashioned race up the river, winner take all!* Somehow, taking dictation from his father, he'd managed to miss the sweeping implications of it all. But how could he help? How could he show his father that he loved him, that he cared, that he could hold up his own end in the great struggle? His eyes shone and he pounded one fist into the other. What if . . .

At the first landing of the great central staircase, Ward Rathbone, his heart pounding fast, grinned in pleased disbelief. He was winning! Little by little he was edging Halsey aside! The year of work he'd put in—grinding, backbreaking, around-the-clock work—was beginning to pay off! His father was even threatening to hand over to him the part of his business that Halsey and Renault had so shamefully mismanaged during the past year!

But how could he follow this up? How could he keep the pressure on Halsey? How could he beat the Brand woman to her knees, beat her so decisively that she'd be finished on the river—and do so in such a way that his father would know it was his work alone and had nothing to do with Halsey?

He chewed his lip in thought. He'd have to work hard on this one. Whatever he decided, it would have to be covert—totally covert. No one must suspect anything at all, right up to the moment when the plan, once set in motion, became completely irreversible. It would take the most careful, most meticulous planning. He'd have to choose his associates with the greatest of care. And there wasn't much time. He'd whistled at the short deadline when Todd, moments before, had told him about the race. There was no time to lose, no time at all.

In the street, Halsey, his strong legs churning beneath him, set so torrid a pace that the two bodyguards had to break into a half trot to keep up with him. Ignoring the danger, he crossed streets as he chose, leaving the drivers to pull their horses up short and curse impotently at him for the disruption. With the original miscreant out of earshot, the bodyguards took the brunt of the cursing, returning some choice epithets of their own.

He followed a twisting, crooked path, dodging horse and wagon alike, taking alley cutoffs, sometimes slipping boldly through a close between two houses. His mind was racing around and around a circumscribed course, and his frustration made itself known in a steady stream of muttered obscenities. Damn Rathbone, anyway! The nerve of the man, calling him to account as if he were some jackleg bookkeeper or menial!

His big fist clenched and his eyes narrowed. *My time will come, Rathbone,* he thought. *And when it does . . .*

God! Imagine him praising that whelp of his! Acting as though the young pup had done a better job of stewardship, when he'd had nothing better to do with his time than manage a bunch of woebegone plats south of the river, where land was virtually worthless! Why, anyone could have done that!

He broke stride. Ward! Ward was the source of his troubles! Likely as not, as a matter of fact, the boy had been behind the attack on Renault. Likely as not he, too, had an assassin somewhere waiting for him—an assassin paid for by Rathbone's cub! But who?

Then the thought came to him of the hand marks on Renault's neck, marks from a hand the size of some circus giant's. He shivered involuntarily at the thought. If a monster like that were on the lookout for him, lurking behind some building some dark night . . .

Bah! he thought. *Get ahold of yourself!* But he did slow his steps, and he did glance back, and, little by little, he let the bodyguards catch up with him as he crossed a brickyard and headed for the Tchoupitoulas Levee. Better safe than sorry. Let them at least stay within sight of him.

But with the water in sight at last, his feet on the boardwalk and his eyes on the long row of docks with their stilt-mounted whorehouses and taverns, Halsey began to relax. He was in his element again. Here, nobody dared strike from cover. If a man were to die in Sailortown, it would be a death dealt out in hot blood, by someone facing him with a knife. He could deal with that sort of thing. He'd done so too many times before.

He was almost grinning as he increased his pace, turning into the long dock that led to his waterfront office. He slowed, stopped, and turned back to the two men who had accompanied him. "It's all right, boys," he said. "You just station yourselves there, where the dock begins. Don't let anybody out here without asking me first. You got me?"

"Yair," one of the thugs said. He looked at his partner; they fanned out on opposite sides of the dock and stood still, relaxed but alert, silent as sentinels.

Halsey nodded in approval. He came to the door and pulled out the big key that unlocked it. Kicking the door open, he lit a lucifer and made for the lamp that hung over the little table.

But something stopped him. There was a sharp report, and Halsey felt a powerful blow in his left arm, one that spun him around and slammed him into the wall. The door lay half open; he fell hard and lay in the pool of light that stretched out from the doorway. Now another figure moved into the light standing silhouetted in the open doorway. A slim figure, womanly in its round curve of hip, long-haired. The light glinted on a shiny-barreled revolver in her hand.

He tried to move and felt a stab of pain in his arm. "C-Cassie," he said.

"Yes," she said in a hard but weary voice. "*You rotten bastard.* I'm going to put you where you'll never lay hands on a woman again." She raised her arms, and the glint of sunlight on polished metal flashed before Halsey's eyes again.

"No," he said. "For God's sake, Cassie, don't." The pistol wavered, steadied, and focused at last on his face. He looked directly into the open barrel. She thumb-busted the revolver, and he noticed with a pang that it was his own gun she was pointing at him. His own gun! He held up his right hand ineffectually, trying to move to one side but wincing with the pain. "Please, Cassie. Please . . ."

Chapter 40

"Arthur!" Ben Samuels said, pausing in mid-stride, looking the young man up and down with those keen eyes that missed nothing. "You're up early."

"Yes," Arthur Gilliam said. His eyes raced right, then left, almost as if avoiding Ben's gaze. "I have an errand. It can't wait. I . . ." He looked into Samuels's eyes and found there only concern, not curiosity. "Ben," he said hoarsely. "Something's come up, something bad. I don't know what to do. I don't know what in God's name I can do."

"Well," Samuels said kindly, "you could try stepping up on the banquette before some dray horse runs you down and tramples you." He guided Arthur to the curb, paused politely to let some people go by, and moved the two of them to one side, out of the press of traffic on the street. "Arthur," he said. "What's the matter? Maybe I can help you."

"Ben," Arthur Gilliam said, "I can't tell you all of it. But it's urgent that I find Cassie right now. She's about to do something. Something terrible."

Samuels's eyes narrowed. "Go on," he said.

"I can't explain," Arthur said. "But I think she's on her way to find . . . to find Simon Halsey. And to try to kill him." He closed his eyes and wiped his face with one hand. "I've looked all over. I have to get to her first. Or get to Halsey. I have to stop her before she—"

"Ah," Samuels said. He looked right and left, then he guided Arthur Gilliam to a doorway. "We can talk here a little without being heard. Cassie? Halsey? What's the connection?'' Arthur did not answer for a moment. Then Ben said, ''Cassie . . . *she's* the connection with Rathbone. Is that it?''

''Yes,'' Arthur said miserably. ''He's been blackmailing her. I found out about it a little while back. Since then I've kept the records under lock and key. The other night she confessed. Halsey has been brutal, ruthless.''

''He would be,'' Samuels agreed. ''And Cassie?''

''She thinks her life is over. She left me this morning before dawn. There was a note. She's going to do something desperate. I don't know what to do. How do I find Halsey? If I ask people, they close up tighter than a drum.''

''I have an address or two,'' Samuels said. ''Whatever the problem is, Arthur, two of us together are better than one. Are you armed?''

''I have a little revolver.''

''Good.'' Samuels patted his inside pocket with one hand as his other gripped the deadly *colchemarde* he carried everywhere. ''I know one place Halsey might be found. Perhaps we can head her off before she gets there and does the—does something that can't be undone. Quickly, man! Follow me!'' Not waiting for an answer, he set off down the street at a pace that was practically a run.

Olivia knocked on the door. ''Miss Brand?'' she said. She knocked again, but the answer came from within before the third knock. She opened the door to find Aurora Brand sitting in dressing gown and slippers before the dressing mirror, a tiny cup of coffee before her. Not for the first time Olivia wondered at the poise Miss Brand could show, even in such dishabille. She thought, *Will I ever look like that?* When she spoke again, it was to say, ''Miss Brand, they handed me this downstairs.'' She passed the paper over.

Aurora smiled wryly. ''What is it, a summons?'' She unfolded the flier and scanned it quickly but unhurriedly. ''Ah,'' she said, ''I was expecting this.'' She looked up at Olivia. ''Rathbone need hardly have gone to the bother of incurring a printing bill for these. One for me alone would have done. I suppose the street is flooded with copies everywhere.''

''Yes, ma'am,'' Olivia said. ''There are little boys going

from house to house with big sheafs of circulars under their arms. Others are pasting them onto walls and light poles.''

"Yes, yes. But he could have spared himself the expense. One copy would have reached me, and I don't have to be stampeded into accepting the challenge. Sit down, Olivia.''

"Yes, ma'am. You're going to accept? But what if . . . ?''

"What if we lose? Well, we could. From all I hear, the *Jackson* is a superior boat by anyone's standards. And Seth tells me Jake Cutler is as good a boatman as any on the river. Yes, it could happen. But why worry? We've got good people too. And we've got the *Memphis*. If I started shrinking away from something like this . . .'' She shook her head with a confident smile. "Don't worry. The stakes will be high, but everything will turn out right. Here, have coffee with me, won't you?''

Ward rode like the wind to the landing of the St. Mary Market ferry, three miles upstream from the New Orleans levees. He took the ferry across to Mechanicsham, a grubby village known mainly as a haven for eloping couples in need of a quick, no-questions-asked marriage, and jogged to the livery stable across the village common.

Inside, the ostler's assistant leaned lazily on a hay rake, looking at him. "Howdy,'' he said.

"Hello,'' Ward said. "I'd like a horse. And I'm looking for Matt Frye.''

"Matt's ailin'.'' The assistant spat into the corner. "Maybe I c'd help ye.''

Ward looked at him narrowly, his mouth set in a skeptical frown. "I was told he could give me a line on how to find a fellow named Henry Olding,'' he said, his words careful and measured.

The ostler's assistant scratched his nose. "I can give you a bay mare. Can't make much time with *her*, though.'' He looked Ward up and down. "You won't need to, lookin' for Henry Oldin'. Don't live far from here. McDonoghville, as I remember.'' He looked Ward in the eye. "I'd have to jog my memory some.''

Ward nodded, dug in his coat pocket for a coin, and tossed it over. "I'm in something of a hurry,'' he said in a flat, impatient voice. "Don't worry, I'm not from the authorities. Very much the opposite. I just happen to require Mr. Olding's services. And his special talents."

The ostler's assistant looked at the coin. His brow went up. "Much obliged," he said. "Special talents, huh?" He grinned. "I don't know the number. It's a little house, painted red, across from the graveyard on Hancock Street, right across from where John McDonough used to bury his freed niggers. You can't miss it. Up in the northwest part o' town. If he ain't home, there's a cocking main 'round the corner, and he'll be there losin' his shirt."

"Good," Ward said, watching him turn out the bay mare. "That means he'll need the work."

Simon Halsey stared at the wavering pistol pointed straight at his eye. "Cassie," he said, dry-mouthed, "my arm . . . you hurt me."

"Hurt?" she said. The gun shook in her hand and she lowered it. There were tears running down her cheeks; her expression reflected the utter desolation in her heart. "You think I care? You think anyone would care? After all the hurt you've given others? Given me? God, Simon. If I thought you'd bleed to death here, I'd just up and leave you. Anything that made your dying slower and more painful. But . . ."

"But you can't do it," Halsey said. He looked her in the eye and saw her wince and turn away. "You can't just stand there and kill me, can you, Cassie? I . . . I know you couldn't. You've got too good a heart." He let his eyes go around the room, lighting at last on the legs of the chair nearest him. If he could get close enough to it to shove it at her legs, hard . . .

She saw his hand slowly slide across the floor. "Simon! You stop that! Stop it right there!" Her panic made her raise the gun again. Halsey saw to his horror that it was still thumb-busted, the hammer pulled way back, and he remembered the revolver had a hair trigger, one he'd filed down himself.

"Cassie," he said in a voice that broke on him, "be reasonable. Can't we talk this—"

The next events happened so quickly, there was neither time, nor the need, to sort them out. What he suddenly saw over her shoulder must have registered on his face. She started to turn. Rough hands fell on her arms, gripping them tightly. The gun dropped to the floor and went off harmlessly, the bullet plowing into the wall of the rickety building. Cassie struggled in the arms of the larger of the two bodyguards while the other helped Halsey get to his feet.

"God!" Halsey said in a tight voice. "You little bitch, you've ruined my arm!" Moving, he felt the pain shoot through him. His face was bathed in sweat. "Ahh! God! God, that hurts!"

"I hope it does," Cassie sobbed. "I wish I'd killed you . . ." She looked down to where the smaller bodyguard was picking up Halsey's discharged revolver and handing it back to him. "Well, you might as well use it," she said bitterly. "Now that I've failed to get you, there's nothing left for me, anyway." She started to say something else, but her voice broke. "K-kill me, Simon! Please. Kill me now. I don't want to live anymore."

Halsey grasped the gun with his good hand. The other arm hung uselessly at his side. His face was drawn, bloodless, and bore an expression compounded of equal parts of hatred and pain. "That'd be too easy," he said. "You've hurt me. Do you think I'm going to let you go out quickly? Easily? So help me, I'm going to find a slow and equally painful way to—"

But he stopped, and through the pained expression on his face she could see a slow and terrible smile beginning to form itself. Her heart beat fast; her mind raced. What could he be thinking of?

The truth, when it dawned, came like a sudden immersion in freezing water. She thought for a moment her heart was going to stop. Panic raced through her mind like wildfire through dry brush. *"No!"* she cried. "Simon, for God's sake. You wouldn't. Please, Simon. *Please* . . ."

"You'd like that, wouldn't you? You'd like it to be just a little matter between you and me. Something that would die and be forgotten when you're gone, and that'd be the end of it. But it isn't going to be so easy. No, Cassie. You got the wrong arm. I still have one I can write anonymous letters with. I still have a couple of addresses to write them with."

"No! No, for God's sake, Simon! Leave him alone! He's just a boy, a child. He hasn't done anything to you. He doesn't deserve to be punished for anything I've done. Don't ruin his life forever, just because . . ."

Halsey smiled horribly through his pain. "There," he said. "There, now. That's better. Now you're coming around."

She hung limp from the big man's powerful hands, looking at him, afraid to hope. "You mean you're . . . you're not going to . . . ?"

"Of course I am," Halsey said harshly. "Of course I am, Cassie. I just wanted you to know beforehand. I wanted you to know before you died."

The horrible smile still on his pain-distorted face, he stepped forward and held the gun to her temple. He spoke to the man holding her. "Step to one side, will you? Grab her by the hair. Hold her just so." He thumb-busted the gun and held it to her head, its icy barrel just touching her upper ear. "Good-bye, Cassie," he said huskily. "I'll say hello to Philip for you."

The docks were all but deserted when Arthur and Ben Samuels arrived. Ben looked around, always cautious, always circumspect. "Wait," he said. "That's Halsey's shack out at the end of the dock. He does a lot of business there. The kind of business he can't do downtown, not without somebody watching him and making certain connections Halsey doesn't want people to make about his activities."

"Yes, but—"

"No, wait. You don't know what kind of trap you might be walking into out there. I'll go ahead. You cover me from here. If I land in trouble, I'll cry out for help." He put a friendly, almost fatherly, hand on Arthur's shoulder. "That little gun of yours, you do know how to use it?"

"Y-yes," Arthur said. "I went out and practiced. But Ben, if you—"

"Don't worry. It'll be all right. Just be ready if there's any trouble. We can take care of ourselves." He smiled reassuringly. "Now cover me, will you, please?" He did not wait for an answer. He walked slowly out toward the stilt-supported shack at the end of the dock, *colchemarde* in one hand, the other near his coat pocket where his own gun nestled, safe and accessible.

Arthur watched him go. His heart was sinking with every step of Ben's well-shod feet. *We'll be too late,* he thought. *We're already too late. If I'd woken up an hour earlier . . .*

Ben Samuels stopped before the shack's door. He rapped twice with a gloved fist. Then he stepped back, his right hand in the coat pocket that held his revolver. There was no answer. He stepped back half a step and, without any preliminaries, lashed out with one booted foot and kicked the door open. There was no response. He entered; from the boardwalk Arthur could see light within as Ben lit a lamp. What had happened? He stifled the sudden impulse to dash forward, throwing all caution to the wind.

Then Ben emerged. His face was set in a grim look. He looked at Arthur, nodded, and motioned him forward.

"Ben!" Arthur said, dashing over the uneven boards, his left hand lightly running along the wooden railing. "Is she . . . ?"

"Wait," Ben Samuels said. "It doesn't look good. She's not there, but there's a lot of blood, and . . ."

Now his own eyes went down to the boards beneath their feet. Boards that bore a red trail of droplets that led out the open door to the far end of the dock, to stop abruptly at the edge, where the handrail lay broken in two pieces. Samuels, moving as swiftly as Arthur had ever seen him move, made his way to the edge and looked down. "God!" he said in a hushed voice. "Arthur, don't look down!"

But the admonition came too late. Arthur looked over the side as Samuels clutched his arm protectively. In the depths there was a pink tint. Pink: the color of the dress he'd bought Cassie not a month before. The wind stirred the surface of the water. Beneath the floating scum on the dirty surface of the water, a pale hand waved in the current, softly, gently, to and fro, as if waving good-bye.

Book Four

Chapter 41

"Seth," Aurora Brand said, pausing at the hall door, "before you go, is everything all right?"

Seth Falkner looked her up and down, smiling, marveling at the precise balance she struck between the studied perfection of her ballroom turnout and the last-minute jitters she seemed to be displaying. "Don't worry, ma'am," he said in his slow, calm voice. "Everything's fine on board. You leave everything to me until morning. You have guests in there, and they'll demand your full attention."

Aurora pursed her lips and—a trifle reluctantly, it seemed—returned his smile in a moment. "You're right," she said. "It's just that . . . well, the race and its possible outcome has been on my mind for two weeks now. I can't seem to relax."

"Yes, you can," he said. "You can be sure I've checked and double-checked everything on board. Security is very tight. I have more bullyboys guarding the *Memphis* than Congress has guarding the mint. Now you go in and preside, as everyone expects you to do. And relax, please. I won't let any gray mares or circuit riders on board to hoodoo the boat."

She put a slim hand on his larger one, and her smile softened a little. "I know," she said, "but there seem to be so many loose ends, and I have people of my own to worry about. We can't find poor Arthur, for instance. He's been missing for a day and a half. Ben's afraid he might do something desperate. I knew I should have had someone look after him."

"It's all right," he said reassuringly. "Really."

"Oh, I know. But, Seth, I had a look at the passenger list. Have there been any new—"

Basil Endicott came up behind them then and put a brotherly hand on her arm. "No, my dear. I knew you'd ask about that. There's no sign of him. But I do have something to tell you, if you'll listen."

He looked at Seth Falkner and winked out of sight of Aurora Brand. Falkner bowed, smiled, and walked away. Basil turned Aurora toward him and looked down into her anxious green eyes. "Ah, how lovely you do look tonight," he said. "If only you were the stupid and malleable type, I'd go get in the queue with all the other men in New Orleans who line up to throw themselves at your feet." He sighed theatrically. "No sign of Boyd, as I say. But, you know, I lied to you some time back, my dear. In Natchez, you know . . . I got *this* dueling on some dreadful mud bank across the river." He held up his scarred hand. "And—"

"I suspected something like that," she said, glancing nervously toward the dining room where the guests awaited her. "But—"

"Silence," Basil Endicott said in a magisterial tone and with panache. "Not another word until I'm done. My second in this sordid little encounter was Dallas Boyd." He waited a moment for this to sink in, then went on, a tiny smile playing on his long face. "He and I met around a poker table. Hit it off immediately. Liked the man immensely. Quite a chap. Aurora, my darling, he's madly, hopelessly in love with you. We had a bit of a chat over whiskey."

"Love?" Aurora said.

"He has the same problem you have, my darling. That damnable, obdurate, stiff pride that makes you step back from the brink. Or is it a sort of fear? Fear of commitment? Fear of making oneself vulnerable? That may be it. The two of you quite simply have to be the most fearless people I've ever met, to the point of foolhardiness. But everyone has his Achilles' heel, and the two of you seem to share this same flaw. It breaks my heart to see it keep the two of you apart, when no more than a word would end this foolishness."

Her eyes were far away now, and her mind was racing.

"Oh, Basil, I *do* know that if I were in need, in trouble, nothing in the world could keep him from my side. But—"

"Then you have the ghost of an understanding beginning to dawn upon you at last, my darling. You may yet achieve a trifling amount of wisdom. What you will do with it remains to be seen." He smiled and leaned over to kiss her forehead. "But keep in that outrageously active mind of yours the fact that the man adores you. No, it's more than that. It's as though there were some sort of bond between you that no separation could sully, no defection could break." He paused and went on. "You know, he knew about MacMaster, and somehow he knew it wasn't serious, wasn't something that could come between you for long. It was as if he understood, and even approved in his own way. He wouldn't want you to be lonely. He'd know you'd serve your needs but would always put things in perspective."

He looked down. Her eyes were shining, and the smile on her face was the old, radiantly lovely one. "There, now," he said. "Do you think you can face the guests now and the race?"

She hugged him impulsively. "Oh, yes!" she said in a new voice, low, strong, full of confidence.

Across town, Ward Rathbone stopped at the door of an abandoned cotton warehouse and knocked three times. The door opened just enough so that Ward could slip inside and shut it quickly behind him.

Henry Olding, bland-faced, paced back to the long table on which his baggage was stacked. "Everything's ready," he said. "Go on home. Relax. You'll read about it in the papers day after tomorrow."

Ward stood, hands on hips, looking at the bags on the table. "You've got everything?" he asked.

"I said relax," Olding said. "I'm a professional. I know my business. I've never failed. I've never been caught. You could run Spain, say, or Portugal for six months on the insurance money that's been paid off on my work so far."

"But the equipment. I wanted to see—"

"No, you don't," Henry Olding said in that flat, patient voice of his. "It's not a recipe for fudge, Mr. Rathbone. One doesn't take it out and play with it between times. When the time's ripe, I'll unpack it and get to work.'' He let the hint of a frown play on his doughy face. ''I'll remind you, sir, our agreement was 'no questions asked.' I'll hold you to that.''

Ward scowled but let it pass. ''All right,'' he said. ''You do come highly recommended. I suppose I'm in your hands. But you mentioned an assistant. I don't see him here.''

''Nor will you,'' Henry Olding said. ''He's not known here. He came in from the East a week ago. I've had him laying low. I don't want him known by anyone here at all. He's my insurance—and yours—that the job will get done even if something happens to me. No one has ever seen us together. But keep in mind, sir, that Henry Olding tells you that next to me, he's the best in the business.'' He looked at Ward sharply. ''Do you remember the clipper *Rappahan-nock*? Burned in Baltimore Harbor a year ago? Well, that was my associate. The owner retired to Charles County and built a house the size of Blenheim Palace on the insurance money. Relax, Mr. Rathbone. I'll do my job. And your *Memphis* will win the race handily.''

''Who says the *Memphis* is mine?'' Ward said. ''It's my father's ship I'm hiring you to blow up, my friend. The *Jackson*.''

Henry Olding's face went completely blank for a moment. It was as close as he had come yet to reacting, whether in shock or surprise or anything else. When he recovered, his poker face was as bland as ever. ''Well, it's none of my affair,'' he said. ''I burn them. It's up to you people to figure out what the profits are going to be.''

''Right,'' Ward said coldly. ''Just make sure you do the job right. I don't want any slipups.''

Arthur Gilliam sat morosely on the sagging bed of his rented room, looking down at the little sheaf of letters spread out on the rickety table before him. He'd read all of them now—in sequence—five or six times. And he'd had his time of weeping, and his time of feeling drained. Now, as he regarded the little stack of paper and the gun beside it, it came to him that both these times had passed.

It was no good weeping for Cassie anymore. It was past time for weeping for his own loss, or for the tragic life she'd told him about, the fruits of which had been laid bare before him in the letters he'd been reading. There was a time for all things, and when their times were past, it was time to move on to other things.

Now it was time for action.

He looked at the gun. For a while he had even thought of turning the weapon on himself, of ending his own sorrows in the most economical and direct fashion possible.

But that was a coward's solution. It was time to be a man, to be a man for Cassie as well as for himself. Yes, and for young Philip Quayle, who'd need him now as no one, not even Cassie herself, had ever needed him.

He looked at the gun, and his eyes burned. Halsey would have to die before he could fulfill the threats he'd made to Cassie so many times before, blackmailing her into doing his dirty business for him. It would take some preparation, some planning. It would do no good at all just to kill Halsey and then get caught for it. No. Philip would need him, and he had to escape in order to help the boy. No matter that the two of them would have to change their identities and go on the run; that was a foregone conclusion. He could always find work; there'd always be work for a good ink slinger. Maybe the thing to do would be to ship out for foreign parts—or, better, to California, where there was plenty of money still to be made, not in prospecting itself but in helping the gold-rich miners to manage the money they'd made up in the mountains and brought back to San Francisco to spend.

But that was the future. Time enough to think of that. Now it was time for action. Decisive action. Halsey had to die.

He reached out and for the fiftieth time picked up the revolver and weighed it in his hand. His face was set in grim lines; his eyes glinted with a new light.

Employees of the Brand Line had fanned out through the company offices in the area, each one guarding a different office. Olivia Soames had elected to sleep on the little couch in Aurora Brand's private office on Royal Street. She even had a little derringer pistol Ben Samuels had given her and

shown her how to use. Now she huddled in her nightgown
and dressing gown before the little fire she'd built in the grate
and thought about the race in the morning.

How exciting! She'd actually be allowed to go along—to
share in the excitement of Aurora Brand's greatest hour of
triumph as she piloted the majestic *Memphis* up the great
river to victory over Rathbone. It would be something to remember the rest of her life. ("Why, yes, children! I do *remember* the great race. Why, land sakes alive, I was *on* the
Memphis, right by Miss Brand's side.")

She turned her head sharply to one side. Was that a tap on
the window?

She turned her whole upper body and looked at her own
pale face in the window glass, the light of the dancing flames
playing on her cheeks. No, it must have been the wind.

Just as she turned her face back toward the fire, though,
the sound came again, this time even more sharply. She
turned, more slowly and apprehensively.

Then she saw a dim face outside on the roof. The body
was barely visible in the faraway light of the street lamp
below. She stood up with a start; her hand went to the tiny
pistol in the side pocket of her dressing gown.

"W-who's there?" she said and stood away from the firelight a bit, warily watching, listening.

The man on the roof moved closer to the window. She
tensed, and then she recognized him. Her eyes went wide;
she put one hand on her bosom, holding the lapels of her
gown together. But she moved to the window and opened it.
"Todd!" she said. "Todd Rathbone, what in heaven's name
are you doing there? You could have broken your neck!"

Todd, shivering and out of breath, climbed in the open
window. "I'm freezing," he said. "C-could I stand by the
fire here for a moment?"

He didn't wait for an answer but moved to the grate, shivering, rubbing his hands together. "Olivia, I had to see you.
Tonight, I mean. Before morning. Tomorrow I'll be . . . well,
I couldn't wait." He looked at her, his usual shy smile giving
way to a new expression: more confident, full of hope and
trust and something else, something she'd never seen in his

face before. "I don't know where I'll be tomorrow, Olivia. I can't tell you about it. But I had to see you before I left."

"But, Todd," she said, "I can't have you up here alone with me like this. What would people think?" As she spoke, she knew how ridiculous her words were—and how contrary to her real feelings. Unconsciously she put her hand over her mouth, as if to stop the flow of falsely "proper" words.

He saw the change in her and impulsively stepped forward to take her hands in his. "I—I don't care," he said. "Olivia, I love you. I have to say it. I have to tell you. I love you. I've never felt this way before about anyone. If I were to leave without seeing you, without letting you know how I feel about you . . ."

Before either of them could think more about the matter, he took her in his arms and kissed her, his lips hot on hers, his hands—strong young hands, gentle and insistent at the same time—running up and down her back and sending delighted chills through her. And she, in her turn, was feeling things she'd never felt before: powerful, irresistible urges that swept through her mind and body like a flash fire through high grass. Her fear of men, of her own sexual nature, that she'd known of ever since Lance Whitmire's assault on her, slipped painlessly away in the wild rush of emotions that ran through her now, and she was kissing him back, kissing him with passion and—yes!—with trust.

Then she pulled back, drew her face down from his, and nestled her cheek against his chest. "Oh, Todd, I can't . . . I can't let myself go. I can't."

But the voice inside her kept asking, What would Aurora Brand do? How would she handle this? And suddenly, in her heart of hearts, Olivia knew the answer. If your young man was leaving on some mysterious trip, if you might not see him again, perhaps never, there was only one thing to do. Follow your heart. Follow your heart. . . .

She raised her face to his, raised her lips once again for his kiss, and now her own hunger was as strong and free and unashamed as his, and the feelings grew within her. The feel of his hands on her flesh was the magical touchstone that released not only the buried passion within her but also something else: a sweet and gentle caring and giving. Yes! This was the way it should be her first time—the first time she gave herself to a man. The time had come. Now, here in the firelight. Now, while her heart raced and her flesh burned under his caresses; now, while her heart seemed fit to burst with love and longing.

"Yes!" she whispered. "Oh, my darling, yes!"

Chapter 42

At noon the next day Olivia, face flushed, heart pounding with excitement, stood before the rail of the texas deck next to Aurora Brand and Seth Falkner, looking down from their high perch aboard the *Memphis* at the crowds gathered on the docks to see the two great vessels off on their epic race up the mighty Mississippi River to St. Louis. On a platform set up between the two ships in their slips, the mayor spun out a seemingly endless skein of almost totally unintelligible fustian, larded with scraps of ill-remembered verse and quotations from inappropriate authorities.

Aurora Brand wasn't listening. She smiled over at Olivia, her own beautiful face showing the flush of excitement. "I was thinking," she said. "What if we bribed the brass band to drown him out?" She looked down at the little watch pinned to the bosom of her dress. "Doesn't he know that we've got a favorable tide just now?" She turned to Falkner. He nodded and signaled to catch the attention of the harbormaster, two seats away from His Honor's podium. The harbormaster nodded solemnly back at him and prodded the mayor discreetly.

Aurora looked back at Olivia, beaming. "Goodness," she said, "you look nice today." Her green eyes narrowed slightly. "Something new's been added," she said. "It's not just the excitement of the race. Something's happened to you that brings something out in you, Olivia. You're positively radiant."

Olivia blushed and turned away. Her eyes, seeking distraction, went over to the great bulk of the *Andrew Jackson* in the next slip, and her face fell.

Aurora's gaze followed hers. "My," she said, "I think that's Rathbone's son Todd, the nice one. But what's he doing on a boat owned by his father—in a crewman's uniform?" She looked back at Olivia, though, and her keen eye caught the precarious mix of feelings visible in Olivia's face. "Oh," she said. "Hmm."

Olivia, her face still flushed, turned away from the scene. She tried to compose herself, but somehow she knew she'd given herself away. How could she have done otherwise, with Todd looking up at her with such a smile? "I didn't know he was going along on the race," she said.

Aurora didn't look at her. Instead she let her eyes keenly scan the crowd gathered on the hurricane deck of the *Jackson* almost as if she were looking for someone. Calmly, almost matter-of-factly, she said in a lower voice only the two of them could hear, "He's a nice boy. Really, there's almost nothing of Laird in him. He's almost entirely Allison's boy. If he has a flaw at all, it's his hero worship, his devotion, to his father. And, Olivia, that's not really a flaw. It's common enough among second sons. It has its positive aspects. It shows he's capable of great loyalty. A woman could find worse qualities in a man."

"I don't know what to say," Olivia said.

"Then don't say anything." Aurora squeezed her hand supportively. "I think the two of you—your relationship's changed somewhat, and very recently. Am I right?"

"Last night," Olivia said, trying desperately not to look at her—or over toward the *Jackson* at him. "It was the hardest choice I ever had to make, I think."

"Follow your heart, darling. Follow your heart. It can lead you astray, but not the way that ignoring it can lead you astray."

"Oh, Miss Brand! You always understand!"

But Aurora's eye had caught something else on the lower decks of the *Jackson*. After she sent Olivia below for her gloves she turned to Seth Falkner. "Unless I'm altogether

mistaken, I think I just spotted Quint Ragland and Mack
Leggett.''

"Not on my ship, you didn't," Seth Falkner said, taking
his pipe out of an inner pocket. "You wouldn't catch me
letting those rogues aboard.''

"No, no. On the *Jackson*. In steerage.''

Captain Falkner's hand paused on the way to his pipe; the
lit lucifer burned almost all the way down to his fingers before he spoke, surprise in his voice. "Now that *is* odd," he
said. "That is indeed one for the books. What do you suppose they're doing there?''

"I don't know," Aurora said. "But look, the mayor seems
to be winding down. We'd better get up to the pilothouse.''

"Ah, yes," Falkner said, pausing to light his pipe. "You
can always tell when he grasps his lapel that way and starts
spearing the clouds with his other forefinger like that. 'And
so, my friends . . .' " He chuckled softly, handing her gallantly up to the little staircase that led to the glittering rococo
pilothouse that surmounted the tall superstructure of the great
vessel.

Jake Cutler, too, took note of the gradual winding-down
of the mayor's windy and flowery screed. He turned to his
first-watch pilot, Edgar Forster, and said, "Is that the passenger list there? Ah, yes. Would you be so kind as to let me
have a look?''

Forster handed the handwritten list over. Jake Cutler
scowled down at the impressive list of patrons and passengers
aboard the *Jackson*. "I tell you, Mr. Forster, if, as they say,
Rathbone's lost ground in the city since he left for the East,
you can't prove it by this list." A burst of tepid applause for
the mayor's speech was interrupted by the brass band playing
a sprightly reel, the trumpets taking the melody over a
vamped bass in the trombones, and the piccolo weaving intricate filigrees around the main melody in triplets.

Cutler raised his voice. "Yes," he said. "Half the cream
of New Orleans and lower Delta society is here on this list.
Some of the best names in the South. There are people here
I'd swear would have either gone on the *Memphis* or stayed
home. I—''

But he stopped dead here and whistled long and low through his teeth. "Well, I'll be billy-be-damned," he said in a puzzled voice. "Now there's one name I think I'd place aboard a Nongahely flatboat headed for hell before I'd imagine finding it on a boat owned by Laird Rathbone. I'll be blowed, Mr. Forster." He shook his head, looking disbelievingly down at the list. "I wonder if he's really aboard. He could just have signed for tickets and then changed his mind. But why in hell's name would he do that?"

"Why would *who* do that, Captain Cutler?" Forster said. It was one of the longest and most complex speeches Cutler had ever heard the pilot deliver when not at the big wheel of a ship.

Cutler looked at him, his face expressionless. "Why, Dallas Boyd, of course. Who in hell did you think I was talking about?"

Mack Leggett was small and wiry; threading his way through the unruly main-deck crowd was easy going for him. For bearish Quint Ragland, following him was a matter that brought to mind the Biblical sayings about the camel and the eye of the needle. "Mack, goddamn yer," he growled. "Slow the hell down there." Finally, pushing through a knot of people, he grabbed his diminutive partner by the collar and held him still until he could draw even with him.

"Let go o' me, yer big bastard," Leggett said, clawing at the big hand on his shirt. "Damn yer. Now I've gone an' lost him."

"Lost who?" Ragland said in a loud voice. Leggett shushed him frantically and drew him aside into an empty space behind a stack of baled cotton.

"Quiet, for chrissake," Leggett said. "God almighty, man, do yer want to tip the bastard off that we're on to 'im?"

"On to who?" Ragland said, moderating his voice to a cavernous stage whisper. "And why in the name of all that's holy are we on this damned boat? 'Come on,' says he, and off we go to Rathbone's boat willy-goddamn-nilly, and never a word why."

"Look," Leggett said. "What would yer say, yer big bastard, if I told yer I seen Henry Oldin' get on twenty minutes ago?'' He paused a moment to let the enormity of the fact sink in. "That's right, Quint. 'Henry the Torch.' The best arson man south o' the North Pole. And, Quint, yer know how Henry dresses? I mean, at home when he ain't workin'?''

"Why, like a dude, o' course. Like a bullyboy in a rich folks' whorehouse. Diamond studs, an' . . . why're yer askin'? You know he usually looks like a riverboat gambler.''

"Not today, Quint. Not today. He looks like a down-at-the-heels coffin salesman. Drabber'n a cracker circuit rider. He'd make a York County Quaker look like a peacock.''

"Ahh.'' It was less a statement than a slow and barely voiced exhalation of breath.

"And, Quint, in steerage. In *steerage*. Quint, Henry don't ride steerage. It's first-class or he don't go. Except. . . .'' He let the words trail off significantly.

"Except,'' Ragland said, "when he's workin'.'' The full enormity of it did not hit him all at once. The expression on his face changed slowly. "But . . .''

"Damn right,'' Leggett said. "And what's Henry doin' workin' *here*? On Rathbone's boat? Minute I seen him go up the gangplank, I said, 'Mack, yer gotta get on board an' find out. So I grabbed yer and run off to the ticket office. No time to explain. But he's here. I seen him.''

"I don't understand,'' Ragland said, scratching his head.

"Neither do I, Quint,'' Leggett said, "but I'm gonna find out if it means stickin' to the bastard like a barnacle on a bateau.'' He dug a friendly fist into his partner's ribs. "Are yer with me?'' he said.

"Damn right,'' said Ragland. "You check the labboard side. I'll check over here.''

"Right,'' Leggett said. "See yer around.''

Aft, on the docks, the gun went off, starting the great race. There was an enormous roar from the crowd, aboard the two vessels as well as on shore.

Basil Endicott, poised on the rickety fire escape outside the window of Simon Halsey's office, tried not to move. His last move had made a resounding creak that had scared him half to death, and he'd been sure one of them would come to the window, look out, and spot him there.

Now, with the sound of the gun and the faraway roar of the crowd, he felt safe enough to edge closer to the window, the general noise covering the sound of his movements. He flattened himself against the wall of the warehouse and edged even closer to the open window, listening through the outside noise for their words from inside.

Now Halsey was talking: ". . . blundering, murderous, stupid little fool! Do you know what you've done? Do you have any idea?"

The other voice, Basil judged, must be that of Rathbone's cub. "Oh, come down off that high horse, Halsey," he said. "You're just jealous because it wasn't you that thought of it—"

"You shut up and listen, you damned fool! You've ruined your father, all of us, yourself! Why, there must be fifty of the biggest people in New Orleans aboard. Do you think that if the *Jackson* blows and *they're* hurt, the authorities aren't going to investigate every scrap of evidence they can find? Goddamn you, you're as good as caught! There's no way any magistrate is going to believe your father and me when we say we had nothing to do with it. Not now. Not after the *Memphis* affair." He cursed and pounded the table with his good hand. "And for God's sake, this is one case we can't fix! We can't bribe anyone to keep his mouth shut now."

Basil's eyes widened. He edged closer to the window.

Ward's voice broke in, incredulous. "What *Memphis* affair? There's nothing wrong with the Brand boat. I specifically gave instructions that—"

"Not this *Memphis*, you mindless puppy! The *other* one. The one we torched and sent to the bottom off Radford Plantation a year ago! Did you think you could buy silence—the same silence—twice in a year? For the same offense? Did you think—"

"I didn't know." Basil, listening, could almost see the thunderstruck expression on the boy's face. "Nobody told me we had a hand in—"

"God! *God!*" Halsey said, pounding his good fist on the table. "There's no way to reverse this. I can't wire ahead without tipping everyone off who was to blame. And I can't sneak anyone on board to stop this Olding fellow."

"It's worse than that," Ward said in a severely shaken voice. "He has a confederate on board. Even if we could get on board the *Jackson* and shoot Olding dead before he could do anything, there's the second man. And no one but Olding knows who he is. Or what he looks like. They won't even meet on board. They've got it settled between them. I gave Olding a set of the plans for the *Jackson*. He must have had it duplicated somehow. Anyway, he'll go to work on his end of the boat, and the assistant will go to work independently on the other. Neither will even know what the other is doing. One has the for'ard hold, the other the aft . . ."

"My God! How could you have done such a thing?"

Ward's voice rose. He was tense and defensive. "I told them to leave evidence to implicate Aurora Brand. There was the earlier suspicion of her, and I didn't know there was suspicion of us too."

"There isn't," Halsey said through clenched teeth, "but there sure as hell will be. *God!* What can I do? How do I stop them?"

Basil flattened himself against the wall, his heart pounding as the door opened suddenly from inside. A new voice bellowed gruffly. "Ward? Ward! What are you doing here?"

"Father," the boy said, "we seem to have a problem."

Basil edged toward the stairs after listening to the loud voices inside repeat virtually everything he'd heard previously. When Rathbone had struck his son, the boy had apparently gone out the door, cursing his father and Halsey. Basil's pulse raced; his mind went around and around in circles. If only he could get down to the ground and get out of sight before the boy managed to reach the street and walk past his highly exposed perch.

A step of the wooden staircase creaked loudly. He cursed silently and, his heart in his throat, stepped off into space. Landing in a patch of tall grass, he bent his knees to cushion the blow; recovering, he slipped hastily inside the open door of the empty warehouse just as Ward Rathbone, muttering angrily under his breath, moved past Basil's hiding place, fists clenched, his mind a thousand miles away.

Basil breathed a deep sigh of relief, and only then did he dare to think about the terrible things he'd heard. When he did, his mind reeled at the implications. How fortunate that he'd followed his instincts and followed young Rathbone this way! But what could he do about it? Somehow he had to stop the *Jackson*—stop it and get the passengers off. There was no other way.

He looked down the alley. Ward was long gone. He bit his lip, thinking desperately. Where was the livery stable? If he could make it to Southport, to the great curve of the river around Nine Mile Point in time—well, perhaps he could signal to the *Jackson*'s pilot and get the race stopped. But he'd have to hurry. Even if no further delays presented themselves, it would take nearly killing even a well-bred racehorse to make it to the old Chauvin Plantation by the time the two great steamers came chuffing around the bend.

There was nothing for it but to do it. Off we go, old boy, he told himself, and set off at a light jog that soon became a dead run through the streets that had been emptied an hour earlier by the festivities at dockside.

Chapter 43

Dallas Boyd turned reluctantly away from the rail and reached into his inner pocket for a cigar. Withdrawing a fine Havana Perfecto, he touched the long cylinder to his upper lip reflectively for a moment, savoring the clean, acrid smell of the tobacco. Then he reached in his vest pocket for a small knife to cut the end with. As he did, he spotted a familiar figure: tall, slender, deadly, gaudily dressed, with a drooping black mustache that was just beginning to show the first signs of gray.

The man recognized him at the same time. Politely, almost deferentially, he nodded hello and started to move away. But Boyd, the cigar between his teeth now, nodded to him: a come-hither nod that very economically said, "All's forgiven, let's talk." He finished lighting the cigar.

The other man moved to his side. "Well, Dallas," he said. "I thought you were still holding a grudge."

Dallas Boyd, puffing a cloud of smoke skyward in the light shipboard breeze, grinned at him. "Bill Schindler, you old pirate. It's good to see you. Particularly if you've got notions of getting a game going up on the main deck in"—he consulted his big railroad watch unhurriedly—"oh, perhaps an hour or so. Or are you going to be working the boats again? I understood . . ."

He let the question hang there. Schindler's spare face assumed a wry expression. "I suppose everybody on the river's heard," the gambler said, "about how Bill Schindler got himself stranded on a bar up by Baton Rouge when some spoilsport of a Missouri puke claimed he'd seen me laying

315

bottom stock." He turned suddenly and spat over the side. "Imagine anyone thinking me a sure-thing man." He grinned conspiratorially. "Besides, I'm a shiner man when I'm working. I don't even use holdouts, and I haven't owned a stripper plate since I was sixteen."

"So, are you working now?" Boyd stepped back and looked him down. He wore the standard black soft hat, black broadcloth coat and trousers, black boots, black tie, frilly white shirt, and the gaudiest vest Boyd had ever seen outside of a hundred-dollar whorehouse, bedecked with diamond buttons. Conspicuous in its absence was the "headlight"—a cut stone many carats in weight, which Schindler had made famous on the river. His hands, however, were heavily beringed, and large stones shone from three fingers of his left hand.

"Ah, you've noticed Plymouth Rock is missing. Goddammit, the blacklist reduced me to the worst of expedients, Dallas. I'm not lucky on land. I wound up putting the little darling in pawn to a gentleman in Cairo when I bet Napoleon's ransom on four of the prettiest sixes a man ever drew. I was sure, dead sure, the bastard hadn't filled the straight flush." He shook his head, still angry with himself. "I have hopes of redeeming it on this trip. I hope you're not still angry with me for—"

"Oh, hell, Bill," Boyd said with a grin. "I don't get angry, I get even. Where's your game? Second table in the main cabin, as usual?"

"No," Schindler said. "I'm still taboo to that extent. But Jake Cutler's an old friend, and he's as superstitious as any man on the river. Thinks it's bad luck to start a race without a poker dealer on board. So he's letting me set up in the texas. I'd say allow an hour for the word to get around. There's big money on this boat. Perhaps you and I can separate some of the best of it from its, ah, current custodians."

"Excellent," Boyd said with that insouciant grin of his. "And then I intend to take you for your boots and drawers, you old thimblerigger. If you've got the deed to your mother's grave on you, I'd advise you to tuck it away in Jake Cutler's safe. Because if you've got anything left that's worth more than the fillings on your teeth by the time I'm done with you, then God's dead and I'm no Irishman.''

"Done," Schindler said. "It'll be a pleasure to pick you clean.''

As Boyd turned away, his eye happened to fall on the staircase leading down to the next deck, and he stopped dead. Down the broad stairs, a small, skinny man in working-class attire beckoned wildly to him, trying to get his attention. To him? Boyd looked around; there was no one else near him. He obeyed the impulse and went down to the hurricane deck to greet the little man.

As he did, a deckhand took the little man by the elbow. "Pardon me, could I see your ticket?" The little man wheeled, looked at his questioner, and turned again to Boyd, his eyes pleading.

"Oh, it's all right," Boyd said. "The gentleman has a message for me. It's about my baggage." He dug into his pocket and pressed a coin into the deckhand's calloused mitt.

"Thanks," the little man said. "I ain't s'posed to be up on the hurricane deck like this. But I seen yer and . . .'' He furtively looked right and left. "Is there someplace we can jabber some?''

"Sure," Boyd said, steering him free of a knot of people and bearing for the lee rail. "But I don't think I know you.''

"I'm Mack Leggett. I work for Miss Brand and Ben Samuels. Yer Dallas Boyd. I seen yer in the city, and I know yer a friend o' Miss Brand.''

"Well, yes," Boyd said. "But—''

"Look," Leggett said, "there's trouble aboard. Big trouble. The worst trouble there is on a steamboat. Me an' my partner, Quint, we been snoopin' around Rathbone's people under orders from Ben, an' this mornin' we saw somebody comin' aboard as shouldn't be here, and—''

"Wait," Boyd said, intrigued. "Shouldn't be here?''

"A torch. A perfessional torch name o' Henry Oldin'. And he's in workin' gear, and he's got his two handbags with him. Never mind how we know him. Just take it from me. Between them two bags there's the makin's of a fire that'll send the *Jackson* to the bottom o' the Mississippi.''

Boyd's eyes narrowed. "Fire? But who would want to burn the *Jackson*? Why?"

"Why's for later, Mr. Boyd. The thing to think of right now is how to stop 'im. My partner Quint's down on the main deck stickin' to 'im like a tick on a dog. But Henry Oldin's a man that can ditch the likes o' Quint, and maybe the likes o' me too. When I seen yer, I figgered we could use some help."

"You could," Boyd said. "And you're right. We'd damn well better get to work." He thought of the poker game and sighed. Bill Schindler would have to wait.

Impatiently Basil Endicott led his rented horse down Protection Levee into Jefferson Parish. From atop the embankment he had seen the towering twin stacks of whichever steamboat had taken the lead; it was still downstream from him. If he could get some real speed out of this nag in the last mile . . .

But the road was too long. He'd make better time simply striking south, following the levee all the way to the river. Grimly he mounted and spurred the horse forward. From a trot he broke into a full-fledged gallop and thanked his lucky stars that New Orleans had never taken to the Western saddle.

Rathbone's downtown office was deserted when he let himself in. The weight of the world was on him as he trudged wearily upstairs and fell, rather than sank, into his big chair behind the broad desk.

The line of filled whiskey bottles on the shelf caught his eye. He hesitated—hadn't he had enough of that, in the months following Allison's passing?—but then a wave of shock, loathing, and fear ran through him again, and he reached up with an unsteady hand for the cut-glass bottle of rye. When he poured into the glass at his side, his hand shook uncontrollably, and he spilled a third of the glass onto the polished desktop. Holding the glass with both hands, he drank thirstily.

The raw taste of the liquor cut through the sick taste in his mouth, but it did little to alleviate the steady ache at the base of his skull. The nausea and dizziness seemed to be gone now, but the general feeling of malaise stayed with him. If there were only something—some laudanum, perhaps, to deaden the pain.

God! God! Where had it all gone wrong? How could it come to this? How could the boy do such a thing?

He reached for the glass again and drained it. He poured again, wondering for a moment at the curious numbness in the hand that held the bottle. When he tried to drink the liquor in the glass, he found himself oddly unable to swallow for a moment. He put the glass down and raised his hands to his throat. He looked at the bottle; there seemed to be two of them for a moment there, wavering before his eyes. There was a strange feeling of numbness in his face, a prickling, particularly on the right side.

He did not hear the footfalls on the stairs until their maker had reached the landing. Then Rathbone's hearing returned miraculously, and the last steps of the man who now paused for a moment at the top of the stairs, looking at him, fell like cannon shots on his ear. He looked up at the man. Familiar, somehow, but who was he? The name . . . the name was . . . He tried to speak but found his tongue thick and his throat dry. He cleared his throat, noting the prickly feeling had spread to his mouth as well, and tried to speak again.

"Well, sir?" his visitor said in a booming voice thick with emotion. "Well? What have you to say for yourself? I suppose you're proud of yourself, eh?" His visitor gripped a stout cane; he tightened his grasp on it and shook it angrily at Rathbone.

"I . . . I w-w . . ." Rathbone said. The words wouldn't come. His head had begun to throb: pulse, pulse, pulse . . . The rhythm was that of his wildly beating heart.

"Goddammit, Rathbone," said his visitor. "Haven't you anything to say to me? Me, who has known you for twenty years? Me, whose wife was your wife's dearest friend for most of that time?" The visitor's voice broke on the next word; he tried again. "My wife—you can imagine how she is taking this! *Mon dieu*, Rathbone . . ."

Rathbone gripped his inert right hand with his left. The tingling was much enhanced. He could feel nothing else in the hand. He pinched it. Nothing, nothing. He looked up at the double image of his visitor. Who was this man? It was somebody he should know, but . . .

"Damn you!" his visitor said. "Answer me! Or haven't you got the guts to speak to me, whom you have wronged? My wife is under a doctor's care. I haven't slept all night. That your *cochon* of a son should do this to me, to Felicite, to our daughter, who was pure before this monster saw fit to defile her! And now—now she must either bear his bastard, or . . ."

Desmoulins. That was the name. Henri Desmoulins. But what was he saying? Something about his daughter . . . about his son. Which son? Certainly not the younger ones. It must be Ward. Ward, who had ruined him today.

Then somehow there was a blank period, and when his eyes opened, the clock on the wall had advanced a quarter of an hour, and it was not Henri Desmoulins standing over him but his son Ward. Ward had a bleeding cut on his face and was holding a handkerchief to it, but there was a thin vicious smile of triumph on his face. Rathbone tried to speak but could not. He tried to move his hands. Neither would obey his command. His eyes blinked up at the boy.

"Well," Ward said. "Well, I'll be goddamned. Look at you now. A stroke! Who would have believed it? Laird Rathbone laid low by something like this."

The boy reached for the open bottle and drank from it, disdaining the empty glass beside it. He put it down and wiped his mouth, still holding the kerchief to his cut cheek with his other hand. "I saw Desmoulins on the stairs. He hit me with his cane. But don't worry, I think he's on the way to the doctor's. There'll be some sort of help for you soon. But not enough, dear Father. Not enough. You're done. Done."

Rathbone watched him helplessly. He tried again to speak, to move, but his body obeyed no command of his at all, none except the command that made his eyes follow Ward's every move.

"Well!" Ward said. "Desmoulins will come around. I'll marry the little bitch, of course—with the proper dot. And I'll pin the *Jackson* thing on Halsey, after I've eliminated him so that he can't talk and tell his side of anything. And then, dear Father, I'll be the master of all I survey." He smiled. "I suppose you think I don't know about the change of will? The one in which Halsey is specifically removed from the proprietorship of any of your properties, leaving the matter open—'up for grabs,' as the street urchins say. That leaves clear sailing for me, as I realized when I opened the safe last night, using the combination you'd taped to the underside of the second desk drawer." He held the bottle up, saluted with it, drank again. "Congratulations, Father. It took me more than six months to find it, going over the room with a fine-toothed comb. But now? Now it's all mine. Even if you survive, I'm a logical choice as conservator, and you'll need one. Because even if you live through this, you'll be a vegetable."

Rathbone looked on with horror. If only he could say something, do something.

Ward patted his cheek. Apparently the bleeding had stopped. "Well, Father," he said, "I'll leave you now. The doctor will be along presently. I've some unfinished business with Halsey. I'll come see you in the hospital. Or in the morgue. I don't suppose it matters all that much, does it?"

Rathbone marked the hurt and anger and malice in the boy's eyes. *We came so close to having an understanding for a while there,* he thought. But it was too late. The boy was lost to him, now and forever. It was too late. Too late for either of them. Too late for anything.

Chapter 44

Basil Endicott, red-faced and winded, struggled to the top of the levee, leaving his rented horse tied at the far side. At the top he gasped for breath and looked right and left, and his heart sank. The *Memphis*, pulling proudly away from her rival, had already made the crossing at Nine Mile Point and was more than half a mile upstream, out of sight of him. He could see her towering stacks emitting irregular puffs of off-white smoke as the great vessel chuffed steadily up the river.

Behind her, the *Jackson* seemed about to cross, and it would pass close to him doing so. He stepped out to a prominent position and waved his arms wildly. "Ahoy the *Jackson*!" he said. "You've got to stop! Stop, do you hear?"

Along the three decks, passengers waved brightly back at him. A deckhand stopped and looked at him. Basil waved all the more wildly. "Stop!" he bellowed, in the parade-ground voice he'd developed while with the guards in his youth. "You've got to stop! There's a bomber on board!"

". . . can't . . . what you . . . louder . . ." came the deckhand's answering cry faintly—too faintly.

Up in the pilothouse the pilot spun the great wheel and called down the tube for more steam. Basil could see him but, significantly, could not hear the words. If only the passengers would leave off their chattering! "Stop!" he bellowed again. "You've got to stop! Danger! Da-a-anger!"

His remarks were buried in laughter from the passengers on the hurricane deck. *Oh, God,* he thought. *I must look fifty kinds of idiot, up here waving my arms like a mountebank.*

The *Jackson* rounded the great curve, shaving the point.

The deckhand, still curious, ran aft along the main deck, his hand on the starboard rail, his eyes on Basil. "Stop them!" Basil yelled, running lightly along the levee as the ship turned sharply away from the outside curve of the river and steamed powerfully away from him. "For the love of God, stop them! You've got a killer aboard! *Bomb! Do you hear? A bomb!*"

The deckhand reached the aft rail and stood watching him, scratching his head. He yelled something across the widening expanse of water, but Basil could no longer make out his voice at all.

"My God," he said, lowering his arms and letting out a deep, dejected breath. What was left? The telegraph. He'd telegraph ahead. But what the devil *towns* lay above him along the river? Which among them would have telegraph offices? Surely Baton Rouge would, but none other. What if the bomb were set to go off before Baton Rouge?

"By heaven," said Aurora exultantly, "she's a wonder, Seth, and no mistake about it." She turned to the captain, and the full force of her radiant smile brought a quiet smile to Seth Falkner's lined old face. "She responds as if she read my mind."

Falkner beamed with pride. "I *told* you, ma'am. This is the ship Ormsby and Flint have been dreaming of making for years. I even added a few touches of my own. And as I told you, it didn't make a bit of difference what Rathbone built into the *Jackson*. We'll take him, anyway. We've the better part of a mile on him now, and Jake's crossing, unless my eyes deceive me, was clumsy back there off the point."

"Seth, I'll never doubt you again," she said. She stepped back, one hand still on the great wheel, and gestured to him. "Here. Do you want to take her?"

"With pleasure, ma'am," Falkner said. He put one bronzed old hand on the wheel, and his smile grew all the wider. "I'll take the next crossing, at least," he said. "I wouldn't want to deprive you of the enjoyment any longer than that." He bent to the speaking tube. "Falkner here, Morris. Give us a little more steam, please."

Aurora Brand looked back at the widening gap between the *Memphis* and its behemoth of a rival, then turned back to smile happily at Seth Falkner. "Steady as she goes, Captain," she said affectionately.

"Easy," Mack Leggett said, grabbing Boyd's arm and speaking in a whisper. "There he is. And, God a'mighty, Mr. Boyd . . . he's still got his bags."

Boyd stuck his head out from behind a stanchion and pulled it back in a hurry. "Well," he said. "I almost did it then. Another split second and he'd have looked me right in the eye." He hesitated a moment, then peeked out cautiously. "Mack," he said, "where's he most likely to go to work? Where's the boat most vulnerable? I don't have occasion to know that sort of thing. On a riverboat I usually spend my time shuffling the pasteboards. Is he likely to blow her this early?"

"Ain't no knowin', Mr. Boyd," Leggett said. "But my feelin' is he'll hit her before we stop at the woodin' station. As fer where . . . well, he could decide to blow the big wheel. That'd sure as hell stop us. Best place to blow us would be in the engine room. Yer could make it look like the boiler blew. But that'd mean killin' the engineer and the striker, and that ain't child's play. Them two is usually the biggest, meanest two bastards on the boat. And the pilot'd notice they wasn't on duty in a minute. But the main thing is, that ain't Henry's style."

"Now we're getting down to it," Boyd said, sneaking another peek out from behind the stanchion. "What *is* his style?"

"Somethin' quiet. Set 'er to blow out the bottom, use a long fuse, an' step over the side nice an' quiet when nobody ain't lookin'. But where? We'll have to stick with him like a couple o' deerflies on a fat cow's ass."

"Right," Boyd said. He looked out again. "Damn! He's gone." He stepped out into the passage and looked down it. "There he goes! Quickly, Mack!"

Leggett hustled after him, his short legs pumping. "Goddammit," he muttered under his breath, "where's Quint? He oughter be right there."

• • •

Halsey, half drunk now, climbed the front stairs to his office again, his good hand on the rail, his face set in a grim mask. Damn! he thought. What to do? What to do about this impossible mess Rathbone's cub had landed them all in? He couldn't think of a thing. Every passing minute brought the moment of disaster closer, closer. . . .

At the top of the stairs he paused, blowing a bit. God! His head was splitting. Perhaps a little laudanum in his drink to ease the ache . . . He pushed the door open and stepped inside. Instantly he knew something was wrong. He'd locked the door earlier.

"There," a voice said behind him. "Just stop right there, Mr. Halsey."

Halsey wheeled. He looked at the slightly built, thin-faced young man with the haunted eyes, at the small-bore pistol he held in his two hands, pointing it unsteadily at Halsey's middle. "You," he said. "You're the Brand woman's ink slinger, ain't you? What the hell are you doing here?"

"I'm Cassie Quayle's friend, Mr. Halsey," Arthur Gilliam said in a voice that shook as badly as his hands did. "That's who I am. And I've come to . . ." His face twisted almost comically, the way a grown man's did when he was about to cry like a child. "W-why?" he said in a broken voice. "She hadn't done anything to you. You ruined her life, and then you k-killed her. And for the love of God, her boy, her innocent son . . ."

Halsey looked him up and down, saw the wavering resolve in him, and laughed contemptuously. "Oh," he said. "So she told you about the brat, did she? I didn't think she'd have the nerve. Then you know about her nigger blood. Well, easy come, easy go, boy. Nigger gals are cheap. The town's full of 'em. And—"

"You! You shut up!"

"Oh, come on now. I like 'em myself, boy. Why, Cassie herself was a hot piece, and all the hotter when she was angry. But then I'm not tellin' you anything you don't know, am I?" His hateful grin broadened. "As for the boy, I don't reckon she had the time to tell you I *sent* those letters she was so worried I'd send? No, she didn't know. I didn't tell her until just before I shot—"

"You cowardly swine . . ." Arthur began. He raised the pistol. But it was a single-action revolver, and he hadn't thumbed back the hammer. Nothing happened when he pulled the trigger, his eyes closed in anticipation of the blast. He winced, stepped back, but then Halsey was upon him, backhanding the gun out of his hands into the far corner of the room.

"Puppy!" Halsey said, driving a fist into Arthur's narrow gut and doubling him over. Halsey's good hand went to Arthur's head, grabbing him by the hair. Simultaneously he brought his knee up into Arthur's face, hard, slamming it into Arthur's nose. Halsey felt the bones break and laughed. Holding Arthur by the hair he threw him back against the wall. The boy's face was a mask of blood. He tried to hold his hands up to protect his face. Halsey's boot lashed out and caught Arthur in the groin. He groaned and began to crumple; his hands dropped, and he let out a piercing groan of pain. Halsey stepped forward, bringing his good right hand up in a powerful uppercut that caught Arthur on one side of the chin, snapping his head back hard against the wall. Arthur collapsed against the wall, sliding slowly down it like a puppet with its strings cut.

"Bravo!" said a voice behind him. Halsey, puffing from the exertion, wheeled and saw Ward Rathbone standing in the open doorway behind him, a cocked pistol in his hand trained directly on the center of his chest. "A fine exhibition! One-handed too!"

"The little bastard," Halsey said. "He was going to kill me!"

"So he was," Ward said. "He failed. Perhaps I won't. Or perhaps I'll let you go. It'll take me a moment or two to make up my mind. Meanwhile, Halsey, back against the wall, and be quick about it, or . . ." He gestured meaningfully with the pistol. Halsey backed up until his shoulders touched the wall behind him as Ward crossed to the corner and picked up the pistol Arthur had dropped. Halsey watched as Ward uncocked his own gun and pocketed it, then cocked Arthur's and leveled it at him with the air of a man who knew what he was doing—or was about to do.

"There," Ward said. "I'd been wondering how I was go-

ing to cover this. The scenario was simple enough except for
that. It went something like this. I surprise you, I shoot you
dead. Then I go to the authorities and tell of uncovering your
plot to fire the *Jackson* and blame it on Aurora Brand. You know,
the idea being that I forced the truth from you and then shot
you when you tried to escape. All right, I turn you in then—
dead, of course, so that you can't tell any tales I don't want
told. And then I'm a hero. But the trouble with *that* one is
obvious. There are too many gaps. I'm a little too closely
connected with the problem. 'How did you learn of this, Mr.
Rathbone?' That sort of thing.'' He shrugged it off, an insolent grin on his face. ''Not so good. But now, this way . . .
look at it; it's wonderful. Young Arthur killed you while you
were trying to beat him to a pulp. And now *I* come along
and find him standing over the body of my father's trusted
business partner and I take action. And only when both of
you are dead do I find evidence proving you've ordered the
torching of the *Jackson*—as well as the *Memphis* last year.

''Oh, don't worry,'' he added casually. ''If there's no evidence, I'll manufacture some. And look! I'm miraculously
metamorphosed into a man who's trying to save not only his
father's reputation and business but also the precious lives of
all those innocent people to boot.''

''Look, Ward. You don't want to—''

''Shut up. I heard some of your conversation with this poor
fish here. My God, you really sold *him*, didn't you? And the
half-caste girl, too, and that brat of hers. Well, your selling
days are over.'' He flourished the gun and then pointed it
dead at Simon Halsey's heart. ''Will anyone on God's earth
miss you, Halsey? Is there perchance anyone, anywhere,
who'll weep at your funeral? I doubt it.''

For a moment—the bare blink of an eye—Simon Halsey
thought Rathbone's rambling discourse was going to take off
on another trail. But then he saw the look on the young man's
face and the tightening of his finger on the trigger of the
revolver he'd taken from the floor where Arthur had dropped
it. All of a sudden Halsey knew the moment was near, the
moment he'd feared for so long. The moment when a man
said good-bye, once and for all, to all of it—all of the hopes

and plans, all of the golden future that would never come true. All the dreams. All the future moments that wouldn't be, ever. He raised his good hand, futilely shielding his face. "No, Ward," he said in a voice whose whining quality surprised and dismayed him. "No, for chrissake . . ."

Then the thunderclap and the sharp, quick pain. Then nothing, nothing at all.

Chapter 45

Basil Endicott wiped his brow and shoved the hair out of his eyes with a single swift movement of his hand. "Now, look," he told the telegrapher, "this is an emergency! You have to understand. Every moment we waste arguing, the closer we come to—"

"I don't care," the telegrapher said. "Goddammit, don't you *hear* that thing?" His impatient wave indicated the clattering key on the table. "I go breakin' into messages like that 'un there and I'll lose my situation. If this was some fancy station on the wire like Memphis or Natchez, it'd be different. If you think—"

"Confound it," Basil said. "If it's money you want—"

"Now, look here, you can't do this."

Basil sighed and balled his big fist. "Up," he said, and grabbed the telegrapher by the lapels, dragging him erect. "I'm sorry, but . . ." His fist lashed out and caught the man on the side of the jaw, sharply snapping his head to one side. Basil watched the light go out of his eyes, then eased him down the counter and let him slide softly to the floor. Then he turned to face the table with its clattering key. Damn, Basil thought, there's a special signal for distress, but what in hell's name is it now? He looked down at the wildly cavorting key and flexed his fingers, hoping he could remember enough code to pass the information along. He'd break in, alert every station on the river, and tell them to wigwag to both ships.

He bit his lip. Might as well tell them all of it, all he knew so far. And if Aurora and the *Memphis* got the message, she'd need to know about his own meeting with Dallas Boyd the night before, about Boyd's plans to go north aboard the *Jackson* "to keep an eye on things." It would mean breaking his promise to Boyd, extracted over drinks the previous night at the St. Louis Hotel, but that couldn't be helped.

As he sat down to the key he listened for a moment to the clicking. His jaw dropped. He reached for pencil and paper and started transcribing: ". . . STRONGLY SUSPECT BOMB ABOARD STEAMER ANDREW JACKSON EN ROUTE ST. LOUIS STOP ALERT ALL STATIONS END RACE ANY MEANS NECESSARY STOP GREAT DANGER TO CREW AND PASSENGERS . . ."

"My God," Basil said. "Who sent this?" He shook his head, listening to the rest of the message, the pencil dangling from his hand. It was all there—well, most of it, anyway. Everything except Ward Rathbone's part in the matter and Boyd's presence on the boat . . .

Slowly, meticulously, Henry Olding checked the fuse, making sure it was securely attached to the suitcase. Then, backing slowly down the middle of the forward freight compartment, he paid out the long fuse a foot at a time. When he reached the end, he paused; then, looking around, he spied a tall container of lamp oil. Better safe than sorry, he told himself silently. He doused the whole area around the black-powder bomb with the oil. The bomb ought to blow the bottom out of the *Jackson*, but it wouldn't hurt to have it accompanied by a nice hot fire, something that would slow down any efforts to plug up the hole. Just in case.

Now he stood, and looking behind him to check his avenue of escape, he dug out an oilskin packet of lucifers and opened it. He extracted one phosphorus match and pocketed the package. He looked down at his handiwork with a small smile of satisfaction before striking the match.

"Get him!" a voice said right behind him. A heavy weight hit him amidships, knocking him flat. A pair of hands the size of two smoked hams slammed into his face—one, two— and across from him someone was diving for the lit fuse, wrestling with it, yanking it free.

The big man atop him got up heavily, dragging Olding to

his feet. "All right, yer little son of a bitch," the behemoth said. "That'll be all for today."

"Good work, Quint," a large, well-dressed man standing nearby said to the roughneck who held him fast. "Another minute or two and we'd have been too late for anything. Mack, douse the place down with sand, will you? And bring the suitcase up. We'll drop it overboard quietly. No need panicking the passengers. Quint and I will get this fellow up to Jake Cutler and see what we can learn from him. If anybody asks, he's a pickpocket we caught stealing my watch."

"Yes, sir, Mr. Boyd," the little man behind him said, and his big fist tightened around Henry Olding's collar.

Seth Falkner rang for the second-watch pilot the moment the message came in. When the pilot arrived at the top of the stairs, puffing and out of breath, he said, "Thank you, Mr. Potter. Take over, please. Miss Brand, I have something to show you. A message wigwagged from the bridge. The mate caught most of it and scribbled it down."

He handed over the paper, his eyes on her face. He caught her sharp intake of breath and noted the change in her expression. "I think we'd better take it seriously," he said. "Somehow we've got to get the message to the *Jackson*. We've got a mile lead on them. That means—"

"I know what it means, Seth," she said, "but you know good and well Jake will think this is a trick. When he gets a message from us to stop the race because he's got a bomber on board, he's going to think it's some sort of double-dealing stunt we worked up to get him to quit. He'll figure we've got some sort of problem of our own and are covering up this way, won't he?"

Seth Falkner frowned. "He might, at that. But we've got to take the chance."

"Of course we do. More than that, if he won't stop, we have to stop him. We have to get him to stop dead until the whole boat's been searched."

"Yes, ma'am," Falkner said, looking back downriver where the *Jackson* was barely becoming visible around a bend, her tall stacks riding high above the ornate superstructure. "And I have to tell you that there's another factor of interest to you."

"Yes?" she said, looking down at the paper again.

"Well, I'm breaking a confidence, but last night Basil Endicott and I had drinks with Dallas Boyd, down at the St. Louis Hotel. He told us not to tell you, but he shipped out on the *Jackson* this morning for St. Louis. He figured that if he were aboard the *Memphis*, you might find it distracting in some way."

Aurora's head slowly rose. Her eyes showed her shock as she looked at Seth Falkner, and the implications came home to her. "Dallas," she said huskily.

Ben Samuels pushed his way through the crowd until he was stopped by a constable. "Oh, it's you, sir," the policeman said. "Over there . . ."

Samuels slowed his pace as he saw the twin litters come down the stairs, a man at each end of each of them. The bodies on them had been hastily covered with blankets. He stopped and nodded to Chief Harrison. "I . . . I heard only a few minutes ago. The word appears to be out, all over town—one version of it, anyway. I thought it'd be best to hear it from a reliable source."

"Right, Mr. Samuels. Well, it looks pretty simple. Mr. Gilliam and Mr. Halsey seem to have got into some sort of argument, and Mr. Gilliam seems to have got the worst of it."

"Halsey was blackmailing a friend of Arthur's," Ben said somberly. "I'll fill you in on that later. Go on, please."

"Well, Mr. Gilliam had a gun, it appears, and he undoubtedly shot Mr. Halsey. Young Mr. Rathbone, coming up the stairs, found him standing over Mr. Halsey's body and told him to drop the gun. Instead . . ." He waved his hand, and his accompanying shrug seemed to express pity rather than indifference. "Afterward, as he went through Mr. Halsey's papers, Mr. Rathbone found a letter leading us to believe he'd planted a professional 'torch' aboard the *Jackson* in today's race. False evidence was to be planted near the bombed area, implicating your Miss Brand. You can see all of the evidence at the station if you want to accompany me."

Ben Samuels thought about the matter. "The bomb. I presume you've—"

"Wired ahead? Oh, yes, sir. We've left messages at all points along the river. 'Stop the *Jackson*.' If anything can be done, we'll do it, sir." The chief took off his hat and wiped the sweat from his forehead. "At least your people are safe, sir. But what a pity about Mr. Gilliam. He seems to have been beside himself. To do a desperate thing like that . . ."

"Desperate," Ben Samuels said to himself as much as to anyone. "Yes." But his face clouded over and his mouth turned down at the corners as he pondered the chief's fantastic tale. There was something about it all that didn't ring true. Everyone involved was a little out of character. Could he picture Arthur shooting Halsey dead? Halsey, himself, leaving behind incriminating evidence? Ward Rathbone throwing away caution and doing his civic duty—and so promptly that the telegraphed message had apparently gone out upriver within an hour and a half of the shootings? What was wrong? Why didn't Harrison's open-and-shut case withstand the most cursory scrutiny?

But then he looked over at the police wagon and saw the remains of Arthur Gilliam being loaded into the back, and there was a sharp stab of compassion in his heart that drove all doubt from his mind, at least for the moment.

On the last flight of stairs leading to the texas deck, Henry Olding suddenly doubled over. "My—my stomach . . ." he said. Sandwiched between Quint Ragland, above, and Dallas Boyd, below, he pulled one hand free of Ragland's grasp and clutched his stomach, his face twisted with pain. "God," he said with a half-strangled gasp, "the pain!"

Boyd, beneath him on the narrow stair, braced him with one hand, while Ragland, leaning down, helped Olding up onto the deck. Boyd waited until the stairs were clear, then he moved up behind them.

But Ragland had let go his grasp on Olding's hand for a moment, thinking the bomber had doubled over with pain. As he reached over to help, Olding's boot lashed out and caught him in the face, knocking him back heavily into Boyd, who was just clearing the edge of the texas deck.

"Damn!" Boyd said. "Quick—after him!"

Ragland recovered and scrambled after the now running arsonist. "Here, you!" he bellowed.

But Olding was in full flight now along the length of the deck. Passing the texas cabin, he added speed. "He's goin' over the side!" Ragland said, pounding after him. "Stop, you! Stop!"

Olding did not hear him. He was at full speed now, gathering momentum for a great leap that would take him far, far out, past the jutting hurricane deck and main deck below, into the rolling waters of the Mississippi. His short legs pounded; his arms swung back and forth, and at the last moment his foot caught in a coil of rope at the edge of the texas deck, and he broke stride just as he reached the edge.

"Stop!" Ragland cried out behind him, but he was too late. Olding stumbled, went over the edge headfirst, and disappeared. There was a commotion below. Ragland braked desperately, stopped just in time, then looked over the edge. Down on the main deck, two levels down, the steerage crowd fanned out from the grotesque sight Ragland looked down upon—the broken body, arms and legs splayed wildly, the neck set at an impossible angle.

Ragland thought and thought, but he couldn't think of a damned thing to say as Boyd, coming up behind him, joined him and looked down at the grisly sight on the main deck. Words simply failed him; he shook his head sadly instead.

Boyd broke the silence between them as the crowd below voiced its shock and horror in a murmur that became a low roar. "Well, Quint," he said, "at least the problem's out of the way, one way or the other. Now perhaps I can get back to my poker game. Cheer up, old man. You did your best. You've probably saved the boat and all of our lives, including mine. I won't forget it, either. Come on down to the main cabin; I'll buy you a drink. You look like a man who needs one."

Ragland bit his lip and let himself be led away from the edge of the texas deck, toward the stairs. What Boyd was saying—it made good sense, it really did. So why did he still feel apprehensive? Why didn't he feel any sense of relief?

Why did a sense of impending danger still hang on his heart, perhaps even more heavily than before?

Fat, balding Oscar Pepper, the very picture of a low-grade commercial traveler, puffed his way through the crush of steerage passengers up near the bow and looked once over a fellow passenger's shoulder at the broken body of the man who'd fallen from the texas deck. He shook his head compassionately and muttered something about it all being a shame, a terrible shame. Then he made his way to the lee deck and stood looking ruminatively out over the Mississippi.

Well, that was that for Henry. He'd always been a bit of a bumbler, for all his reputation in the trade. He'd just been lucky most of the time, steering as close to the wind as he did. Without some sort of lucky star above looking out for him, he'd have been caught years ago, jerked up to Jesus by a couple dozen feet of hemp line, and left there to dry like Maggie's Drawers.

At least Henry hadn't had the chance to blab everything he knew under pressure of some constable's truncheon, including all he knew about his confederates in any given operation. More to the point, about confederates in the *present* operation. This way Henry's mouth was sealed in the most efficient manner imaginable.

All the better, Oscar Pepper told himself. All the better that it had gone this way. For one thing, they'd think they'd already gotten their man—and they'd relax. And he, Oscar, could get back to work, unhurriedly finishing the little project Henry Olding had been too damned clumsy to finish by himself.

He smiled. It looked like clear sailing from here on in. When the bomb was placed and the fuse burned down to the halfway mark, he'd step unobtrusively over the side, aft of the great wheel, and make for the far shore.

Chapter 46

Olivia's dark head appeared at the top of the stairs. Overcome with diffidence at the door of the one inviolable sanctuary aboard a Mississippi steamer, she paused. But Aurora Brand, turning, saw her and gestured: *Come on up! Quickly!* She put one hand to her mouth and hesitated again, but after a moment she obeyed.

"Miss Brand," she said, "someone told me you wanted to see me."

"Yes," Aurora said. She looked at Seth Falkner, at the second-watch pilot at the great wheel, and let her tensed shoulders fall. "Olivia, we've got a problem. And since you're in this as much as I am . . ."

"Me, Miss Brand?" the girl said. "But—"

Aurora waved her hand as if to say, "Silence please." "You and I both have someone very dear to us on board the *Jackson*. Your young man, Todd, is in the crew, and Dallas Boyd's on the passenger list. And there's a bomber loose aboard the *Jackson*."

Olivia's eyes went wide. "A bomber? But how . . . ?"

"Never mind how." Aurora Brand's face showed her perplexity as she paced back and forth in the little cabin. "We just know. But we don't know when the bomb is supposed to go off. And we've signaled the *Jackson* repeatedly, without results."

"You mean, they don't see the signal?" the girl said, hardly believing what she was hearing.

"They see it, and they seem to think it's some sort of sharper's trick. Instead of reversing engines, they've poured on steam. They've gained a quarter of a mile on us since the first signal.''

"Oh, my God," the girl said. "Todd . . . Mr. Boyd . . . all those innocent people . . ."

"Exactly. I'm trying to figure out what to—" Her face suddenly changed. Her eyes lit up. "Seth!" she said, turning to face forward again. "The narrows up ahead, in the upriver channel. If we stalled her there, would we block the channel?"

"Eh?" Falkner said, pausing in the middle of lighting his pipe and looking at her so long, his eyes only half focused, that his match burned his fingers. "I'll be damned. I . . . excuse me, ma'am. Mr. Potter?"

The second-watch pilot frowned and thought about it. "Hmm. I ran this water six nights ago, on the *Carondelet*. She wasn't drawing near the water the *Jackson* must be. She's shoal there, everywhere but the main channel." He looked up ahead, at the twisting stream, at the wind-reef ripples in the brown water. "Jake Cutler and his man must know that. I don't know his pilot, but on the first leg of a river race he won't have any apprentice cub at the wheel. He'll have a man who knows the river, knows what you can do with passengers aboard and what you can't. I think you can block her. But, ma'am, it'll be dangerous. Maybe too dangerous."

"I know," Aurora said. "The *Jackson*'ll be coming around the bend under a full head of steam, thinking she's chasing a boat going hell-for-leather, and she'll find instead a boat stalled in the only channel. The question is—and I ask the two of you as professionals—has she time to back water? To stop? Or does she go plowing into us and hit us broadside?"

The two men looked at each other long and hard before they looked back at her. Seth Falkner pursed his lips and fiddled with his pipe. Then, with measured words, he said, "It's risky, ma'am. It's the riskiest thing I've ever been asked to do. Given my druthers, I'd rather run a twenty-mile stretch full of snags on a dark night. But—"

"But?"

"You're right. I can't think of anything else to do. Not with three hundred of New Orlean's best on board back there." He lit his pipe with a hand that came closer to shaking than Aurora Brand had ever seen it do. "Mr. Potter?" he said.

The pilot looked back. "I wouldn't do it on my own initiative," he said. "But—"

"Damned right you wouldn't," Aurora said with a tense smile. "I'd have your head, your gizzard, and your license, in no particular order. Quite right, Mr. Potter. It's a decision only the owner of a ship has the right to make. And I'm making it. Stall her in the narrows, Mr. Potter. Block the channel."

Inert, only his eyes mobile, Laird Rathbone lay on his downstairs bed, watching the doctors and nurses scurry about him. He had given up listening to their chatter; it seemed to have little to do with him. Now a new voice cut into the talk, a voice thick with a new authority and confidence. Laird closed his eyes and listened as his son Ward entered and, one step at a time, took over.

"I don't care. If you can't take just as good care of him here as in a hospital, you're incompetent and should be discharged. I'll pay for round-the-clock care, and all the watches will have a full household staff to run errands for them. Every nurse will have six niggers at her beck and call. Do you think you can improve upon that at any hospital? Eh? Then don't give me any medical folderol. Do as I say. And keep in mind who the biggest donor to the hospital fund is, eh? If you can't remember that fact, I'm sure the hospital administration will be delighted to remind you, with a little help from me."

Rathbone rolled his eyes and opened them. He heard the door pushed shut behind him, and Ward's voice came closer. "Father," his son said, "I'm going to have you looked after here. There'll be people watching after you all the time. There won't be a moment when you're alone."

Now he could see Ward standing over him. Surprisingly he could see something new in Ward's face: a protectiveness, a genuine concern, even a certain affection that he could swear had never been there before. Rathbone's eyes searched the young man's face; his mind reeled at the change.

Ah, but of course. Ward had won. He had won the battle between father and son, and definitively. He could *afford* the largesse of affection, of filial respect, of solicitude. His father could no longer hurt him, could no longer threaten him, could no longer grant or withhold delegated power, praise, or reward.

The door opened suddenly behind Ward. The boy turned and said, "Oh, Alex. I thought it was . . ."

Rathbone strained, but not being able to turn his head, he saw neither of his two sons. "It doesn't matter what you thought, Ward. I wanted to tell you I'm leaving for good. I'm all packed and—"

"Leaving?"

"Oh, spare me the brotherly concern. You don't give a damn, and neither do I. I just wanted to tell you. And do me one last favor. It'll pay me back for the thirty dollars you stole from under my mattress six months ago. Tell Marcella Hays I've gone. Discreetly, if you can. Tell her—"

"Marcella who? *Hays*?" Ward's voice seemed ready to break out into wild laughter. "Is *that* who it's been? The wife of . . . oh, my God, this is rich. You randy little bastard."

"Whatever." Alex's voice was flat, emotionless, impatient. "I won't bother saying good-bye to the old man. He won't even notice I'm gone. He never noticed I was here. If it hadn't been for Mother, I'd have gone long ago. As for the past year, well, I've been spinning my wheels in the mud here. Time to go, to get out from underfoot. Oh, don't fret yourself, dear brother. I won't contest anything. I don't want your damned money, or your damned power, or anything you'll pry out of Father's hands now that he can't do anything about you anymore. None of this matters. It's your world, Ward, not mine. I have enough money to get by until I've established myself."

"Well, I'll be damned," Ward said. "The puppy asserts himself. All right, go. I won't make a move to stop you."

"Thank you," Alex said sarcastically. "Say good-bye to Todd for me when you see him. He ought to be back in a month or so."

"Todd?" Ward said. "I've been so busy, he's slipped my mind. Back in a month? Where's he gone? Off to the bushes with the little Soames girl, I suppose."

"Why, didn't he tell you?" Alex said, the sound of his

voice moving farther away from Laird. "He shipped out on the *Jackson* this morning as an ordinary deckhand. He thought it might impress Father or something like that. Good-bye, Ward." The door slammed behind him.

"On the *Jackson*?" Ward said out loud, thunderstruck. "Todd? But they don't know about the second man! Even if they get Olding, there's always . . . oh, my God. Oh, my God!"

Rathbone could see him now, upside down, standing behind his father's bed, both hands pressed to his face and covering his lips, mouth, and chin. "Oh, my God," he kept saying over and over again.

"Russell!" The voice broke into Todd Rathbone's thoughts; for a moment he didn't realize the name bellowed at him so precipitately was his own. "Russell, God damn your hide, don't sit there like a bump on log! Get busy!"

Todd snapped to and faced the mate. "Sorry, sir. I told the leadsman, just like you told me to."

"Then get aft! Hop to it! See the striker in the engine room. He needs some muscle to help repair the doctor engine. That ought to be about your speed. If he said he needed brains, I'd send someone else." The mate looked him up and down. "Well, don't just stand there! Double time!"

"Yes, sir!" Todd said, and set out at a quick clip. Why, he asked himself, hadn't he picked a name he was used to? Every time someone yelled Russell at him, he went off into a funk for a moment or two, trying to figure out who they were talking to. He'd have to watch that. *Russell,* he told himself. *You're Tad Russell. Get that through your damned thick skull.*

Edgar Forster, first-watch pilot of the *Jackson*, bent over the speaking tube again. "Mr. Casey," he said to the engineer, "I asked for more steam."

The voice came back up at him, a little annoyed. "Striker's working on the doctor," he said. Forster stood up and stared at Jake Cutler. He said nothing but shook his head slowly, his expression revealing his anxiety.

Cutler stepped over to the tube. "Mr. Casey," he said, "is this a garbage scow or a New Orleans packet, sir?"

"Why, it's a New Orleans packet, sir. But—"

"Well, then, damn your eyes and your black heart, treat her as though she was one. Stay awake down there! For the love of God, have you dozed off and let chips get into the doctor? Is the water supply from the boilers shut off? What in hell's name is going on down there?"

"Little mechanical difficulty, sir."

"That's enough. No excuses. Stay alert! Check the gauge cocks! Stay on top of things!"

"Yes, sir, but . . ."

Cutler didn't wait for the answer. He stepped back to the aft end of the pilothouse and addressed his guests again. "Sorry about that, gentlemen. Sometimes the crew lets things get away from them, and one has to shake things up a bit."

"That was the engineer, wasn't it?" Marcel Trudeau, a big trader on the Bourse, said. "I mean, is there any danger? After all, a race . . ."

"Rest easy, Mr. Trudeau," the captain said. "The days of the dangerous races are over. There are strict regulations these days, restricting each vessel to just so many pounds of steam to the square inch. No, it's the slow runs where things get dangerous, where people get careless. On a big, important cruise like this one, virtually everyone in the crew has five or six people bellowing at him, keeping him up to the mark. You're as safe as if you were sitting in your own parlor at home, sipping good chicory coffee." His smile remained serenely confident, but his hand, deep inside his jacket pocket, had two fingers crossed. So far the word hadn't got out about the bomber. The commotion had, so far, been passed off as the antics of a madman bent on suicide.

"Captain," the pilot said behind him. "Up ahead, sir, around the bend. Look, sir. The *Memphis*."

Jake Cutler excused himself and moved forward to the big wheel and the broad window before it. "Why, what in hell's name is going on?" he said. "What is that damned fool woman trying to do? She's blocking the confounded channel!"

"Yes, sir," Forster said tensely, wishing the captain hadn't brought visitors into the pilothouse. He bent over the speaking tube, but then he hesitated and straightened up again. "Back her, sir? Stop her? Or—"

Cutler frowned and pondered the question a moment. "Can we get into the downstream channel, do you think? Is there time?" He peered out over the broad expanse of water before them.

"Not much chance, sir," the pilot said. "Shoal water. See the ripple?"

"Yes, yes. Damn the woman! Damn her eyes! She'll try anything, won't she?" He spoke from between clenched teeth. "Well, all's fair in a run for the antlers, eh? Mr. Forster, pass her on the right. Cut it fine, but pass her."

"On the right, sir? But—"

"Two bells, Mr. Forster! Pass her on the right! That's an order!"

Up in the pilothouse of the *Memphis*, Aurora Brand watched unbelievingly, her eyes wide with horror. "Seth!" she said. "They're going to try to pass! They'll never make it! They'll go aground!"

"Oh, my God," Seth Falkner said. "He can't do this!"

An identical shock went through the both of them as they watched the great bulk of the *Andrew Jackson* slide swiftly atop the underground sandbar and go aground on the drowned reef with a terrible, grinding shudder.

Chapter 47

When the *Jackson* hit the bar, the forward inertia of the great vessel threw to the decks virtually every man, woman, and child on board. After a moment's shocked silence their reactions came, loud and strong: cries for help, screams of pain, and the general commotion common to any disaster. Adding to the noise was the sound of the great ship itself reacting to the intolerable strain put on her by the grounding. The hull and deck alike showed immediate signs of hogging. The deck timbers arched; the hog chains, fastened to hull timbers at bow and stern and carried over a series of struts rising from the keelson, drew taut. One snapped, the chain flailing wildly about, its iron connecting rod striking a crewman and killing him. Listing hard to port, the great ship began to die a little at a time. The engineer was already dead, his head smashed against the boiler by the lurching motion of the boat, and the striker shut down both the main engine and the doctor.

From both the *Jackson* and the nearby *Memphis*, the ships' yawls—lifeboats—were lowered from the davits. Those of the *Memphis* were first in the water; Aurora Brand had called out the order to lower away the moment it became obvious the other vessel was doomed. Now, having directed the first lowering-away, she prepared to climb down into a lifeboat herself. Her own ship lay at anchor now, relatively secure. Half the crew had taken charge of calming her own passengers and making sure the balance of the vessel was not disturbed by the rush of gawkers to the starboard rail; the other

343

half of the crew was in the water, making for the other vessel, ready to help with the evacuation.

Behind her, a voice cut into her consciousness. "Miss Brand! Miss Brand!" She wheeled, hand on the gunwale. Olivia Soames made her way toward her through the milling crowd. "Please . . ."

Aurora Brand waited, biting her lip. As the girl approached, she said, "Olivia, if you could help with the survivors as they come over . . ."

"Miss Brand," Olivia said, "I have to go with you."

"But, Olivia—"

"No. I have to. You've got Mr. Boyd over there. I have Todd. If I didn't go along, and if anything happened to him, why, I'd never be able to live with myself." The girl's voice broke. Aurora smiled and clasped her shoulder.

"All right, but do as I say. And, Olivia?"

"Yes, ma'am?"

"I understand. More than you think."

As she spoke, her thoughts were still on Dallas Boyd.

On opposite ends of the stricken boat, Boyd and Todd Rathbone struggled with the passengers, trying to keep the evacuation orderly. The stairs above them, leading to the boiler and hurricane decks, were clogged with people trying to descend. Boyd, coming down from the texas, had simply slid down the vertical stanchions that rose from the deck rails; others less agile than he were now finding their descent blocked by the glut of panic-stricken people. Turning from the loading of a half-filled yawl, he went to the foot of the steps and, standing squarely in the way of the oncoming horde, bellowed in a voice of command, "All right, there! Slow it down! You in back! Take it easy, now." With one hand he liberated a child from the knot of people and passed him over the heads of the passengers to a crewman loading the near yawl. "Here! Get this little lady on board, please."

Then, looking up, he happened to let his eye fall on the second wave of lifeboats coming across from the *Memphis*. Standing in the bow, fearless and determined-looking, was Aurora Brand. Boyd grinned; he'd never seen her look lovelier, even though that red hair was disheveled and one sleeve was torn. He couldn't resist yelling over to her: *"Aurora! Over here!"* His reward was a smile and a look of relief that his heart could read even at this distance. *My God,* he thought. *And I thought she didn't care.*

Now, prompted by the girl behind her—Soames's child, was it?—Aurora cupped her hands around her mouth and cried something out to him. He didn't make it out at first over all the commotion. With his free hand he put his hand to his ear as a sign to her that he hadn't heard her the first time. She shouted again: "Rathbone, find Todd Rathbone!"

"Louder!" Boyd bellowed across to her. "Can't hear you!"

She tried again. "Rathbone's son, Todd, the second son, he's in the crew!"

"Ah," Boyd said, and nodded. He looked at the Soames girl and understood. He grinned and thought, Well, a chip off the old block. What woman wouldn't be a little better off with a trace of Aurora's fearless and independent spirit? He waved at the two women and, breaking free, headed aft. Rathbone's boy on board, eh? An officer? No, his old man would have heard of it. A deckhand, then, a cub. That would mean he was down here on the main deck somewhere. Boyd stepped up to the port rail, jumped lightly atop it, and peered down the length of the big vessel. He'd have to be back there somewhere.

Stepping down onto the badly warped deck, he began making his way back toward the aft passageway and the great paddlewheel.

Amidships, Oscar Pepper, his satchel in hand, pondered his situation. The *Jackson* was doomed, and her bottom hadn't been blown. His chances of collecting that fat fee were almost nil now. Unless, technically, he could make a claim based on his having performed the feat in good faith, anyway. If he went ahead and blew the boat, blew the bottom out of her, perhaps he could qualify as having fulfilled his end of the bargain. Then, if his anonymous patron were to renege on the deal he had made with Olding, the criminal code of the river underworld could make it hot for the man who'd backed out on his end, on rightful payment for services rendered.

He looked around him. There was no one to be found except at the two ends of the slowly foundering boat. Forward and aft were where the lifeboats were. Back here . . .

Yes, there. There was a protected spot, out of sight, in the narrow well beside the great paddle box. If he could set the charge just so, it would blow the buckets right off the wheel and the bottom out of the *Jackson*. If he gave it a long fuse, that would give him time to get aft to the boats and make his way off the stricken ship just as if he were any other passenger.

He knelt, opened the satchel, and went to work. He'd thought ahead; everything was set except for the paying-out of the fuse and the lighting of it. He set the charge in place and backed down the narrow passage, laying out the fuse.

"Hey," said a voice behind him. Oscar turned, startled. A young crewman, maybe twenty or so, stood there, aghast at what he saw. "Hey, you can't . . ."

Oscar Pepper attacked. He reached out one hand and grabbed the boy by the hair. His other hand took hold of the young man's uniform lapel. He ignored the flailing arms; pulling the crewman forward, he ran him headlong into the bulkhead just forward of the paddle box. His head hit the stout wall with a sickening sound; his body went limp, and Pepper eased him down to the deck. He looked around furtively. My God, he thought, someone's sure to be along any minute now. No time to waste . . .

He returned to the strung fuse, picked it up, and lit it with a lucifer. He waited until the flame was flickering brightly, burning its way slowly down the line, before he dropped it on the deck and began walking unhurriedly away from it. Now, he told himself, just walk away as though nothing had happened. Don't hurry. Get out of sight of the whole thing, and then, when nobody is looking, slip into the crowd back by the boats. If it's too crowded, jump in and start swimming. Plenty of others were doing that, after all.

Suddenly, without warning, the deck moved violently under his feet, just as he passed a pile of baled cotton. A bale

tipped and fell heavily on top of him, knocking him flat on
his back. He felt something snap, and when he tried to move
his legs, they would not obey his command. "My God," he
said. He pushed with his arms, but the weight was too great
for him to shake off. He turned his head desperately and saw
the bomb, not ten paces from him, past the inert body of the
young crewman. The bomb was set to blow the guts out of
the great steamer, and him with it! The sputtering fuse continued to burn. . . .

"This way! This way!" Aurora Brand cried, waving her
arms without rocking the boat. The rowers brought the *Jackson*'s yawl clumsily along and made for the swimmers in the
water. "Here they are!" she said, pointing. Strong hands
reached down for the swimmers, pulling them clear. Only
when they were safely in the lifeboat did she turn to her
rowers and call out softly, "All right, boys, over there, near
the paddle wheel."

She was in the middle of another order when her words
froze in mid-syllable. She raised her eyes to the level of the
main deck, taking in the whole scene in three quick flashes:
the sputtering, burning fuse sending up feeble sparks; the
unconscious boy lying close by it; and—her heart almost
stopped—Dallas Boyd making his way down the passage toward the bomb.

"Dallas!" she screamed. "Get back! Get back!"

Olivia, standing in the stern of the little boat, had seen it
all, too, and had recognized the inert form of the boy in
uniform. "No!" she screamed. "Todd—it's Todd!"

Boyd turned. His eyes narrowed, and he strained to catch
their words. At his feet a bale of hay lay atop a passenger, a
man who struggled feebly. He stooped, lifted it free with a
powerful motion so precipitate that the bunching of his mighty
shoulders split his shirt up the seam in back. "Here," he told
Oscar Pepper, "let me get you out of here."

"Quick!" the man said. "I can't move my legs. And
there's a bomb back there. By the paddle box. It'll go off any
moment now."

Boyd stood erect, and looked around quickly. His gaze

took in the flickering fuse and the unconscious boy lying near it. The choices flashed through his mind.

Then he recognized the boy's face, and he remembered Olivia Soames's anguished cry to him. The multiple choices suddenly melded into one now. He vaulted over the cotton bale, sprang to the boy's side, and lifted him up with a mighty wrench. He climbed to the railing and bellowed: *"Aurora! Get back!"* Balancing on the rail with the boy in his arms, he leaned far out over the river, tossing the boy free only to dive off after him.

Just then the bomb went off with a tremendous flash and a deafening boom. Timbers, panels, and the buckets of the great wheel went flying every which way. A ten-inch piece of railing was torn from the ship and caught Boyd on the side of the head just as his body hit the water.

"Dallas!" Aurora screamed. Tossing caution to the wind, she dived straight out from the prow of the little boat to cleave the muddy waters of the Mississippi with a splash. One of the rowers, steadying the boat, stood and dived in after her. Swimming with powerful strokes of her arms, she made for the place where the two bodies had gone down. As she did so, Todd Rathbone came to the surface, spluttering; she grabbed him by the hair and held him up, treading water, until the crewman could take Todd from her. Then she looked around. *"Dallas!"* she called desperately again. There was no sign of him. Taking a deep breath, she dived again.

Below the surface, the bar sloped off sharply. She breast-stroked blindly through the muddy water, her hands stretched far in front of her. *Please, God,* she thought, *let me find him. Let me bring him up. Don't let there be something wrong.*

Nine feet down, the length of a sounding pole, she hit weeds. Her hands, poking through the greenery, closed on an ankle. It was a man's ankle encased in a soft leather boot. *Dallas!* She pushed forward, her lungs straining. She cursed the clumsy skirts she was wearing and kept moving. In a moment she was beneath his body, trying to get some purchase, her feet mired ankle-deep in soft mud. His deadweight bulk was too much for her. Too large. Too heavy. She was running out of breath . . . running out of strength.

• • •

Then, from the darkness, there came a blinding light overhead. Aurora blinked, and tried to raise a hand to shield her
eyes; but her arms seemed to be pinned down by something.
She looked down, and saw that she was wrapped tightly in
blankets. People were looking down at her, people whose
anxious faces she couldn't quite make out.

"Oh, thank God," someone was saying. "Thank God she's
alive." The message spread back through the crowd. "She's
alive! She's alive!" From the distance there came a rousing
cheer from many throats.

"Miss Brand," someone said closer to her. "Miss
Brand?"

Others chimed in: "Now don't worry. Don't try to get up.
You just lie there and . . ."

"There, now, Miss Brand. We're bringing . . ."

"Something under her head, please? Somebody bring a
pillow. . . ."

She blinked again, trying to remember. Down in the water.
Down in the water trying to pick something up. Something
too big, too heavy. Running out of . . .

She struggled, trying weakly to sit up. "Where is he?"
she said, panic-stricken.

"Everyone's all right, Miss Brand," someone replied.
"We've got virtually everyone. Thanks to your quick work,
we've got through this tragedy with a minimum of—"

She pushed against the blankets, trying to free her arms.
"Damn you!" she cried. "Let me go! Where is he? Where's
Dallas? Take me to him! I want to see him."

A new face was with her now, one she recognized. "Olivia!
I've got to—"

"Easy," Olivia said in a soothing voice, forcing her with
gentle hands back down onto the newly brought pillow.
"Easy, now, Miss Brand. He's been hurt, but you saved him.
You got to him in time, and, oh, yes. Todd's safe. Almost
everyone on the *Jackson* made it. You're a heroine now."

"She sure is," a man said. "Why, if she hadn't . . ."

Olivia ignored him. "You're on board the *Memphis* now,"
she said, taking Aurora's hand. "Boats are coming from the
shore to take the passengers off now. By dark the word'll be
out all the way up to St. Louis, all the way back to the Gulf.

They'll be talking about this on the Mississippi for years. You'll be a real queen of the river, ma'am.''

Her words trailed off, and her hand continued to stroke her mistress's brow. Aurora closed her eyes, letting tears of relief roll down her cheeks. He was safe. Dallas was safe. Nothing else mattered. Nothing else at all.

Chapter 48

A week later Henri Desmoulins stood before the big desk Laird Rathbone had occupied for so many years and looked down at its present occupant with an expression full of obvious hatred and scorn. "Monsieur," he said, "if it were not for my long history of dealings with your father and my concern for his present situation, you may be sure I would have no hesitation in—"

"Oh, for the love of God, sit down and spare me the oratory," Ward Rathbone said. "We both know why you're here. It has nothing to do with outraged paternal this and that. You're here to make some sort of marriage settlement. The only sensible thing to do is get on with it, without all this sawing the air with one hand and turning the air purple with penny-dreadful prose." He stared the banker in the eye insolently. "Well, sit down, won't you? Have a cigar. Genuine Perfectos from Oriente province, the best available. Or perhaps you'd prefer a drink."

"I don't believe what I'm hearing," Desmoulins said. "You have the nerve to stand there and—"

"Sit *down*," Ward said, and for the first time Desmoulins, looking in the younger Rathbone's eyes, could see something of the elder one. The ruthlessness, the cold disregard for human feelings, the callous practicality. "This is a business deal like any other. You have a daughter to bail out of trouble. I have a partnership to forge. We might just as well get right down to details."

"P-partnership?" Desmoulins said, wide-eyed. "Good God, *monsieur*. Partnership?"

"You gain a son, and your daughter retains her good name. We make a financial settlement. Seems simple enough."

"Settlement?" Desmoulins said, apoplectic. "You expect me to settle money on you? On *you*?" He pounded the desk before him. "You have taken leave of your senses!"

"Calm down," Ward said with his father's old basilisk smile, the deadly one Desmoulins remembered from so many years before. "Who said anything about your giving me any money? Quite the opposite. What I am discussing is partnership, and with a man who stands to profit nicely from becoming my, ah, 'father.' "

Desmoulins stepped back, his eyes blazing. " 'Father'?" he said. "You go too far!"

"The hell I do," Ward said. He took a paper from the top drawer of the desk and tossed it across. "See if this reads properly, will you?"

Desmoulins scanned the paper unbelievingly. " 'Mr. and Mrs. Henri Desmoulins are pleased to announce the marriage of their . . .' " He looked at Ward and threw the paper back on the desktop. "You're very sure of yourself, aren't you?" he said.

"Oh, very much so," Ward said. He sat back and looked at his visitor with no trace of a smile on his face; it had been replaced by a sinister, even frightening, bland expression. "You see, I've been doing a little research this week. Specifically I've been going through my father's business papers." He reached inside the drawer again and withdrew a file. "Sit down, please. Does the name Theodore Parsons mean anything to you?" He took note of the startled look on the banker's face. "How about Horace Catlin? Or perhaps the Marcus Pfeil Development Company? Or, let's say, Jacob Quine and Associates?" He smiled again, the same reptilian smile Desmoulins had noted earlier. "Eh? Shall I jog your memory? Shall I, dear 'Father'?"

Desmoulins sank heavily down into the chair opposite him. "How did you come across those names?" he said. "How much do you know?"

"Most of it," Ward said. "Now you realize why I insisted on your coming here. At your office all sorts of people are scurrying about. Never know when someone's going to hear something he shouldn't. Whereas here—well, you can see we're alone. I took some pains to make sure we would be.''

He waved a hand expansively at the row of bottles behind him. ''You're sure about that drink?'' he said. ''Imported cognac? Sherry? Port? Well, suit yourself. You ask what I know. Well, one thing I *do* know, and that's that each one of those names represents a bad loan you've made with the depositors' funds, a loan you'll never see repaid. A loan given without security you can show when the investigation begins.'' He smiled an even more deadly smile. ''*If* the investigation begins, dear 'Father.' ''

''Look here—''

''*You* look here. Tell me what would happen if a big depositor or two were to close an account? A note holder?'' The smile was almost a grin now. Almost. ''Shall I show you the bankbook on just one of your big accounts, dear 'Father'? Why, the Rathbone account—the one in my mother's name alone—has over a hundred and sixty thousand dollars on deposit with your bank. What if I were to close Mother's account tomorrow morning? Demand cash?'' He opened the file and withdrew a stack of papers. ''And what about these? What if all these accounts were to demand cash tomorrow?''

''But they can't,'' Desmoulins said. ''You wouldn't. Of course—''

''Of course one doesn't do that sort of thing? Eh? But what if, while waiting for payment, I were to put it about that Henri Desmoulins's bank can't meet its obligations? What if the rest of the depositors were to lose faith in your solvency? What if they were to demand an audit and learned about the state of your bank's finances? Where would you stand, then? Eh, 'Father'?''

Desmoulins's shoulders drooped. ''My God,'' he said. ''My God. How did you—''

''Find out? Why, Father had the whole thing figured out some time back. He's had you watched, ever since I started paying attention to Odile. He knew damned good and well you'd try something. He had you in the bag shortly after he returned from the East. His investigators presented him with enough evidence to put you in jail for the rest of your life for various crimes. Only he didn't have much time to do anything about it. I'm not sure he even had a chance to read the report carefully. When he got back, there was the business of the boat race to attend to, and then he had the stroke. But the report was here in his desk drawer when I came in to take over."

"My God. What are you going to do?"

Ward smiled. "Why, become your partner. It so happens that some enterprises I have in mind for the future will require having a legitimate-looking bank as a front. Oh, don't worry. Along with this comes my agreement—not in writing, of course—to bail you out in case one of the depositors has the same idea I did and tries to pull out. If we're partners, of course I'll cover you."

"P-partners," Desmoulins said heavily.

"Yes. I take it we're in agreement? Yes! Well, then let's get down to business. Before all else, one thing I need right now is a good lawyer, someone to replace Renault. I wonder if you could advise me . . . ah . . . 'Father.' "

"Lawyer?" Desmoulins said, his voice empty of emotion. "Oh, Mahaffey, I suppose. Judd Mahaffey."

"No, no," Ward said, dismissing him with a wave of the hand. "Small-time. I want someone good. Who represents you in New York?"

"Why, there's a man named Etienne Legras," he said. "But he never—"

"Bring him here," Ward said. "Make him an offer he can't refuse. I've been stymied too long by that damned Jew Samuels. He's outflanked us at every turn. If this Legras is any good . . ."

"He's the best," Desmoulins said. "But he'll never leave New York."

"All right. Leave that to me. Just get him here. I'll talk to him." Ward rose and paced back and forth behind the big desk, his hands behind his back. "I've lost one to the Brand woman," he said. "I'll not lose another. I'm going to get her. *Get* her. I don't care how. And you're going to help me. As a silent partner in your bank—"

"Partner? But your investment . . ."

"My investment is my not telling on you, and perhaps my covering your rear end if trouble appears. That's worth half the business, my friend. Or would you rather I—"

"No, no! I . . ."

Ward ignored him. "I'm going to get that damned greasy Christ killer Samuels too. I don't know how, but I'm going to cut out his damned Jew tripes." He pounded one fist into the other palm. "Father had the right idea; he just didn't go far enough. Mother always held him back." He smiled that shark's smile at his new partner. "Never fear, Odile won't have the same effect on me, dear 'Father.' This is a marriage of convenience, pure and simple. Not that she won't be treated well enough if she's content to mind her place."

Desmoulins looked at him, at the monster Laird Rathbone's illness had unleashed upon the earth, and shuddered. Then, however, he thought of the alternatives Ward had presented him with—and the horrid thought he had been trying not to think formed itself inside his head. *Relax and learn to enjoy it as best you can. It's the way the whole rest of your life is going to run.*

"You can see Mr. Boyd now," the doctor told Aurora. "But I must tell you he can withstand no shocks. There must be no movement. His head . . ."

"I understand," she said, smiling. But as she went in the door she felt tension that her composed smile did not reveal. How would he react to her? Would the two of them still feel compelled to yield to their own foolish pride, to hold themselves apart from each other? For a moment she hesitated, afraid to enter; she looked back at Ben in the waiting room.

"Go on," he said with a smile.

She nodded and entered, closing the door behind her. She closed her eyes and composed herself, but when she opened them and saw the man on the bed, her composure deserted her. He was so thin and drawn.

"Dallas," she said, and rushed to his side. One of his big hands lay on the coverlet. She held onto it gently and sat down by his bedside.

His eyes opened. He looked at her, and a succession of expressions passed across his face. He smiled wanly, and then the smile became a grin. He squeezed her hand with a little of his old strength. "Aurora . . ."

She looked at him, at the white bandages on his head and the pallor of his face. She tried to speak to him but her voice broke. Instead she held his hand to her cheek. "I . . . I'm trying to say something, but I can't seem to find the words."

He squeezed her hand again, and she kissed it. "Maybe I can help," Boyd said in a husky voice. "You could start off with 'welcome home.' "

"Oh, my dearest. I thought I'd lost you."

Boyd looked into her eyes, and the impression of weakness, of sickness, disappeared. "Lost me, Aurora?" he said. "How could you lose me without telling me to go? And I'm not sure that I'd obey you even if you did." His voice gathered strength. "Look," he said, "you risked your life for me out there. I owe you one." His grin was the old familiar one now, but there was something new in his eyes. "You and I aren't the marrying kind—not now, at least. Six months of domesticity and you'd shoot me with my own pistol. But, Aurora, my darling, is that the only possible bond? Isn't there another sort of arrangement a man and a woman can have if they know each other—and themselves—as well as we do?"

She kissed the big hand in hers again, her eyes shiny, her heart full to bursting. "Oh, Dallas," she said. "Yes, my darling. Yes."

Out in the street again, Aurora dawdled her way down the banquette with Ben Samuels, happily taking in the myriad sounds and smells of the infinitely seductive New Orleans streets. "Oh, Ben," she said, "I'm so happy. So very happy."

"Then he's all right? The doctor will let him go?"

"Yes. We'll sail in three weeks. He'll be under orders to rest and recuperate for a time, and I'll see that he does. But we'll have time together, three glorious months of it. We've never had more than a few days at one time." She put her hand affectionately on Ben Samuels's arm. "And you? Are you going to go upriver to see Sarita while I'm gone?"

"I wish I could spare the time," Samuels said, "but some-one has keep watch here. Young Rathbone will be laying in wait for us, and he'll be infinitely more dangerous than his father ever was, just you watch. He's tough and resourceful. I had no idea how much. Look at the way he covered himself on the *Jackson* business. I thought we had him boxed in, and look at him. If Endicott could only tell what he knows, but he can't. Who'd believe him? It would be his word against Ward's, and young Rathbone is a hero now. The whole thing has been blamed on Halsey."

He thought about what he'd just said and glanced hastily at Aurora. "I'm sorry. I didn't mean to remind you. I'm working on clearing Arthur's name for his parents' sake—and for ours. Poor devil, he deserved better."

"He did," she said, "but I promised myself I wasn't going to think about anything unpleasant. I—oh, did I tell you? Dallas has a new foreman. Jean-Marie Leblond. The people on Bayou Lavache are ecstatic; this is the first time anyone has named a Cajun to oversee a major plantation. Olivia's so happy. She's going down to visit Jean-Marie and Inez while we're gone."

"Oh?" Samuels smiled at her. "She has a surprise coming, I think, one that may well complicate her life just now."

"Well, perhaps," Aurora said. "It seems young Todd was deeply affected by his father's stroke. He's going upriver with Laird and his nurses. There's a hospital in St. Louis where they've had some success with stroke patients. Todd thinks, against all odds, that if he tends his father carefully enough, watches over him night and day, Laird may come back from that nearly helpless state he's been in ever since the stroke."

"God help us all," Samuels said. "I hate to wish that sort of ending on anyone, even Laird Rathbone. But if the alternative is seeing him back in action . . ." He shuddered visibly. "Imagine father and son working in tandem." He shook his head. "So Olivia and Todd won't be seeing much of each other for a while."

"No, and I can't bring myself to think that's a bad thing. Todd's a nice boy, but he *is* a Rathbone. And he *does* have that streak of fierce loyalty to Laird. Sooner or later he's going to be faced with a serious and very difficult choice."

She thought a moment and shook her head lightly. "Or maybe it's Olivia who'll be faced with the choice, not Todd."

Samuels smiled. "Just wait," he said. "You'll see." He looked at his watch. "Oh, look at the time. I have a stop to make—would you mind making it with me? It's at the St. Louis Hotel, just down the street, a minute or two away."

Aurora beamed at him. "Ben, I'm so happy, I'd go along if it took six hours. Certainly. Then . . . well, I suppose a businesswoman can take her lawyer to dinner now and then? How about escorting me to Moreau's, or perhaps Antoine's? *Pompano en papillote*, perhaps? *Suprêmes de volailles avec . . .*"

"I'd be charmed, of course. But first the errand." He took her arm and gallantly steered her up the steps of the imposing building. In the rotunda they were intercepted by a formally dressed member of the hotel staff. "I'm Mr. Samuels," he said, "and this is Miss Brand. We have an appointment."

The man bowed and led them away. "We?" Aurora Brand said. "You didn't tell me. . . ."

"It'll only take a moment," Ben said. He let the hotelier lead them through a pair of curtained doors into the grand ballroom of the hotel. Aurora stopped, looked with puzzlement at the great throng of guests and the printed streamers hanging from the chandeliers. She could not recognize anyone for a moment. Then, little by little, she picked out some of the faces: the cream of New Orleans society, many of them, and better than half of them recognizable as former passengers on the one and only river cruise of the steamship *Andrew Jackson*.

She turned to Ben Samuels, one hand pressed to her cheek, as it dawned on her slowly. "It was the only way I could get you here," he said. "I hope you don't mind. They wanted so much to do this."

Someone handed him a glass of champagne then, and he faced the crowd and held it high, speaking in a loud, clear voice filled with respect and affection. "Ladies and gentlemen, Miss Aurora Brand!"

The glasses were raised and the guests drank. The cheers rang out, and Aurora Brand thought her heart would burst with the wild mixture of emotions that ran through her at that moment. Now she could make out the words they were saying. They were the same words they had painted on the streamers that hung above their heads: "Long live Aurora Brand—Queen of the River!"

Chapter 49

Behind Todd Rathbone the whistle hooted peremptorily. He looked back, annoyed. "Oh, confound it. I suppose they won't wait any longer." When he turned back to Olivia, his smile was the old warm and good-hearted one, with only the smallest trace of his irritation showing. "You'd think that with the steamship line in the family I'd command more respect than that. But . . ."

"I understand," Olivia said. "These things run on schedules. Todd, write to me, will you? I'll miss you. Really I will."

He took her hand in his left one; the right, still bandaged after his second operation, lay in its sling, pinned to his coat front. "Every day if I can. I'll have plenty of time to think about you but not much time for fooling around with anyone else. Taking care of Father full-time will keep me true to you, even if my inclinations didn't already run that way." The whistle blew again. "Damn!" he said. "I mean—I'm sorry . . ."

"No," she said. "Run for it. They're going to pull up the stage plank." She pressed his hand warmly and released it. "Run!" she said, and watched him go, feeling sad for a moment. If this thing hadn't happened to his father—if he hadn't had that good loyal heart that made him think of others first—what might their relationship be like now?

"Why, hello, Miss Soames," a voice said nearby. She turned. Ward Rathbone stood before her, resplendent in a dark broadcloth coat and a businessman's vest. He'd let his sideburns grow; that aged him a little, despite the still youthful cut of his features. His eyes, though, were no longer those of a boy.

"Miss Soames?" Olivia said. "We've grown formal, Ward."

He grinned, but the grin was a new and harder one. "Oh, all right. I took it for granted you were mad at me." He watched the steamboat prepare for debarkation over her shoulder. "So you came to see Todd off. Lucky man."

"We're friends," she admitted. "Did I read something about your betrothal the other day? To Odile Desmoulins?"

"You did," he said. His smile was a strange one these days; it did not quite reach his eyes. "Time to merge the fortunes. Time to consolidate." The grin was back. "I've decided to give your friend Miss Brand a run for her money, and there's no time for starting like the present."

"Well, strike while the iron is hot," she said. "If you're going to steal a march on her, the time is now, while she's gone." Something malicious in her made her add, "Of course, Ben Samuels is here. He'll have an eye on you."

"Ah, yes," Ward said. The half smile remained as the eyes darkened under knit brows. "The Jew. Well, I'll take care of him when the time comes. All in good time, eh, Olivia? Well, see you around." He saluted, turned, and briskly walked away.

Olivia shook her head, looking after him. How could Todd have come from such a family? It was almost as though he shared none of the blood that ran through the veins of Laird and Ward.

"Oh, I say, Olivia . . . Miss Soames . . ." She turned with a warmer smile to see Basil Endicott bearing down on her, with a man even larger and better dressed than himself in tow. It took her a moment to recognize the tall man beside him. Then she stared shamelessly, her mouth open.

The two of them pulled up beside her. "Why, look, Miss Soames, this is an old friend of yours, I believe. We met on the boat coming down from St. Louis." Basil's eyes twinkled as he gallantly bent over her hand, but her eyes, still wide with surprise, remained on his companion. Zach McClellan!

"Why, Zach," she said, "I hardly recognized you." She thought about this and bit her lip. "Goodness, that was an ungracious thing to say, wasn't it? But you look wonderful, if you'll pardon my saying so.''

He bowed slightly, and she marveled at the change in him again. He was dressed to the nines in apparel of the finest and most expensive cut; he looked like a man born to this sort of affluence. "Times change," he said. "It's good to see you again, ma'am." She looked in his eyes and saw a new reserve there, as well as a new poise. But there was no mistaking the hunger, the devotion, that lay beneath these. No doubt about it, he was still in love with her.

"How fortunate to have run across him," Basil was saying now. "Small world, you know. He's an old black sheep like myself, only one with perhaps a bit more character than I had. I like the easy life. I have my solicitor deposit the checks, even if I seldom draw upon them. Bad form, you know. But Zachary, here—he went me one better. He refused the family stipend altogether. Went out and made it for himself. Did a damned good job of it.''

Olivia, flustered now, stammered a little as she spoke. "I— I heard Mr. Boyd had a new partner. I had no idea.''

"It's all right. As a matter of fact, I took payment for that first year in land. We're partners on some ventures now, but I have acreage of my own too." He smiled. "Your friends in Bayou Lavache have asked about you constantly. They want to know when you're coming down to visit." The smile was really a very nice one: more confident, more secure. Her heart beat a little faster for it. "So do I.''

"Why, what a coincidence," she said. "I'm leaving to-morrow night. You wouldn't have had time to hear up in St. Louis. Inez asked me down after Miss Brand left with Mr. Boyd for the islands.''

"How splendid!" Basil Endicott said, impulsively throwing his long arms around the both of them. "I'm going along too. Zachary invited me on the way downriver. He says that a confirmed gumbo addict like myself will go mad with joy on the bayou; I'll eat myself into a stupor." He smiled wryly. "I do believe he also made mention of certain charms the Cajun women are said to have.''

Olivia looked up at Zach, smiling for the first time. "Oh?'' she said.

He made a face, and his eyes sparkled. "Rumors," he said, "rumors I haven't had the time to check out, making a place for myself. Of course, my schedule is beginning to open up a bit these days. Perhaps the finer things of life won't elude me much longer."

Her eyes caught his now and held them, and she made room for a new feeling in her heart, one she'd never felt before, not with Todd, not with anybody. "Perhaps they won't," she said.